PRAISE FOR
1 RAGGED
RIDGE ROAD

"An innovative and gripping novel. Readers will find themselves totally captured in the spell. . . . The novel provides
an otherworldly feel that allows readers to believe they are
reading two stories for the price of one novel. . . . A winner
encapsulating the full range of human emotions inside a
mesmerizing mystery. . . ."

—Harriet Klausner, Amazon.com

"Loads of fun. . . . A classic. . . . I devoured *1 RAGGED
RIDGE ROAD* with the same gusto I've shown to a not-
quite-defrosted Sara Lee."

—Kiki Olson, *St. Petersburg Times* (FL)

"This coauthored debut is adroitly constructed . . . eerily
riveting. . . . [A] clever tale with resonant irony."

—*Publishers Weekly*

"The skillful weaving of threads from the past with the
present creates a fascinating tapestry of events filled with
intrigue and mystery."

—Angela Lansbury

"Entertaining. . . . Two stories skillfully woven together.
One is an old-fashioned whodunit and the other is a
contemporary suspense story. . . . Resist the urge to peek at
the last few pages. Anticipation is half the fun of this
mystery."

—Linda L. Heinzman, *Florida Times-Union* (Jacksonville)

1 Ragged Ridge Road

Leonard Foglia and David Richards

POCKET BOOKS

New York   London   Toronto   Sydney   Tokyo   Singapore

POCKET BOOKS, a division of Simon & Schuster Inc.
1230 Avenue of the Americas, New York, NY 10020

Copyright © 1997 by Leonard Foglia and David Richards

Originally published in hardcover in 1997 by Pocket Books

All rights reserved, including the right to reproduce this book or portions thereof in any form whatsoever. For information address Pocket Books, 1230 Avenue of the Americas, New York, NY 10020

ISBN: 0-671-00355-0

First Pocket Books paperback printing May 1998

10 9 8 7 6 5 4 3 2 1

POCKET and colophon are registered trademarks of Simon & Schuster Inc.

Cover art by Neal McPheeters

Printed in the U.S.A.

For Elizabeth and Lillian

Acknowledgments

—⚬—

Mary Pope Osborne—not just a friend, but a writer's best friend—was there from the very beginning. Gail Hochman never wavered in her enthusiasm, and Pete Wolverton kept a sharp eye on every detail. We're indebted to all three.

For their ideas and support, we also owe thanks to Hannah and Jim Heyle, Peter Hagan, Donna Knight, Sally Smith, and Alma Viator.

1 Ragged Ridge Road

One

---✦---

At first, the snow came gently—in dry, feathery flakes that slid off the gabled roof and floated down the chimneys. Those that collected on the windowsills or lodged in the corners of the windowpanes didn't remain there long, before the wind picked them up and set them on their downward drift again. In a few hours, it would become one of those hard, icy storms that the community held accountable every winter for at least two broken legs and countless twisted ankles. For now, it settled over the slopes surrounding the mansion like gossamer silk—silent, graceful, and deceptive.

Not even the hatch marks of the chickadees marred the perfect whiteness. Their jerky movements amused her, whenever she caught sight of them hopscotching across the lawn. They reminded her of tin windup toys. But it was growing dark and they seemed to have disappeared under the bushes or beneath the front porch. She couldn't tell. Although the chandeliers in the house cast oblong sheets of light onto the yard, what was bright and cheerful indoors turned grayish and opaque when mixed with the snow.

She sighed contentedly. Christmas was her favorite

holiday, and not just for the gifts, which all her life had been extravagant and were likely to be so again this year, judging from the mounds of packages at the base of the Christmas tree. She welcomed the peacefulness of snowy nights that sealed up the mansion in a cocoon and the good spirits that overtook the butler, cantankerous as he was the rest of the year.

Her husband had spotted the perfectly shaped tree on the northwest corner of the property. It had taken three workmen to chop it down, drag it out of the woods, and maneuver it through the front door without scratching the chestnut woodwork. Nearly ten feet tall, it sat in the large, open stairwell and filled the whole house with a fresh forest scent. The maid and the kitchen help had spent several days hanging the delicate crystal ornaments and draping the garlands of cranberries and popped corn, so that no swag drooped lower than the next and no ornament detracted from its neighbor. Later this evening, they would light the tapers that stood like sentinels at the tip of each branch.

How unfortunate it all had to come down by twelfth night, she thought as she climbed the wide staircase that wound around the tree and led to her bedroom on the second floor, then corkscrewed up another flight to the servants' quarters and the attic under the gables. If she had her way, the Christmas decorations would never be packed away. From the parlor, she heard the strains of "God Rest Ye Merry, Gentlemen." Someone was at the player piano, pumping the pedals vigorously. The notes came in loud, blustery gusts. A ragtag choir of carolers from town would be making the rounds before long. From past experience, she knew that a few of them, emboldened by the gin in their back-pocket flasks, would be more than a match for the huffings and puffings of the mechanical piano.

Her fingers went instinctively to her neck. Tonight she would wear the necklace. Her guests would ooh and aah—the women envious of so many fine diamonds and sapphires, the men drawn to the pale décolletage that showed them off so well. She relished the attention in advance, knowing that as soon as the holidays were over, the jewelry would go back into her husband's vault at the bank.

Once she reached the second floor, she glided down the long hall, entered her bedroom, and shut the heavy door. A freshly stoked fire in the fireplace threw reddish yellow shadows over the room and made the brass fender and fireplace tools shine like antique gold. Two small lamps, reflected in the mirror behind them, formed circular pools of light on the dressing table. The thick velvet curtains had been drawn against the chill by the maid, who was waiting in the kitchen for the bell that would summon her back upstairs to dress her mistress for the evening's festivities.

The woman sat down before the mirror, removed the necklace from its case, and held it up to her cheek. Glints of silver and blue danced across the ceiling. She studied her image in the mirror, allowing a smile to break across her face. How could she not be happy? All the dreams she secretly harbored for the new year were about to come true. Voices from the living room, accompanying the music, washed up against the bedroom door: "Oh, tidings of comfort and joy, comfort and joy . . ." She hummed along with them.

A burst of wind rustling the curtains cut her reveries short. She turned to look and noticed a thin dusting of snow on the floor. The window must have blown open while she was daydreaming. She parted the curtains and checked. No, the latch was shut tight. Then something moved in the pane, a dark reflection that caused her to whirl around.

On the far side of the bedroom stood a figure in a heavy blue topcoat. A knit cap was pulled down over the eyebrows, and a checkered scarf was wound tightly around the lower half of the face. All she could make out were the eyes, which were red and watery. The gloved hands gripped the brass poker from the fireplace set.

"Who are you? What are you doing here?" she asked indignantly.

The figure was silent.

"Didn't you hear me? Who are you?"

The only response was a long, protracted moan. Louder, it would have been a growl.

"Get out of here immediately or I will have my husband throw you out." Even as she spoke, she sensed the idleness of her threat. If her husband had returned home from the bank, she hadn't heard him. With that infernal player piano making such a racket, who could hear anything? She backed up and reached for the button to call the maid. In an instant, the figure was upon her, the poker raised high like a hatchet. But it wasn't the weapon, flashing in the firelight, that made her body go weak and dried out her mouth. It was the look of pure malevolence in the eyes,

"Oh, my God, please don't—"

The poker came down with a furious thwack, carving a deep gash in her forehead. The next blow sent her sprawling at the foot of the bed. Short gasps of pain escaped her lips, then little bubbles of purple blood. The person was bellowing at her now, *"Whore, filthy whore . . . you've got everything . . . I'm not going to let you . . ."* The words entered her consciousness like broken fragments of sounds, shards cutting the inside of her head. They had no more meaning to her than the gruntings of animals.

What was happening? Where was her husband? Why this savage fury?

She curled herself into a ball as the merciless beating continued. After a moment, she saw black. Then felt nothing.

In the parlor, the player piano fell silent.

The only sound the woman might have heard, had she been alive to hear it, was the flap-flap-flap of the music roll, turning on itself.

$\mathcal{T}wo$

—⁂—

Carol Roblins loved the mansion at first sight when she and Blake drove by it that late-October afternoon. They were living in three cramped rooms on the army base at the time, the latest in a long line of temporary quarters that stretched from Georgia to southern California and now to rural Pennsylvania. Sundays, they took to exploring the towns in the area in the hope of finding a home more to their liking. At the very least, a bigger one. And this was surely the biggest one in Fayette.

The Kennedy mansion, it was still called, although the original owner, a local banker, according to the real estate agent, had died in the 1920s and his descendants no longer resided in the state. Three stories tall, it sat on a sturdy foundation of Pennsylvania fieldstone. The stucco walls were of a color and texture that reminded Carol of yellow cake. A wide veranda wrapped around the front and one side, terminating in a screened-in gazebo that was strategically situated to catch the breeze.

Summers, the windows had been hooded by green canvas awnings, but all that remained were the corroded metal awning frames, and then only some of the windows could lay claim to that bit of architectural coquetry. The canvas

5

had long since rotted and blown away. On the sharply pitched roof, the fieldstone made a reappearance in the form of two stolid chimneys, capped with little tin roofs of their own.

In all, the mansion was grand from a distance, shabby up close. During the Depression, it had stood empty, a monument to the kinds of quick, flashy fortunes that had been prevalent a decade earlier. Then, after World War II, it had been turned into an apartment house, and the real decline had begun. The spacious rooms had been carved up, doors had been walled over, and fireplaces bricked up. Closets were made into kitchenettes, introducing smoke and cooking grease into parts of the house that had smelled only of cedar and rose-petal sachets before.

Still, Carol knew a potential beauty when she saw it. Although the years of neglect had taken their toll, the damage was not irreversible. The grand staircase was missing some spindles from the banister, and the treads and risers were badly scuffed. But the wood was fine-grained chestnut, something you just didn't see these days, and could easily be brought back to its original luster. The folding mahogany doors that used to divide the living room and the dining room had been stored in the basement. Poking around in the gloom, she and Blake even came upon a couple of chandeliers, entwined in a corner like bejeweled spiders, that must have hung in the main rooms.

When they returned to the foyer, Carol immediately went to the staircase again and ran her hand lovingly along the banister. Just the feel of the aged wood was enough to set her dreaming. This glorious place could actually be theirs. Far from being put off by its tumbledown condition, she found herself thinking that it would give her something to do, besides taking care of Sammy. Not that she wasn't devoted to her son. Sammy came first and always would. But the notion of having a house to take care of, too—this house—lodged in her head and wouldn't leave.

Part of her acknowledged how old-fashioned she was being. Well, theirs was an old-fashioned marriage, wasn't it? Blake went to work; she stayed home. He was the man of the family; she, the woman. They operated on a clear, if

antiquated, division of the sexes and an even clearer deline-
ation of duties.

Her head tilted back, she turned around slowly and gazed
up into the open stairwell, marveling at what seemed to be a
stained-glass, octagonal skylight. Decades of filth had dulled
the colors, and a thick layer of dead leaves blocked out any
sunlight. But her guess was right: three flights up, the
original skylight was still intact. Flowers and ribbons made
for an elegant pattern. Or maybe the ribbons were letters.
From the distance, Carol couldn't tell.

Blake could see the excitement in her eyes and felt an
unexpected surge of tenderness for her. Her emotions had
always been so transparent, unlike his. He'd loved that
about her once. Perhaps he still did, deep down. Then, the
tenderness abated.

The hard truth was that, more and more, he felt as if they
were going through the motions of married life, making
empty gestures and small talk and gliding over what really
mattered. He wondered if all married couples had that
sensation after a while. If they did, the guys on the base
never talked about it. Blake certainly wasn't one to bring up
the subject. He'd buried himself in his job, instead. At least
that was paying off. The rumors of his advancement had
been growing louder lately.

"What do you think, Blake?" Carol said, determined to
keep her tone neutral. Her excitement was palpable anyway.

"Is this really the answer?" he asked himself. He looked
at his wife, then diverted his gaze. She hadn't changed much
in the fifteen years they'd been married. There were a few
lines on her forehead, some wrinkles around the eyes, but
nothing that makeup didn't easily cover, when she bothered
with makeup, which wasn't often. She was still as slender as
she was the day they had first started going out. Her blond
hair had darkened since then, enough so that Carol periodically felt compelled to "help it out a little," but she hadn't
attended to that recently, either.

All told, she was a much prettier woman than she allowed
herself to be. He couldn't remember the last time she'd
really dressed up and shown off her figure. He speculated
that it must have been the spring party at the officers' club,

but he had no image of her to go with his memories of that event. It seemed to him that she was more intent these days on being Sammy's mother than his wife.

Suddenly, he was aware of the silence and realized she was waiting for an answer. "It's awfully big," he replied. "I'm sure we can find some place smaller. More manageable."

"But no place is going to be this special. We deserve something special."

He wanted to say, "No kidding," but suppressed the urge. "You need money for special, Carol. A lot of money. Do you have the slightest idea how involved a renovation would be? And you know how much they've got me working now. When am I going to find the time to redo a house?"

"I'll do it. This could be my project. Please?"

"And Sammy?"

"What about him? He's not a baby, Blake. He could help. It would be good for him."

She was pushing and it made him nervous. He raked his fingers through his hair a couple of times, as he always did when he needed to calm himself. It was thick and black, with a sheen that was actually the beginnings of gray. He was wearing a plaid shirt and a tan golf jacket, but even when he was in civvies, the brush cut was a dead giveaway that he belonged to the military.

Carol recognized the nervous gesture and it occurred to her that she had never seen him with his hair grown out. It had always been short. Even in his childhood pictures. If there was any wave to it, she would be the last to know.

"The whole idea is crazy," he said, less assertively than before. He was weakening. Carol took him by the arm and walked him back into the living room. "Just look at those beautiful bay windows. They're just like the ones we had on Thatcher Avenue. Think how much fun we had fixing up that place."

"Thatcher Avenue was a one-bedroom apartment. This is a twenty-two-room house."

"So, it will take us a little longer, that's all."

"Like the rest of our lives."

She wasn't going to back down. Of course, it would take

time, but she could picture them rehabilitating the old mansion, working side by side, cementing their marriage along with the driveway. Sammy would have the woods and the fields to explore, and the stream that cut through them, its waters as pure and chilly as icicles.

"You always said Sammy needed a yard to play in."

"A yard. Not his own forest. I can just see him wandering off and getting lost."

"Blake, be serious. I really want this."

Two days later, he gave in. It was the ridiculously low price that clinched it. Apparently, their potential beauty was, in the view of most, if not all, of the prospective buyers, a white elephant. When word got around the town of Fayette that the Roblinses had signed on the dotted line, there was general amazement and some outright laughter, while Mr. Beldman, the pharmacist, noted dryly that he didn't want to be present when they got their first heating bill.

Blake blew his stack when it came. But then, he blew his stack about so many things that winter that Carol wondered if he wasn't having his midlife crisis ten years early. His feelings for the mansion had never matched hers, and he seemed to resent it that he had allowed himself to be swayed by her arguments. It soon became apparent to her that the renovation wasn't going to be the wonderful collaborative venture she had envisioned. He was not merely used to order. He thrived on it. It was what had attracted him to the military in the first place, why he had risen through the ranks to captain with such ease. And the mansion was in a perpetual state of disorder.

They appropriated the old library on the ground floor for their bedroom. A cozy office, which opened off the library, made the perfect bedroom for Sammy. Hard as they tried, however, they couldn't keep the clutter and the dust, generated by the renovation, out of either room. There was unwanted symbolism in that, if either had chosen to recognize it. Blake grew testy and Carol's optimism started sounding forced, probably because it was. Somebody had to keep up the family's spirits, though.

Even she had a brief sinking feeling when part of the

entryway wall crumbled on her. She was patching a large crack when the old plaster fell away in large, dry chunks. Before she knew it, she was staring at a sizable hole. Her attempts to contain the damage only made it worse. By the time Blake arrived home, she was up to her ankles in debris, and a cloud of chalky dust hung in the air.

Blake stood in the front doorway, refusing to enter. He had put on his formal dress uniform for some official ceremony that day and the polish on his black shoes gleamed like wet tar.

"What the devil is going on here?" he barked.

Carol tried to inject a little lightness into the situation. "What does it look like? I'm tearing down a wall. Bob Vila has nothing on me now."

"Except common sense."

"It's just plaster, Blake."

Angrily, he kicked a slab of plaster with the toe of his shoe. "Biggest mistake I ever made," he muttered. "I never should have bought this place."

"*We*, Blake. We bought this place. Remember?" It infuriated her when he talked like that. As if she didn't exist. He turned abruptly and started down the front steps.

"Where are you going?"

"I'm going around to the back door because I'm not about to track through that mess. Unless, of course, you want to get this uniform cleaned and pressed again. If we have any money left over, after pouring it all into this dump, that is."

Carol chased after him, the conciliatory expression on her face at odds with the smears of plaster war paint on her cheeks. "You're exaggerating, Blake. This place is going to be absolutely beautiful when we're done. You'll see."

"Get real, Carol." He stomped off toward the back of the house.

Carol took a few deep breaths, then mumbled to herself, "Loosen up, Blake."

"Get real" had always been his response to her flights of enthusiasm, even when they were young. "Loosen up" was her usual retort. Although both commands were uttered in fun, they served nonetheless to define the fundamental difference in their temperaments. Blake was solid, reliable, a human bulwark. (His square shoulders were one of the first things she had noticed about him.) She was so much more impulsive.

For a long time, she believed their personalities to be mutually enhancing. Her imagination, her curiosity, her sense of adventure, made life more interesting for him, just as his dependability, his pragmatism (although she didn't like the word itself), made life saner and safer for her. It was a perfect fit. Of course, relationships were more complicated than that, but as capsule analyses went, that one struck her as accurate enough. Until they began to change.

Marriage and motherhood grounded her, and while her romantic side never withered away, she learned to give it less expression, knowing how easily it was mocked and eventually telling herself that it belonged to another, simpler period in her life, like the portable pink-and-white vinyl record player she'd prized in high school. Little by little, Blake's dependability hardened into a kind of inflexibility. Rigor, even. "Get real" lost its playfulness. So did "loosen up." What had started out as good-natured gibes evolved into veiled criticisms. The perfect fit wasn't so perfect, after all.

Mid-February, the promotion Blake had long been angling for came through. Carol knew how much it meant to him. He would be assistant army attaché at the American embassy in Bonn, a posting that was bound to expand his contacts. If he performed well—and here Blake took care to quote his commanding officer exactly—he could expect "a career-enhancing billet at the Pentagon in the not very distant future." Carol tried to get excited for him, but the thought of packing up again and leaving a spot that had fired up her dormant imagination dampened her enthusiasm.

"What about the house?" she asked, trying not to sound too disappointed.

"What about it?"

"I don't want to sell it and move again."

"We won't have to."

"How can we afford to keep it? Who'll rent it in this state? One peek at this kitchen . . ." She let the sentence trail off with a vague gesture at the surroundings. The old-fashioned kitchen appliances and the chipped linoleum floor put it better than she could.

"I . . . uh . . . I . . . thought . . . uh . . ." He stopped. As a child, he had stammered badly, but he had gotten over the habit in high school when he learned not to rush his thoughts. One of the few occasions Carol had heard him succumb to the stammer was at his mother's wake, and it had been painful to hear. She hoped he was just fumbling for the right words this time.

He sounded them slowly. "I . . . uh . . . well . . . I thought that I would go alone."

Instantly, Carol realized what was happening. The long, festering discontent was about to surface. In fact, it just had. It was out. Spoken. There could be no pretending otherwise. "Oh" was all she could manage.

"It's only a temporary position," he rationalized. "A year at most. You know how fast things can change over there. Why uproot Sammy one more time? The year will be over before any of us knows it."

He rocked awkwardly on his feet and cleared his throat before adding, "We need the time apart, Carol. To figure out where we stand with each other."

She couldn't bring herself to face him. "Where do we stand, Blake?"

"I don't know."

"And so you're going to run away to the other side of the world. Is that it?"

"I'm not running away. This is work. My career. It's important to me."

"More important than your family?"

"Look at me. Are you happy?"

The question caught her unaware and her heart contracted. She was incapable of giving him an easy answer. Sure, she was occasionally disappointed in their lives together, as was he. But did that qualify as unhappiness? Or was it a sign of carelessness, of inattention, on one another's part? And when had disappointment become grounds for a separation, anyway?

As she sank to a kitchen chair, her tears began to flow,

slowly at first. But the more she tried to bring them under control, the faster they came, and before long she was sobbing audibly. Blake paced back and forth, confining his steps to the worn patch of linoleum in front of the sink. Displays of emotion made him acutely uncomfortable. Pacing was how he coped.

"I'm sorry. I can't help it," she apologized, but that only made her sob all the more.

He came up behind her and placed his hand on her shoulder. She reached up and clutched it, and they stayed that way for several minutes, not saying anything, until Carol's crying subsided. Then she released her grasp, went to the sink, and splashed some cold water on her face.

"I must be a sight." Why was she always the one to cry, never Blake?

He held out his handkerchief, but she rejected it with a shake of the head.

"Have you given any consideration to Sammy?" she asked, the faintest trace of accusation creeping into the question.

"He spends so much time with you, he probably won't even notice I'm gone."

"How can you say that? The boy worships you."

"That so? You could have fooled me."

"He just doesn't express himself like other kids. You know that. You keep expecting him to wake up one morning and have this animated conversation at breakfast with you about the Yankees. That's never going to happen. You've got to stop waiting for him to come to you and take the trouble to enter his world. That is, if you want a relationship with your son."

They'd been over this ground so often in the past she could hear Blake's response before he uttered it.

"You coddle him too much."

"Please, let's not have that discussion again. What are we going to tell him? Or rather, what are you going to tell him? Because I'm not handling this one. Sammy's going to have to hear this from you."

They talked late into the night—sorting out their relationship and how it had come to this impasse. Once they got beyond the anger and the accusations, they actually addressed some problems that should have been tackled long ago. Simple things such as how Carol felt about moving every couple of years. (She had never liked it.) Or why Blake was so reluctant to express his emotions. (He considered it a weakness.) Little was resolved, but the rift no longer struck Carol as this fearsome chasm, ready to swallow them up. She could see its shape and its depths—and its perils—more clearly, and that consoled her. Sad as it was to think how long they had been drifting apart, somewhere in the back of her consciousness was a spark of relief that the truth had finally been acknowledged.

By the early-morning hours, they were talked out and exhausted. Resigned to Blake's leaving, Carol had convinced herself it was just another army assignment, not a trial separation. Blake was no longer feeling such hangdog guilt. They even allowed themselves to look back on better days. Carol laughed out loud when Blake recalled the first time she had prepared her special apple-cinnamon soufflé. They had been married only a few weeks and she had slipped out of bed at sunrise, hoping to surprise him with her culinary skills. She had put the two soufflés in the oven and then tiptoed back into the bedroom. Blake had reached out for her and they had started to kiss. The kissing got out of control and one thing led to another. Not until their desire was appeased and they lay spent and contented on the bed did they smell smoke coming from the kitchen.

The soufflés were ruined. Carol was distraught, even though Blake assured her that their time in bed was better than any soufflé could ever be. He was finally able to calm her down only by picking the few edible pieces out of the charred pan and proclaiming them delicious. The episode had given birth to a long-running joke: "Do you want sex or a soufflé this morning? Because you can't have both."

Sex usually won out in those early years.

The day Blake left for Germany, it snowed, and then the snow turned to slush. Carol had decided to make the departure into a going-away party, mostly for Sammy's sake, and she'd gone to the trouble of preparing three of the famous soufflés. But the festive mood soured when Sammy stayed in his room and refused to come out for breakfast.

Blake went in to fetch him. Seated by the window, Sammy was absorbed in the task of polishing a small silver object. It was typical of his son, thought Blake, to be lost in his own world. But did it have to be today of all days? He tried to stifle his annoyance.

"Hey, buddy. Don't you want some breakfast?"

"No."

"Aren't you hungry?"

"No."

"Mom made our favorite soufflés." Sammy said nothing and continued diligently to rub the silver object. Blake saw that it was a spoon. "Where did you get that, Son?"

"Found it."

"Where?"

"Outside."

"Do you like it here, Sammy?"

"Yes."

"Well, so does your mom. That's why I'm going abroad alone. So you guys don't have to move again. I'll get my work done as soon as possible and then I'll come back. That way, we can keep the house. Do you understand that?"

Sammy raised his head. The expression on his face was blank. Blake wondered if his son believed him.

"Besides, I couldn't take you, even if I wanted to."

"Why?"

Blake leaned down and whispered conspiratorially in Sammy's ear, "I'm going on a secret mission."

Sammy perked up. "What's the secret?"

"Well, it wouldn't be a secret if I told you now, would it? But you know what we're going to do?"

"What?"

"We'll have a special code, you and I."

"What's that?"

"That's something that no one else understands. Just us. I'll call you every week, and if I say, 'The weather was good this week,' you'll know I'm okay and the mission is going well."

"That's silly." Sammy giggled.

"Well, what should the code words be, then?"

Sammy mulled over the question seriously. Then he held up the object in his lap. "Shiny spoon."

"Shiny spoon?"

"Yes. If you're all right, say 'shiny spoon.'"

"Okay, it's a deal."

"And if you're not all right . . ." Sammy thought long and hard before chirping brightly, "Say 'shiny knife.'"

After breakfast, Carol hugged Blake on the veranda and babbled something ridiculous like "Take care of yourself." Sammy ran down the steps and waved until the car that had come to pick Blake up had rounded the bend in the road and disappeared from sight. As she turned to go back inside, Carol looked up at the house. It was a big, old mess, she thought, but it was her big, old mess. In the few months they had lived there, she had a stronger feeling of belonging than she had experienced anyplace else. Even if things were never repaired with Blake, in some strange way she couldn't articulate, she felt that she'd come home at last.

Three

The sergeant had seen his share of dead people—those claimed by accidents or disease or old age—but he'd had few dealings with murder victims in his career. A vagabond knifed in a drunken brawl, a farmer who had drowned his wife—that was about it. They had been tawdry killings and attracted little attention.

The woman who lay at the foot of the canopied bed belonged to another class. She had elegance, wealth, breeding. The bedroom alone attested to that. He recalled tipping his hat to her when they had passed on Main Street and had trouble reconciling that image with the body that lay on the floor. She looked like a smashed china doll—fragments of her beauty floating in a pool of crimson blood. He felt the nausea rising in his throat, swallowed hard, and turned away.

He could see that the murderer had escaped by a side window, which was still open and gave onto the roof of the veranda. One of the red velvet curtains had been partially torn from its rod, and snow was blowing into the room. Faint footprints were discernible on the roof, but the storm was filling them in fast. The sergeant knew they would be *completely covered over before they could provide any significant clues.*

"It's gone." The maid, visibly shaken, hovered in the doorway. "I don't see it. It's gone," she repeated shrilly. The sergeant had immediately put the bedroom off-limits to the staff of the mansion, but in the maid's case, it was an unnecessary precaution. Her eyes were round with terror and she had no intention of venturing any closer to the dead body.

"What's gone?" The sergeant cast his eyes about the room, not certain what she was referring to.

"The necklace. The necklace she was going to wear tonight. There's the box." The maid pointed to an empty velvet jewelry box on the dressing table. "Someone's taken it." She crossed herself several times and began chanting "Holy Mary, Mother of God, pray for us sinners now and at the hour of our death." Over and over. The litany sounded like whimpering to the sergeant and aggravated his nerves.

"Where is Mr. Kennedy?" he snapped. "Does he know what's happened yet?"

He turned back to the maid, not really expecting an answer. She had buried her head in the neck of the butler, who was attempting to comfort her and remain stoic, although the grisly sight of his mistress's battered body upset him no less deeply. Suddenly, a flurry of activity could be heard below. The forensic specialist—or the mousy gentlemen who fulfilled that function on the small police force—a photographer, and half a dozen other officers had arrived on the scene.

"He was here," the butler spoke up. "Then he left."

"Left?"

"Yes."

"Where the hell did he go?"

"I don't know," the butler replied, sounding more stupid than he would have liked.

A jolt of energy coursed through the sergeant. He bolted out of the bedroom and started for the grand staircase. "What kind of a car was he driving?" he called back to the butler and maid, who were following after him.

"No car. He was on foot," the butler said.

"He didn't even bother to take his overcoat," added the maid, who had regained some of her composure. "He just left. We couldn't stop him."

"Which way did he go?" barked the sergeant as he reached the foyer. The butler gestured toward the front door. The sergeant promptly ordered two young officers into the night to see if they could spot any traces of the man's flight. With the snow coming down harder and harder, it seemed unlikely. He cursed to himself. The irritating "Holy Mary, Mother of God" had resumed. He cursed again. The investigation was not off to a promising start.

Within the hour, the mansion was swarming with policemen and detectives who had been summoned from Harrisburg. The upper floors of the mansion were cordonned off, and the help, less terrified now than dazed, collected in the kitchen. The cook had brewed a large pot of coffee, but nobody was drinking it.

Some officers, at a loss at what to do, milled about the living and dining rooms, trying to look purposeful but mostly taking in the furnishings. There had been a lot of talk in the town when the mansion had gone up. Now they were getting a chance to see for themselves how bankers lived.

In the dining room, on a long table covered with antique lace, heavy silver and crystal glasses caught the light from the chandelier and sparkled. Chafing dishes on the cherry sideboard suggested the generous amounts of food that would be served later in the evening. Or would have been. Boughs of pine trees adorned the mantelpieces, adding to the fragrance of the stately Christmas tree in the foyer. It was festive, opulent, lifeless.

A spanking new 1928 Ford, driven by a well-dressed man, chugged into the driveway. Next to him sat a woman in a sable coat. Packages were piled up on the backseat.

"Oh, my god, the guests," the maid wailed. "What are we going to do?"

"How many are you expecting?"

"*About fifty.*"

The sergeant singled out a chubby-faced officer barely in his twenties, standing in the foyer, one of the few men who had chosen not to go upstairs and view the corpse. "Billy," he ordered. "Don't let anyone up here. Block off the end of the road."

"*What do I tell them?*"

The sergeant felt a great weariness come over his body. A murder like this was terrible enough, but that it should happen now, during the season of peace and goodwill, made it doubly awful to him. "Tell them," he said with a wry nod of the head, "that Christmas has been canceled this year."

Outside, there was a stomping of boots on the veranda, then the front door opened. A frostbitten policeman stumbled in, out of breath, shaking snow from his cap. "We found him."

The house went silent.

"*You found who?*" *the sergeant asked.*

"*Charles Kennedy. The husband. We found him.*"

Four

—~m—

In the weeks that followed Blake's departure, it began to sink in how impractical the place really was. *Folly* was a word that Carol had to keep banishing from her mind. She told herself that was Blake talking, then she'd shuffle through the bills and concede that maybe he'd had a point. A small inheritance from her parents had covered the down payment, and she and Blake had taken out a home-improvement loan to cover some of the basic construction costs, but that money wasn't going to hold out forever. She calmed herself with the notion that a warm spring would put an end to the astronomical heating bills.

Fortunately, there was the rent from the second-floor apartment. Paul Clemson had been living in those three rooms on the west side of the house for years, when the Roblinses moved in. He had yellowing skin, tobacco-stained teeth, and a gnarled body that could have been whittled out of driftwood. Six days a week, he worked as a mechanic at Broadbent's Automotive Center on the out-skirts of Fayette, and the seventh day, he kept mostly to himself, shut up in his apartment. His hands were callused and permanently stained with oil, which made them look a little like relief maps.

His surliness had bothered Carol. But Blake had said the man was just taciturn and agreed to let him stay on, while they redid the rooms around his. Then Germany had called and she was left to handle Clem, as everyone called him. He had already grown lax with the rent payments. Each time Carol tried to bring it to his attention, he responded with a monosyllabic grunt. This month's rent was already nine days late.

Just another of life's little travails, Carol murmured to herself as she wandered out on the veranda. The trouble was, if you started adding up life's little travails, you had one big travail on your hands before long.

"Sammy?" she called into the dusk. "Supper."

The mountains off in the distance were inky black against an orange sunset. She breathed in the tangy March air, a mixture of pine needles and fresh earth redolent of spring. Being the owner of the biggest, partly renovated mansion in the county had its consolations. Sammy had taken to the fields and forest with all the vigor of a twelve-year-old boy who, for the first time in his life, wasn't being reminded to watch the traffic, wait for the red light, and look both ways before crossing the street. "Don't wander too far," "Stay out of the stream," and "Leave the dead animals alone" were the rules that Carol now laid down.

While she stood there, rubbing her arms briskly to fend off the chill, Clem's dented pickup snarled up the driveway and lurched to a stop by the kitchen door. She thought about asking him for the rent, but no sooner had she got her courage up than he had pushed through the kitchen door. All the months she had known him, Clem had never used the front door or the main staircase. He came and went by the back—skulked in and out like a dark shadow. Sometimes, she didn't even hear him descending the stairs in the morning. She would glance up and catch him standing there, staring at her with those milky eyes of his, as she prepared Sammy's breakfast.

An electric light went on in one of his rooms and threw a yellowish glow on the lawn. Clem's bedroom was located just over the library, where Carol slept. He clumped around a lot at night, and the clumping carried through the ceiling.

Once she had gone upstairs and asked him to turn down his television, but he'd been so unpleasant about it that she had never asked again.

The sound that made her prick up her ears right now, however, was the squish-squishing of her son's sneakers as he rounded the corner of the mansion. She knew what that meant: Sammy had been wading in the stream again. The sheepish expression in his brown eyes confirmed it, even before she checked out his feet. Carol permitted herself an exasperated sigh, then relented and gave him a hug. How important, after all, were wet sneakers?

More serious problems faced them. Blake was gone and she and Sammy were living in a torn-up house with a stranger who hardly spoke to them.

As they trudged up the front steps, hand in hand, she told Sammy they would be having fresh apple cobbler for dessert that night. What did he think of that?

"Cobbler?"

"You know. Like apple pie. Soggier."

He considered the prospect gravely. "Okay."

She could have proposed rhubarb pie or Jell-O pudding, and he would have been just as amenable. Sammy Roblins, she reflected, was the most cooperative man in her life right now.

As soon as he was born, Carol gave herself over totally to motherhood. Samuel Grover Roblins, she proudly informed anyone who would listen, was a special baby. He hardly ever cried. Whenever he awoke in the middle of the night, it was no effort putting him back to sleep. He had such an innately sweet disposition, such a contented look in his soft brown eyes (courtesy of Blake), that several times every day Carol would lean over his crib and coo, "What are you dreaming about, my little man?"

That was how she and Blake explained it to themselves when his first words were so long in coming. Sammy was a dreamer, off in his own world, but so good-natured! "He's just like Fred when he was a kid," said Carol, referring to a cousin who'd grown up to be a fairly prominent nuclear physicist. Blake countered that Sammy's temperament came from his side of the family and had a whole list of kindly aunts and benevolent grandparents to support his claim.

Sammy was six before he could tie his shoes, and then he needed constant reminding to do it. "Your laces, Sammy!" Carol would point out time and again. And time and again Sammy would look down and say, "Oh, yeah." But his attention would immediately be drawn to something else and the laces would be forgotten. He had the concentration of a butterfly.

"Didn't you hear your mother?" Blake barked at him one morning. Sammy turned back, surprised, and answered, "Yes." But when Blake asked him what she had just said, Sammy couldn't remember. In retrospect, that was a sign. There were a lot of signs in those early years. Carol and Blake misread them all. "Late bloomer" got added to Sammy's character description, as the explanation for his erratic behavior. That, and "his head is always in the clouds." But his bursts of energy and his insatiable sense of curiosity were enough to convince them that in most other respects, he was a perfectly normal child.

It was a first-grade teacher in Costa Mesa, California, who recognized that Sammy might have a problem. As delicately as possible, she pointed out that he didn't follow directions very well and she had difficulty getting him to join in group activities. He seemed to mix up left and right, forward and backward, up and down—simple opposites like that. And were they aware how terribly confused he was by numbers?

Seeing a scowl on Blake's face, she quickly backed off. "Of course, it may mean nothing at all. He could just be young for his age."

The child psychiatrist was more forthright. After giving Sammy a battery of tests, he informed Blake and Carol that their son was learning disabled.

"You mean retarded?" Blake asked bluntly.

"No, he is not stupid, Mr. Roblins, but he definitely has a neurophysiological problem and severe attention deficit disorders."

"In ordinary words, Doctor, please."

"Well, his central nervous system isn't working right. He has difficulty processing information, language. He doesn't take it in the way other children do. That's why he seems unfocused so much of the time and why his thoughts sometimes come out fragmented. He can't express all he knows. There's a lot more inside Sammy's head than he is able to share with you."

The doctor reassured them that there was no reason to despair. With proper tutoring and guidance, plenty of learning-disabled children achieved great success. The important thing was to build on their strengths, their imagination and their creativity.

Blake looked distressed, nonetheless, as the doctor went on to explain that learning disability is often passed through the male genes. "Or it could come from a virus the woman contracts during pregnancy. We don't know enough, really, to say for sure."

Later that night, after Sammy had gone to bed, Blake confronted Carol with his suspicions. "I suppose you think it's my fault. Well, it's not. There's never been anything like that in my family before."

"It's nobody's fault, Blake. It just is."

"All that stuff about the male genes—that doctor doesn't know what he's talking about. So don't blame me that our kid's abnormal."

"I'm not blaming anybody. And anyway, he's not. He just needs a little extra help," Carol said as reassuringly as she could. Blake didn't appear persuaded.

From then on, she noticed subtle changes in their relationship. They no longer talked about the big family they would have someday. Whenever she brought up the subject, Blake replied that it cost enough to raise one kid as it was. How could they ever afford two? But she sensed that wasn't the real reason. Somewhere inside him—in a place so hidden she could never reach it—he was afraid. The son he had produced was deficient. He held himself responsible.

Each time Sammy lost his mittens or tripped on his untied shoelaces or disappeared into his dreamworld, Blake regarded it as his own failure. It was as if the sins of the son

LEONARD FOGLIA AND DAVID RICHARDS

were being visited on the father. Blake pulled back emotionally and began to hold Sammy at arm's length. Carol saw it
happening and rushed in to fill the void.

She became Sammy's teacher and his best friend. Someone had to, and his flights of fantasy didn't disturb her the
way they did Blake. In the doctor's politically correct words,
Sammy was an "exceptional" child. Carol took it to mean
that he was unique, his own special person, and relished his
pluck and his oddly poetic view of the world. If only Blake
could see him through her eyes.

She never regretted the hours she spent with her son or
the patience she lavished on him. Several years before the
move to Fayette, however, even she had to recognize that
Sammy was relying on her less and less. His solitary side
became steadily more pronounced the older he got, and he
shied away from children his own age, content to spend
hours alone. With a growing sadness, she observed that he
was his own best companion. As for school, specialized
instructors, far more knowledgeable than she, had taken
over his education. Carol found herself becoming just a
mother again. There was nothing wrong with that. But once
she had aspired to something more.

She couldn't remember when the idea first came to her.
It seemed the logical thing to do, though. Fayette was
surrounded by Civil War battle sites, and the Gingerton
State Forest drew its share of visitors, especially in the fall,
when the leaves turned and a mountain of pumpkins
marked every roadside stand.

Outside of the Motel 6 on Route 30 and a Holiday Inn
that had seen more festive days, there was no place for
tourists to spend the night, so most of them pushed on to
Harrisburg. A bed-and-breakfast stood to prosper, if it was
attractive and friendly and had some kind of historical
connection.

Carol had always wanted a career—not just an office job,
but one that brought her into contact with people. Retailing
seemed the logical choice—she could see herself as an
executive for a big department store—but at community
college, a series of dreary economics classes, taught by

cheerless professors, had gotten the best of her enthusiasm. Surprisingly, the nutrition course she had taken only because she needed the credits proved more to her liking. Organic foods were becoming the rage, and the rewakening interest in regional cuisine intrigued her. At a small culinary institute in Boston, where she signed up for night classes, she discovered that she had a real flair in the kitchen. Then she met Blake, fell in love, and became an army wife and mother. When she gave up night classes, she promised herself it would be just for a while. But "a while" stretched to months, then to years, and the idea of a career was now little more than a hazy memory.

It must have been the display in the window of Browser's Corner, the bookshop on Main Street, that planted the seed. The theme was "Voyage Far and Wide with Books," and the window was decorated with flags, maps, and various travel guides. Carol was running a quick errand to Beldman's Pharmacy next door, but one book in particular—*The Bed-and-Breakfasts of North America*—had attracted her attention. On her way home, the inspiration hit her. The Kennedy mansion had all the requirements of the ideal bed-and-breakfast. God knows it was big enough. It had charm, or would by the time the renovation was finished. And its past was rich and romantic, or so she had been led to believe by the real estate broker.

The more she turned the idea over, the more excited she became. It did seem the best solution. What were her options, after all? Either she could rattle around the mansion for a year, fretting about the state of her marriage, or she could make something of the place. If the itinerant army lifestyle had taught her anything, it was how to set up a comfortable home, meet strangers, and make them feel welcome. The cooking would be a breeze.

She convinced herself that her marriage wasn't foundering so much as that she and Blake had simply chosen to pursue separate careers. In different ways, opportunity had struck for both of them.

She brought up the idea to Blake during one of their weekly phone conversations. Sammy always spoke with his father first, then she came on the line and caught him up with the news. She still felt obliged to run things by him. Some habits never died. She eased into the subject casually. "You know, I've given a lot of thought to the house since you've been gone . . ."

There was silence on the other end of the line.

". . . and, well, it seems to me that . . ."

"What?"

She blurted it out. "That it would make a great bed-and-breakfast. Now just listen for a moment." Her enthusiasm took hold, and in a rush of words she laid out her plans for the house and grounds.

"That's a pretty major undertaking, Carol. Do you really think now is the time?" She chose not to pick up on the condescension in his voice.

"You always thought this place was too big for us alone. And the area needs a nice bed-and-breakfast. With all this Civil War stuff, a lot of tourists come through here. There'd be nothing like it in Fayette. I've checked around." She went on and on, not wanting to stop, for fear that Blake would belittle her dream or reject it out of hand.

At last, she put the question to him, phrasing it as positively as possible. "Don't you agree that it's a fabulous idea?"

"I think . . . we should think about it."

That wasn't what she wanted to hear. "Believe me, that's all I've been doing. I've put a great deal of research into this."

"Can't it wait until I get home?"

"And when is that going to be?"

He paused. "I don't know."

His nonchalance struck a spark of anger in her. "Well, I can't wait around for you to decide what you're doing with your life and what part Sammy and I will play in it."

"That's not fair. We both agreed we needed time."

"Yes, Blake. And I've made up my mind that this is what I want to do with my time."

"So you really don't need my opinion. Why did you bother to ask?" There was the old Blake, making her feel inadequate with his superior attitude. How often in the past

28

had she held herself back because of a flip remark he had tossed off? Well, she wasn't going to buckle.

"Blake, what do you expect me to do for the next year? Just sit here? You hadn't thought about that, had you? You only thought about what you needed."

"Starting a business is not a hobby you can drop the minute you get bored with it. It takes commitment. Day in, day out. And money."

She knew that those weren't the real issues. She was the issue. Could Mrs. Blake Roblins really manage on her own? Without him? Once again, she was asking for his approval, his permission, but for the first time in their marriage, she realized she didn't need it.

"Do you have so little faith in me, Blake?" she said softly.

For a while, the only sound on the line was the low crackle of static. "I'm afraid we have a bad connection," he finally noted. "I told you what I think. What else can I say? Good luck."

From that point on, the mansion became the focus of her days and her recurring dreams—a preoccupation that helped stave off darker thoughts about the future with Blake.

She estimated that the living and dining rooms, end to end, measured thirty by eighty feet. What better spot for wedding receptions! She imagined the guests chatting brightly and getting tipsy on champagne. On a nice summer's day, they could spill out onto the veranda, which she would line with pots of red and pink geraniums. Not that the mansion wouldn't be a perfect place for business conferences, too. It was quiet, spacious, and spoke of prosperous times. Or did once. Businessmen liked that. As an extra attraction, she'd work out a tie-in with the Fayette Golf and Racket Club.

More than anything else, though, she would make the mansion into a romantic weekend getaway for couples from Washington and Philadelphia. What had been apartments she would turn into bedroom suites and give each one a name. The most luxurious would be the Kennedy Suite, after the original owners. If she could locate an old photograph of them, she'd even hang it on the wall over the bed. Assuming they were attractive, of course. If they weren't, well, Currier and Ives would have to do.

"One of the Christmas scenes," she said to herself.

The Kennedy mansion would be the showplace of the county again, pictured in all the best architectural digests. And she'd be sitting on the veranda in a wide-brimmed hat, toasting the photographer with an iced tea.

"Cheers!" she said, hoisting her paintbrush. She felt a few droplets of paint land on her face.

Painting the inside of the linen closet in the downstairs bathroom was an inconsequential job that didn't have to be done today. But addressing trivial tasks now and then gave her a needed sense of accomplishment. She had met with a few contractors in the area, and getting someone to take on such a long-term project at an affordable price was proving to be less of a snap than she had hoped. Tim Holmes, the owner of Fayette Remodelers, quoted her a bid that was twice what she had anticipated.

"Isn't there any way to do it less expensively?" she asked him.

"Sure," he growled. "Hire a couple of college kids to come in and slap some paint on the walls. If you want a professional job, it's going to cost you."

She said she would have to think about it.

So here she was: The Handywoman in spite of Herself. It sounded like a bad comedy.

She balanced her paintbrush on the edge of the paint can and listened for Sammy. The house was still. Where had he gone to this morning? She was pretty sure he wasn't in the basement. That was last week's hideout. The week before, she'd found him in the closet in one of the back bedrooms on the second floor. But a twelve-year-old boy had a hundred other places to hide. That was the trouble with an old mansion like this. Along with the plumbing that needed repairing, of course, and the faulty wiring, and the dry rot in the pantry. She stopped herself.

No, she wasn't going to get into all that again.

Not today. It was too nice out, a perfect sunny day, unseasonably warm for March.

On a hunch, she went to the foot of the stairs and shouted. "Sammy, I'm giving you ten to get down here. One . . . two . . . three . . ." Faint footsteps on the third floor indicated that she had flushed her son out of hiding. Just to make sure, she continued counting.

"Seven, eight, I'm at nine, young man. Nine is one away from ten, and if I get to ten, the television goes off for a week. Trust me. Nine and one-half . . ."

Sammy bounded into sight.

"Hiding." He smiled gleefully. "Way up. High as the trees. Do you want me to show you?"

"No, sweetheart. I would like you to go outside and get some fresh air. You're not going to spend the first sunny day of March in a closet. Why don't you go see if the violets have come up by the stream."

"Violets?"

"Yes, violets. The little purple flowers."

"Okay."

"And stay out of the water."

Arms flying, Sammy scampered down the final flight of stairs, paused, then took the last three steps in one leap. His sneakers hit with a thump, and a silver angel, blowing a trumpet, tumbled to the floor.

"Mind the Christmas tree," his mother said. "How often do I have to tell you? And take your windbreaker."

She retrieved the angel and refastened it to the branch from which it had fallen. The tree was one of those artificial pines that required no water, no care, only the occasional dusting. Time was, Carol would never have let such a thing in the house. But that was when she took her tree down after the holidays like everyone else. A real tree was out of the question now. A real tree, she knew from experience, barely lasted through the end of February, and spontaneous combustion was always a danger in the summer.

Anyway, unless you felt the needles, she rationalized, you couldn't tell the difference.

Sammy escaped into the sunshine, and Carol returned to her painting, finished off the inside of the linen closet, and briefly thought about tackling the medicine chest before calling it quits. She plunged her paintbrush into a can of turpentine, then wiped her hands on her baggy overalls, resolving, as she did, to start paying more attention to her appearance. With Blake gone, she had little inducement to look her best. And yet she prided herself on her hair, silky blond with no trace of gray—and her face still retained that all-American freshness that had so displeased her as a youth, when ethnic was in and she would have killed to look more exotic—like Cher.

Her ancestors had been pale, blue-eyed Englishmen and women with flawless skin, and the lineage showed. Plump as a child, she'd shot up in adolescence—"just like a patch of nettles," her mother used to say—to her present height, a little over five and a half feet, and acquired the lithe figure she had maintained ever since. Her high cheekbones gave her an aristocratic air, slightly at variance with her full lips, which were responsible for the sensuality of her face and suggested that sometime in the past a Mediterranean or two had managed to get a toehold on the family tree.

Most people were surprised to learn that she was thirty-eight and would have guessed ten years younger. She considered herself plain nonetheless, and the baggy overalls weren't doing a whole lot this morning to improve her self-image.

She heard Sammy laughing and hooting on the front lawn. So he wasn't checking for violets. It was still better than having him shut up in the attic with the bird's nests and acorns and rocks that he was forever dragging in from the woods. A regular scavenger, her son.

She went out on the veranda. A tall, rugged-looking man wearing a baseball cap was playing catch with the boy. His black hair was thick and curly, and a tuft of dark chest hair poked out of the neck of his khaki work shirt. He moved with the kind of loping, loose-limbed grace she admired. She couldn't decide if he had failed to shave this morning or was simply one of those men who had to shave twice a day.

"What can I do for you?" she shouted down at him.

"Mrs. Roblins?" He removed his baseball cap and ambled toward the veranda.

Sammy was yelling, "Throw it back. Throw it back."

The man stopped, pitched the ball high in the air, and said, "Pop fly to center field."

Sammy squealed with joy, as he did whenever he got overly excited, and danced on his toes while he waited for the ball to come down. He caught it with both hands, then shrieked, "Catch! Catch! Catch it again."

"Just a minute, son. I want to talk to your mum, okay?"

Sammy contented himself by spinning in wide circles on the grass.

"I'm Walker White, Mrs. Roblins. I work for Tim Holmes down at Fayette Remodelers. I couldn't help noticing you the other day."

He reached out and shook her hand firmly. As he let go, she realized that this was the first contact she'd had with an attractive man since her husband's departure, and for a second she actually found herself comparing the stranger with Blake. Physically, he was larger, but he had an ease about him that contrasted pleasantly with Blake's military bearing. His chin was strong, but his mouth turned up at the corners, softening his face and giving the impression that he was about to break into a smile at any moment.

So there were other possibilities out in the world, she thought. Handsome possibilities with dark hair, dimples, and tight jeans. And here she was in baggy overalls without a trace of makeup, only splatters of white paint on her face. Figured!

She checked her thoughts. It was only a handshake, after all.

"I'm sorry Tim was so rude," she heard him saying. "Nothing personal. He gets that way sometimes. Anyway, I'd like to talk to you about the job."

"From what Mr. Holmes said, I'm not sure I can afford you."

"Maybe you can't afford him, but don't rule me out so fast." He flashed a big grin and the dimples reappeared. "Maybe we could negotiate a price acceptable to both of us."

"Should you be going behind your boss's back like this, Mr. White?"

"Call me Walker, please. Way I look at it, it's more like getting out from under his thumb."

He went on to explain that he'd been thinking of striking out on his own for some time now and had just been waiting for the right opportunity. The renovation would give him a good chunk of work up front. Five or six months' worth, from what he estimated. That would allow him plenty of time to rustle up other jobs for the future.

"I don't have Tim's overhead, so I'm willing to work for what he was paying me—fifteen dollars an hour, give or take a few minutes. I have my own tools. And I'm dependable."

Good as the idea sounded to Carol, she felt obliged to offer a few objections on principle. "You can't do this all by yourself. It's not a one-man job. I'd pitch in, of course, do my share. Still . . ."

"I know lotsa guys to hire for any special work. You can pay them direct, like you'll pay me. Frankly, Mrs. Roblins, I think it's a good deal for everyone, don't you?"

What other prospects did she have? "Well, I suppose it's worth a try. We could see how it works out for both of us . . . Walker." They shook hands again.

"Monday, then?"

She tucked a rebellious strand of blond hair behind her ear and smiled nervously.

"Monday."

So Walker became a big part of their lives, swiftly taking over the role of decision-maker. Carol had to remind herself periodically that she was the employer and he was paid help. He had a habit of just plunging into his work, no questions asked, and she had never been one for giving orders. In her mind, it made for some awkwardness, but she was going to have to learn a lot of things. How to take charge was only one of them.

There was no question that Sammy came alive in Walker's presence, absorbing the male energy he gave off and drinking in the least bit of praise, like one parched for it.

Every morning, the boy waited eagerly for Walker's pickup truck to arrive, and as soon as the wheels hit the gravel driveway, he would announce to the whole house,

"He's here! Walker's here!" After school, he'd tag along with the workman, going from room to room, carrying his tools and making a nuisance of himself. Walker never let on that the boy was anything but a big help.

"When I start my own company, you'll come work as a contractor for me," he promised Sammy, and clapped him on the back.

"When is that?"

"Someday soon."

Sammy crowed delightedly and darted off to tell Carol. "Guess what?"

"What?"

"Walker says I can be a compactor for him someday."

Carol devoured every book she could locate on home improvement, and her head was soon swimming in confusion. The language was foreign to her, and the technical drawings didn't help. If she was going to make any progress at all, she realized the renovation was going to have to be carried out in an orderly manner. She and Walker sat down at the kitchen table and drew up a battle plan.

They decided what parts of the house would be attacked first (the kitchen, the living room, the dining room, and the foyer). Then, carefully assessing the chosen areas, they determined what should be saved (the double sink, the cabinetry, and obviously, the fireplace mantels) and what shouldn't (every last kitchen appliance and the horrid fluorescent lighting).

With Walker's guidance, she weighed bids from various subcontractors. After that, her chief function was the coordination and scheduling of the work itself. She had always thought of herself as organized. But getting a kid and a husband up and started on their day was no preparation for keeping a half dozen workmen busy and on schedule, especially when they regarded her with a thinly masked skepticism that, maddeningly, vanished if Walker was by her side.

There was more to it than pulling down old walls and putting up new ones, but little by little, she figured it out. She learned that the electricians and the plumbers had to start their work *before* the new walls were closed up. Once the wallboards were hung and plastered, they would come back and do the rest of their job—installing the surface outlets and switches, the fixtures and appliances. As for the moldings, baseboards, doors, and cabinets, they were the province of the carpenters (Walker and a good friend, Joey Burns, whom he kept talking about) and came next. After that, new flooring would be laid wherever it was needed. Then, and only then, would they tackle the best part, the sanding and the woodworking and the painting, all the finishing touches that would make the old place good as new. (She blushed to think that she had once considered those finishing touches to be the lion's share of the job.)

With an overall plan in her head, the project no longer struck her as quite so overwhelming, and after a few weeks the signs of progress multiplied rapidly. Walker opened up the fireplace in the dining room and pronounced the chimney in operative condition. As rotting plasterboard walls were ripped down and carted away, Carol could start to see where the original rooms had been. The day new appliances were ordered for the kitchen, she decided it was her job to strip the cupboards in the pantry. A few layers down, she came upon a coat of psychedelic orange.

"Hippies!" she said, laughing.

When she finally hit the original wood, it was a rich molasses color, delicately veined. The discovery filled her with new resolve. If she was going to do this job, she was going to do it right. Everything would be as authentic as possible, so that the minute guests crossed the doorstep, they would be transported back to a more gracious era. She'd be providing them with more than comfortable lodging. She'd be offering them escape.

"We're not just going to renovate this place, Walker. We're going to *restore* it," she announced one morning as she was serving him coffee in the kitchen. Sammy had his nose in his oatmeal and wasn't listening, but Carol noticed a funny expression on Walker's face.

"I really mean it," she insisted. "Every square inch of this house is going to be put back exactly the way it was when that couple moved in here seventy years ago."

Suddenly, she realized Walker wasn't looking at her. He was looking past her at Clem, who was standing, immobile, at the foot of the stairs. Before she had time to say anything, the mechanic elbowed by her and banged the kitchen door with such force that the Christmas wreath nearly came unattached.

Five

—••—

Despite his fortune, he never felt he deserved her. The money had accumulated too quickly, and prosperity had not required great efforts on his part. Although he was a serious worker, he had come to believe that luck, more than his own industry, had shaped his success. He could easily remember a time in his youth when his family lived modestly. His mother had regarded money with some suspicion, born of her sober New England heritage, and she'd passed that suspicion on to him, along with a fine nose, chestnut hair, and eyes of a blue so dark they verged on black. He could have lived luxuriously, but didn't, and that made him seem eccentric to many.

Women would have flirted with him, had he given them the least encouragement, but he barely noticed their presence and had little sense of himself as pleasing. Long ago, he had convinced himself that he had no aptitude for small talk and the intricacies of courtship. "Too busy working for anything else," he'd reply when his friends chided him on his solitary ways. After a while, it was just assumed that he was destined to be a bachelor.

"What a pity," sniffed mothers with eligible daughters

when they saw him emerging from the Fayette Guaranty and Trust.

Veronica changed all that. As outgoing as he was reticent, as sure of her appeal as he was ignorant of his, she was by common consent the most desirable young woman in the county. Also one of the more headstrong. One day, she turned to her closest friend and announced abruptly that her mind was made up. After a careful assessment of all the single men in the county, she had concluded that Mr. Kennedy was the only one worthy of being her husband. Thereafter, while she didn't exactly connive to get him, she did see to it that she crossed his path whenever he came out of the bank, or that she was seated to his right at the rare dinners he was coaxed into attending.

In no time, he was smitten—as much by her outgoing manner as by her startling beauty. Her hair was a lustrous black and she wore it in a bob, a style popularized by the screen star Louise Brooks. The cut emphasized Veronica's porcelain skin and the mischief in her eyes and also contributed to her reputation for daring in the conservative town, where movie goddesses were viewed by many as creatures of abandon, if not outright sin.

Despite a tendency to speak whatever was on her mind, Veronica never commented on the banker's stodgy past or badgered him to change his ways. But he became decidedly less standoffish in her company, as if her sociability were somehow contagious. The big difference that had come over Mr. Kennedy replaced the size of his fortune as the major topic of conversation in the parlors and on the street corners of Fayette. He was no longer deemed solemn, and his awkwardness in a crowd was now considered part of his special charm.

It became evident that he had been frugal in the past only because he had had nothing, or no one, to spend his money on. She awakened his latent generosity and he showered her with presents—silk scarves, jewelry, and for Christmas, a beagle whose mournful appearance recalled his own disposition before she had entered his life. His biggest gift to her, however, would be the house he would construct on one hundred acres of land outside Fayette. The property straddled Ragged Ridge Road, a dusty one-lane byway named for the faintly sinister outcropping of rock that dominated the northwest corner. Removed from Fayette, surrounded only by rolling fields and stands of fir and pine, and in the distance, the jagged, toothlike rocks that seemed at sunset to be taking a bite out of the sky, it would be their dream house.

It scared him sometimes how much he loved her. He placated those fears by sparing no expense on the building, insisting on the best materials and then hovering over the teams of workmen, who were soon laboring eighteen hours a day, seven days a week, under his vigilant eye. He saw its rooms as a projection of the future they would have together. They had to be perfect, because their lives would be perfect. The elegant chestnut staircase was designed with only her in mind—how her hand would look on the banister, how the large leaded-glass window on the landing would silhouette her. The risers mustn't be too steep, he instructed the architect, or the treads too narrow. Details obsessed him, right down to their entwined initials, which he had a glazier etch into the glass of the front door.

The living room would be closed off from the dining room by large mahogany doors that glided on metal tracks. When the doors were open, the two rooms would accommodate the big parties she liked, the dances and the holiday receptions. Also on the first floor, he wanted a sitting room for her, a paneled office for himself, and a library for them both. Even though the house would have the latest gravity hot-air furnace—the warmth rising up through filigreed grates that bore their initials, as well— he saw fireplaces in every room, giving off the golden glow and sharp crackle of pine logs burning.

On the floors above, he mapped out a whole configuration of bedrooms—a master suite with a spacious dressing room; sunny, bright bedrooms for the children she would bear him; and even a pair of guest bedrooms with a shared parlor for the relatives who'd come visiting. He was fascinated by the latest bathroom fixtures one day. The next, the properties of marble from Carrara, compared with that quarried in Vermont, were his overriding concern. Nor did he forget the servants, who would inhabit the third floor, connected to the rest of the house by an intricate web of wires and bells. If she were to ring a bell in the library or the master bedroom, an electric board at the head of the third-floor hallway and another in the kitchen would automatically light up, directing the servants where their services were required.

Everything was for her, the woman who had drawn him out of himself and given his fortune a purpose. He could barely wait to show it all off—the house, his bride, their happiness. The engagement lasted a year, during which the architect was afforded no rest and the workmen were urged to greater and greater speed. Six weeks before the wedding, invitations went out, announcing that the marriage would take place at two o'clock on the afternoon of Saturday, June 4, 1927, at the First Presbyterian Church of Fayette. Following the ceremony, a reception would be held at 1 Ragged Ridge Road, soon to be known as the Kennedy mansion.

Six

—◆◆◆—

The Fayette Historical Society was just a desk in a corner of the Fayette Public Library, which had been built, like the town's elementary school, in the late 1950s, when its long, low lines and brick and glass walls passed for the height of modern. Now it looked dated, although in no interesting way, and people regretted more of an effort had not been made to save the original library, a fanciful Victorian structure with thick stone walls and turrets. The argument for pulling it down—or at least the one advanced at the time by Mr. Beldman from behind his pharmacy counter—was that the high-ceilinged rooms simply cost too much to heat. The old building had required constant upkeep and a full-time janitor just to see to it that the floors were oiled, the shelves dusted, and the plumbing functional.

So it had been leveled and replaced by a nondescript shoebox with green, scuff-resistant vinyl floors that could easily be buffed with an electric polisher. The original library survived only in photographs. One, taken in 1910, was featured prominently on the wall behind the desk belonging to the historical society and helped define the society's jurisdiction in a building that kept interior walls to a minimum. The irony was not lost on Carol.

Sammy loved going to the library for story time. Every Wednesday afternoon, the children gathered on the oval carpet under the central skylight to listen to the adventures of horses that could fly and dolphins that could sing. Sammy sat there spellbound, unaware that most of the other kids were five or six, half his age, or that he towered above them. Carol tried not to notice, too. Afterward, still under their thrall, he would repeat the day's stories all the way home in the car.

Carol couldn't remember anyone telling her stories when she was growing up. Her mother hadn't read much—just the occasional biography and the obituaries. Fiction was frivolous. Her father, a taciturn man, usually turned on the television set after dinner and dozed. Books had offered her an early escape from the dull world of uncommunicative parents, and they had been an important part of her life ever since.

Soon after she had started taking Sammy to story time, she had become aware of the desk with the historical-society lady seated sternly behind it. That's what people actually called her—the historical-society lady. She was always slightly overdressed, as if she were presiding over a formal tea, not a dozen wooden filing cabinets stuffed with documents and a couple of shelves of books by local authors, who had a passion for Civil War taverns or Indian artifacts unearthed in the hills beyond the town dump. She was probably in her late sixties, wore too much powder, looked vaguely sexless, and obviously took her duties seriously.

While waiting with the other mothers for story time to finish, Carol had observed more than one person approach the desk and innocently ask the historical-society lady for the location of a best-seller or manuals on gardening. In a sharply whispered admonition that could be heard by everyone, the misguided souls were informed that libraries were for reading and maybe it was time they started with the sign before their very noses. Thereupon, a bony hand connected to a thin arm lifted itself off the desk and pointed dramatically to the brass plaque under the photograph that said "Fayette Historical Society, Founded 1903."

The gesture, worthy of the ghost of Christmas future, had

its effect. Chastised, the confused patrons usually slunk away without another word. The mothers all shook their heads, amused and a little put off by the woman's haughty manner. When Carol decided to start delving in earnest into the history of the Kennedy mansion, though, she knew where to go first.

Standing in front of the desk one crisp Monday morning that March, she waited while the lady finished making cryptic entries in a ledger, carefully screwed the cap back on her fountain pen, and then deigned to look up.

"Yes?" she hissed.

"I wonder if you could give me some information," Carol said, feeling a bit like an errant first-grader in the principal's office.

Automatically, the bony hand rose up and pointed to the plaque on the wall.

"Oh, I know. That's why I'm here. I'm looking for information about the former Kennedy mansion on Ragged Ridge Road. My name is Carol Roblins and I recently bought—"

"I know who you are."

"You do? What a nice surprise. And who might you be?"

"Esther McPherson."

"How pleasant to meet you, Mrs., uh, McPherson," replied Carol, momentarily taken aback to learn that the historical-society lady had a name. "I'm sure you'll be able to help me. I'm interested in finding out whatever I can about the Kennedy mansion. You know, pictures of the house when it was built. The inside, particularly. I thought you might help me track down the original blueprints. Anything, really."

"Whatever for?"

"I'm planning on restoring the house. Actually, I've already made considerable progress."

"We don't have anything on that house," snapped Mrs. McPherson, turning her attention back to the ledger.

"You don't? How odd." The thought that the historical society wouldn't be a treasure trove of information hadn't crossed Carol's mind.

"May I ask why you don't?"

"We don't have information on every house in the county, Mrs. Roblins."

"But, Mrs. McPherson, from what I can tell, this isn't just any house. It was one of the most splendid houses of its day. Can you imagine the money that went into it? It must have been quite a showplace. I can't believe you wouldn't have any information about it."

The main librarian and a couple of browsers glanced over. The historical-society lady drew herself up tall.

"Mrs. Roblins, the Fayette Historical Society was founded so that our children, and our children's children, would have a record of who built this county and so that we might preserve some of the beauty of the past. There is no beauty worth preserving on Ragged Ridge Road. And now if you will excuse me . . ."

That was obviously the end of the conversation. Startled by the edge in Mrs. McPherson's voice, Carol turned and made her way out of the library. She paused on the steps. Had she been naive to think that the historical society would welcome her with open arms? How many valuable buildings had the town already lost because no one cared? The mansion was certainly going to enhance the community, once the restoration was done. Of all people, Mrs. McPherson should appreciate that. Why then had she been so uncooperative?

Carol retreated slowly down the concrete walk to Main Street. Glancing back, she could see the historical-society lady talking on the telephone. Her face was flushed and she seemed to be speaking fast. Her mouth looked like an angry rubber band. Carol had the uncomfortable feeling that she was being talked about.

Instead of returning home immediately, she walked up Main Street and tried to shake the image of Mrs. McPherson snarling into the receiver. She told herself not to take it personally. The old lady was having a bad day, that's all. Still, the incident at the library pointed up how few people she knew in Fayette.

She and Blake had introduced themselves to the neighbors on Ragged Ridge Road shortly after they'd moved in. But the house was too much of a mess at the time to invite anyone over, and the neighbors for some reason stayed to themselves. There had been no covered dishes, no welcome wagon, no one popping over in the morning for a quick cup of coffee. She hadn't expected people to behave as they did in southern California, where even the checker in the supermarket called you by your first name and told you to have a good day. But she hadn't anticipated quite this many cold shoulders, either.

How many times had she attempted to strike up a conversation with the other mothers at story time? They smiled, returned her hello, then withdrew. Was it because of Sammy? she wondered. Parents were kind to him and seemed to enjoy his high spirits. But they kept their children at a distance, as if his disability might rub off on them. And heaven forbid that Carol might actually invite their precious children to come over and play some afternoon! Apparently, it was simpler for them to fend off that troubling prospect by remaining politely aloof.

Passing by Beldman's Pharmacy, Carol spotted the pharmacist's bald bead glowing under a fluorescent light at the back of the store. She resisted the urge to go into Browser's Corner, next door, which was flogging stacks of the latest Danielle Steel in the window under a banner that said "Put a Little Passion in Your Life." A housewife pushing a shopping cart filled with groceries barreled out of Meadowbrook Market, and Carol had to jump nimbly aside to avoid a bruised shin.

"Pardon, dear," called out the woman, who was having trouble keeping the cart on a straight course. "These damn things have minds of their own." Almost by way of illustration, the cart hooked dramatically to the right and the front wheels skidded off the curb into the gutter.

The sign for Linehan's Candy Kitchen across the street caught Carol's eye, and she decided to stop feeling sorry for herself and indulge in a sundae. The gold-leaf script on the door boasted that the establishment had been "serving our own ice cream since 1908," but sometime in the 1960s, the interior had undergone an unfortunate remodeling. Orange leatherette booths and fake Tiffany lamps set the tone. Still, it was bright and clean and smelled pleasantly of caramels.

Carol seated herself by the window and ordered a dish of French vanilla with chocolate sauce. As soon as it arrived, her mood improved. Maybe she was exaggerating. Things weren't that bad. There was Walker, after all. He was proving to be a godsend. The other day, when he'd removed a wall of discolored Sheetrock in the parlor and come upon a strip of original molding, his excitement over the discovery was almost greater than hers.

One fussy crone presiding over a musty historical society was no measure of anything. Lots of people would be thrilled by what she was doing, if they knew. She took another spoonful of ice cream and gazed out the window. A delivery truck had just pulled up before the office of the *Fayette Weekly Register*.

The idea came to her in a flash. An ad. How simple. She'd put an ad in the *Fayette Weekly Register*, asking anyone with information about the Kennedy mansion on Ragged Ridge Road to get in touch with her. There were bound to be plenty of old-timers in the county with stories about the house. Maybe even pictures they'd be willing to share. It would also be her way of officially announcing that she intended to put down roots here, become part of the life of the town. Who knows what people she'd meet this way?

Eager to get on with it, she polished off the sundae. The first step in her new community-relations program, she decided, as she fished in her coat pocket for her change purse, would be to introduce herself to the woman at the cash register.

"Hello, I'm Carol Roblins," she said, pushing two dollar bills across the counter. "I've just moved to town. Well, not just moved . . . I've been here a few months, actually. I'm from California."

"Are you, now? I'm Nance Linehan and my son owns this place." She was an ample woman whose figure was in no way enhanced by the absurdly frilly, brown-checkered apron that was apparently the mandatory uniform for the female employees. She lowered her voice. "That's my grandson Chet over there."

She nodded in the direction of a surly teenage boy with a paper hat on his shaved head, who was having trouble forcing a scoop into a rock-solid block of pistachio ice cream. He glanced up and grunted.

"Of course, he'd rather be chasing after the high school girls, but we all take turns working here. Family tradition. I'm not objecting, mind you. It keeps me out of trouble. If I could just stay away from the pecan pralines." She gave a little snort that was meant to convey the impossibility of the task. "We make them right here on the premises. I don't suppose you'd want to sample one, would you?"

"Not on top of the sundae, thanks."

"Sure wish I had your discipline," Nance Linehan sighed. "They've always been my downfall, the pecan pralines . . . Them, and the peanut butter truffles and the cherry nougats."

She handed Carol her change, then asked, "By the way, you're not the one that bought the big house out on Ragged Ridge Road?"

"Yes, I am," said Carol, surprised.

"My, my. What are you going to do with a big barn like that?"

"Actually, I've been thinking of making it into a bed-and-breakfast."

"You mean, a hotel?"

"Well, sort of . . ."

"Who's going to stay in a hotel on Ragged Ridge Road? It's nowhere near the main highway. Nobody will know it's even there. Look, I'm not objecting. But have you really thought this through? It seems kinda foolhardy to me."

"Well, maybe it is," Carol replied, wondering how the conversation had taken this turn. "It's just a thought. Anyway, it was nice meeting you, Mrs. Linehan, and your grandson. I'll see you next time."

She pulled her coat around her and pushed open the door.

"Don't you need a permit for that sort of thing?" Mrs. Linehan shouted after her.

As she crossed the street to the *Fayette Weekly Register*, it occurred to Carol that maybe she was going to have to rethink this good-neighbor policy.

Seven

—⁂—

The *Fayette Weekly Register* was published every Thursday and allowed its subscribers, 3,409 according to the most recent audit, to keep up on news they already knew.

By the time the winning score appeared in the paper, most everybody who had an interest in such matters had personally congratulated the high school basketball team. A fire or an automobile accident on Route 30 usually drew a crowd of onlookers, eager, afterward, to give a firsthand account of the disaster. The readers of the *Register* were rarely taken by surprise. Its pages merely confirmed what they had been discussing over back fences or at the Molly Pitcher Coffee Shop, generally recognized as the best place to get in on a breaking story.

No one held it against the *Register*. The paper was appreciated as the unofficial record of births, deaths, and high school graduations. It served as a community bulletin board. (That's how Carol had learned about story time at the library.) The Meadowbrook grocery ads were carefully studied and the coupons faithfully clipped. Dear Abby and Marmaduke, the cartoon, were among the more popular features.

Carol was hardly prepared for all the activity when she

walked in. Several phones were ringing and people were scurrying about. Something was in the air. A man in his fifties was pacing back and forth nervously. His shirtsleeves were rolled up and his paisley vest was unbuttoned. "Is it definite? Make sure it's definite," he kept repeating. This was directed at a heavyset woman who was attempting to do several things at once: cradle a telephone on her shoulder, listen to the person on the other end of the line, take notes, and ignore, at least temporarily, the man behind her.

"Just an hour ago, you say? . . . Was anybody with him? . . . I see. Thanks Evvy. We'll probably want to get back to you." She hung up the phone and announced, "It's official. He filed papers this morning."

A young man huddled over a nearby computer let out a whoop. "Maybe we'll see some action in this burg at last."

"Don't get carried away," said the man in the unbuttoned vest, who seemed to be in charge. The publisher, Carol guessed. "See if you can get him on the phone. If there's an official statement, we'll print it in a sidebar on the front page. I want a draft of the story by this afternoon. Do we have any recent pictures of him? If not, send Scotty over to get a head shot, pronto."

Having issued his orders, he looked up and noticed Carol. "Can I help you?"

"I'd like to place a classified ad."

"Tony," he barked at the young man at the computer, "help this lady, would you?"

The publisher promptly focused on more important matters, while Tony pushed back his chair and jogged up to the counter. He had a spiky haircut and a broad smile and gave off youthful energy, like a pinwheel.

"Is it always this exciting here?" Carol asked him.

Tony sneaked a peek at the others in the office, then whispered, "We just found out someone may be running for mayor." His eyes widened, as if to say, Can you believe it?

"Is that unusual?"

"Running against Mayor Quinn? You bet it is. Except for his first election, no one has ever run against him. And that was before I was born. People call him Mayor for Life. It's a joke. But not really."

"So this is news then."

"About as big as it gets around here." Tony laughed. "It'll be our lead story this week."

Carol felt she was being let in on a secret. Her ad suddenly seemed insignificant.

With a touch of embarrassment, she explained the situation. From under the counter, Tony pulled out a chart, showing the different formats for classified advertising and the cost. Together they decided on a small box and drew up the copy:

> **INFORMATION WANTED**
> concerning the history of
> **1 RAGGED RIDGE ROAD**
> especially photographs
> and original architect's blueprints
> Please write or call Carol Roblins
> 555-9534

"That should do it, Mrs. Roblins," said Tony. "It'll be out on Thursday. I hope you get results."

"Are you finished up there, Tony?" came the publisher's voice from the back of the office. "Let's get cracking on this story. Foster's wife said she expected him home in a half an hour. Why don't you be there when he returns. Talk to him. Pick up some color for the story."

Tony needed no further encouragement. He grabbed a reporter's pad and couple of ballpoint pens off the desk and was halfway out the door when the publisher called after him:

"What are you going to ask?"

Tony stopped in his tracks. "What do you mean?"

"What are you going to ask him? What's the important question?"

"If he's running for mayor."

"We know he's running for mayor, numskull. Find out why he's running. Why?—that's the angle you're after. See if he'll say something about Mayor Quinn. God knows nobody else in this town dares to. And make sure you tell him first that he's talking on the record. Got it?"

"Got it," echoed Tony, and he disappeared down the street.

Carol stood there watching, transfixed. The publisher approached the counter.

"He's a good kid. He'll make a fine journalist someday. I gather he took care of you?"

"Yes, he did," said Carol. "I chose to go with a small box. Would you mind taking a look?"

While the publisher read her ad, she checked him over discreetly. He was compactly built and had begun to bald in a way that made some middle-aged men sexy. His cosmopolitan air definitely set him apart from the average male in Fayette. Carol decided he must have worked on a glamorous, metropolitan newspaper once as an investigative journalist. Maybe in New York. And then he'd given it all up, the glamour and the power, for a simpler life and the chance to run his own weekly journal. She liked that scenario a lot and for the time being preferred to forgo the truth, whatever it was. One thing for sure, men were certainly more attractive to her than they had been for some time.

"Reads fine to me," he said, rubbing his chin. "You know, I just may be able to help you. Can you spare a few minutes?"

He led her to a room at the back of the office, furnished with dull gray metal filing cabinets, oversize bookshelves, a small reading table, and a chair. "This is the morgue," he explained. "We keep bound copies of the *Register* going all the way back to 1912. Ten years ago, we started putting the paper on microfilm. But before that, every article in every newspaper was also clipped by hand and filed according to subject. The next step, if we can ever afford it, I suppose, is to computerize the operation."

He pulled open a filing cabinet drawer, ran an eye over the folders, closed it, and opened another. It took him a few minutes before he located what he was searching for. He removed a manila envelope marked "Kennedy, Charles and family" and laid it on the table.

"This ought to have something," he said. "The Kennedys were pretty prominent around here once upon a time. You don't hear the name much anymore. Anyway, you're free to have a look."

The heavyset woman appeared at the door.

"Sorry to interrupt. Mayor Quinn's on the line. Says it's urgent."

"Ten to one, I know what that's about. He's heard about Foster and wants to know how we're going to play the announcement. Not that the old fox will come right out and ask me. I'll tell him we're doing nothing special. Just putting out a full-color edition, doubling the press run, and distributing the paper for free this week. Think that'll get a rise out of him?"

"An apoplectic fit, is all," remarked the heavyset woman wryly.

Chuckling to himself, the publisher left to take the phone call. Carol sat down at the table and eyed the folder. For a second, she had the uncomfortable sensation that she was prying into someone's private affairs. She could hear her mother's raspy voice admonishing her, "Sticking your nose where it doesn't belong, as usual. When are you ever gonna learn?"

Carol opened the folder anyway.

Several dozen articles, yellowed with age, tumbled out. The paper had the fragile texture of dead leaves. She unfolded the articles carefully, half-afraid that they would snap in two. Some already had and were held together with Scotch tape that had taken on the color of amber.

A banner headline, published on December 28, 1928, jumped out at her.

Bloodshed on Ragged Ridge Road

Community Stunned
by Murder and Suicide

In a tragedy without precedent in the history of Fayette, two of the town's most prominent citizens met their deaths on Christmas Eve.

As she was preparing to receive guests for a holiday supper, Mrs. Charles Kennedy was brutally murdered in the bedroom of her elegant home at 1 Ragged Ridge Road. Robbery is believed to have been the motive.

Upon discovering his wife's body, Mr. Kennedy, the well-known banker and town benefactor, fled from the house and committed suicide less than two hours later by throwing himself in front of a train headed for Erie. His body was dragged several hundred feet. A doctor, arriving on the scene shortly afterward, said that death came instantly.

A statewide search is under way for Mrs. Kennedy's murderer. Meanwhile, Fayette police officials continue to investigate the circumstances of both tragedies. Mr. Kennedy was 38. His wife, the former Veronica Childers, was 25.

Servants Provide Details

From the testimony of the Kennedys' servants, the following picture has emerged. Mrs. Kennedy's body was found just before 7 P.M. on December 24. Megan O'Hare, Mrs. Kennedy's personal maid, told the *Register* that she had gone upstairs to help her mistress dress and was knocking at the bedroom door when Mr. Kennedy arrived home. Stepping aside, she let him pass before her. The lights were low, so initially neither noticed anything unusual. Then Mr. Kennedy spotted his wife curled up in a pool of blood at the foot of her bed. Both he and the maid rushed to her side. She appeared to have been bludgeoned to death. "It was obvious there was nothing to be done for the poor woman," said Mrs. O'Hare, adding that "it was as horrible a sight as any I've seen."

A necklace of diamonds and sapphires that Mrs. Kennedy was to have worn that evening was missing from her dressing table. A wedding gift from her husband, it is conservatively valued at $10,000. Otherwise, the bedroom and its contents were undisturbed.

The butler immediately telephoned the police, who arrived twenty minutes later. Before their arrival, Mrs. O'Hare continued, Mr. Kennedy began to scream, "Why would anyone do this?" She said she tried to comfort her employer, but he proved inconsolable and ran out the front door of the house, "wailing in a frightful manner."

Police Pursue Leads

The police were investigating the scene of the crime when word arrived that Mr. Kennedy had been crushed by a train. The suicide occurred at approximately 8:30 P.M., minutes before the train was scheduled to arrive at the Fayette depot.

In a brief statement issued yesterday by Sgt. Michael Stevenson, it was officially confirmed that Mrs. Kennedy was struck multiple times with a blunt object about the head, neck and shoulders. The assailant escaped out a second-story window giving onto the roof of the porch on the west end of the house. He then headed into the woods and made his way toward Ragged Ridge, where his trail disappeared.

When asked why no one heard the attack, Marjorie Potter, the cook, said that the staff was playing Christmas carols on the player piano and that "God Rest Ye Merry, Gentlemen," Mrs. Kennedy's favorite, must have drowned out any noise coming from the bedroom.

Sergeant Stevenson pointed out that the deep gashes inflicted on Mrs. Kennedy suggest that the murderer is possessed of uncommon strength. Other clues to his identity are few right now. Since the missing necklace, made up of twenty-four diamonds and sapphires, is readily identifiable, it is believed the murderer will try to sell the stones individually.

Shock spread quickly throughout the community Monday night as friends and neighbors of the popular couple learned the news. Wed a year and a half ago, the Kennedys were widely admired professionally and socially, and close friends described their marriage as "perfect." This week, however, a storybook marriage ended in tragedy.

Eight

To my best friend and business partner, I can honestly say today is a day few of us thought we would live to see. You have shown us what can happen when a man meets the right woman. Who has not seen the change that has come over you, who has not welcomed it, envied it even? The beautiful woman who captured your heart has captured the hearts of all who know her. Ladies and gentlemen, I present you the former Veronica Childers, now and forevermore, Mrs. Charles Kennedy."

The best man paused and made what he felt to be an appropriately grand gesture. Veronica blushed and looked up at her new husband.

The living and dining rooms were filled with small tables, draped with white linen cloths and decorated with stalks of blue and white iris. All the doors and windows had been thrown open to take advantage of the clement weather, so even those who had been relegated to tables on the veranda could convince themselves they were inside with the others and that their position on the fringes of the festivities carried no social taint. On the lawn, bright green with the summer's first growth, nannies watched over rambunctious children and tried to keep starched *party frocks from getting stained and chubby knees from getting scratched.*

Inside, someone began tapping a piece of silverware against a crystal champagne flute. Others followed suit, and the wave of softly tinkling glass spread through the rooms, then outdoors, where it blended with the children's cries. As custom demanded, the groom kissed his bride, and the tinkling noise stopped immediately, supplanted by a general murmur of satisfaction.

The best man stood by patiently through all this, reluctant to spoil the drama of the moment, but eager to finish his toast. He'd worked on the speech for weeks and wanted it to be right for his closest friend, a man he regarded as a brother. But he was also aware that some of the most important businessmen in the county would be present, and it never hurt to make a good impression.

"As for Charlie Kennedy," he resumed once the murmurs had subsided, "I think I can say, as well as anyone here, that he stands for commitment. We have both worked hard the past fourteen years. But it's Charlie's dedication to the bank, day and night, that has allowed us to grow and prosper as we have. Yet even when he was putting in eighteen hours a day, he would encourage me to spend more time with my dear wife, Polly, and our two dear children. Of course, Polly would probably say a few more hours wouldn't have hurt."

A dark, ripe-looking woman in her mid-thirties acknowledged the joke with a tight smile, self-consciously brushed back a lock of her coffee-colored hair, and tried not to show her irritation at being singled out. Phillip had a habit of holding up his family in public that made them all seem part of an advertisement for the soundness of the bank or the security of its safety-deposit boxes. The joke got a few laughs and Phillip moved on.

"Now we're seeing another expression of Charlie's commitment and his generosity in this splendid mansion he has built for Veronica. Could there be a more loving gift to a bride than this, the elegance that is One Ragged Ridge Road?"

Charles Kennedy held up his hand, as much to stop the

applause that threatened to break out as to bring the best man's speech to a close. Phillip was a good and loyal friend, but the flowery rhetoric was embarrassing, and Phillip wasn't exactly one to underplay it.

"I'm sorry to interrupt," he said, clapping Phillip affably on the shoulder to indicate that no offense was intended. "You know how impatient I can be. I'd planned my little surprise for later. In private. But this just seems to be the right time. Veronica, if you'll allow me . . ."

Suddenly without a function, the best man cleared his throat nervously and took his seat next to Polly, while the guests, aware that Mr. Kennedy's "surprises" were almost never little, angled to get a better view. From the inside pocket of his tuxedo, the groom produced a red velvet box, opened it, and removed a necklace, glittering with diamonds and sapphires. The stones were so brilliant they seemed to pierce the air with little shafts of light. The platinum setting shimmered.

Most of Fayette's citizens would have objected strenuously to being described as rustic, yet few had seen jewelry of such magnificence, except perhaps in magazine illustrations. Involuntary gasps of admiration and sighs of envy could be heard, followed by a collective exhalation of air. Then, the buzzing: Had not Charles Kennedy truly given his wife everything? Spoiled her beyond the wildest imagining? A couple of men toward the back speculated on the cost of such a necklace, only to be shushed by their spouses, desirous of prolonging the romance of the moment.

Unvarnished talk about the price of the gift, the folly of it, the sheer ostentation, would come later, behind closed doors at home. Old Mrs. Meadowbrook, who considered jewelry a vanity, mainly because she owned none of value herself, would tell everybody that Mr. Kennedy was turning into a big show-off, and there was nothing worse in her book. Faced with the luxurious object itself, however, most of the guests responded with the kind of stupefied reverence that untutored museum-goers reserve for works of high art.

Tears welled up in the bride's eyes. "Oh, Charles, it's

too much," she said as he placed the necklace around her neck and fastened the clasp.

Polly glanced away. How splendidly everything was going for Veronica Kennedy. A storybook courtship, the perfect wedding, and now this. She couldn't help contrasting it with her own wedding, a hastily arranged affair fourteen years earlier, with only the immediate family in attendance. She and her sisters had sewn their own dresses, and her mother had baked the wedding cake. There had been no honeymoon, just the two-day train trip to Fayette where Phillip was to join his boyhood friend in a new business venture.

She noticed her husband, beaming as usual. He was utterly without envy, she thought. Charlie really was his idol. Nothing he did, or would ever do, would be found wanting in Phillip's eyes. Well, the alliance had proved lucrative for all concerned, that was undeniable. Their two-story colonial house a mile away was no match for 1 Ragged Ridge Road, perhaps, but they lived prosperously by Fayette's standards, and their two children were well provided for. Being a pragmatist at heart, Polly knew where to take her consolation and ignored, as she always had, whatever pangs of jealousy might have gnawed at her soul.

In the early days of Charles and Veronica's courtship, she had realized that she could never compete with the younger and prettier woman. So she hadn't tried. Supporting roles suited her better anyway. Veronica, like many beautiful women, needed reassurance, and Polly was more than willing to supply it, offering encouragement when encouragement was needed and showing concern when concern was politic. If Veronica's place was in the spotlight, Polly knew that hers lay in the shadowy area just beyond the bright circle, and she took to it naturally.

Initially, there may have been something forced about the relationship, but with time, a bond of complicity had united the two women. Polly was fascinated by Veronica's *plomb, and Veronica came to appreciate what she called *'s unfailing common sense. They exchanged confi-

dences and told each other their dreams. As wives of the town's most successful business partners, they would now be thrown together even more often.

Waiters with bottles of chilled champagne circulated among the tables. Phillip leaped to his feet again, quick to reclaim his role as toastmaster. As the guests raised their glasses, Polly felt she could honestly raise hers, too. She had always wanted the best for Charlie. Now she told herself she wanted it for them both.

"To the Kennedys, Fayette's first couple," she heard her husband cheer.

"To the Kennedys," she repeated firmly, with the conviction of one who had long since made up her mind where her best interests lay.

Nine

—❦—

Images of the murder and suicide flashed through Carol's mind as she drove down Main Street and headed out of town. The Fayette Guaranty and Trust loomed on the right, and although she had passed it dozens of times in the past, it dawned on her this time that it was Kennedy's bank. Or had been once. Except for the automatic teller machine and the Speedy Cash sign with its green neon lettering, the sober facade remained unchanged from the 1920s. Suddenly, the deaths she had just read about in columns of yellowing newsprint no longer seemed so remote.

Five minutes later, she guided her Toyota onto Ragged Ridge Road and tried to imagine it as a long driveway to the house she now owned rather than a two-lane paved street that thirty hastily built, expensively priced homes shared as an address. The property was mostly farmland back then, and the oaks that now arched over the road had to have been mere saplings. She pulled the car up to the kitchen door, switched off the ignition, and sat for a while. She wasn't a superstitious person, and the idea of living in a haunted house didn't trouble her. With all the banging and sawing going on, any ghosts would have shown themselves by now. But somehow the mansion struck her as different, a place of sadness and pain, a beautiful dream cut short.

Weren't real estate agents supposed to inform you of things like that?

She got out of the car and walked around to the west side of the house. The Kennedys' bedroom was on the second floor, and the murderer had escaped through one of the windows onto the roof of the veranda. From there, he had either jumped to the ground—a good fifteen feet, she estimated—or shinnied down one of the rainspouts. Looking up, she realized that the rooms were probably configured differently now. Clem's apartment took up most of the area.

"Why you standing there?"

Sammy had poked his head out of a dormer window on the third floor.

"Oh, just looking at the house." There was certainly no reason to share any of her discoveries with her son. It had taken years to get him to sleep in his own room, and occasionally she still woke up to find him crawling into her bed in the middle of the night.

"What do you see?"

"Well, I see Sammy Roblins, for one thing. What are you doing up there? Where's Walker?"

"Downstairs."

"Where downstairs?"

"Down one stair."

"You mean on the second floor?"

"Yup."

"What's that you're holding in your hand?"

"Nothing . . . mine." And he was gone.

The first floor was shaping up nicely, Carol thought, as she paused in the foyer to take off her coat. Even the workmen, who tracked back and forth all day long, had begun offering appreciative comments. Most were along the lines of "Sure don't build 'em like this anymore, Mrs. Roblins," although one journeyman, letting out a low whistle just as she happened by, had crowed, "Damned if the old gal ain't a looker, after all." Startled by such effrontery, Carol was all ready to say something back when she saw that he was admiring the restored fireplace mantel and its delicately fluted columns.

The second floor was a different matter. Expediency had governed its transformation into apartments, and the families who had lived there over the years had not been respectful of the past. Gouged walls and scarred floorboards bore witness to countless domestic dramas, and the vintage kitchens were of the trailer-park variety—so compact as to have been virtually unmanageable.

Clem's apartment, of course, was still occupied. Of the remaining four—two on the front of the house, two on the east side—Walker judged the latter to be the least damaged, so they had been targeted as the first guest suites. But even here, some of the walls were in such poor shape that it was simpler to pull them down and start over. Walker had the new framing pretty much up by now.

The sound of his buzz saw rent the air. She followed the whine up the front stairs and down the corridor and found him cutting two-by-fours in the suite farthest back. Fine dust flying off the saw filled the air with a white haze. A milky plastic drop cloth over the doorway kept the dust from spreading to the rest of the house.

She watched him through the dirty plastic for an instant. He had knotted a checkered bandanna around the lower half of his face, like a Western desperado, and removed his shirt, something he was doing more and more as the weather warmed up. She had to admit he had the build for it. Usually she didn't allow herself to fantasize about other men, the way her married girlfriends did. Much as they insisted there was nothing wrong with letting your imagination run a little wild, she thought of it as a form of cheating. She knew she had felt cheapened the few times she had caught Blake looking at another woman. Was that just one of the many old-fashioned ideas she was going to have to sacrifice, now that she was on her own?

Pushing the plastic aside, she ducked into the room.

"How's it coming along?" she shouted above the whine.

Walker flicked off the saw and tugged the bandanna down

around his neck. Jesse James turned into the Marlboro Man.

"Hi, there. Welcome to our first guest suite. I was just putting up the last few studs. A sauna is going to fit in the bathroom just fine. And we'll still have plenty of room for a sizable dressing area." He strutted around the room, his arms extended wide. "So what do you think? Pretty impressive, eh?"

The smirk on his face prompted Carol to wonder if he was referring to the studs or to his rippling biceps. He seemed inordinately proud of both.

"It looks swell," she replied, purposefully avoiding any double meaning, if one was intended. "So where's Joey?"

"Down at the lumberyard, picking up more Sheetrock."

Walker pulled a T-shirt over his muscular torso while Carol made a definite point of averting her gaze and inspecting the newly defined bathroom area. A puritan upbringing died hard. When she finally looked back at him, his cock-of-the-walk attitude was gone. He was all business again.

"This stuff makes a real mess," he said. "Do you mind if I have Sammy lend me a hand, cleaning it up?"

"Fine with me. It will give him something to do. How long has he been in the attic?"

"Couple of hours, I guess. You know that's where he hides his stash these days."

Carol nodded.

Sammy's habit of collecting things had started after the family had been transferred a couple of times and it was no longer possible to pretend they were just going for a trip. Sammy knew a move meant you weren't ever coming back. He cried so hard the day they were to leave Georgia for southern California that Blake and Carol had to think fast to get him into the car. So they told him they were all going to take three things with them to remember the town by. That way, Carol pointed out, they wouldn't really be leaving it behind at all. They'd be bringing it with them. Sammy jumped at the idea.

Thereafter, he began his collections early. The hard part

was getting him to pick only three objects from the piles he squirreled away in his secret hiding places.

"Walker, did you know a murder took place in this house?"

"No kidding! When?"

"Seventy years ago. The first couple that lived here. The wife was murdered."

"Who did it? The husband?"

"No. The husband killed himself after he found her body."

"That doesn't mean he didn't do it. Domestic violence has been around for a long time. There was a whole thing about it on *Oprah* the other day. Women who beat up their husbands, though. How's that for a switch?"

"It was a robbery, Walker. The Kennedys were pretty well off. Mr. Kennedy was a big banker."

"He would have to be to build this place. Where did you find all this out?"

"At the *Weekly Register*. I saw the original clippings. It happened on this floor in a bedroom on the other side of the house."

She paused. He could see her mind clicking away.

"Is Clem around today?" she asked.

"Who knows with that creep!" Walker went over to the window. "His truck's gone."

"Keep an eye out for me. Let me know if he comes back."

Walker's reproachful expression indicated that he knew what she was up to.

"And don't stare at me like that, Walker. I've never been in his apartment. Blake checked it out before we decided to buy the place. Anyway, I'm not going to pry into his affairs. I just want to see what that end of the house looks like." With that, she ducked out of the room and vanished down the hallway.

"Be careful," he yelled after her.

For safety reasons—a fire or a burst water pipe—Blake had informed Clem they had to have a duplicate set of keys to his apartment. Clem objected until Blake swore that he would use them only in case of an emergency. Well, Carol thought, Blake promised. I didn't.

Her only purpose, as she fitted the keys into the locks, was to figure out where the Kennedys' bedroom had been and how much of that section of the house had been altered. No sooner had she stepped inside than she was overcome by the chaos. The door opened directly onto a dining room. Carpeting that might once have been beige ran from wall to wall. A Formica table with two chrome and vinyl chairs sat in the middle of the room, but it was so littered with old pizza boxes and empty beer cans that Carol wondered how anyone could possibly eat off it. Stacks of newspapers were everywhere, listing precariously. A large, half-filled Hefty bag suggested the extent of Clem's housekeeping.

To the right, a narrow hallway led to the bathroom and a small kitchen. Peering down it, Carol could see a sink stacked with dirty dishes. She could only imagine the state of the stove. There was no avoiding the rancid odor—like curdled milk in a warm refrigerator. Didn't Clem ever air the place out?

An archway on her left gave onto what appeared to be his bedroom and living room combined. The windows had thick, olive-colored army blankets over them, so it took a while for her eyes to accustom themselves to the gloom. She was hesitant to turn on a light; that would be snooping.

An ugly oak table occupied the middle of the room. On top of it sat a large television set and on top of that a smaller one, which apparently allowed Clem to watch two programs at once, if he wished. This he did from a large overpadded armchair that had already yielded up much of its stuffing and had grease stains where he leaned back his head. A couple of dressers formed a barricade between the TV sets and a sagging double bed with dirty sheets. Carol had the impression of being in a secondhand furniture store.

No attempt had been made to arrange the room attractively. Everything was positioned to require the least effort from its occupant. It didn't matter if a table butted up against a dresser or the back of the dresser was exposed to the room or one wooden chair served as a nightstand, while another functioned as a clothes rack. For someone like Carol, who prided herself on her attention to details, the apartment was a nightmare.

The voice rang out of the darkness. "Boo!"

Carol's feet left the ground. She spun around to find Walker in the archway, roaring with laughter.

"Walker! What are you trying to do? Give me a heart attack? You're supposed to be my lookout."

"Talk about a dump," he said, picking up a girlie magazine from a large stack. "I think we may have a potential serial killer on our hands here."

"That's not funny." Carol grabbed the magazine out of his hand. It was called *Juggs* and featured on the cover a picture of a woman with the largest breasts she had ever seen.

"How does she stand up?" Carol said, embarrassed.

Walker peered over her shoulder at the lewd cover. "She probably doesn't much," he chuckled.

Carol put the magazine back on the pile. "Please don't touch anything else. I don't want him to know anyone's been here."

"Fine by me," Walker said, raising his hands over his head. "So what have you found out?"

"Nothing. I'm just curious where the old master bedroom was. I guess this is it. According to the article I read, the murderer made his getaway out a window. It must have been one of those two windows over there. The veranda is just below. You wouldn't even need a ladder."

"This is just like that *Murder, She Wrote.*"

"No more from you, Walker. It's bad enough that I'm in here. Will you please keep an eye out."

"I was going to get Sammy to help me clean up."

"Fine. Just go."

"Aye, aye, Inspector Roblins." She shot him a nasty look that sent him packing and resumed her investigation.

From what she could tell, the two rooms had been made out of one. Otherwise, why would the fireplace be jammed in a corner as it was. It had obviously been the focal point of the bedroom once. She ran a finger over the mantel, thick with dust and lumpy with layers of old paint. The fireplace looked as if it might still work, once the grate was emptied of Clem's oily workboots.

Mindful not to upset anything, Carol inched her way

cautiously along the walls, getting the impression, as she did, that the Kennedys' bedroom had been something much bigger, probably more in keeping with the downstairs living room. Even in the gloom, she could make out the fine ceiling moldings.

She tried to put Clem's possessions out of her mind and picture the bedroom as it might have been furnished seventy years ago with a canopied bed, a dressing table, and perhaps a plush divan before the fireplace. The dimness helped by obscuring the squalor before her. She closed her eyes and let her imagination drift, sensing the house around her, grand and solid and enfolding. It had been built to withstand the years and the elements. Not like today's flimsy, thrown-together houses, which would be lucky to last a decade or two. This one, she felt, was meant to span the generations.

A picture of Veronica Kennedy, reclining languorously by a winter fire, formed in her head. The army blankets turned to lush velvet. She could almost feel the warmth of glowing embers on her skin.

A whirring sound brought her back to reality. Walker had turned on a power drill in the other end of the house. Enough daydreaming! She had seen what she had come to see. She turned to go, then stopped.

There was just one more thing to check out before leaving—the murderer's escape route. She crossed the shadowy room carefully, weaving around broken-down furniture that jutted every which way. The nearest window was partially blocked by a plywood bookcase that contained a plastic coffeemaker, an assortment of cheap paperbacks, and the most unexpected item of all in the whole apartment, a Bible with a white leather cover and embossed lettering. She pulled back a corner of the army blanket and looked out, as best she could. A few dead branches had fallen on the roof, but it was difficult to see much else.

The view would be less obstructed from the other window. She felt her way to it and pulled back the makeshift wool curtain again. A pair of pouter pigeons, startled by her appearance in the glass, flapped their wings furiously and took flight.

"Sorry," she apologized. "I didn't mean to scare you guys like that."

She pressed her nose against the pane and looked down. She was right. It was no distance at all to the veranda roof. Even Sammy could negotiate it. From there to the ground was a more severe drop. But a snowdrift would cushion the fall. Or a clump of bushes.

She let her eyes run across the lawn. Immediately, her heart started pounding faster. Clem's truck was parked in the shade under a tree. As if propelled by a jolt of electricity, she leaped back from the window and struck her elbow on the corner of a dresser. "Damn," she swore.

"That's what you get for breaking into people's homes."

Clem was standing in the shadows on the far side of the room. His face was like stone. How long had he been there?

"Oh, Clem," she stammered. "I'm sorry. I, uh, smelled something burning. I thought maybe you left something on the stove."

"The stove's not in here."

"Well, yes, I know. When I realized the smell wasn't coming from your apartment, I let myself take a peek. I mean, I've never seen this part of the house before."

"You're full of shit. There's no burning smell."

"Oh, yes, there was. Even Sammy smelled it." She was no good at this. "I guess it must have been some of the power tools that Walker was using."

"What did you touch?" His voice was hard and flat.

"Nothing, I swear."

"What did you come in here for?"

"I told you Clem, I thought I—"

"Why are you in my house?" It had been so long since someone had screamed at her like that, she lost her breath. Instinctively, she retreated up against the wall. Worse than being caught in Clem's apartment was being caught in a lie. And Clem knew she was lying. His jaw tightened.

"What were you looking for behind my bookcase?"

"Behind your bookcase? Oh, no, I was looking out the window."

"You lying bitch," he bellowed.

"Hey, just a minute. What's the problem here?" Walker

had materialized in the doorway. Sammy hovered right behind him. Normally, the boy's natural curiosity would have propelled him into the room, but he sensed something was wrong. Not wanting to run away and be thought a coward, though, he ended up dancing nervously in place.

"What is this, a party?" Clem snarled.

"I was just explaining to Clem how I smelled something burning in the apartment, but everything seems to be fine." Carol slipped by the angry renter and joined Walker and Sammy at the door. "Come on, Sammy. Let's help Walker clean up. I'm sorry to have disturbed you, Clem. I promise it won't happen again."

Without looking back, she pushed Sammy ahead of her, then grabbed Walker's arm and pulled him out into the hall. She was trembling. She hoped it wasn't too visible.

The fury of Clem's voice stopped them all in their tracks. "If I ever catch you in my rooms again, you and that idiot son of yours will be sorry you ever heard of Ragged Ridge Road." With that, he slammed the door so forcefully it sounded like a cannon going off in the house. Frightened, Sammy started to cry.

Carol gritted her teeth to keep from crying herself. Clem was right. She shouldn't have been in there. But he was such a horrible man. He'd given her the willies from the very beginning. She resolved to ask him to leave. She would just have to find the right pretext and the right moment. The sooner, the better.

She forced a smile. "The lady of the house is going to prepare fried chicken and mashed potatoes for dinner tonight. Walker, can we interest you in staying?"

"Sure." Her jocular tone didn't fool him. He could see how shaken she was. For her son's sake, she was acting as if she'd had nothing more than a little neighborly misunderstanding with Clem.

"Okay, enough loafing, you two. Let's get on with the cleanup." She gave Sammy a pat on the behind.

Once they disappeared behind the plastic curtain, Carol let herself acknowledge the depth of her fright. Having Walker stay for dinner would delay the moment when he'd go home and leave them alone, which she dreaded. It would also give Clem a couple of hours to cool off, which certainly wouldn't hurt matters. If only she could figure out how to ask Walker to spend the night without giving him the wrong idea.

Clem was probably all bark, but she wasn't sure. Walker was a gentleman, though. Of that, she was fairly certain.

Ten

———

Walker spent the night and the rest of the week, too. Carol made up the fold-out couch in the parlor for him and had coffee and Danish waiting every morning when he stumbled, tousled and sleepy-eyed, into the kitchen. He humored her by saying the arrangement saved him a forty-minute commute every day, but it was for her he stayed. The episode with Clem had shaken her up badly, although she put up a brave front and even tried to joke that she was no Miss Marple.

A new familiarity developed between them, and they quickly fell into a domestic routine. Carol was a little surprised how quickly. In a matter of days, Walker had made the transition from chief carpenter to houseguest to family man. One morning, she came into the kitchen to find him preparing breakfast for Sammy.

"I got up earlier than usual," he said, as if that explained it.

She had been so wrapped up in her own problems and the house that she hadn't given a whole lot of thought to the life Walker led away from work. Now it occurred to her that maybe there wasn't all that much of a life there to begin with. The only phone calls he made had to do with business—never anything personal. Perhaps the reason he had been able to move in with them so effortlessly was that he had no encumbrances, no ties, no loyalties, elsewhere. If so, it was none of her business, she reminded herself.

What counted was that Walker was an easy man to have around. Not a whole lot upset him. Because he was used to dealing with tumbledown walls and crumbling ceilings, he expected a certain amount of chaos in life and, consequently, wasn't surprised when he encountered it. His attitude had a calming effect on Carol.

Of course, they were still a man and a woman living under the same roof. She couldn't deny that she was drawn to him, and from the way she would sometimes catch him gazing at her, with a half-grin on his boyish face, she surmised that his interest in the mansion extended beyond the chestnut paneling to include its now-and-then-bedraggled owner. But there was no point making too much of that.

It was natural that she would feel something for Walker. Blake was overseas indefinitely, Clem was behaving badly, and she was—practically, if not technically—a free woman. Other than Sammy, Walker was the only male with whom she was sharing her thoughts these days. The important thing was not to mistake loneliness for desire, or to confuse the pleasures of a budding friendship with the stirrings of love.

Sometimes, they worked well into the evening, then ate a late dinner. Afterward, Walker would watch TV until Sammy nodded off and had to be carried to his room. The awkward moment came when it was time for the two adults to turn in. But they soon hit upon a routine there, too. Carol would bid Walker a quick good-night and head into the kitchen, where she prepared the automatic coffeemaker for the next morning. Walker would stroll out on the veranda for a look at the stars or a breath of fresh air. What they were both really doing was putting a little space between them, making sure nothing came of their proximity in a drafty mansion, hugged by the inky darkness.

During the day, their conversation revolved mostly around the ongoing construction. Carol had heard from Joey that Walker was divorced, and Walker was certainly aware of Blake, but neither felt compelled to engage in heart-to-heart talks. Lighting fixtures seemed a safer, more appropriate topic.

Clem was nowhere to be seen. He rose early, returned late, and slithered up and down the back stairs more surreptitiously than usual. Maybe Walker's presence scared him. Maybe they were all scared of one another in this big old house. Part of Carol, the peacemaker, was tempted to talk to Clem, see if she could smooth things over. If she explained about the murder and the newspaper clippings, he'd understand why she had been drawn to his rooms. But she knew that was wishful thinking. She had never had an honest conversation with him before, and it wasn't about to happen now.

So she did what she always did when she was upset. She threw herself into work. Her reasoning was simple. Either you could sit around all day long, feel sorry for yourself, and do nothing, or you could polish the kitchen floor, weed the garden, and sort out Sammy's socks. You might not feel any better by the end of the day, but at least the floor gleamed, the socks matched, and the zinnias stood in a nice, neat row.

The one ritual that unfailingly revived her, however, was walking with her son to the foot of the driveway every morning and waiting with him until the school bus came. As it pulled away, Sammy would squash his nose up against the window and make a funny face, then Carol would make a funny face back at him and wave. Some days Sammy wouldn't say a word, but he always made the face. And she always laughed and made her face. She couldn't say why the exchange was so important to her, but it was, and afterward, all the way back to the house, she was acutely aware of how much she loved her son.

Walker's calling from the kitchen door broke the spell this morning.

"Telephone, Carol." She picked up her pace. "It's Blake," he said as she came up the steps. He poured some coffee into his mug and took it out on the back porch to give her some privacy.

"Hi, Blake. How are you?"

"Fine. Who was that?"

"That was Walker. I told you about him."

"Does he always start this early?"

All of a sudden, it just seemed too complicated to explain—Clem's threats, her fears, Walker's moving in. She'd barely had her coffee, and the plumbers were going to be putting in the new bathroom fixtures today, if the bathroom fixtures arrived on time, the work was piling up everywhere, and anyway, there was absolutely nothing between her and Walker.

"Yes," she said. "He's very conscientious. He makes a point of getting here as early as possible." And that was that. Not a lie, in her estimation, not even a white lie, just a necessary . . . simplification of the situation. They talked a few minutes more, hesitantly, without connecting.

"I'm sorry I missed Sammy."

"I'll tell him. He thinks about you a lot, you know."

"Yeah. I think a lot about him, too."

She hung up the phone, feeling unsatisfied, the charm of the early morning broken.

Walker ambled in from the back porch and put his coffee mug in the sink. "So that's the mysterious Blake. He actually exists."

"Oh, yes, he definitely exists."

"Are you two still together?"

"We're married, if that's what you mean. Blake's on a special assignment right now."

"Yeah. Secret mission was what Sammy told me. Actually, that's all he said he could tell me. James Bond stuff, eh?"

"Oh, that's only a game his father plays with him. It helped Sammy understand why we all weren't going to Germany."

"So you all could've gone?"

"We could have, I guess," she replied limply. "But with the house and everything . . . it didn't seem the time."

"Well, I'm glad you stayed right here." He smiled and waited for a reaction. "Or I still would be working for Tim Holmes!"

"So it's turned out well for all of us."

"Sure has."

Carol could see that he wasn't just being polite. He meant it. He was becoming attached to the old house, too.

"What about you, Walker? Have you ever been married?" she asked impulsively.

"Sure was . . . oh, yeah . . . I sure as hell was." The smile left his face and he clenched his jaws involuntarily.

"Sorry. None of my business," Carol added hastily.

"No. It's fine. It was a while ago. Ancient history by now. She wasn't the girl I thought she was, that's all . . . You couldn't trust her. I know that's not a nice thing to say about somebody, but it's true. She was just a terribly . . . untrustworthy individual."

Carol thought she detected a quiver in his voice. Without meaning to, she had apparently struck a raw nerve. She wished she hadn't brought up the subject. What was she supposed to say now?

They were both relieved to hear Joey Burns's truck, then the thud of the truck door, and finally his voice singing out, "Is anyone gonna give me a hand, or do I have to carry all these tiles myself? I get a hernia, I sue."

"The bathroom tiles," Walker said.

"Are you putting them down already?" Carol asked, her eyes bright.

"Not until the fixtures are in. A couple of days, maybe."

Struggling under the weight of a heavy cardboard box, Joey pushed clumsily into the kitchen. "I was beginning to wonder if everybody was still in bed! So you are up! I was passing by Chalmers Marble and Tile this morning and I thought I'd save them a delivery."

He tore back the flap of the carton. The tiny square tiles were attached to sheets of meshing, like so many lozenges. "Eggshell. Nice."

"They're for the border," Carol said.

"The ones on the truck must be white. Did Walker tell you the trouble I had breaking up the old floor in that back bathroom? Damn thing was cement! Solid as a concrete bunker."

As Carol watched the men unload the tiles, her optimism revived. They were actually making headway, not just costly mounds of rubble. She could envision the possibility of paying guests climbing the grand staircase, admiring the Christmas tree, complimenting her on the handsome decor, then, over breakfast the next morning, promising to spread the word about the Ragged Ridge Inn.

She had a few qualms about the name. The Ragged Ridge Inn didn't sound particularly hospitable. But she was confident she would hit upon the right one. Until then, she informed her son that, yes, they would all call it Sammy's Big Hotel.

With the signs of progress, her rancor toward Blake was no longer so keen. She reasoned that he was doing what he had to do. So was she. The bed-and-breakfast would be tangible proof of her taste, her vision, her refusal to give up. And if the Ragged Ridge Inn failed—the name was going to have to be changed, no question about that—well, it would be her very own failure. Nobody else's. Even that was a heady prospect.

Friday morning, she drove up to Harrisburg to pick out paint and wallpaper samples and scout a few antiques stores along the way. She had never believed in interior decorators and put them into a class of expendable people—personal shoppers, financial planners, consultants of any sort—who simply did work that other people were too shiftless to do for themselves. On the car seat next to her was a folder in which she kept magazine photographs and sketches of rooms she liked, advertisements that had caught her eye, swatches of pleasing fabric. No interior decorator was necessary. The rooms would look the way she wanted them to look.

When she returned early in the afternoon, the workmen were sprawled out in the wicker chairs on the veranda, eating the chicken-salad sandwiches she'd left for them.

"The phone's been ringing off the hook while you were gone," Walker yelled as she crossed the lawn.

"Why? What's the matter?"

"Nothing's wrong. It just shows you the power of advertising."

"Oh, the ad! I almost forgot about it. People really called?"

"One lady tried to tell me the story of her life. Most of them said they'd call back. Three people left their names and numbers. I jotted them down on the pad by the telephone. By the way, there's a copy of the *Register* in the stack of mail."

Joey piped up, "Good time to advertise, Mrs. Roblins. Big news in the paper this week. Everybody's reading it. You see that, Walker? Ned Foster is actually going to run against old man Quinn. He must know something that the rest of us don't know."

Walker snapped, "Foster's some big liberal, you know."

"Really? I did work on his house. He seemed like a nice guy."

"He's a liberal."

"Where'd you get this?"

"That's what I heard," Walker said, letting the volume of his voice stand for his argument.

"Is that so? And who are you? Mr. Walker Cronkite or something? At least, the Mayor for Life will have to get off his butt for once and campaign for office." Joey chuckled.

Hurrying inside, Carol deposited the wallpaper samples on the kitchen counter and retrieved the *Register* from a small stack of mail—bills, mostly, and a postcard from Blake to Sammy. The postcard showed a man holding a performing bear on the end of a leash. The bear wore a pointed hat and was standing on its hind legs. "How would you like this for a pet, Sammy?" Blake had written.

Carol picked up the paper. Splashed across the front page, big letters proclaimed, NED FOSTER ANNOUNCES CANDIDACY FOR MAYOR. Under it was a photograph of a man Carol judged to be about her age, mid-thirties. Well groomed. Friendly smile. She scanned the story, then opened to the jump on page four. There was her ad, surrounded by a dark box. You couldn't miss it. No wonder she'd gotten so many calls.

She made herself a sandwich out of the remaining chicken salad, poured herself an iced tea, and pulled a stool up to the counter. The pounding from the second floor meant that

Walker and the plumbers were back on the job. As she reached for the pad with the numbers of the people who had called, the telephone rang.

"Hello," she said brightly.

There was no response, just a rustling noise that sounded like static.

"Hello," she repeated, wondering if anyone was on the line. Still, no response. She was about to hang up when a muffled voice finally spoke up.

"What do you think you're trying to do over there?"

"Excuse me. Who is calling, please?"

A long silence followed. "I said, what do you think you're trying to do?" Then she heard a click and the line went dead.

Startled, she held the receiver in front of her and looked at it. "What am I trying to do? What I am trying to do is restore a house and start up a business! Do you mind?"

It was bound to happen, she reassured herself. Publish your phone number in the newspaper and you get crank calls. She put the receiver back on its cradle and turned her attention to the names on the pad. Who were these people and what pleasantries would they have to say to her? Hopefully, something a little more helpful than the man— for it had been a man's voice—who had just hung up on her.

She dialed the first number on the pad. No answer. An answering machine clicked on at the second number. Carol left a message. At the third number, a woman picked up.

"Could I speak to Mrs. Sue Whiley, please?" Carol asked, checking the name on the notepad.

"Speaking."

"This is Carol Roblins. I had a message that you—"

"Oh, the lady from the Kennedy mansion."

"Yes, I guess you read my ad in the—"

"You got a big family, dear?"

"Ah, no . . . I . . ."

"Well, I just thought with a house like that someone with a big family would come along and put it to good use. That's what it was built for, you know."

"Yes, I gather—"

"Course, they split it up into apartments. That was after the war. Probably before your time."

"A little."

"How old a girl are you?"

"Thirty-eight."

"You got children?"

"One. A son."

"Well, you better hurry up if you're going to fill up that house."

Mrs. Whiley allowed herself a hearty laugh. "Don't take me seriously, honey. You do what you want. Everybody has their own ideas these days. In my time, you started early and had as many kids as you could. Made for the death of a lot of poor women, though. So I guess you youngsters have it right. Two is enough. Isn't that what you all want? One of each. So you can have a career. Well, I had four. Thought four was a good, round number. But I tell ya, I wasn't sorry when they were grown and out of the house. Course, my husband's dead now. But I have nine grandchildren to keep me occupied."

"That's nice," Carol interjected, just to signal that she was still on the line.

"You know, growing up, we all thought that house of yours was haunted, 'cause of what happened there. That's kids and their imaginations for you. On Halloween, we would always dare one another to go up and ring the front doorbell."

"Who was living here then, Mrs. Whiley?"

"Nobody. No one for a long time. Place was all boarded up tight as a drum. It was forbidden for any of us to go near the house. So that's just what we did. Guess it's a natural instinct for children to disobey."

"Do you mind if I ask you your age?" Carol sensed that she had better take control of the conversation before Mrs. Whiley embarked on her theories of child psychology.

"Seventy-nine next month. Never thought I'd see the day. And don't you know, I feel the same as I did when I was thirty-nine. Not the body, of course. But the mind. The time goes by fast, honey. *Pfffffttt!* Before you know it, it's over."

Carol thought she heard the light clink of glass against

glass and speculated that Sue Whiley might just be nipping at the cooking sherry as she nattered on. "So you were alive when the Kennedys lived here."

"Not only that, dearie, I was at their wedding. I was only seven, mind you. But I can see it all clear as day. Prettiest wedding I ever went to. I thought they'd all be like that. Well, I lived to find out different. But that's another story."

"Do you remember anything about the house?"

"I remember there was a beautiful stairway. Is it still there?"

"Yes, it is."

"And I seem to recall a large living room with a fireplace big enough to walk into. Well, big enough for a seven-year-old girl to walk into. I wish I could tell you more about the inside. But, you see, the children ate outside. Only grown-ups and important people were permitted inside."

She sounded like a live wire to Carol, who decided that it was time to implement the good-neighbor policy and invite her over for lunch. Seeing the house might jog her memory.

"Oh, I couldn't do that, honey. My legs gave out on me years ago. Talking on the phone is about all I'm good for. I probably don't remember that much anyway."

"Don't hang up yet, Mrs. Whiley. How did your family happen to go to the wedding?"

The woman paused long enough to take a swig of whatever she was drinking. "My father worked for Kennedy and Quinn at the bank."

"Kennedy and Quinn?"

"Yes. He took it real bad, Mr. Quinn, what happened in that house. Never really got over it. They were boyhood pals, you see. My father used to say Mr. Quinn never forgave himself for not saving his best friend."

"What do you mean, not saving him?"

"Well, I'm just reporting what went around years later. After Mr. Kennedy discovered his wife's body, he ran to his friend's house. To Mr. Quinn's house. Guess he didn't know where else to go. Mr. Quinn was in deep shock himself and tried to comfort Mr. Kennedy. To no effect, apparently. 'Cause the next thing we all heard was Mr. Kennedy had thrown himself in front of a train. After that, poor old Mr. Quinn was never the same. A broken man. He continued to run the bank by himself, but he lost all his money in the crash of '29. Like everyone around here. Thing is, Mr. Quinn had a lot more to lose than most. The bank collapsed, but he still had plenty of land. Cash poor, I think they call it. He and Mr. Kennedy owned a big chunk of this town back then. The Quinns still do. But that's enough of my talking for one afternoon."

Carol couldn't let the old lady stop now. She threw out another question.

"This Mr. Quinn you're talking about wouldn't be any relation to Mayor Quinn, would he?"

The crackling voice on the other end of the line went silent again. Finally, Mrs. Whiley mumbled, "Honey, you don't know a thing, do you? Mr. Kennedy's partner back then, Phillip Quinn, was the mayor's grandfather. He's been dead a long time now. Probably forty years."

Carol wasn't certain what to make of the information. Why should she be surprised that Mayor Quinn, the Mayor for Life, was a descendant of Charles Kennedy's closest friend? Fayette was a small town and families stayed put in small towns. Still, something about the woman's tone seemed to imply there was more to it than that.

"And they were best friends, you say?"

"The very best. Like peas in a pod. It all came apart in one horrible night, Mrs. Kennedy getting murdered. Mr. Kennedy, crazed with grief, committing suicide, and Phillip Quinn not much better off for grieving himself. We were on our way to the mansion that very evening for a Christmas party, my parents, my brother, and me. It was snowing something fierce. And the police were stopping cars at the foot of Ragged Ridge Road, turning people back. My father got out of the car and talked to one of the policemen. When he got back in, he told us Mr. and Mrs. Kennedy were ill and the party was canceled. Course, they weren't ill at all. They were dead. But my parents didn't tell us until much later. Parents thought about things like that back then. Nowadays they tell their kids anything.

"I do remember this. My father turned to my mother and said, 'It's the devil's envy that brings death into this world.' I can't even say for sure what he meant. Odd, isn't it. Forget my phone number half the time, but that's stuck with me all these years. 'The devil's envy.' Kinda gives you the chills, don't it?"

Eleven

—⚬—

The storm had picked up in force and volume. What earlier in the evening was a gentle falling of snow that promised to be picturesque and nothing more was being whipped up to a frenzy by winds out of the north. The flakes came down thick and heavy, then, caught by an upward draft, were swirled around violently before they settled at last on the ground. The weather forecast was revised hourly, and the talk in Fayette was now of five or six inches by dawn.

The engineer knew that Chaldrake Tunnel was up ahead, but the locomotive's usually blinding headlamp was ineffectual under these conditions. The yellow beam shone fifty or sixty feet into the distance, then stopped so abruptly one would have thought it had hit a solid white wall. The engineer wasn't too worried. He knew this stretch of the route well. In another mile or so, the tracks would curve to the right, then enter Chaldrake Tunnel. Another half mile after that and the train would be pulling into the Fayette depot. He glanced down at the clock on the instrument panel. It read 8:23. He was only a few minutes behind schedule, not bad considering the unexpected vigor of the storm.

The snow was building up fast everywhere. Tree branches sagged lower and lower. Roads blended into the fields on either side and disappeared. Anyone darting from barn to farmhouse, stalled Model T to back door, left only the briefest traces of his passage. It was as if the world were being made all smooth and undulating for Christmas morning. The snow filled holes, masked the irregularities of the landscape, softened nature's hard edges.

No one would ever find the footprints of the person trudging toward Chaldrake Tunnel or the curious furrows that accompanied them. Had it been spring and the ground muddy, they might have been mistaken for the tracks of a clumsy farmer and his plow. But spring was months away. And it was not a plow that was being dragged laboriously through the snow. It was the unconscious body of Charles Kennedy.

The engineer noticed several patches of gold, glowing off to the right, and recognized them through the wintry swirl as the last houses before the tunnel. They looked warm and cozy. Then the train roared into the dark hole and the Christmas wonderland disappeared. Freed of its snowy shroud, the headlamp sprang to life, sweeping the granite walls and forming strange shadows that raced ahead of the locomotive like terrified animals.

By now, the body of Charles Kennedy lay on a rocky promontory that overlooked the far end of the tunnel. The figure beside him, exhausted by the exertions of the last few minutes, was breathing heavily. A minute more and it would have been too late. The muffled sound of the approaching train grew louder, while the faint yellowish light coming from the tunnel gained steadily in brightness.

The wind died down for a second. Then a horrible scream of anguish echoed among the frozen boulders as the body was pushed into the void.

At first, the engineer saw nothing but the tumbling whiteness of the storm. What he saw next were limbs, flapping helplessly in the air. It took him a moment to realize that someone had leaped onto the tracks. Auto-

matically, he reached down and yanked on the emergency brakes with all his strength. The locomotive shuddered like an injured beast. Sparks flew off the tracks and bored little sizzling holes in the snow.

The engineer could only close his eyes, knowing that this powerful machine, the most sophisticated of its day, would never stop in time.

Twelve

———m———

The ad in the *Fayette Weekly Register* produced results. They just weren't the results Carol had expected. Besides the call from Sue Whiley, she heard from two antiques dealers who claimed to have authentic furnishings from the mansion, which they would be willing to part with for a price, of course. A man who had rented an apartment in the house in the 1950s promised to send snapshots. A painter phoned, looking for part-time work, while a Mrs. Grubbick, after identifying herself as a concerned neighbor, expressed her hope that Carol wasn't planning anything drastic that would alter the congenial nature of Ragged Ridge Road.

The mail wasn't much more helpful. On a postcard, someone had scribbled, "I always thought it was a lovely place!" but the signature was illegible. The local laundry sent a prospectus for daily linen service. In addition, the Fayette Office of Business Permits and Regulatory Assistance, which presumably was not responding to the ad, felt duty-bound to alert Carol that her application to open a bed-and-breakfast was missing several crucial documents.

Her dossier, according to their official checklist, was lacking DOS*3 (Receipt of Registration of Corporation) and 76-19-3 (10/97) (Certificate to operate exhaust and/or ventilation system), plus fees totaling $97.85. Once the enclosed forms were completed and processed, however, the office assured her that it would be most happy to issue her Gen-129*06, otherwise known as a permit to operate a temporary residence.

Carol saw a visit to the Fayette town hall in the future, a prospect that filled her with mild trepidation. Securing a Gen-129*06 was proving only slightly less complicated than getting an MBA from Harvard. And she still hadn't settled on a name for the establishment. The Ragged Ridge Inn sounded too sinister, as if it were part of a motel chain run by Norman Bates. She avoided hurting Sammy's feelings by telling him that Sammy's Big Hotel was perfect in all respects, save one. They were running a bed-and-breakfast, not a hotel, and he didn't want to trick the customers, did he?

"Pick something warm and hospitable," counseled the author of "So You Want to Start Your Own Bed-and-Breakfast," a vaguely patronizing brochure that the Office of Business Permits had seen fit to send along with the delinquent forms. If that was the chief requirement, one name had always lingered in the back of Carol's mind. She printed it in block letters on a piece of paper to see how it looked. Then, wavering no longer, she entered it on all the forms.

With the renovation in high gear, nearly a week went by before she found time to run the papers down to the town hall. The sky was a prophetic gray, and she grabbed a yellow slicker off the hook as she left the house.

The Office of Business Permits and Regulatory Assistance was on the second floor of the town hall, which automatically became the most impressive structure on Main Street the day the library was torn down. It still retained an aura of majesty, although the paint had begun to chip off a large Civil War mural in the marble lobby and the bulbs in some of the hanging globes had burned out.

The bureaucracy was just as Carol had feared. Paperwork and the authoritarian personality seemed to go hand in hand. You didn't fill out line three! You are required to use black ink, not red. Sign where all the *x*'s are! Big city, small town, it didn't matter. To cap it off, she was missing PH-129*07, a permit to serve food, and a health inspector would have to check out her kitchen before it could be issued.

This was explained to her by a middle-aged woman with a sharp nose and close-set eyes who clearly prized neatness in all things—her dress, the office she ran, and the applications that were submitted for her consideration. "Health Department first. Then pay the fee. Then come to me," she said. As for the liquor license—no wedding receptions or parties could be held on the premises without one—it was subject to approval of the community. After all, Carol would be introducing alcohol into a residential area. There would have to be an open hearing, discussion, debate, a consensus among the neighbors.

"That should be fun," Carol muttered to herself.

"I'm terribly sorry," said the woman. "But the rules are the rules. If you just follow them, we'll be more than willing to license the"—she glanced down at one of the forms—"the, uh, Christmas Inn. Is that what you'll be calling it? I guess that's why you have Christmas decorations up in May."

"Excuse me?"

"I heard you still have your Christmas decorations up."

"Really? And who did you hear that from, may I ask?"

The woman didn't blink. "I don't remember."

Yes, there were wreaths on the front and back doors for all to see. And a ten-foot tree in the stairwell. And holly and bayberry candles on all of the mantelpieces. It was no secret, and Carol had never considered herself an eccentric, whatever gossip was making the rounds. Over the door hung a needlepoint sampler that read, "Keep Christmas in your heart all year long." That's all the explanation she felt obliged to give anyone.

The truth was that her parents had been agnostics who refused to celebrate the holiday and considered it a deplorable commercial invention. According to a deeply held family prejudice, people who erected mangers on their front lawns were no better than those who planted plastic flamingos in their gardens. Every year, the neighbors across the street decorated their bushes with blue lights. "Gas jets," her mother scoffed. "They look like gas jets." The day came and went, like any other day, without presents or a special meal or wishes of any sort. Carol hung around with her Jewish friends at that time of year just so she wouldn't feel so alone, even though half of them had trees and exchanged gifts.

After Sammy was born, Christmas entered her life in a big way. She was so enchanted with the colored lights, she objected every time Blake went to dismantle their tree. That first tree stayed up past Twelfth Night. The following year, it stayed up until the end of February. Now it never came down. Perhaps with The Christmas Inn on a sign out front, people would stop giving her strange looks. She would have an official excuse—it was good for business. Funny how most people had no problem handling that.

Carol thanked the woman behind the counter for her help—the irony went unnoticed—and was halfway down the corridor when she spotted a gleaming brass plaque that read Office of the Mayor. Ever since Sue Whiley had pointed out the connection between the Kennedys and the Quinns, Carol had been meaning to ask the mayor about his grandfather. She was here. Why not pay him a call? Kill two birds with one visit, to borrow a phrase. No question that the lady in the Office of Business Permits was a hawk. Under what plumage would the good mayor present himself?

Laughing, she slipped inside the office. An all-too-pretty receptionist talking on the telephone gestured for her to take a seat. Carol did as instructed and casually surveyed the surroundings. The most distinctive feature was a large, tinted studio photograph of the mayor, sixtyish and very pleased with himself, above the receptionist's desk. A pompadour of silver rose dramatically off his broad forehead. The style hadn't been fashionable for decades. Definitely a puffin or a plover, Carol decided. Whatever it was those strutting, full-breasted birds were called.

Without intending to, she found herself eavesdropping on

the conversation. The person on the other end was upset, and the receptionist was having a hard time getting a word in.

"Yes, I know . . . It's just like your father . . . Yes, I understand . . . I know . . . Would you please listen to me for a moment." She rolled her eyes. "He said he doesn't like his new rooms. He hates the nurses. I told him I'd let you know as soon as you came in and that you'd look into it . . . No, I didn't say you'd go out there. I said you'd *look into* it. It's not the same thing."

The receptionist, miffed, glanced over at Carol, who pretended to be lost in contemplation of the mayor's portrait.

The conversation resumed. "Of course, I know you can't run out there every five minutes. But what was I supposed to tell him? Frankly, I feel sad for him. He's lonely. He's a sweet old man . . . I know he's not my father, but still . . . Third floor . . . the new rooms are on the third floor . . . Okay, I'm sorry. Next time I just won't take his call."

She rolled her eyes again. "By the way, don't forget you've got an appointment at four."

She hung up the phone and directed her attention to Carol. "What can I do for you?"

"I was hoping to talk to the mayor. It's not urgent. I'm redoing the house on Ragged Ridge Road and I—"

"You're the one who put that ad in the paper," the receptionist interrupted. On her desk lay several copies of the *Fayette Weekly Register* with the picture of Ned Foster smiling confidently on the front page. The contrast with the mayor's lacquered portrait couldn't have been greater. "You have to understand this is a pretty bad time for Mayor Quinn, if you know what I mean. It would probably be better to wait until things have settled down. Anyway, I don't expect him in for a while."

"I see," said Carol, sensing a brush-off.

"You can leave your name and number, if you want. Actually, you don't have to bother. It's in the ad, isn't it?"

Carol nodded.

"I'll give him the message," concluded the receptionist, who suddenly had important business with a filing cabinet.

Just another friendly public servant, Carol reflected on her way out. Why were they so uncooperative? You'd think she were starting a brothel at 1 Ragged Ridge Road. Now that she'd decided to call it the Christmas Inn, they'd be hauling her up on charges of blasphemy before long.

For the moment, she didn't care. She was pretty certain she had just learned something exciting. The mayor's father, the son of Kennedy's business partner, was alive. That possibility had never occurred to her. He would have to be—what?—in his early eighties, Sue Whiley's generation. People lived long in this part of the country. He must have spent time at the mansion. "What were they like, Charles and Veronica Kennedy?" was the first question she would put to him.

Curiosity was starting to get the better of Carol again. There was no reason to wait for Mayor Quinn to get back to her, not when his father was . . . where?

She stopped short. Where was he?

It sounded like a hospital from what the receptionist was saying. No, she said he didn't like his rooms. Plural. And she mentioned nurses. It had to be a nursing home. Or possibly one of those assisted-living places. In the lobby, Carol checked the directory of municipal offices on the wall. The Council on Aging was on the first floor. A gleam came into her eye. She was batting zero for two today and had nothing to lose. It was worth a try.

The door was locked.

"It's not locked. It just sticks," came a voice from within. "Push hard."

The door gave abruptly and Carol was catapulted into the room, where she collided with a slight man wearing a pink shirt, a polka-dot bow tie, and a pinkie ring. From a distance, his hair registered blond. Up close, the roots showed.

"Well, don't we know how to make an entrance! You okay?"

"I'm fine," said Carol, catching her breath. "How about yourself?"

He patted his arms and legs as if checking for broken

bones. "Other than I'll never dance again, I seem to be all right."

"Why? Are you a dancer?"

"Used to be." He broke into song. " 'What I did for love' . . . that's from *Chorus Line*. You heard of it? A musical."

"You were in that show?"

"Auditioned seven times. Made the final cut twice. But you know the old saying: 'Many are called, few are cast.' Anyway, enough of my sad life. What can I do for you?"

He swept around behind a counter, leaving a trail of sweet cologne.

"I'd like some information about, um, housing in the area for the elderly," she began tentatively.

"Planning ahead, are we?"

"Oh, no. For my mother."

"It was a joke. What does she need?"

"She's eighty-two and she really can't take care of herself. She's not senile or anything. On the whole, her health is quite good. She still makes her bed every day, does the dishes. Or attempts to. But she's beginning to drop things. This morning, she broke a . . . a coffee cup. The third one in a week. It seems time for us, my husband and me . . . to explore some other living arrangements for her."

Lying didn't come easily to Carol. The more she rambled on, the more transparent she felt. From the way he pursed his mouth, she could tell the man didn't believe her for a minute.

"I've certainly heard that story a thousand times," he said. Carol's heart sank. She'd been found out. "Take my own parents. Who would have thought I'd be back here taking care of them? Not me. I was supposed to be on Broadway! A big star! Things don't turn out the way we plan, do they?"

"No, no, they don't," Carol concurred hastily.

"But we mustn't dwell on that." He rustled up some brochures from under the counter. "I can give you some options."

He explained that the county maintained housing for

senior citizens, but there was a two-year wait. Nursing homes in the Fayette area ran the gamut—from the posh to the strictly utilitarian. Like most things in life, it all boiled down to how much you were willing to spend.

"I'd really like the best for my mother," Carol said. "You understand."

"Then you might consider Lowell Farm. It was a working farm once. Now it's more like a retreat. Pretty fancy-schmansy. Wouldn't mind living there myself."

He showed her a picture.

Her eyes glued to the brochure, Carol asked, "This wouldn't be where the mayor's father is?"

"No."

"Oh. I heard he was there. Not that it matters, of course."

"No, old Mr. Quinn is over at Oakdale, I believe. That's not exactly what you'd call a dump, either. Condos for those who are still independent. When they're less able to take care of themselves, they can be transferred into the main building, sort of like a hotel with nurses on call round-the-clock."

"Oakdale?"

"Yes, here's the brochure."

Carol tried not to show her delight. It was like a game, a big puzzle, putting the Kennedy mansion back together and uncovering its past. Maybe she'd picked the wrong profession. She should have been a private eye. Instead of her yellow slicker, she would wear a trench coat and a beret pulled rakishly over one eye. She suppressed a giggle, which the man mistook for a muffled sob.

"It's hard to accept our parents getting older, isn't it?" he said. "It seems like yesterday that my mother was sending me off to dancing lessons and telling me I was going to be somebody famous. Now I'm back home, taking care of her and my father, trying to keep their spirits up and convince them tomorrow's worth living for . . . Heigh-ho! . . . That's Shakespeare."

He gathered up the brochures and slid them into an envelope. "You can take all this with you. You don't have to decide anything today."

"You've really been more helpful than you know."

"I live to serve." He removed an imaginary hat from his head and made a deep bow, as if he were taking a curtain call before an adoring audience.

She felt sheepish about having misled the one nice person she had encountered in the town hall. "I think *A Chorus Line* made a big mistake" were her parting words.

Thirteen

———m———

On impulse, Carol decided to drive out to Oakdale that very afternoon. According to the map on the back of the brochure, the facility was located just off exit 16 on I-81, a forty-five-minute trip at most. Walker had said he'd be gone most of the day, picking up supplies and ordering lumber. Sammy wasn't due back from school until four. There was no reason to be home for hours.

The sun breaking through the clouds was the final argument. The yellow slicker had been a needless precaution. An overcast spring day was promising to turn out glorious. Clumps of jonquils had recently burst into bloom on the hillsides, and a soft green down covered the fields. As the Toyota whistled down the highway, Carol felt like a kid playing hooky.

Old Man Quinn will welcome the chance to reminisce, she told herself. Old people like nothing better than to talk about the past. Look at Sue Whiley. Now there was a championship talker. She was probably on the phone this very instant, giving someone the latest update on the state of her legs. Carol wondered if Sue and Old Man Quinn knew one another, growing up. She would have to ask. It would be good for openers. She was going to have to stop thinking of him as Old Man Quinn, though, or she would slip and call him that to his face.

Oakdale looked exactly as it did in the brochure. It could have been a well-manicured resort or the sort of upscale housing development that gets built around a golf course in the California desert. The lobby was sleek and modern, a far cry from those linoleum and plywood nursing homes, where the sharp stench of urine hit you as soon as you crossed the door and rows of listless patients in wheelchairs were lined up against a wall for what was optimistically described in the promotional literature as the social hour. Several Chinese urns of freshly cut flowers guaranteed Oakdale visitors a different olfactory experience. Except for a starchy receptionist seated behind a teak desk, no one was to be seen.

"Good morning, I'm visiting Mr. Quinn," Carol called out to her, and headed straight for the elevators on the far side of the lobby.

"You know he's been moved, don't you?" the receptionist managed to say to the speeding form.

"Yes, third floor," Carol replied, all business, as she disappeared into the elevator. She popped her head back out.

"Which room was that again?"

"Three eleven," said the receptionist automatically.

"Right."

The doors closed. Carol congratulated herself. It wasn't as if she were up to no good. She was doing what the historical-society lady should have been doing, putting together an oral history of a significant mansion. That was the extent of her sleuthing. No need to bring the receptionist into it. The Kennedy mansion happened to come with a few skeletons attached. Most houses did. How did the old expression go? "If the walls could talk . . ."

Well, Carol thought as the elevator reached its destination, they can't. People talk.

She hunted for the door marked 311 and found it. A card slipped into a metal holder to the right confirmed that a Lyle Quinn was the resident. She rapped several times with the brass knocker.

"Hold your horses!" answered a gruff voice. The door flew open.

"I hate it when you people arrive early. I'm not one of those vegetables you've got around here. Don't think you can parade in and out whenever you damn well please! You'll learn that with me! I say one o'clock, I mean one o'clock. Not a minute before!"

With that, the man Carol took to be Lyle Quinn marched off into the bedroom and slammed the door behind him. He hadn't as much as looked at her. Startled, she stood there in the entranceway, not knowing what to do next. Her watch read 12:40. Apparently, he'd mistaken her for someone who was supposed to show up in twenty minutes. She thought about leaving. No, she decided, that would be silly. She'd driven all this way. She would simply explain the confusion when he reappeared, then offer to come back another time. The sound of water running could be heard from the other room.

The living room was attractive, although the furniture was clearly of another age, a bit too heavy and overstuffed for Carol's tastes. Family heirlooms, undoubtedly. Dominating them all by its sheer mass was a rolltop desk that might have seen use in the early days of the *Weekly Register*. Or, more likely, the Fayette Guaranty and Trust. Lined up along the top were a dozen or so black-and-white photographs, fading faces from the past, peering out of ornate silver frames.

Two of the older pictures looked like enlargements of smaller photographs that had been about to fritter into pieces when a restorer got his hands on them. One was a family portrait—a couple with two children at their side, standing in a garden. The boy was thirteen or fourteen with a cowlick, the girl about ten. The woman wore a knee-length flapper's dress and a chic cloche hat, but the awkwardness of the pose suggested that she was uncomfortable before a camera. Her husband had his thumbs hitched in his vest pockets and appeared more at ease. The other photograph seemed to have been taken five or six years later and showed the same woman with her son, who had grown into a serious young man. Her expression was pinched and severe. But the most notable aspect of the photograph was the way she was gripping her son's arm—tightly, her fingers crinkling the fabric of his jacket sleeve, as if she were afraid and lonely and needed someone to cling to.

Carol was about to pick them up and examine them when a harrumphing Lyle Quinn emerged from the bedroom. He was using an umbrella as a cane, and it made metallic tapping noises on the floor as he walked. "I curse the day I stopped driving. Have to depend on people like you to take me everywhere. I might as well be in prison. Hell, I might as well be dead for all the liberty I've got. I'm going to tell that son of mine to get me a car again. Man of my age having to sit around and wait for a driver who shows up too early or sometimes doesn't show up at all. Ridiculous!"

For emphasis, he stabbed the floor with his umbrella. Lyle Quinn had a heavily lined face, beady eyes, and tufts of white hair growing out of his ears. Jimmy Cagney at eighty without the star quality. Carol pegged him for one of those feisty codgers who are constantly railing against the world and their own decaying faculties. She didn't envy his nurses.

"Mr. Quinn," she said, "I think there's been a mistake. I'm not who you think I am."

"Oh? Who do I think you are?" He was immediately suspicious.

"I'm not sure exactly. I guess you think I'm supposed to drive you somewhere."

He mulled over her answer for a while, legitimately confused, then erupted again. *"Don't play those games with me.* You know you're supposed to drive me somewhere. Why did I ever listen to that big-shot son of mine? 'You need supervision,' he told me. 'You'll be better off in an apartment with proper care.' Ha! He should live here then. He should eat this crap."

Quinn was working himself into a state. Flecks of white spittle formed at the corners of his mouth as he shouted.

"No one can fool me. I know what goes on around here. I see all those people drugged up. Vegetables! If you think I'm going to let myself be turned into a . . . a turnip, you've got another thought coming. No, I'm not the crazy one around here."

"Mr. Quinn, please calm yourself." Carol started toward him, but he waved his umbrella menacingly in her face.

"You remain right where you are, lady. Do you hear me? I'm not staying here another goddamn moment."

He bolted for the door, leaning on the umbrella with his right hand, while throwing his left hip forward, which gave him the slightly comic sideways gait of a sand crab. For one who appeared so decrepit, he moved surprisingly fast. Almost before Carol realized it, he was out of the apartment and down the hallway. With the tip of the umbrella, he punched violently at the elevator button.

All the years with Sammy had accustomed her to erratic behavior, but Quinn was a veritable quick-change artist. She reminded herself not to panic. The irrational outburst would play itself out sooner or later.

"Mr. Quinn," she said in her most soothing manner, "I don't work here. I just came to visit. I wanted to talk to you about your family, that's all. I'm awfully sorry to have bothered you. I'll be leaving now. So you don't have to go anywhere. You can come back into your apartment."

He eyed her suspiciously, wanting very much to believe, the hard, crusty face lost and vulnerable once again. Carol could have sworn he was on the verge of crying. Slowly, she reached out to take his hand, but her gesture merely provoked a switch back to the arrogance and cockiness. Lyle Quinn wasn't going to be fooled. Oh, no, he sensed the trap. He had it all figured out. Just then, the elevator arrived and the codger vanished.

Her only choice was to follow after. Clattering down the stairwell, she burst into the lobby just in time to see him hobbling in his curiously effective crablike fashion toward the front entrance. The receptionist had seen him as well and come out from behind the teak desk to greet him.

"Aren't we looking bright and chipper this morning, Mr. Quinn," she cooed in a saccharine tone better suited for communicating with children under three or puppies.

With a grunt of disgust, Quinn turned his back on her and beat a retreat, before realizing that Carol stood in his path. Trapped, he snapped his head back and forth from one woman to the other. The receptionist, unaware that anything was amiss, continued to bear down on him, her smile as wide as it was synthetic.

"I think the car is waiting out front, Mr. Quinn. You certainly do have a lovely day for your ride. Here, let me give you a hand."

The umbrella came down sharply on her knuckles, putting an end to her effusions. She backed off immediately and her smile vanished. "Security!" she shrieked. "There is a problem in the lobby. Someone call security!"

Seeing his escape route opening up, Quinn bounded out the front door and headed onto the well-tended grounds. The umbrella sank into the moist grass each time he leaned on it, inhibiting his progress. His hobbling motions were less brisk now. Fatigue was setting in as he reached an ornamental pond, which an ambitious landscape artist had planted with cat-o'-nine-tails and lily pads. The design was meant to simulate nature's, but somehow failed.

At that moment, three orderlies in tight formation came running around the corner of the building. Spotting their patient, they fanned out to prevent his escape. Quinn picked up the pace of his sidelong scuttle and made for the cluster of cat-o'-nine-tails on the far side of the pond. His shirttails had come untucked and were flapping behind him. The whole episode was taking on the aspect of a silent-movie chase—jerky and farcical. All that was lacking were the pratfalls.

Carol watched, her dismay deepening, as the orderlies closed in on Quinn. They were making placating gestures with their hands and telling him not to worry, that everything was going to be all right. Quinn didn't look as if he believed it, but he had, at least, stopped striking out with his umbrella.

"Would you like us to call the mayor?" volunteered one of the orderlies, a thin, sinewy man, who appeared to be the chief.

"Why?" snapped Quinn. "He's in on it with the rest of you. Don't think I don't know what goes on here. How you turn people into vegetables and then, all of a sudden, they disappear."

"Nobody disappears, Mr. Quinn."

"What happened to Joe Proux, then?" Fright filled Quinn's eyes. He was rocking back and forth on his feet unsteadily. Carol was afraid he would tumble over.

"What happened to Joe Proux? Won't answer, will ya?"

"You know very well that Mr. Proux passed away. We told you the day it happened," said the chief orderly.

"You killed him."

"Nobody killed Mr. Proux. Joe Proux had a heart attack, and you'll have one, too, if you don't quiet down." The orderlies' patience had run low. They began to inch in on the raving man.

"Lies! Lies! Lies!" bellowed Quinn, as if he had been stuck all over with pins. His breath was coming in short spurts. During the brief confrontation with the men he regarded as his captors, his face had gone from apoplectic red to ash white. All at once, he made a horrible gulping sound, his head sank down into his bony shoulders, and he crumpled in a heap.

Carol gasped. From her vantage point on the sidelines, Quinn's collapsed body reminded her of a scarecrow blown off its pole—a pile of rags and brittle bones that might as well have been sticks. And it was all her fault.

Minutes later, an ambulance drove onto the lawn and a pair of medics leaped into action. Quinn was strapped to a stretcher, and an oxygen mask was clapped on his face. Two of the orderlies helped hoist him into the back of the vehicle, while the third signaled to Carol that she could ride with the patient, if she wished. She waved no, and the ambulance sped away, its siren screaming.

In a daze, Carol started for the parking lot. There was something about the spectacle she had just witnessed, something that spoke about the frailty of age and the futility of flight when time, not men in white uniforms, is the real aggressor. She didn't know Lyle Quinn, but to see him reduced to such a pathetic caricature of a human being disturbed her profoundly. Did old age necessarily have to lead to this ignominy?

The chief orderly ran after her and put a hand on her shoulder. "Don't worry, miss. He'll be okay. He's going to bury us all. Is he a relative of yours?"

"No." Carol hesitated. "I'm just a . . . um . . . friend of the family."

"I guess I didn't get your name."

"Roblins. Carol Roblins."

"Well, Mrs. Roblins, it wasn't your fault. Try not to be upset. I just need to know if you want to call his son or should I?"

"It's probably better that you do it."

She sat in the Toyota for a while, gripped the wheel tightly to prevent her hands from shaking, and tried to gather her thoughts. What was she doing, interfering with other people's lives? People she didn't even know. Treating the past like some big treasure hunt devised for her amusement. What difference did it make who lived in that house seventy years ago? It certainly wasn't worth this. The grotesque episode with Lyle Quinn escalated in her mind to encompass her entire life.

What she was doing was distracting herself, allowing herself to get caught up in some forgotten drama because her own life was such a mess. She could fill the house with all the carpenters and plumbers she wanted, fill her head with complex tax codes and building regulations. She even had people ringing her up at all hours with their half-baked memories of the mansion. None of that was going to change the emptiness she felt. She was living as a single mother with a twelve-year-old son. Her marriage was a failure.

At first, she thought her tears were for Old Man Quinn. But the longer she sat there, the more she cried for herself, for Blake and Sammy and the happy life they were all supposed to have had together. The Christmas Inn was such a preposterous idea. And this was how she was going to prove to Blake that she could make it on her own. What made her think she could pull it off? She had never run a business before. She had never even held a paying job.

The grounds were empty and serene now. The temperature had gone up several degrees and a faint haze rose off the pond. A pair of sparrows swooped down from a nearby tree and settled into the rushes. It was as if nothing unpleasant had happened. Carol murmured a prayer for Lyle Quinn, asking God to please let him pull through and not suffer any pain because of her.

The clock on the dashboard told her that Sammy would be getting home from school shortly. She didn't want him walking into an empty house, although he never seemed to mind. She fished a Kleenex out of her purse and wiped her eyes. Self-pity wasn't something she usually went in for. It made her feel foolish afterward, in addition to which it was hell on the makeup.

She inserted the car key in the ignition and was preparing to back out of the parking space when a vision in her rearview mirror caused her to switch off the motor. Walker's truck was coming up the driveway.

He breezed right past the Toyota without noticing it, pulled up to the front entrance, and disappeared inside the building. Everything had been so surrealistic up to now, Carol just sat there and watched. Then after several minutes—it may have been longer, she hadn't thought to look at her watch—Walker strode out of the building, a frown on his face, climbed into the truck, and drove off.

Fourteen

—⁕—

By the time Carol arrived home from Oakdale, the school bus had come and gone. Walker, who was unloading sheets of plywood from his truck, nodded and shouted out a greeting. Sammy had dropped his backpack in the middle of the driveway and was struggling with a small carton.

"Nails," he yelled. "Heavy."

"We got a regular he-man here," Walker said, laughing.

Sammy beamed, so proud of himself. Around Walker, Carol noticed, he tried hard to be grown-up and do a grown-up's work. The boy really needed a role model. Much as she loved him, she couldn't provide what Walker did by his mere presence.

She was tempted to ask Walker what he was doing out at Oakdale, but an instinct prompted her not to. She had succeeded in keeping things professional between them, although at moments they still came dangerously close to crossing the lines that separated worker and employer, friend and confidant. It was one thing to be personable, but quite another to get personal, and she was careful, when they talked, never to delve too deeply. It was best that way. It made her realize how little she actually knew about him, though. Was he visiting a relative? Maybe he had a girlfriend who worked there. If so, he had never mentioned one. And he had only stayed a few minutes before leaving, troubled, from what she could see.

Part of her, the curious side, wondered why, but if she asked, that also meant she would have to explain why she was there, and she didn't feel like revisiting that debacle anytime soon. Walker's private business was his private business, she reminded herself as she climbed the back steps to the kitchen.

Sammy followed excitedly, dancing on his toes and squealing, "Messages! Messages!" as he did each time Carol was about to check the answering machine.

He took television in his stride, but for some reason, voices coming out of the answering machine transported him with delight. After Carol and Blake first purchased the PhoneMate, weeks sometimes went by without any messages, which struck them as odd. Then they discovered why. Sammy was inadvertently erasing them. He couldn't leave the buttons alone. So a rule was established: Sammy was in charge of playing back all phone calls, but an adult had to be present.

"How many?" asked Carol as she hung up her slicker.

"Three . . . Ready?"

She walked over to the counter.

"Ready?"

"Okay, ready."

She eased herself onto a stool, more exhausted than she'd realized. Sammy pressed the play button and stared raptly at the machine, not daring to look away for a second for fear that the voices might stop talking if he did.

Beep.

There was nobody to be heard—just a rustling noise, as if someone were shuffling papers while preparing to talk. Carol thought she recognized the sound and waited for a man's voice to say something. The rustling was broken by a cough—at least it seemed like coughing to her—and then the muffled voice spoke up.

"What are you trying to do?"

Silence returned and the person hung up.

"Who was that?" Sammy asked.

"I don't know. I guess somebody dialed a wrong number." Carol suspected it was the same crank caller who'd phoned a few days ago, much as she wanted to believe otherwise. A call out of the blue was nothing to worry about, after all, but two calls were harder to dismiss. Two calls meant someone was thinking about her more than she liked.

Beep.

"Hello. I'm leaving this for Carol Roblins. My name is Tina Ruffo. I'm calling about your ad in the *Fayette Weekly Register.*"

Carol cringed. Enough with that ad.

"My grandfather Christopher Ruffo designed your house, and I think I have the original blueprints. Anyway, I'm going to be in the area over the weekend. I thought I could bring them by. I'll be driving down from New York today, so maybe it's best I call you in the morning. I hope they're helpful. Okay? Well, good-bye."

The message was the first good news of the day. Suddenly, Carol no longer felt quite so tired. The original blueprints! That's just what she was after. Now she'd be able to put Clem's apartment back to its original state. That ad wasn't such a dopey idea after all. "Ruffo, Tina Ruffo," she said, making a mental note. Wait until she told Walker!

Beep.

"Hi, everybody. It's Blake."

"Daddy!" said Sammy, eyeing the machine with renewed wonder.

"Sorry I missed you again. They still haven't settled me in one place. As soon as I have a number, I'll let you know. Until then, you can leave messages at the old number and I'll call you back."

It seemed so long since Blake had left. So much had happened. Wasn't that always the danger when people went different ways? The moments they no longer shared and the conversations they no longer had drove them even further apart, widened the gap, until it wasn't arguments and misunderstandings that separated them, but emptiness.

"So how is everyone? Hi, Sammy."

"Hi," Sammy whispered.

"I got the birthday card. Thanks for remembering. You're becoming a real artist. We're going to have to put your pictures in a museum soon."

Sammy's face glowed.

"Let me know all about the new school, all right? I just mailed you off a package. You should get it in about ten days. Just something small. I hope you're taking care of your mom. Remember, you're the man of the house until I get back. Okay, then . . . I . . . um . . . I love you."

"Love you," echoed Sammy, his voice barely audible.

"So, Carol, how's the big restoration coming? Send some pictures, if you get a chance. Things are fine over here. The job is turning into a lot of long hours, though. I don't mind. You know me. Well . . . I guess I should go now. I wish I had gotten you in person. I hate talking to these damn machines. Maybe next time. . . . I, ah, I . . . hope you're well. 'Bye now. 'Bye, Sammy."

The machine clicked off.

"'Bye," Sammy mumbled, the corners of his mouth twitching. He ran to the calendar on the wall, counted off ten days, and put an X on May 21. Then, he bolted up the back stairs, not wanting Carol to see him cry. Just minutes earlier, he had been tagging gleefully alongside Walker. The mood swings came so fast sometimes. Would it be any different if Blake had stayed with them? Carol honestly didn't know.

The sound of Sammy's footsteps faded. Silence came over the house. He had probably shut himself in a closet or crawled under a bed like a hurt little animal.

"Sammy," she called out. "*Sammy!*"

"Hiding," came a faint voice in reply.

Looking for him was one of their rituals, and Carol usually made an elaborate point of searching in all the wrong places. "Are you there?" she'd sing out each time she opened a door or lifted the corner of a bedspread, knowing full well, of course, that he wasn't. So it would go until his giggling became so loud it was impossible to keep up the charade. Carol sensed he wasn't playing a game today.

She checked all his usual hideouts on the second floor with no success. Then she remembered a small door in one of the dormer rooms on the third floor that gave onto a storage space under the eaves. The floorboards were warped and cobwebs hung from the beams in long, gray tendrils. Steamer trunks, footlockers, and old hat boxes had probably been kept here once—the sharp slope of the roof precluded the storage of anything much larger. As it was, an adult had to crouch or run the risk of a fierce rap on the head. It was just the sort of refuge—dark and cozy and a little mysterious—that Sammy managed to find wherever they lived.

Carol stood outside the door. "Sammy?"

There was no giggling, but a faint thump told her she had guessed right. She peered through the opening and saw her son, curled up where the eaves met the floorboards.

"That's nice that Daddy is sending you a package, isn't it?"

"Yup!"

"Do you miss him?"

"Yup."

"So do I."

"What is in the package?"

"I don't know, Sammy. We'll have to wait and see. He sends you packages because he loves you. Do you know that?"

"Yup."

Her son was so difficult to read at moments like this, when his emotions were pulled in close and he seemed wrapped in layers of stillness. It wasn't sullenness, which required more self-awareness than he possessed. To be sullen was, in a way, to be manipulative, and Sammy inflicted his moods on no one. They just happened abruptly, without those transitions that complicate and color normal behavior. Sammy could be ineffably happy or inconsolably sad. The in-between states he either couldn't or didn't express.

The wedge-shaped space under the eaves had become his new hiding place. He had already amassed a number of artifacts, which were neatly arranged in a row. Carol had to crawl on all fours to get through the door, which was barely three feet tall and two feet wide.

"You want to show me your things?" she asked.

There were the usual assortment of stones, a rusty Pennsylvania license plate from the year 1962, and a gnarled piece of wood that resembled a giraffe. The heavy silver spoon, polished to a high shine, was more unusual, a valuable heirloom, maybe. Where had Sammy picked that up?

Then she noticed the antique frame and the photograph of a young couple, laughing on a boardwalk in the summertime. The image had suffered some water damage, but the carefree spirit came through anyway. The woman, quite beautiful, was looking directly at the camera and had struck a pose of mock flamboyance. With her right hand, she held a wide-brimmed straw hat high over her head, the way a gypsy might hold a tambourine, and her right hip was thrust forward seductively. The man was in profile to the camera, down on one knee and gazing up at the woman with rapture. Their clothes looked almost like costumes. Indeed, were it not for the railing behind them and beyond that the sparkling ocean, they could have been emoting in an amateur theatrical. A breeze blowing off the ocean ruffled their hair. Hers was jet-black and lustrous, cut short to fall just below the jawline. His—dark and full and curly—reminded Carol of a young Charlie Chaplin's.

She turned the photograph over. On the upper right-hand corner, someone with elegant penmanship had written "Atlantic City, September 1928," followed by the letters *VCK* with a heart around them. The ink had faded badly.

"My God, Sammy, where did you find this?"

Sammy bit his lip and stared at a knot in the floorboards.

"I'm not scolding, sweetheart. I'm just curious. It's such a lovely old photograph. Where did you get it?"

Sammy lifted his head. "Here."

She turned it over again, not quite believing what she saw. The handsome couple frolicking on the boardwalk in Atlantic City were Veronica and Charles Kennedy. Here they are, Carol thought to herself, without a worry in the world, laughing and carrying on in the sunshine. So young and so very blithe. Little did they suspect that in three months they would both be dead.

Fifteen

F*antasy always had a special appeal for Veronica. It was one of the things Charles found charming about her. Often he had the impression, when she swept down the stairs to greet their guests or recounted her latest shopping expedition to Harrisburg, that she was playing a role. A flush rose in her cheeks, her voice took on a heightened vibrancy, and her gestures became larger and grander, as if she were addressing him or their guests over a row of invisible footlights. She was a natural actress, and since his was the least histrionic of temperaments, he relished the times when she drew him into the performance and made him a fellow player.*

Like many young women, she had dreamed of going on the stage. But the hard work and long hours had been apparent to her from the start. Unlike most young women, she came to realize that the dream was probably no more than an adolescent craving for attention more fruitfully satisfied in other ways. And then she had met Charles Kennedy. Ironically, he had made her a rich and glamorous star in the eyes of the townsfolk at least.

For their sake and his, she conducted herself as a banker's wife was supposed to. Now and again, though, either because she was bored or because the youthful sparks of ambition had not been thoroughly extinguished, her imagination would take hold. During a stuffy dinner party, she would find herself secretly pretending to be someone else. While the conversation at the table revolved around certificates and debentures, she was hearing wicked anecdotes and titillating gossip. The bespectacled accountant to her left became a Russian prince. Should she whisper in his ear that his wine was laced with poison? Too late, he had just taken a sip and would be dead by dawn.

Eventually, she would hear Charles clearing his throat and proposing that the men join him in the parlor for a cigar. The spell was broken, the dinner was over. She was herself again, a banker's wife in Fayette.

So it was that September weekend in Atlantic City, a resort she'd visited once or twice before and never much cared for. The crowds that might have lent some animation to the place had returned to New York and Philadelphia. Only a few straggling vacationers populated the beach and the boardwalk, which seemed more raffish than usual in the slanting sunlight.

It wasn't long before she decided they weren't on the New Jersey shore at all, but in the south of France. Yes, that was it. They were romping with the international set at Antibes. She was a celebrated chanteuse. He was the elegant double agent who steals state secrets to win her favors. She called him François and told him that she would be Mireille.

Soon after their arrival, they drifted into a gift shop, crammed with tasteless souvenirs. "Would you like me to buy you this, Veronica?" he said, holding up a particularly horrid trinket for her inspection. She was only a few feet away, but didn't respond.

"Veronica!" he repeated, louder.

She turned slowly, her face uncomprehending.

"Apparently, you've mistaken me for someone else, monsieur," she said in a heavy French accent. "My name is Mireille. This Veronica, she is an old flame, perhaps? Do I look so very much like her?"

That was all the prompting he needed. "You are much too beautiful to be confused with anyone else," he said, bowing low. "Excuse my unfortunate error. If I may introduce myself, François de la Villette. At your service."

She extended a hand. He kissed it. The proprietor of the store, a buxom woman, gazed up from behind the counter, the disapproving expression on her fleshy face signaling that no hanky-panky would be tolerated on the premises.

"Can I show you something?" she barked.

"Not a thing, madam," he answered. "For I have just found her, my lover and soul mate. The long search is over, and it has ended here, among your fine goods and precious mementos. We shall never forget you, shall we, Mireille."

Hand in hand, they slinked dramatically out of the store without so much as a backward glance at the disconcerted owner.

For the rest of the weekend, they were Mireille and François, members of the demimonde, throwing caution to the September wind and living out their illicit romance with no thought for the consequences. The resort was theirs. They were free. In another week or so, the saltwater taffy stands and beach umbrella concessions would close down. A few photographers not yet willing to pack up their gear continued to canvas the boardwalk for customers, but they were easily brushed away.

Only one persisted. "Have your picture taken with the lovely lady? Yes, you, sir. Do a man a favor," he pleaded, tagging along after them. "I take the picture now, deliver it to your hotel later, and you've got a memory to bring back home. You and the missus right here on the world's most famous boardwalk. What do you say, lady?"

"Oh, let's, François," she replied impetuously. Arching her neck and throwing her head back proudly, she gave the camera a smoldering look, then burst out laughing. Her good spirits were contagious. He couldn't resist the fun. Like a Victorian suitor, he went down on one knee and clutched both hands over his heart. The wind ruffled their clothes and mussed up their hair.

"Be mine, Mireille, be mine till death do us part."

"Nobody move now," said the photographer.

With a click, they were captured forever against the cloudless sky, the singer and the spy, two playful people very much in love. Even the photographer could see that, and he was squinting through a viewfinder.

After dinner that night, they walked along the edge of the beach and made a game of keeping just out of reach of the waves, until one washed up around their ankles and soaked their shoes. They had drunk a bottle of champagne and were feeling light-headed and irresponsible. She took off her shoes and stockings, and soon after, he had, too.

The moon had slid behind a cloud mass, but the sand was soft between their toes, and a warm breeze, blowing in off the dark water, added to the sensuality of the night. He could feel the longing in his body, growing stronger by the minute. How much he desired her—this mysterious, childlike woman he knew so well and sometimes didn't know at all.

She untied the chiffon scarf about her neck and started to run down the beach, away from the deserted boardwalk toward the dark at the far end. In the breeze, the scarf waved sinuously—beckoning him, daring him, to follow.

"Wait, Mireille, wait," he called out.

Up ahead, she stood facing the sea—eyes closed, arms outstretched—and drank in the salty air.

The twinkling hotel lights were mere pinpricks in the enveloping blackness, and the distant sound of the roller coaster seemed an echo from another world. He came up behind her and pressed his body against hers.

"François adores Mireille," he moaned as he nibbled greedily at her neck and reached up his hands to cup her breasts. She turned around and they were quickly lost in one another—her yearning melting into his, just as his limbs entwined with hers.

She broke away long enough to unfasten her dress,

which fluttered to the ground. Clumsily, he hopped about, struggling to remove his pants, then able to contain himself no longer, he clawed off his shirt. That night, with the waves lapping up against their feverish bodies, they made uninhibited love in the ocean's shallows.

The next day, they would return to Fayette, to the bank and Ragged Ridge Road. To reality.

Sixteen

———

Ring!

Carol was too deep into her dream for the telephone to awaken her right off. It was snowing in the dream and she was running after a man, trying to convince him not to kill himself. She couldn't see his face, only the back of his head, but she knew it was Charles Kennedy. If only she could catch up to him and talk to him rationally, she could prevent a terrible tragedy. But her feet kept bogging down in the snow and brambles grabbed at her clothes. Why wouldn't he stop and listen to her?

Ring!

"Remember me. Don't forget me," the man shouted over his shoulder. She could barely see him through the snow now. The trail was getting harder and harder to follow. Yet, even as he disappeared from view, she felt close to him. He was bequeathing a great legacy to her. "It's yours," his disembodied voice said. "No longer mine. Yours. Cherish it." Then she heard a train whistle, sharp and urgent. Only it wasn't a train whistle.

Ring!

She reached out a hand from under the bedcovers, fumbled for the telephone, and managed to mumble a hello into the receiver. She felt as if she were emerging from a coma. Tina Ruffo was on the other end of the line, asking if it was okay to drop by this afternoon at two. Who the hell was Tina Ruffo? Oh, yes, the lady with the architect's plans. Of course, two was fine. Carol replaced the receiver in its cradle after a couple of tries and checked the alarm clock. It was nine-thirty. How had she slept so late?

She lay back in bed and let some of the images swirling in her head subside. Yesterday at Oakdale had been such an emotional day. She felt spent. Slowly, the world came into focus. Rising, she slipped on a paint-spattered workshirt and a pair of jeans and went down to the kitchen to make herself some coffee. Walker was taking the day off. Clem was at the garage; he always worked Saturdays. Where was Sammy? She hoped he wasn't hiding. She didn't have the energy to go hunting for him this morning. A dirty juice glass and a cereal bowl in the sink told her that he'd already made himself breakfast.

She poured herself a cup of coffee and wandered out into the living room. It still wasn't totally furnished, but several large leather armchairs gave it a nice, clubby feel. The mahogany walls had a deep shine to them, and the fireplace was primed and ready for its first fire in decades. The room was starting to look as if it belonged to another age.

Walker had done an expert job on the staircase. It was whole again, and you couldn't tell where he had fit in the missing spindles. From the landing, Carol glanced out the window and saw Sammy, crouched on a rock by the stream, skimming stones on the water. He needed friends. Restoring the mansion had consumed so much of her time and concentration. She was going to have to devote more attention to him. She decided to take him to a movie later in the afternoon, after the woman with the plans came by.

Coffee cup in hand, she climbed the remaining stairs and continued her inspection. In the two suites at the back, the bathroom fixtures had been installed and rolls of wallpaper in boxes were stacked up in a corner, waiting to cover the naked walls. She'd chosen a small rose print for one bedroom; a finely checked pattern, more masculine, for the other; but for the moment, smooth, cream-colored plasterboard was all that covered the framing. The seams were neatly sealed with tape, which gave Carol the odd impression of being inside a very large package.

The rooms were identical now, and a little sterile, but after the wallpaper went up—and the curtains and furniture were added—they would have distinct personalities and would appeal to different people. Interior decoration, she thought, was really a kind of trickery, just another instance of illusion triumphing over reality, like the makeup she almost never wore any longer. (The sight of her unwashed morning face in one of the gleaming new bathroom mirrors must have prompted that comparison, she decided.) Next week, Joey would put in the baseboards and the trim, and the wall-to-wall carpeting was on order. If they all made a concentrated effort, the rooms would be ready for guests in a few weeks. The library and office downstairs where she and Sammy slept were going to have to wait. And Clem's bedroom—she shuddered—was a project all its own. But nobody had to see that part of the mansion yet.

She would start slow. Open on weekends only. That way the work could continue during the week. She remembered reading someplace that the Marriott hotel chain had grown from a single coffee shop in the Washington suburbs. Well, the Christmas Inn would begin with these two suites. She'd have to put a sign out soon and get herself listed with the Chamber of Commerce.

The doorbell brought her back to the moment. Tina Ruffo had arrived early and Carol wasn't even properly dressed. Shrugging off any last notions of vanity, she padded down the stairs and pulled open the heavy wood-and-glass door. And was more than startled to find a portly, middle-aged man standing there. He looked to be about sixty, well-dressed in a light gray suit with a club tie. Beyond him, she could see an expensive car parked in the driveway.

"Mrs. Roblins? Bill Quinn." He extended a large, well-manicured hand.

"Mayor Quinn?" she burbled, giving the hand a limp shake and cursing herself inwardly for not having put on shoes, at least. This was no ordinary social call. Troubling images from Oakdale immediately raced through her mind—Lyle Quinn, hobbling pathetically across the lawn; his ashen face, twisting into a grimace of pain; the medics, lashing him to a stretcher and driving him away.

If the mayor held her responsible in some way, the smile on his face gave no clue. It was wide and friendly, although a little too synthetic to put Carol completely at ease. He probably turned it on and off at will. Most politicians did.

"May I . . . ," he asked, indicating with a half-gesture that he would like to come in.

"Oh, of course. Where are my manners? I was just, um, just doing the laundry," she said, hoping that might explain the bare feet. No sooner had she closed her mouth than she realized how stupid the words sounded. "Can I offer you a cup of coffee?"

"Please. You know, in all my years I've never been in this house before." He looked around the foyer slowly and methodically, as if he were committing the details to memory. "I heard you were restoring it."

"Yes, I am."

"Making it into a bed-and-breakfast, I heard."

"Yes."

"Fine, fine. Good thing for Fayette. I trust you haven't had any difficulty with the official paperwork . . ."

"Well, just a few little—"

"Because if so, I'd be happy to do whatever I can to help out. There are always ways to cut through the red tape, speed a permit along, that sort of thing." There was that condescending smile again.

He was far more imposing in person than the portrait in his office suggested. Probably six feet two inches, beefy, what people usually referred to as "a big man." But it was the air of unassailable self-confidence that unsettled Carol. She suspected that the smooth, ingratiating manner masked a terrible temper. He was definitely not someone to cross.

The staircase had attracted his attention and he was running his hand up and down the banister, admiring the wood.

"It's chestnut," she explained. "It was very popular back then. American chestnut trees were among the most common in the hardwood forests of the East. They're rare now.

An epidemic almost wiped them out in the 1930s. Almost, but not quite. We searched and searched, because we had to replace some of the spindles. We ended up using something very close. I bet you can't tell which ones are new."

"I'm sure I can't."

"Anyway, chestnut is not used for building any longer because it's an endangered wood."

"Oh, so we have endangered wood now, do we?" he said with a quiet chuckle. "My, my. If we believe these environmentalists, there isn't going to be much of anything left before long. But I do see you have a Christmas tree. So I guess we don't have to worry for them yet."

"Well, since I decided to call the place the Christmas Inn, a tree struck me as—"

"I believe you mentioned a cup of coffee, Mrs. Roblins?"

"Yes, how forgetful of me. Won't you take a seat?"

He sauntered into the living room while Carol escaped to the kitchen, grateful for the opportunity to collect herself. Why was Mayor Quinn suddenly so interested in her house? His secretary had said he was a very busy man, but today he certainly seemed to have all the time in the world. She took her best china out of the cupboard, filled a large pitcher with hot coffee and a smaller one with milk (the cream in the refrigerator had soured). She rooted around in a box of sugar cookies and managed to find half a dozen that weren't broken. She arranged everything on a silver tray and carried it into the living room. Bill Quinn had settled into one of the leather armchairs.

"So," he said, staring her straight in the eye, "how did they die?"

"Who?" Carol put the tray down with a clatter.

"Why, the chestnut trees, of course. How did they die?"

"Oh, it was a fungus. A fungus that attaches itself to the tree when it's a sapling and prevents it from attaining maturity. Strangles it, actually. Did you know there is an American Chestnut Foundation that searches out healthy young saplings and tries to shield them from infection?"

"How interesting. How very, very interesting." He took a sip of his coffee, then placed the cup on the table beside him. Everything he did, he did deliberately. His voice reminded Carol of an old-time radio announcer's. It was deep, resonant, vaguely phony. He seemed to be sizing her up as he talked.

Carol thought that maybe she should just apologize for what had happened at Oakdale before he raised the subject. Be up-front. Wouldn't that be best?

"Tell me, Mrs. Roblins." Too late. He leaned forward. "Just what is it you want from me?"

"I beg your pardon?"

"My secretary said that you dropped by yesterday, that you wanted to see me."

"Oh, yes . . . Well, it's about the house, really. I was told that your grandfather was in business with Charles Kennedy, the man who built this place, and I thought—"

"What did you think?"

Before she could reply, she heard the kitchen door slam. Sammy scurried into the room, breathless, his eyes bright with an excitement that usually prefigured one of his mood swings. There was a bulge under his windbreaker, and a tuft of white fur poked out of his collar.

"Look," he squealed. "A doggie."

"Where did you get that, Sammy?" Her tone was harsher than she intended. Bill Quinn made her nervous.

"A man."

"What man?"

"Down the street. He said I can keep him. Please?"

"We'll talk about it later."

"Please? Please? Please?"

"Sammy, can't you see we have company? This is Mr. Quinn. He's the mayor of Fayette."

Sammy barely looked up. His disappointment risked turning into tears.

"What a cute little pup you've got there," intervened Quinn. "Do you want to show him to me? What's his name?"

"Doesn't have a name."

"What do you mean? Everybody needs a name, son. We'll have to come up with one. Maybe your dad will have a few ideas."

"My daddy's gone. Far away."

"Oh, that's too bad."

"Special mission."

"Where's that?"

"Europe."

"That's enough, Sammy," said Carol sharply. There was no need for Bill Quinn to know their personal business.

"Well," the mayor said, "I bet your mother will let you keep the pup for company."

"Can I, Mom?"

"We'll discuss it later. Take him outside now." Reluctantly, Sammy obeyed. Carol thought she detected a flicker of triumph on the face of the mayor when she turned back.

"Every boy should have a dog, don't you think? Of course, I don't mean to interfere. I didn't realize Mr. Roblins was away. Will he be gone for a long time?"

"It's hard to tell with the army."

"Not too long, I hope. Separations can be so difficult." A note of sympathy had crept into his voice.

"Well, we'll see. At any rate, as I started to say earlier, I thought you might know something about this house. That's all. But I'm sure you have far more important matters to tend to today. It was very kind of you to drop by."

"No kindness at all. I was driving by. You're one of my constituents. This is an election year, remember."

That isn't it. That isn't it, at all, Carol heard herself thinking. He was playing some cat-and-mouse game with her, and she wished he would leave.

"Look, Mr. Quinn—"

"Bill, please."

"Look . . . Bill. I'm very sorry about what happened at Oakdale."

His eyebrows arched quizzically as he waited for her to continue.

"Yesterday . . . with your father. I should never have gone out there."

"You were at Oakdale yesterday?"

"Well, yes. I thought you knew. I went to speak to him about the Kennedys. Isn't that why you're here?"

He shrugged his shoulders almost imperceptibly, the picture of calm. "I told you. My secretary informed me that you had come by my office." If he was toying with her, she was dealing with a master.

"Is he all right, then? Your father?"

"Oh, he's fine, thank you. And did you? Speak to him?"

"Well, no, I never really got the chance."

"I see. But what exactly did you hope to find out?"

"Nothing in particular. I mean, I didn't have anything specific in mind. What it was like back then, I guess. Impressions. I don't know really."

"Impressions?" The mayor allowed himself a little laugh. "I daresay that's about all my father remembers these days. He is an old man, as you may have noticed. Easily agitated. I believe it's important that his life be—how shall I put it?—as uneventful as possible. Surely, you understand."

In the heavy silence that followed, Carol sensed she had better say something or she would find herself in trouble. Some men had the power to threaten without ever doing anything threatening. It was a function of their size and their unexamined assumptions about their place in the world. They didn't just take up space, they took it away from others. Bill Quinn was one of those men.

"I guess I, well, I sometimes get carried away with this restoration," she stammered. "I want it to be as authentic as possible. But I may have located the original blueprints."

"How fortunate for you."

"So I won't have to bother you or anyone in the future."

"I think that's best." Had Bill Quinn gotten the promise he'd come for? He stood up, visit over, and instinctively adjusted his suit jacket. "Of course, if my father ever tells me anything about the house, I'll be sure to pass it along," he added, the consummate politician again.

Carol accompanied him to the door, acutely conscious of her bare feet on the wooden floor.

"You've done an admirable job, Mrs. Roblins," he said, casting a final look about the foyer. "I know how maddening our town bureaucracy can sometimes be. If I can run interference for you, don't hesitate to call my secretary." The wide smile reappeared.

Sammy was seated on the bottom porch step, staring at the sleeping puppy curled up in his lap. Bill Quinn paused to take in the sight. "It must be hard for the boy without his father."

"Yes, he misses Blake. But he'll be back soon."

"I hope so, Mrs. Roblins, I hope so. For the boy's sake and for yours."

"Got to get a good name for you," Sammy said as boy and dog trudged over clumps of matted grass, the boy moving more surefootedly, though no less eagerly, than the dog. "I'm Samuel Grover Roblins, but they call me Sammy. The men who work on the house are Walker and Joey. Everybody's named something. Except you."

The dog, a black-and-white-spotted mutt, had short hair and wire whiskers, which betrayed the terrier in his lineage, and large, soulful eyes, which bespoke of the spaniel. Judging from the paws, he was not likely to remain small for very long, although, right now, he was having difficulty keeping up, despite a considerable expenditure of energy that propelled him in erratic bounds over the recently thawed landscape.

"Come on. Stay close. I'll show you the stream first." Together they approached the bank. Sammy knelt down and dipped his hand in the chilly water. "Wanna drink?"

The dog swished his tail vigorously and licked the boy on the chin.

"Hey, pay attention," Sammy said with the sternness of a seasoned soldier imparting survival skills to the new recruit in his platoon. "You can drink the water, but you can't walk in it. Ever, ever, ever. Understand?" His mother didn't like it when he came home with soaking sneakers, and he knew she wasn't going to make any exceptions for a dog.

"So, no wet feet. Okay? Now you say, 'Aye, aye, sir.'"

The dog cocked his head sharply, which Sammy took as a sign of assent. From the stream, they slipped deeper into the woods, a motley of browns and grays, speckled yellow by the sun, with budding branches providing a light wash of green. Sammy's sneakers crunched into the earth, which smelled fresh and damp and set the dog's nose twitching.

There were so many places he wanted to show the animal—the open pasture in which cows had begun grazing only last week; the rusty railroad tracks that disappeared into a tunnel if you followed them far enough; and the big boulders up on Ragged Ridge, where you could hear your echo if you stood in the right place and shouted into the hollow in one of the rocks.

"Sammy," he called out.

"Sammy-ammy-ammy" came back the reply.

"Dog!"

"Dog-og-og-og."

"You see? That's why we gotta get you a good name."

The dog collapsed on his haunches and yawned, exposing a tongue that looked like a pink ribbon. He had, apparently, seen enough for one afternoon. "Tired already?"

The dog flopped over on one side.

"Okay, I'll carry you then." Sammy scooped up the animal and deposited him down the front of his windbreaker, so that only a shiny snout and two blinking eyes were visible. Then, making sure that his passenger was in place, he galloped down off the ridge and penetrated the woods again.

No longer army buddies, boy and dog were scouts astride an imaginary horse, racing to reach the fort before the Indians headed them off at the pass.

"Giddyap," Sammy hollered, lashing his invisible steed. Barely breaking gait, he ducked under a low-hanging branch, leaped over a fallen log, and eventually, having outwitted their pursuers, emerged on the lawn on the east side of the mansion.

By the back door, Clem was tinkering with the motor of his truck. Sammy reined in his horse and hid behind a tree to observe. The hood of the dented truck was propped up by a metal rod, and the mechanic disappeared under it for minutes at a time, before resurfacing to rummage around in his toolbox or to spit a gob of brownish liquid on the ground.

"That's Clem," Sammy whispered in the dog's ear. "He chews baccy." That's what he'd heard the mechanic call the brown stuff—although what baccy was and why anyone bothered to eat it, when it tasted so bad you had to spit it out of your mouth all the time, Sammy didn't know. That was something to ask Walker.

After a while Clem's tinkerings reached a successful conclusion. He unhooked the rod holding up the hood, which fell shut with a clang. Satisfied with his work, he reached through the window, took a can of beer off the front seat, and yanked up the flip-top. A few swigs later, he looked around and caught a glimpse of Sammy's windbreaker behind the tree. "Hey, eejit, I see you over there," he called out, wiping his mouth with the back of his hand. "What's that you got in your jacket? A water rat?"

Sammy said nothing.

"I wanna see the water rat. Why don't you show 'em to me," he repeated with a hoarse laugh as he cut across the driveway in the boy's direction.

"Shiny spoon, shiny spoon, shiny spoon," Sammy chanted to himself. Then, hugging the dog close to his body, he turned and bolted into the woods.

Clem came to a stop with a shrug of disappointment. "Hell, kid. Just trying to be friendly, that's all."

Seventeen

—⁓—

I'm sorry I was late. But I've been meeting cousins I didn't even realize I had. And now after meeting them, I'm going to have to pretend I don't know them. My nerves! Everybody is so white here. I feel like I'm from the old country and I'm just from Brooklyn. No offense. Did you grow up in the area?"

"No."

"I didn't think so. You look too much like a normal person to me."

Tina Ruffo was experiencing what Carol diagnosed as severe culture shock. She had arrived at four, instead of two, flying up the driveway as if it were the Indianapolis Speedway in a rented, cherry-colored compact. Then, while parking, she had managed to take out a corner of a petunia bed Walker had planted only weeks before. She had gotten no farther than the veranda before she collapsed into a white wicker rocker, where she was now seated, gulping down a glass of ice water and trying to regain her bearings.

"It's just so hard for me to believe that I am related to these people," she said between gulps. "The highlight of their day is going to the feedstore. And these are people who do not need to feed, if you know what I mean. Blimps! Their idea of 'low fat' is a short pig. Of course, they think I'm the big slut from New York. I can tell by the way the women look at me whenever I'm talking to their husbands. I want to say, 'Don't worry, honey, I wouldn't lay a finger on that fat fuck you call a husband, even if he were the last man on earth. I'd become a lesbian first.' No offense. You're not a lesbian, are you?"

"Er . . . no."

"Lesbians always want me. Why is that? By the way, do you think I could have another glass of water? I'm absolutely parched."

Carol disappeared into the kitchen. It didn't take a sleuth to know that Tina Ruffo came from a world beyond Fayette. The accent alone screamed Brooklyn. She had done her time at the aerobics studio, and her body, which was squeezed into a pair of black jeans and a form-fitting T-shirt with gold stars, attested to every sidebend and stomach crunch. She was in her early thirties, but could easily pass for twenty-five. Her brazen manner was what most people meant when they said that New Yorkers were a pushy breed: she obviously didn't have a whole lot of truck with the social niceties. After the mayor's veiled threats, Carol found the candor refreshing.

"Are you sure you don't want something else? Coffee? A soda?" she said as she returned with the ice water.

"No, thanks. The water is fine. I need to flush my kidneys. They had the meal from hell waiting for me when I got in last night. Hot dogs! And one of those Jell-O salads with the mayonnaise on top. Thank God I packed some rice cakes in the car or you'd be looking at a dead person right now."

In the afternoon sun, the mountains stood out in sharp relief. A leafy green freshness was everywhere. It was another of those days when Carol couldn't imagine a prettier landscape than the one before her eyes. They didn't have this in New York. She sneaked a glance at her visitor, who had pushed her black, wraparound sunglasses up on her head and was taking in the idyllic view. A breeze stirred the wind chimes at the far end of the veranda.

Tina Ruffo broke the silence. "Jeez, my back is killing me. From sitting in that car for six hours straight. I guess I shoulda rented a bigger one. I picked it because it looked cute. And the color matched my nail polish. Just kidding, hon. I'm not that much of a bimbo. Tell me something. How do you people ride in cars all the time? All the way down from New York yesterday, I could feel my ass spreading. I should have gone jogging this morning. I know I'm going to put on ten pounds this weekend. Do I look fat to you?"

"No, you look in great shape to me."

"Thanks, doll. I just hope I make it through this wedding in one piece. My cousin is nineteen and she's marrying a twenty-one-year-old apple-grower. What year is this? I wanted to scream, 'Are you out of your mind? You're a baby. Run for your life!' But who am I to judge, right? She's got the husband. I don't. The wedding's tomorrow at three and then I'm outta here. Jeez, I hope they don't expect me to eat any of the wedding cake."

Tina glanced up at a sky of perfect blue.

"You don't think it's going to rain, do you?"

"Not likely," said Carol, unable to keep the grin off her face.

"We don't have a lot of weather in New York. What I mean is, we don't pay it much attention. So now you must be wondering if this broad ever shuts up and did she bring the blueprints." Tina reached down, picked up a cardboard tube at her side, and waved it like a drum major's baton. "Tah-dah!"

Carol's heart skipped a beat. "How did you find out I was looking for them?"

"One of my aunts. Great-aunt, really. Aunt Clara. She lives over in Gingerton, but she was raised here in Fayette and still keeps up on the hometown news by subscribing to the paper. That's how she learned about you. She gave us a call in Brooklyn a couple of weeks ago. 'You'll never believe this,' she says. 'They're fixing up the place Christopher built over in Fayette.' Christopher Ruffo—he was my grandfather, Aunt Clara's brother-in-law. He's always been the big deal in the family. What do you expect? A famous architect! Everybody else grew fruit. Or sold it. This isn't boring you, is it?"

"No, it's fascinating."

"I wouldn't go that far, doll." Tina drained her glass before picking up the account. "My father inherited all of grandfather's stuff. So after Aunt Clara's call, I went over and checked in my mother's attic. Sure enough, there were all the original drawings of just about every house he ever designed, neatly labeled and filed away in a couple of trunks. It was easy enough to find the plans marked Kennedy Mansion. I had copies made. And violà!"

She handed the tube to Carol, who unscrewed the metal cap and slid out a dozen sheets of blue paper tightly rolled together. Floor plans, elevations, details of casings and moldings—it was all there. Transported back in time, Carol examined the plans with a kind of reverence. Even Tina was momentarily silent. Here was the house the way it was meant to be, the way Charles Kennedy had intended it for his young bride.

"I can't tell you what this means to me," Carol finally said.

"You're really into this restoration thing, huh? Well, somebody else is gonna be pretty happy, too. Aunt Clara. It killed her to see this house falling apart over the years. As far as she was concerned, it was an insult to the memory of her sainted brother-in-law. Christopher Ruffo could do no wrong in her eyes. She still talks about him like it was yesterday. Just this morning, she was saying that he was real friendly with the people who built this house. They stayed close after it was finished. She even seemed to think he was a pallbearer at the funeral. They're buried out at Woodbridge Cemetery on the edge of town in a big family crypt. Vinnie, Aunt Clara's husband, is buried there, too. In the ground, though. It looks like we'll be paying our respects tomorrow before the wedding. Death? Marriage? What's the dif, right? The weekend's shot, however you look at it. Let me ask you something. Doesn't it spook you that there was a murder here?"

Carol carefully rolled up the plans and replaced them in the tube. "That was such a long time ago."

"But what if the place is haunted?"

"I think I would have seen any ghosts by now," Carol replied lightly. Evidently, this was no joking matter for

Tina, who bent forward in the rocking chair and lowered her voice to convey the gravity of her beliefs. "You never know. These ghosts can be tricky. Once in the middle of the night, I saw my dead aunt Rose standing at the foot of my bed. As near as you are to me. I swear it. She had come to tell me not to worry, that everything was all right on the other side. Not that I was overly worried at that point. When I woke up the next morning, the whole room smelled of Desert Flower."

"Desert Flower?"

"The talcum powder. They used to sell it at the five-and-dime. Real cheap. You couldn't give Aunt Rose the good stuff. She always swore by Desert Flower. Now she's dead and she's still using that shit."

Tina paused to let the full significance of the story sink in. "Did you ever think that maybe this house got changed so much that the ghosts are confused? They lost their bearings, got turned around, which is why you haven't seen them. If you put the house back the way it was, they might recognize the old place and move back in. Better watch out. Grandfather Chris may pop in for a visit some night."

Tina let out a guffaw and trotted down the porch steps, her high-heeled black boots making sharp clicking noises as she did. Carol followed, thanking her profusely for everything she'd done.

"Oh, please! You're the first sane person I've met down here. I was beginning to think all of Pennsylvania was crazed. Now I know it's just my family." The cherry-colored compact zoomed off as fast as it had come.

Carol turned back and admired the house for a moment. There was something fundamentally grand about it, but it wasn't at all show-offy. Christopher Ruffo had been a man of good taste, and now, with the plans in hand, the years of neglect were officially over. She felt a momentary kinship with him. But ghosts popping up at the foot of the bed? Carol laughed. No thank you. She had quite enough problems as it was.

Just then, Sammy emerged from the woods in back of the house with the puppy still tucked in the front of his windbreaker. Maybe she would let him keep it, after all.

They'd already bonded. A pet would make a good companion and teach him responsibility.

"So how's the little doggy doing?" she asked.

"Charlie."

"What?" She stooped down and stroked the animal's head.

"I named him after the man in the picture. The man who lived here first. His name's Charlie."

Eighteen

---〰〰---

Christopher Ruffo gripped the brass handle of the coffin and looked straight ahead, the blank expression on his face giving no indication of the anguish he felt as the procession made its way over the frigid ground to the burial site. A path had been laboriously chipped out of the snow, but patches of ice still made the footing precarious. He tried not to imagine the remains of his friend inside. The train had dragged the body of Charles Kennedy along the tracks for several hundred feet, mangling it so badly that even the painstaking efforts of several morticians had been unable to put it back together.

At the visitation, the casket remained closed. So did that of Veronica Kennedy, although her death, if no less grim, was reported to have been less disfiguring. Ahead of him, Christopher saw one of the pallbearers carrying her casket slip and almost fall. He tried not to think of her, either, to empty his mind out, make it cold and numb until he was back in the privacy of his own home and could let his grief flow freely.

In that, he was not alone. The town, as a whole, seemed to be emotionally paralyzed. The spirit had quickly drained out of the holiday as accounts of the Kennedys' deaths had spread from house to house. By Christmas night, it was totally gone. The decorations stayed up and presents were perfunctorily exchanged. But few people sat down to Christmas dinner with relish. In the days that followed, the horror set in like a dull ache. The town dignitaries had no consoling words. The police had no leads.

The snow had long since turned into an ocean of frozen ripples and waves that made travel treacherous and lent a bleak note of eternity to the landscape. Had Charles Kennedy not constructed a mausoleum two years earlier, after the passing of his mother, it would have been necessary to wait for the spring thaw before committing the bodies to rest. A small chapel in the high Gothic style, the mausoleum was set into the side of a steep hill at the south end of the cemetery. At the time of its construction, townsfolk criticized it for being pretentious and a waste of money. But now a more modest shrine would only have added to the mounting despair. The cold, sculpted stones were a solace to those who stood shivering in the twelve-degree temperature and listened dumbly while the minister struggled with little effect to draw some meaning from recent events.

They were like so many splotches of ink on parchment, their mourning garb contrasting starkly with the brittle whiteness over which they had joylessly trudged. All of Fayette's best families—the Waynes, the Knights, the Whileys, the Fullers, and the Beldmans—were present. Veronica's relatives huddled near her casket, too stunned to do much more than mouth silent responses to the minister's prayers. Charles's family was smaller—cousins, mostly—and was scattered among the crowd. It was the presence of all the bank's employees and so many of its regular customers that attested to his standing in the community. And, of course, Phillip Quinn.

As the service droned on, Christopher Ruffo glanced out of the corner of his eye to see how Phillip was holding up. Even a fleeting look revealed a broken man. The architect had never been one for psychologizing; he preferred to deal in realities, stone and brick and mortar. But it crossed his mind that the greatest loss had been suffered by Quinn. Veronica and Charles were joined in death and would never know the agony of living without one another. Phillip Quinn was the one who had been left behind; the patterns that gave purpose and organization to his life had been shattered.

Polly stood at his side, her head tilted down, her arm linked around his in the posture of the dutiful wife. But Christopher read it differently. She seemed to be steadying her husband, holding him up, and the expression on her face, to the extent that it could be discerned under the black veil, was one of hard resolve.

Positioned in front of them, their children were on their best behavior and kept the fidgeting to a minimum. Now and then, Polly Quinn reached out with her free hand to adjust the coat collar of their son or to give the shoulder of their daughter a reassuring pat. Phillip appeared unaware of his offspring, but Polly was determined to get through the funeral as a family.

Christopher tried to refocus his attention on the minister, who was extolling the infinite wisdom of God that so surpasses mankind's ability to comprehend it. Even a tragedy like this one, he promised in a voice that trembled either from emotion or from the cold, would be revealed in the hereafter to have served a glorious function. In the meantime, the Kennedys had found peace in the bountiful embrace of the Lord.

A noise from the back of the crowd caused the minister to look up. Automatically, the heads of the mourners swiveled to determine the source of the commotion. The boot heel of a young woman had broken through the hard crust of snow, and she had taken an ungainly spill. Her mortification at having disturbed the solemn ceremony lent a violent flush of red to her face. Christopher Ruffo recognized her as the Kennedys' maid, Megan O'Hare. Several men rushed to her aid and, with some exertion, succeeded in righting her. A child giggled and was promptly shushed up.

The time had come. The minister nodded imperceptibly to the pallbearers, who hoisted the two caskets to shoulder *height and prepared to place them on the stone catafalques inside the mausoleum. It was a delicate maneuver, fitting them through the narrow door. Christopher Ruffo banished all thoughts of the deceased from his mind, concentrated instead on the costly wood, and told himself over and over that it mustn't get scratched. Concern for the burnished ebony replaced all memories of his dead friend for the time being.*

Once the caskets were lodged within the marble sepulchre, the ornate metal door with its tiny stained-glass window was closed and locked. Forever sealed off from the living, Charles and Veronica Kennedy had entered a timeless realm beyond death, which few of the mourners understood, but almost all acknowledged and feared. They turned to retrace their steps over the unforgiving terrain. And then, it began—a piercing wail that stopped them instantly in their tracks.

Phillip Quinn had hurled himself against the facade of the mausoleum and was clutching at the grated door that kept him from Charles Kennedy's casket. There was nothing for him to grab on to, just the sharp edges of the metalwork, which tore his fingers. Magnified by the marble wall, his cries echoed out over the whole cemetery like the lamentations of a shaman.

Polly's astonishment at her husband's behavior gave way to embarrassment, then humiliation. Silently, she implored the minister for help, but he was busy thumbing his Bible aimlessly, as if in search of a verse that might arrest what appeared very much to his eyes like the devil's own handiwork. Everyone shifted awkwardly and waited for Quinn's sobbing to abate. Instead, it grew more frenzied.

Wanting to shield her children from the sight, Polly pulled them to her breast and rocked them back and forth. It occurred to Christopher that that's how she must have solaced them when they were little and came running to her in the middle of the night with their bad dreams. The gesture was awkward and ineffectual—the children, after all, were adolescents and her son was nearly as tall as she—but it seemed to permit Polly to think she was doing something useful, taking charge in some small fashion. Or maybe it was just a reflex action.

Soon, however, her husband's grief was too much even for her to bear. Grasping her children by the hand, she made her way as rapidly as possible to the cemetery entrance.

The rest of the mourners took this as their cue to leave. The shuffle of shoes on ice resumed, and the procession, less dignified now, beat an unsteady retreat. The Kennedys' deaths had been painful enough to deal with. Now Phillip Quinn's outburst was making them squirm with discomfort, and they were eager to return to the warmth of their homes and ponder other things. Or nothing at all.

Only Christopher Ruffo lingered behind, and he was not sure why. A sense of duty had something to do with it, if not a sense of compassion. But stronger than either, perhaps, was that perverse compulsion that drives people to look where they oughtn't.

What he saw made him wince.

Phillip Quinn had collapsed at the foot of the shrine. His wan face was contorted by indescribable sorrow, and his fingers, shredded by the metal grate, were bleeding on the snow.

Nineteen

———

By Monday morning, Carol's mind was made up. She would give Clem his notice. She had the blueprints now, so his gloomy, gerrymandered rooms could be converted back into the elegant bedroom suite that the Kennedys had built for themselves. Also, she'd be having her first paying customers before long, and the prospect of anyone's running into Clem in his oily overalls, grumbling sourly and tramping up and down the stairs at odd hours of the night, was not one she wished to entertain. Clem and the Christmas Inn were definitely incompatible.

Telling him would be the hard part. He had spoken to her only twice since catching her in his apartment—once, when he gave her the March rent (eighteen days late); once, when they had accidentally collided in the second-floor hall and he had muttered something under his breath that sounded suspiciously like "bitch" to her. She pretended she hadn't heard, but a self-protective instinct prompted her to keep as far away from him as possible. He didn't like women. Who knew what he was capable of? Fortunately, Walker would be there tonight while she gave Clem the bad news.

The workman was ensconced at the kitchen table, examining the blueprints and whistling occasionally with admiration for Christopher Ruffo's work.

"Do you think a month's notice is enough?" Carol was already beginning to worry.

"I'm surprised you let him stay on this long."

"I want to give him time to find another place."

"Carol, the guy threatened you in your own house. I was a witness. Just kick the bum out."

"Well, he's got his rights, too. As a renter, I mean. I'm not sure what the law says on the subject."

Walker just looked at her.

Why did she dread confrontations so much? Was it something in the genes? Or the cumulative impact of all those years, growing up, during which her mother regularly admonished her, "Don't make a scene, dear." Not making a scene was the hallmark of good breeding in New England, but Carol sometimes wondered if it wasn't really a form of faintheartedness, cowardice masking as manners. A few flat-out scenes might have helped the marriage with Blake. So much had gone unsaid for so long. Problems had been allowed to fester, unaddressed. The air never got cleared, until finally it was so heavy with low-hanging storm clouds that they both doubted the sun would ever break through.

No, unpleasantness didn't go away of its own accord, and if unpleasantness didn't, Carol could rest assured that Clem wouldn't, either. She tried to put him out of her head and imagined his rooms, instead. Not as they were now, squalid and dark and filled with broken-down furniture, dirty dishes, and dog-eared porno magazines, but as the spacious, airy, two-room suite that would be the pride of the Christmas Inn. The Kennedy Suite. She even had a photograph of Charles and Veronica, radiant in their happiness, to hang in a place of honor, once the work was finished.

"You sure that's what you want to do?" Walker asked her.

"Yes, why?"

"Just thinking. It's such a big area, and we're going to have to gut it, start over from scratch, from what I can tell."

"Yes, but we've got the blueprints!"

"I realize. But don't you think it makes more sense to turn that part of the house into two or three separate bedrooms? Bring in a lot more money that way. As it is, we're going to have to rip down a couple of walls and move some doors. The pipes are probably shot to hell."

"That's not the point, Walker. This was Charles and Veronica Kennedy's bedroom, the one part of the mansion that was theirs alone. The other rooms are different somehow, less intimate, more public. Their bedroom is the heart of this house. It has to be put back just as it was, don't you see?"

He shook his head, then said brusquely, "You'll be re-creating the scene of a crime, you know. Is that what you really mean to do? Put it back like it was the night of the murder? Bad enough you're naming it the Christmas Inn."

"What do you mean, 'bad enough'?"

"Carol, this Charles and Veronica were killed on Christmas Eve, right? And now you're restoring their room and you want to call this place the Christmas Inn. Wake up."

The words brought her up short. She didn't look upon the mansion as a place of death. Why did others? Come to think of it, the historical-society lady had been quick to dismiss the house, as if it carried an unmentionable taint. Then there was Tina Ruffo with all her talk of ghosts. Now Walker seemed to be warning her not to proceed with her plans. He didn't even look like himself right now. Carol thought she detected a remoteness in his eyes, and the strong, masculine jawline she usually found so appealing merely seemed stubborn. An image of him leaving Oakdale, a scowl burned into his face, flashed through her mind. There was a side of this man she clearly didn't know.

"I'm thinking about the future of this house, Walker," she said. "Why are you bringing up a murder that happened seventy years ago?"

The tautness in his face vanished. He smiled, his typical casual self again.

"People just may not want to sleep in there, that's all."

"Then we won't tell them."

"I guess we won't."

That afternoon, she stopped by the sign painter's shop on Whippoorwill Lane. "So you're calling it the Christmas Inn, eh?" mumbled a grizzled man covered with moles that closer inspection revealed to be flecks of dark blue paint. "Cute. Real cute. Would you believe I once dated a woman named Noele Holliday?" Carol couldn't tell if he was pulling her leg or not, but when he promised to have some preliminary designs to show her by the end of the week, she decided he wasn't. The lady at the Chamber of Commerce seemed less captivated by the name. However, she dutifully wrote down the address and the phone number and said that she would be delighted to pass along the information, if any tourists came in looking for "that sort of place."

Carol thought it better not to ask her what she meant by "that sort of place" and informed her instead that the Christmas Inn would officially open for guests on Memorial Day, but weekends only at first. "If the permits come through," she added under her breath. While leaving, she noticed a large rack of brochures by the wall. Figuring she might as well know the competition, she helped herself to a handful.

"You've Never Seen the Likes of Mr. Bill's Elephant Museum," trumpeted one, which promised "one of the largest and most unusual collections of elephants in the world," including Miss Betty, a twelve-foot-tall talking elephant, whatever the hell that was. The brochure for "The Land of the Midget Horses" showed two laughing children cavorting with "a picture-perfect, fully grown miniature performing horse" no bigger than they were. By comparison, the portrait of Dwight and Mamie Eisenhower, posing staidly by a bed of flowers before their "only permanent home" in Gettysburg, was a model of taste, even if the house itself, judging from the pictures, was a decorator's nightmare.

All Carol needed to do to fit right in with the Christmas Inn was to put Santa Claus on the roof, Mrs. Claus in the kitchen, and a herd of itsy-bitsy reindeer in the backyard. The notion made her laugh and distracted her for a while from what was really occupying her: Clem. How was she going to tell him? And what was it going to be like living under the same roof, once she did? She worried the rest of the afternoon.

Walker stayed for supper and helped clean up afterward.

Sammy's entire life was now centered on Charlie, the puppy, who, Carol explained with as much patience as she could muster, could not have dinner at the table with the rest of them, but would have to settle for his own dish next to the refrigerator.

"Can I eat next to him, then?"

"Sammy Roblins, be sensible!" Furthermore, she painstakingly explained, as soon as Charlie had eaten, it was Sammy's responsibility to take him outdoors immediately so there would be no accidents on the carpets.

She and Walker relaxed on the veranda, while Sammy followed Charlie around the front lawn expectantly, waiting for something to happen. Each time the puppy sat down, Sammy propped him up on his legs again. Down, up, down, up—it was a stalemate. Which of the two, boy or pet, was more frustrated was difficult to ascertain. Finally, Sammy uttered a cry of joy and, clapping his hands as he raced back to the veranda, announced triumphantly to the neighborhood, "He peed!"

Sammy ran off again, and Walker went into the parlor to catch the evening news, leaving Carol to her thoughts and the fading light. Across Ragged Ridge Road, a cornfield had recently been plowed. At this time of night, the rich earth looked like a dark pond. A few minutes passed, then Carol heard the familiar rattle. Clem's battered pickup chewed its way up the driveway and lurched to a stop by the back door. Determined to catch him before he disappeared into the house, she jumped up and called his name.

"Could I have a word with you, Clem?"

There was no reply, just that sullen stare, made more intense by his dark, bushy eyebrows, although the pint of whiskey in his back pocket probably had something to do with it, too. He sauntered around to the front of the veranda, purposefully taking his time and prolonging the silence between them. The theme music of the *ABC Nightly News* reminded Carol that Walker was not far away and shored up her faltering will. She began haltingly.

"Clem, remember when Blake and I bought the house? We said we'd let you stay here as long as we could . . . that we didn't want to have to put anyone out, if we didn't have to. . . . We meant it, but, well, as you can see, I've been doing a lot of work these past couple of months. I'm very close to opening the bed-and-breakfast, and it's quite important to me that the house look as it did when it was first built."

"Cut the bullshit. You've decided it's time to kick me out, haven't you?"

"I wouldn't call it kicking you out. However long it takes you to find someplace else——"

"Sure, like that! I'm supposed to find another place to live." He was glaring at her, and Carol could feel the perspiration breaking out on the nape of her neck. He was such a volatile man, and he had been living right above her all these months.

Clem made a fist and began pounding it into the palm of his left hand, the way a baseball player breaks in a stiff mitt. "Where the fuck do you suggest I move? Got any bright ideas, lady?"

Carol heard Walker's footsteps coming up behind her.

"Mr. Tough Guy to the rescue," sneered Clem.

"Can it, Clem. She's giving you notice. You got thirty days to get out of here. That shouldn't be too hard to understand." Walker spread his feet and planted his hands on his hips. The stance didn't invite a protracted discussion.

"I understand," snickered Clem. "Boy, oh, boy, do I understand! Don't think I ain't seen everything that's been going on around here. Mornings in the kitchen! Late nights in the parlor! Oh, I seen it all."

"Thirty days, Clem," repeated Walker. "No more. Now scram."

The mechanic backed off. He knew Walker could beat him in a fight, if it came to that, but he didn't want to advertise his fear. So he kept the stupid grin on his face as he moved away, until there was enough distance between them for him to feel safe. Then he pointed a grimy finger at Carol and bellowed righteously, "You should be ashamed of yourself. Carrying on behind your husband's back. Carrying on under your eejit kid's nose, for chrissake. What the hell kinda mother are you?"

Carol's mouth dropped open.

"Don't act Miss Innocent with me. When the cat's away, the mice will play, huh? What would your husband do if he found out? He could, you know, find out. A letter is all it would take. One little postcard. 'Dear Blake, I regret to inform you that your wife is—'"

"That's enough, Clem. Don't cause any more trouble around here than you already have." Walker started down the stairs, but the mechanic was already loping toward his pickup. "Sluts, they're all sluts," he muttered loud enough for Carol to hear. He climbed behind the wheel and the truck shot backward. Then, with the whine of rubber spinning on gravel, it tore down the driveway, hurtled left, and vanished, leaving a cloud of blue exhaust fumes behind. The roar of the motor faded in the distance, and the sounds of the night reasserted themselves. The wind stirred in the trees. Several houses away, a dog barked.

"Well, this is going to be a fun month," Carol said, trying to lighten the mood.

"What a jerk!" cursed Walker, staring down the road. He turned back. "I'll sleep over tonight. You do want me to, don't you?"

"Thanks, I'd appreciate that," she said, but the question struck her as unnecessary. They already had an unspoken understanding. It was customary for him to work right up to the dinner hour, and no less customary for her to invite him for supper. Afterward, he helped with the dishes and then Sammy usually had something important to show him (his newest find), which Walker examined with all the seriousness the boy expected. Invariably, the evening hours slipped by so quickly that Walker, after a glance at his watch, concluded that it wasn't worth the long commute just to sleep in his own bed and plopped down on the couch.

As Walker went indoors, Carol realized that the idea of his spending the night had a different connotation to it now, a nasty subtext. She had always been so careful to keep everything professional between them. They hardly even discussed their personal lives with each other, and now Clem had poisoned the atmosphere with his insinuations. Funny what words could do, especially lies.

The color of the sky had deepened to a dark navy blue. Carol lingered on the veranda, thinking the neighbors had probably been keeping tabs on her, too. Had they seen Walker's truck parked overnight in the driveway and jumped to the same conclusions as Clem? How many had witnessed the scene tonight?

She put her head against the back of the wicker chair and closed her eyes. The soft spill of light from the parlor, catching her hair, turned it from blond to golden. Only a faint creasing between her finely arched eyebrows betrayed her concern. Otherwise, she looked like a pretty teenager, lolling away the minutes before her boyfriend arrives to take her to the Saturday-night movies.

Clem was wrong, but there was just enough truth in what he had said to disturb her. Oh, nothing had gone on between her and Walker. The relationship was all aboveboard. Strictly platonic. She had no apologies to make on that count. That didn't mean her mind hadn't wandered now and then. But if she had occasionally asked herself what kind of a lover Walker might make, she had sinned in thought only, as the Catholics put it. Had Clem picked up on that, or was he just hurling charges, willy-nilly, hoping that some would hit their mark?

She was going to have to be more prudent in the future. In more ways than one.

The front door swung open and Walker joined her on the veranda. He had showered and put on a clean pair of dress pants and a plaid, button-down shirt. Carol thought she smelled the scent of aftershave lotion.

"Are you going somewhere?"

"No. Just felt like getting cleaned up for a change. All my jeans were dirty."

"I'll put them in the wash, if you like." She got up and started inside.

"I did it already. I didn't think you'd mind."

"Why should I?"

Carol knew that he kept an extra set of work clothes in the closet in the parlor. Apparently, he had brought a few of his good clothes over, too.

"Don't worry about Clem. I'll make sure he doesn't cause

any more problems before he moves out." Walker leaned up against the veranda railing, his hands in his pockets and his feet crossed at the ankles. He had combed his hair and parted it neatly on the right-hand side. It flashed through Carol's mind that he had gotten cleaned up just for her. The confrontation with Clem had clearly established him as king of the hill.

"I'm sorry you have to go through all this, Walker. You're here to renovate an old mansion, not to be my protector."

"Is that what I am now?"

"Well, you're a lot more than a carpenter. That's for sure."

"I should hope so. We're friends, at least. Well, aren't we?"

"Of course we are. And I'm very grateful for all you've done for Sammy and me."

"I haven't done anything."

"You have, too, Walker. Look at what just happened. I never could have handled that alone. You have no idea what it's like to be a woman in that kind of a confrontation. You feel so small. I mean that literally. You feel physically small and completely vulnerable. That man could hurt me."

"He's not going to hurt you. I can guarantee you that." With no further prompting, he reached out his arms and pulled her close. She gave in to the embrace and laid her cheek up against his chest. His arms were clasped behind her back, and for a moment she enjoyed the sensation of being enveloped by a strong man. His strength was like a shield, guarding her from harm and Clem's invective.

As she lifted her head, her chin brushed the tufts of hair poking out of the triangular neckline of his sports shirt. The scent of his aftershave was sweet to her nostrils, and she was aware that one of the lines she had tried so hard to keep between them had been crossed.

She pulled back, but he held on to her tightly—his lips pressed up against her temple. The sudden intimacy made her uncomfortable. Were the neighbors seeing this? Was Sammy?

"I'll bet you regret you ever got involved with the Christmas Inn," she said, hoping to break the mood.

"Best thing that ever happened to me."

She looked up at him. He gave her that big, engaging grin.

"Oh, you probably say that to all your employers," she quipped, and squirmed out of his arms. "I think I'd better check on Sammy."

Once she had slipped inside the door, she paused in the foyer to collect herself. That had been a close call—too close. For a split-second, she had been tempted to give in, to do away with that fine line, erase it altogether. She couldn't let it happen again. Checking on Sammy was such a lame excuse; Walker had to know. She risked a glance out the bay window to see what he was doing. She could see his back as he stared off into the darkness and could only imagine what was going on in his head.

Sometime in the middle of the night, as she tossed and turned in a restless half-sleep, she thought she heard a thumping and sat bolt upright in bed. Someone was walking directly overhead. Clem had returned home. She slipped out from under the covers and cracked open the parlor door to see if Walker was still there. He was snoring on the foldaway couch, dead to the world. He hadn't bothered to crawl under the covers.

"Pssst," she whispered, hoping the noise had awakened him, too, but the snoring continued rhythmically.

She returned to her bed and sat in the dark, listening to Clem clomping around his rooms. He was making no effort to be quiet. All at once, there was a loud thud.

"Sonavabitch," he yelped. Something must have fallen over. Then came the sound of heavy objects being dragged across the floor or pushed up against the wall. Two people were talking. One, the louder one, was issuing orders. Carol couldn't make out what the quieter one was saying, but whatever it was, it wasn't appeasing the loud one. Their discussion was heated. What is going on up there? she thought.

She tiptoed into the foyer and peered up the stairs. She could hear more clearly now. It wasn't two people at all. It was Clem, carrying on a conversation with himself, taking both sides. "You understand, don't you, that it's real important for me to make the house all nice and pretty. Can't have your type around here no more," he said in a high-pitched voice that Carol recognized as a bad imitation of hers.

His own snarly voice answered mockingly, "Yeah, I understand. Gotta make the place nice and pretty for lover boy. Can't have the kid catchin' you doing it with somebody who's not Daddy. Old Clem's rooms gonna make the perfect love nest." The banging resumed, punctuated by Clem's hoarse, whiskey-soaked laugh.

Without warning, the door to the apartment opened, throwing a shaft of light into the hall, and Clem stormed down the back stairs. The kitchen door clacked. Carol darted back into her room. She was tempted to sneak out on the veranda to see what he was up to, but quickly thought better of it. Only moments later, Clem was back in his rooms, and the banging and cursing were louder than ever.

"You got thirty days, understand, thirty days." It was Walker's voice he was imitating now. "Don't worry, big man, I get it. I'll be outta here by then. I'll be outta here so damn fast you'll feel the breeze," he replied in his own voice.

A moment of quiet ensued. Then, "Forgive them, Great White Father, for they know not what they do." The boozy laughter bounced off the walls.

How long would this last? Afraid to get back in bed, Carol pulled her terry-cloth bathrobe tight and curled up in a ball on top of the bedspread. In that position, she drifted off for an hour at a spell, only to be awakened by another thud. The last time she remembered looking at the digital alarm clock on her bedside table, it registered 5:25, and the faint orangy glow that preceeds the sunrise was lapping at the curtains.

At 6:57, she came to with a start. The first thing she was aware of was the silence. It was like the stillness after the hurricane that tore through central Florida, when she and Blake were living there early in their marriage. Absolutely nothing had seemed to stir then, not an insect, not a blade of grass, not a single palm frond. Even the birds were mute. She had the same eerie impression now that life had ceased.

In the bedroom abutting hers, she peeked in on Sammy.

Charlie was nestled in the crook of his arm. Kids and puppies could sleep through anything. It surprised her, though, when she checked on Walker, that he had barely shifted on the foldaway couch in the parlor. She could have sworn that his body was in the same position five hours earlier. The bedcovers weren't wrinkled and one of the two pillows was still freshly fluffed up. Had he been too exhausted to budge?

She ventured into the foyer, concluding from the silence that Clem had finally fallen into an alcoholic stupor and stumbled to bed. A hangover would put him in an even fouler mood today, if that was possible. Tentatively, she climbed a few steps, arching her neck as she did, trying to see his apartment door without being seen herself. Up a few more steps. The ridiculousness of having to sneak around her own house like an intruder made her angry. Only when she reached the landing could she tell that the door was ajar.

Mindful of the noise her slippers made, she shuffled nervously down the hallway, her courage waning fast. The last time she had marched boldly into the apartment, Clem had frightened the living daylights out of her. The door was like the entrance to a cave then. It seemed brighter inside this time. Bracing herself, she entered and looked to her left. The olive army blankets had been torn down and light was streaming in through the windows. Most of the furniture was gone. During the long, noisy night, Clem had carted everything off. That's what the frenzied activity had been about.

All that he had left behind were a varnished bureau, minus its drawers, a couple of sorry wooden chairs, and a table that tilted badly to one side for want of a leg. And trash, everywhere. The newspapers, no longer in a pile, covered the floor. Several upended Hefty bags spewed forth their unsavory contents: tin cans, chicken bones, rags that had probably been T-shirts once, even the remains of a pizza. There were wire coat hangers, a crumpled-up girlie calendar, worn-out shoes. And chunks of plaster! Gazing up, Carol saw why: the light fixture, a bare bulb on a long cord, had been ripped from the ceiling.

A sour stench of garbage filled the room. She rushed to

the nearest window, threw it open, and drank in some of the sweet morning air. It had been horrible, but the nightmare was over at last. Clem was gone. No more looking up from the kitchen stove to find him standing there accusingly, like some oil-stained apparition. No more pleading with him for the overdue rent. She was preparing to go back downstairs when all at once she felt a horrible sickness in her stomach. The walls were covered with green spray paint. As she gaped in disbelief at the ugly squiggles and splotches, she realized that it was writing. No, not just writing, words of warning.

And the words screamed, FLEE OUT OF THE MIDST OF BABYLON, FOR THIS IS THE TIME OF THE LORD'S VENGEANCE.

Twenty

———

The first task Carol and Walker tackled that morning was to slap a coat of paint on the walls in Clem's bedroom. It was wasted effort in a sense. The walls were in poor condition and badly damaged in places and were going to have to be replaced with plasterboard. But having put Clem out of the house, Carol was determined to eliminate all traces of his presence, especially the spray-painted threats that he had left behind as his parting gesture.

Her hair was tied up in a yellow kerchief, and she had deep circles under her eyes from what had been a fitful night of sleep. The relief she felt, as she guided the roller back and forth over the walls, more than compensated for her fatigue, though, and she attacked the job with enthusiasm. One coat of white paint did only so much. The dark green graffiti still bled through, but, fainter, it no longer had the same frightening immediacy.

Outside, the sun was blazing in another cloudless sky. Summer seemed determined to crowd out spring this year. Walker had peeled off his shirt and was working in his T-shirt and jeans.

"I can't believe all the racket Clem made last night. You really didn't hear anything?" Carol asked.

"Nope. Nothing at all. When I conk out, I conk out."

"Well, you certainly looked out for the count, I'll say that."

"What do you mean?"

"At one moment, when Clem was really raving, I stuck my head in the parlor door. Looking for reinforcements, if necessary."

"So you saw then."

"What?"

Walker laughed. "That a team of wild horses couldn't have roused me."

"I guess not."

Carol laughed along with him. With each passing hour, her spirits rose. Clem's poisonous presence had been worse than any ghost, but the house was being cleansed, exorcised, with broad strokes of Devonshire Cream. Walker busied himself cleaning up the mounds of trash. The wall-to-wall carpeting in the dining room area and the bedroom was filthy, and Carol proposed ripping it up immediately, until Walker pointed out that it would at least protect the floorboards for the time being. The carpeting was granted a reprieve. The warped linoleum in the kitchenette and bathroom told another story. The wood underneath appeared to be rotting.

Walker plucked a deflated inner tube out of the rubble, shrugged his shoulders in disbelief, and threw it down. "Looks like Paul Clemson brought his work home from the office," he joked. Before long, he had filled up five large garbage bags and raised a fine cloud of dust that clung to the back of their throats.

Carol called a break and announced she was going down to the kitchen to get something to drink. "Want a soda, Walker?"

"Just some cold water. While you're at it, do you mind bringing up some more trash bags? I think there are some in the toolbox in the back of my truck."

Carol let the tap water run until it was icy cold and prepared a snack of sliced apples and Gouda cheese, before going outdoors. Walker's toolbox contained a little of everything—tools, of course, but also extra work clothes, a roll of paper towels, sandpaper, a can of motor oil. She was surprised at how much stuff he carried with him. "That's a workman for you. Ready for any emergency," she told herself. She had to root around before she found the Hefty bags. As she reached for them, her hand touched a small canister. Curious, she picked it up. It was spray paint. She examined the label: "Forest Green."

What was it doing there? Had Clem tossed it in the back of the truck? It was absurd to think that Walker had anything to do with the writing on the wall. He had been asleep all night long. She'd seen him. Anyway, there were dozens of reasons for a workman to keep spray paint in his toolbox.

Offhand, she couldn't think of one. And forest green? It wasn't a practical color, like black or white. Then the afternoon at Oakdale came back to her and Walker's truck speeding up the driveway. She'd never been able to put that out of her mind.

It was time to clear up a few of the mysteries.

She slipped the spray paint in her pocket and carried the pitcher of water, the snacks, and the trash bags upstairs on a tray. Happy for a rest, Walker laid his broom aside and settled into the open window.

"Look what I found," Carol said, producing the paint canister.

"What? Oh, yeah. That's mine," he replied without much interest. He planted one foot on the sill and tilted his head back to catch the sun's rays.

"I know it's yours. It was in the truck."

"Yeah. So? That's where I keep it."

"Is this what Clem used?"

Walker sat forward abruptly. "Let me see." He grabbed the can and gave the wall a quick spritzing. The color matched that of the graffiti. "Damn! He must have taken it last night." He reflected for a moment, then burst out laughing. "Son of a gun!"

"What's so funny?"

"Well, I guess old Clem is too much of a God-fearing man to actually steal the paint. So after he was through, he put it back where he found it. Mighty thoughtful of him, wouldn't you say? It's all right to scare the shit out of people and deface their property, but whatever you do, don't steal the paint!" Laughter seized him again.

"This is no joking matter, Walker."

"Sorry. I thought a little humor would help. People are pretty messed up. They do crazy things. Clem went bonkers last night. There's nothing more to it than that."

Walker returned to his perch on the windowsill, took a swig of water, and nibbled on the cheese. Carol realized he was probably right. Despite her proclivity for complicating things, there was no need to look any further. Nine times out of ten, the obvious explanation was the correct explanation.

Idly, she raised the question, "Walker, who do you know at Oakdale?"

He drained his glass and didn't reply right away. "How do you know I know anybody at Oakdale? Do you follow me around? Jeepers, what's with you today, Carol?"

Her face reddened with embarrassment. Some investigator she was! She was going about everything the wrong way this morning. She should have brought up Oakdale that very day. Guess who I saw this afternoon, Walker? The playful approach. Now it sounded as if she were making an issue out of absolutely everything, including a paint canister in Walker's toolbox.

"Of course I don't follow you around. I was there a few days ago, that's all, and I happened to see your truck in the parking lot. I keep forgetting to mention it. I don't know what made me think of it now." She wasn't telling the whole truth, that she'd watched him disappear inside and come out only minutes later with a highly disturbed look on his face.

"I have an aunt there. What were you doing there?"

"Oh, one of my dumber ideas. I went to talk to the mayor's father. You know how obsessed I am about finding out the history of this place. He wasn't very helpful. He wasn't helpful at all. I don't think he remembers anything. It's too bad."

"Yeah, it is too bad."

"Is your aunt sick?"

"No, just old. I take her out for drives now and then."

"In the truck?"

"Yes. She's grateful for the chance to get out, see something besides her room."

"Where do you usually go?"

"Wherever she wants."

"What about the other day?"

He paused to pop a slice of apple in his mouth. "We didn't. She took a spill and wasn't up to it."

"I'm sorry. Was it serious?"

"Could have been worse. She's her old self again."

And that was the end of it, another perfectly legitimate explanation, even if Walker didn't seem to come from a family that had money, certainly not the kind of money to keep someone at Oakdale. But then Carol didn't really know anything about his family. He occasionally mentioned his parents, so they were still alive. But that was all she knew.

The subject of Oakdale didn't come up again.

They made small talk the rest of the afternoon. By the time the school bus dropped off Sammy at the foot of the driveway, they had cleaned up the apartment, which was now just three empty, somewhat desolate rooms in bad disrepair. Most signs of their former occupant had been obliterated.

"Charlie, I'm home." Sammy came bouncing up the stairs, wearing the Monte Carlo T-shirt that Blake had sent him. He'd worn it to school every day since it had arrived, a week ago.

"Hey, just the man I was looking for," said Walker. "You want to give me a hand with this trash?"

As they carted the bags down the back stairs, Carol felt as if a big load had been lifted off her back. This bedroom belonged to her now, and the memory of Charles and Veronica Kennedy. Clem would never bother her again.

For the next two weeks, she stayed out of the apartment and occupied herself by decorating the two completed suites at the other end of the house, which she decided to call the Rose Room and the Hunter's Retreat in keeping with their respective decors. The former, frilly and feminine, had a color scheme of soft pinks and pale greens that she had taken from a photograph of an English garden in a morning mist. The latter was done in shades of browns with black and white accents, aimed, she felt, more at the male sensibility.

She went in opposite directions with the furniture, too. The spindle bed and the vanity in the Rose Room, she painted white to go with a white wicker armchair. She outfitted the bed with an antique skirt and spread and lots of fluffy pillows. On the top of the vanity, she arranged a matching brush, comb, and mirror, all made of hand-painted porcelain, and nestled a nineteenth-century china doll in the wicker chair. The Hunter's Retreat, on the other hand, could have been lifted from a cabin in Maine. It featured a wrought-iron bed, a wooden chest with leather hinges, and an oversize rocking chair by the window. But the crowning glory was the pair of antlers she had picked up cheap at a yard sale in Brickton. The day she hung them over the bathroom mirror, she pronounced the first rooms in the Christmas Inn officially ready.

"All I need now are the guests," she noted, surveying the results with pride.

The crashing and pounding that echoed down the hallway suggested that Walker and Joey had their work cut out for them. With crowbar and sledgehammer, they went at temporary walls that proved remarkably resilient and ripped out kitchen appliances encrusted with years of petrified food. A built-in china cupboard from the 1950s was torn from a corner of the dining room with a screech of rusty nails and a clatter of glass. Armed with Christopher Ruffo's plans, the two workmen slowly reestablished the floor plan of the original suite—the sumptuous bedroom with its elegant fireplace, the dressing room big enough to double as a sitting room, and of course, the imperial bathroom. Carol popped in regularly, marveling at how generous architects had been with space back then. You had a different slant on life when the walls weren't closing in on you and the ceiling wasn't two feet above your head. It was no surprise that people crammed into tiny apartments were always at one another's throat. Rooms like these made you feel freer, more generous, more open to the world somehow.

Carol certainly felt that way as she stood at the bedroom window and looked out at the foliage, an umbrella of green that would shade the house and help keep it cool in the sizzling months ahead. Although the winter had been hard on the silver birches, the oaks and the maples had come through splendidly. The lawn was already an emerald green, and Charlie was making the most of it—arching his back and rolling in the moist grass almost like a dolphin cavorting in sea foam.

The traffic on Ragged Ridge Road, Carol noted with satisfaction, was barely visible from this part of the house now, and the leaves muffled the sound of the rare automobile horn. She could hardly make out the truck that had pulled over on the shoulder, where her driveway joined the street. She squinted.

"Come here quick," she called out to Walker. "See down there. To the left of the driveway. Someone's watching. Someone with binoculars. Isn't that Clem's truck?"

She stepped back from the window while Walker inched forward cautiously, trying to stay out of view.

"Yeah, that's Clem's truck, all right. It looks like Clem behind the binoculars, too."

The old fear welled up inside her. "Well, he's got no business being there. I'm going to call the police." She was almost out of the bedroom when Walker stopped her.

"What are you going to tell them, Carol? That Paul Clemson is parked on the edge of the road? There's no law against that, you know. It is a public thoroughfare."

She turned back. "After all the threats he made? He's stalking me, Walker."

"He was pissed off. He probably still is. That doesn't mean he won't get over it. He needs time to cool down."

"Tell me something," Carol said, fixing Walker in the eye. "Whose side are you on?"

The question was unexpected. Momentarily short of words, he shifted uneasily on his feet. Then the familiar, unassuming smile appeared on his face, a smile that accentuated his boyishness and almost dared people not to trust him. "Come on, Carol. Be fair. I don't want you to make this into a bigger deal than it is."

At that moment, the truck started up with a sputter. The throb of the idling motor floated up through the window. As if to prove the wisdom of Walker's words, Clem had apparently seen enough and was preparing to pull away.

Led on by the pungent scents of earth and new grass, Charlie had moseyed to the edge of the lawn. Ungluing his nose from the ground, he padded onto the shoulder of the road where a clump of ragweed attracted his interest. Clem revved the engine several times, and in a split instant Carol knew what was about to happen.

"Oh, my God," she yelled to Walker. "He's headed straight for the dog. He's going to hit Charlie." The worn wheels of the truck spun on the gravel before grabbing hold, then the battered vehicle pitched forward onto the macadam. The dog was less than seventy-five feet away.

"Charlie!" Carol leaned out the window as far as she could and bellowed. Oblivious, Charlie lifted his leg, intent upon leaving his mark on the ragweed. The truck was picking up speed, swerving from side to side. Clem hunched over the wheel, his face pressed up against the windshield, as he bore down on the animal.

"N-o-o-o-o!"

The force of Carol's scream tore at her vocal chords. The right side of the truck caught the shoulder, producing waves of dust. The animal's leg muscles jerked instinctively and he skittered sideways with a piercing yelp. The truck lunged back onto the pavement. For several seconds, the dust made it impossible to tell what had occurred.

Carol hung in the window, appalled, waiting for the air to clear. How would she ever be able to explain something like this to Sammy? Then, she heard her son's voice as he rounded the house.

"So there you are, Charlie. Naughty boy. Naughty!"

Unhurt, the dog had scampered back onto the lawn and was cowering under a hydrangea bush.

"Come out of there, Charlie. No more running away."

Sammy coaxed the pet out of hiding and shooed him toward the veranda. "No, no, no. Understand? I'm not going to tell you again. Okay?"

Carol breathed deeply and collapsed against the wall, shaken by what she had just witnessed. Then her whole body began to tremble with the realization that it could just as easily have been Sammy, not Charlie, dallying at the edge of the road. Would Clem have borne down on her son, too? What was going on here? The mansion was supposed to bring her happiness and a sense of security, not these feelings of queasiness that gnawed at the pit of her stomach.

"Narrow escape, eh?" Walker came over and put his arm around her shoulders.

She stiffened at his touch. "Narrower than you think. I knew that man was dangerous."

"You're a bundle of nerves. Let me give you a massage."

"That's all right, Walker." She shook off his hand with a shrug of the shoulders.

"What's the matter? Can't I touch you?"

"It isn't that."

"What do you mean, then?"

"Well, just that there's touching and there's touching."

She heard the phone ringing downstairs and Sammy running to get it. Grateful for the distraction, she pulled away from the workman and shouted, "A 'hello' would be appropriate, Sammy."

"Hello...yup...what?...yup...yup." Sammy dropped the receiver on the kitchen floor and shouted, "For you, Mom."

"Who is it?"

"Don't know." He scooped up Charlie, stuffed him down his shirt, and carried him off to his room.

Carol sprinted to the kitchen and retrieved the phone. "Hello."

A woman's voice asked hesitantly, "Ah, yes . . . is this the Christmas Inn?"

"Yes, it is." It was the first time anyone had used the name.

"Do you have a room this weekend?"

Carol checked the calendar. It was Friday. Memorial Day

weekend. According to the Fayette Chamber of Commerce, at least, she was officially open.

"This weekend? Like today?"

"I'm sorry it's so last-minute. I suppose you're all booked up, too."

"No, no. How many?"

"There are two of us. Just one room though."

"That will be fine."

"We'll be there in about an hour. We're in downtown Fayette right now. We thought we'd stroll around a little. Sightsee."

"That's terrific. I'll look for you in an hour then."

"Don't you want our names?"

"Oh, yes, of course."

"It's Bayshore."

Carol hung up the phone in a panic. She was wearing dirty Bermuda shorts and one of Blake's old white shirts. Her hair was a mess. She had to take a shower. Walker and Joey were still making debris in the Kennedy Suite. Breakfast! What was she going to serve the . . . the . . . their name had something to do with the ocean. Beachman! No, that wasn't it. Bayshore! Yes, what was she going to serve the Bayshores in the morning? She should have asked them what they liked. And the Christmas candles! She hadn't put out Christmas candles in either the Rose Room or in the Hunter's Retreat. The bathrooms had towels, though, didn't they? She dashed up the stairs, becoming more discombobulated by the second.

"Sammy! Walker! Joey! Everybody!"

There were plaster-dust footprints the length of the hall. She grabbed a broom and started sweeping furiously. Walker came running, half-expecting to find a corpse on the landing. Joey was right behind him. Seconds later, Sammy materialized, wide-eyed, at the top of the stairs with Charlie. Carol looked at them all.

"Guests!" she announced proudly.

The Bayshores turned out to be a nondescript couple in their sixties. His abiding passion was the Civil War. Hers wasn't, but she had a sweetly accommodating nature, which allowed her to tag quietly along at his side as he trudged over battle sites and re-created for her benefit violent and bloody clashes out of the past. As a respite from their weekend agenda, perhaps, Mrs. Bayshore opted for the Rose Room, but they spent little time in it, and Carol hardly saw them, except in the morning. Although she had laid in enough food to feed one of the armies that held such fascination for Mr. Bayshore, they proved to be as timid at the breakfast table as they were intrepid on the battlefield. On Monday morning, declaring themselves eminently satisfied with the Christmas Inn, they wrote out a check for $240 and departed. A breeze, Carol thought, this is going to be a breeze.

Walker and Joey were back in the Kennedy Suite on Tuesday, and the cheap wall-to-wall carpet that had been laid down God knows how many years earlier, before Clem even, finally came up. It was so filthy that Carol would have burned it right there in the backyard as an act of public sanitation if the law had permitted. Walker pointed out that, disgusting as it was, it had served a useful purpose: the floors were in remarkably good shape. He gave a tug to a last remnant clinging stubbornly to the baseboard between the windows. It yielded with a rip. Underneath was one of the cast-brass grates from the original heating system.

"What do you know!" he whistled, and called for Carol to come take a look. Instead of the usual grid of squares, the grating was formed by the initials VCK, repeated in a handsome pattern. Carol had seen renderings of the grate in Christopher Ruffo's plans, but she had assumed the grates themselves had been sold to an antique-brass dealer at some point in the past. None were to be found in the mansion. Until now, that is.

While Joey and Walker carted off the rug, she knelt down and cleared some of the dirt off the grate. Then she ran her fingers over the letters VCK. It was the same VCK that had been etched in the frosted-glass window of the original front door (it, too, long gone); the same VCK that a good scouring had revealed in the stained-glass skylight in the foyer. Certain people marked by doom—romantic poets, especially—were supposed to know in some secret part of themselves that their lives would be brief. She wondered if

Charles Kennedy was one of them. Had he sensed that he and Veronica would not be together long? Was that why he had made such an effort to leave an imprint of their union on the house? "Remember me," he had said to Carol in her dream.

She gazed about the empty room. The sunlight pouring through the windows transformed the motes of dust in the air into magical bits of phosphorescence. There was that tug again. She had the distinct impression that Veronica and Charles were reaching out to her. She would never admit it to anyone—it was too crazy—but she felt joined to the dead couple all the same. It was no coincidence that she had bought this mansion or that the restoration had become such a compulsion. She told people it was a wise business decision. Old was in these days. One of those magazines, *House, Home, and Garden* or *Martha Stewart Living,* had said so only the other month. But it was far more personal than that.

She wanted to find out what had happened to Charles and Veronica, help them in their distress, silly as that sounded. How could she possibly help people who were dead and buried, people who had lived seventy years ago? Still, long before she had known their story, something had prompted her to bring Christmas back to this big old house. Tina Ruffo would say it was ghosts. Maybe it was some old romantic ideal she had clung to obstinately since childhood, despite the evidence of a prosaic world. Despite the evidence of her own marriage. Only a shrink could tell.

Walker and Joey trudged through the door, interrupting her reveries. They were covered with dirt from the carpet, and Joey was carrying a vacuum cleaner.

"Let me help for a while," she volunteered, taking the vacuum cleaner from him.

"Why not? Have we ever been known to refuse another pair of hands?" Walker cracked. He unscrewed the brass heating grate and lifted it out, so that Carol could begin there. Six inches below the floor level were a series of cast-iron louvers that regulated the amount of hot air rising up from a furnace in the basement. The furnace was nothing but a historical curiosity now, and the louvers had been closed for decades. With her hand, Carol scooped up the debris of another time—carpet tacks, splinters of wood, nuggets of plaster the color and hardness of coal. Then, she opened the louvers and peered into the blackness.

At first, she assumed the heating duct went straight to the cellar. But it couldn't. The duct was almost a foot from the wall, and her bedroom was directly underneath. She took a piece of wood and stuck it through the louvers. About eighteen inches down, it struck something metallic, the bottom of the duct, apparently, which angled off toward the wall. In what seemed to be a three-sided box, layers upon layers of dirt and soot had built up over the years. The floor brush of the vacuum cleaner was too big to fit through the louvers, so Carol had to use the long, flat attachment. As she wiggled it around, she could hear the dust being sucked up.

"Don't overdo it, Carol. More crap is just going to fall down there." Walker had an armful of rotten planks and was stoically preparing to descend the stairs again.

"I'll be done in a second. Then we can seal it off with plastic," Carol answered him over the roar. But Walker was gone.

Suddenly, the vacuum cleaner emitted a loud squawk and varoomed into high gear. The nozzle was blocked.

"That's all I have to do—suck up a nail in this machine," she said to the empty room. "It's so old it will probably explode." She yanked the plug from its socket and the motor died down with a pathetic whine. Carol carefully lifted the attachment up from between the louvers, and sure enough, an object was lodged in the end. Even caked in grime, it gave off a luster.

She knew what it was instinctively. Before the words had even formed in her head, she knew. It was a necklace. The necklace. The one she had read about in the pages of the *Weekly Register*. The one that had been stolen the night of Veronica Kennedy's murder.

But how could that be? The killer had made away with the jewels. The newspaper article said so. Was the article wrong? Perhaps the robbery hadn't gone off as planned. Or perhaps there never was a robber. The police hadn't been able to find him, and they had scoured the state. All at once,

Carol's mind started to reel. What if it had been murder, pure and simple? She tried to conjure up a vision of that awful night. Someone had beaten Veronica Kennedy to death. Who? And what could possibly have been the motive for such a crime? Whatever it was, it wasn't theft.

She removed the necklace from the end of the vacuum cleaner and laid it across her wrist. Then, gently, she blew on it and wiped away the dust with her index finger. The diamonds and sapphires started to sparkle, as if they had been awakened from a deep slumber.

"I'm gonna take a beer, okay?" It was Walker's voice, coming up from the kitchen. "Want one?"

She quickly dropped the necklace in the pocket of her jeans. "No, but you and Joey go ahead and help yourselves," she called back.

As she finished cleaning the duct, she could feel the jewels burning her skin. She packed up the vacuum cleaner, slipped down the front stairs to her room, and locked the door. With great care, she took the necklace from her pocket and laid it on a towel at the foot of her bed. Then with a toothbrush, slowly, painstakingly, she caressed the precious stones.

All sorts of questions would have to be answered. Did the necklace belong to her or to Veronica Kennedy's descendants, wherever they were? Should she turn it over to the authorities? Could it still be considered legal evidence, when the murder had gone unsolved for seven decades? Dazed, Carol sat on the edge of the bed and moved the jewelry around until it trapped the light and made little rainbows on the wall.

Then she took off her workshirt, stood before the mirror in her bra, and fastened the necklace around her neck. She shook her hair off her shoulders and slowly lifted her chin. The present fell away. She was back in the past, hypnotized by the heirloom that had unexpectedly come into her possession. Not a muscle moved. Charles Kennedy's voice breathed in her ear, "It's yours now. Not mine. Yours."

The sound of Walker's truck going down the driveway brought her back to herself. How long had she been standing there? She couldn't say. Quickly, she placed the necklace in a small jewelry case and slipped the case under her mattress. The rational thing would have been to store it in a safety-deposit box, but reason had nothing to do with her decision. It just seemed wrong somehow to take the necklace out of the mansion. Besides, nobody knew about her discovery. No one in the whole world.

Twenty-One

—∾∾—

Megan O'Hare held the dress high over her head as she went down the hall to the Kennedys' bedroom, careful that the hem didn't touch the floor, although no harm would have come if it had. Every last hint of dust had been hunted down and swept up, and the floors had been waxed and polished, and waxed and polished again, so that their gloss equaled that of the dining table.

The cook pretended that she could just as easily set out tonight's repast on the dining room floor, spanking clean and shiny as it was, and the guests would never know the difference, save for the fact that they would have to get down on all fours to serve themselves. Even then, she noted wryly, a few would be none the wiser. Just whom she meant by that, she refused to say, but she knew what she knew. Not everybody who would be putting on elegant airs tonight at the Kennedys' annual Christmas party came by them naturally.

Once inside the bedroom, Megan carefully laid out the dress on the bed, making sure no creases or folds were in the fabric. Mrs. Kennedy's appointment at the beauty parlor had been for two o'clock, and it was now three. She would be home in another hour and would expect to find

*the bedroom warm and cozy. Megan put another pine log
on the fire and gave the embers a vigorous stirring with the
brass poker. An orange flame rose up out of the ashes and
soon the bark began to burn, while the pitch made angry,
sputtering sounds.*

*She crossed to the window and glanced up at the sky,
gray and lowering and heavy with snow about to fall. It
was getting dark earlier and earlier. She figured she might
as well draw the velvet curtains now and spare herself
another trip later. She switched on the lamps at either end
of the dressing table and prepared to return downstairs
when her eyes alit on the oblong jewelry case. She knew
what was inside: the diamond and sapphire necklace. She
had seen Mrs. Kennedy wear it only once before—at last
year's Christmas party—but she remembered exactly
what it looked like.*

*The few times in her life that Megan had been to a
museum, it was the exhibits of gold and jewels that had
enthralled her. Others rushed off to see the monumental
paintings or the classical sculptures, but she searched out
the cases where the bracelets and rings and necklaces of
ancient civilizations were displayed. Once at the National
Museum of Dublin, she had gazed so long and so hard at
the Brooch of Tara, entranced as she was by the sunken
pearls in the delicate gold filigree, that a guard had asked
her if anything was wrong. Embarrassed, she had moved
on. But she came back later to marvel at the Celtic
ornament and wondered for a long time afterward what it
must be like to possess such a magnificent piece of
jewelry.*

*She only owned trinkets, herself. Worthless baubles.
Glass beads. She sat down at the dressing table and stared
at the oblong case, imagining its contents and trying not
to open it, but knowing that eventually she would. Well,
what wrong was in that?*

*Mrs. Kennedy was away for the afternoon, and she was
the only servant permitted in the bedroom, other than
Jimmy, who sometimes doubled as Mr. Kennedy's personal groom, when he wasn't acting as the butler. No one
would know she had been snooping, least of all Mrs.*

Kennedy. Half of the clothes hanging in the dressing room, she had never worn. On the shelves, there were things still in boxes that she had probably forgotten she'd even purchased. When you had so many possessions, that was what happened: you lost track of them.

Like the perfume bottle with the onyx top. Mrs. Kennedy didn't notice that it was missing for two months. When she finally asked what had become of it, Megan confessed that she had accidentally broken it and apologized profusely. Only she hadn't broken it at all. She had sent it to her sister in Dublin for her birthday. Mrs. Kennedy had scolded her and told her she would have to make an effort to be more careful in the future. But she'd let it go at that. Hardly a scolding at all, really.

Megan caught sight of herself in the oval mirror over the dressing table. She disliked seeing herself in her black-and-white maid's uniform. It was hard for her not to think of it as a stigma. Not that she was resentful toward the Kennedys. She wasn't. Mr. Kennedy, at least, treated her well, and she was grateful to be in America, away from the poverty of her family back home in Ireland. Still, a twist of fate and things could have been different. She might have been the wife of a wealthy banker with a necklace of twenty-four diamonds and sapphires all her own.

At last, she allowed herself to open the oblong box. Gently, almost reverently, she ran her finger over the stones. She could almost feel their brightness on her skin. She undid the first three buttons of her uniform and folded the cloth under, so as to give the severe dress a neckline and expose her cleavage. Then, she scooped up the necklace and held it in her open hand, savoring its weight. The notion occurred to her that she could walk out of the house with it right now and never come back. There was nobody to stop her. But she realized she was thinking pure nonsense. An inexpensive perfume bottle with an onyx top was one thing, but a priceless necklace like this . . .

Instead, she fastened it around her neck and, turning her head slowly from side to side, allowed herself to imagine the life she might have had. Wasn't she, in her way, as pretty as Veronica Kennedy? Wasn't her neck as graceful? Her skin as fair? All that made her a maid was the drab uniform. With a dress like the one she had just spread out on the bed and jewels like these, she, too, could charm the elite of Fayette.

"Caught you!"

Startled by the voice, she jumped up, knocking over the padded bench on which she had been sitting. Jimmy had come up from the laundry with the freshly starched white shirt that Mr. Kennedy would wear tonight. When she saw who it was, she blushed violently.

"She's not back, is she?" she asked.

"Not yet."

Megan reached behind her neck, undid the necklace, and started to put it back in its case.

"No wait," he said. "Let me see how it looks on you."

"Turn around then."

As he obeyed, she reattached the clasp and boldly opened her uniform another button, exposing the tops of her breasts. She took Veronica Kennedy's silver brush off the dressing table and ran it briskly through her auburn hair several times. Then borrowing the crystal atomizer, she sprayed herself with a light mist of lilac scent.

"Ready," she said, satisfied with her primping.

He turned around and his eyes were attracted instantly to the glittering necklace. After a while, he lifted his gaze to meet hers.

"It suits you," he said. And she knew he was right. It did.

Twenty-Two

—m—

N̲ow?" shouted Sammy, who stood impatiently by a large, boxy contraption in the living room and stared at it with the fascination he usually reserved for the answering machine.

"Not yet," Carol replied from the upstairs hallway. "The first guests won't be arriving for another hour. Take Charlie outside and play."

Sammy flopped down on a leather chair and kicked his feet aimlessly. The hour couldn't pass fast enough for his satisfaction. In his hand, he held what appeared to be a scroll of cream-colored paper, riddled with holes. He tapped it repeatedly on one arm of the chair, then on the other. Then he tapped it on his knees and kicked his feet again.

He heard his mother go into the Rose Room, come out, and go into the Hunter's Retreat. In the kitchen, two women in white aprons were busy arranging crackers and cheeses and crisp vegetables in fancy patterns on silver serving platters. A bartender with a red bow tie and green cummerbund was setting up the bar, soft drinks and fruit juices, on a table by the window in the dining room. The bustle belied what was elsewhere in Fayette just another lazy Sunday in the offing, the first one of August, and the occasion for nothing more strenuous than leafing through the Sunday paper or rocking in a hammock. For Carol, though, it was an important day, bordering on the nerve-racking. She had put on her best slacks and her one Ralph Lauren blouse and pinned a sprig of holly to it.

During the months of restoration, there had been little reason and less time to dress up. She usually just scrubbed her face and pulled her hair into a convenient ponytail or tucked it under a kerchief. This morning, she'd actually spent fifteen minutes before the mirror, brushing on the blusher that accentuated her cheekbones and applying the mascara that deepened the blue of her eyes. The big decision, however, was to let her hair hang loose about her shoulders. It was the style she had favored all through college. That she could still get away with it and not look, as some women did, as if she were trapped in a time warp gave her a certain measure of satisfaction.

Having paid little attention to her appearance for so long (the house, she was always saying, was the real beauty in the family), she rediscovered the pleasure of feeling pretty, although a certain amount of vanity was excusable in this case. It behooved her to look good: the whole town was about to show up at her open house.

Well, not the whole town, perhaps. But anyone who had read the notice in the *Weekly Register*—announcing that the Christmas Inn, Fayette's historic bed-and-breakfast, was open for guests—was invited to drop by and celebrate from one to five. In reality, the Christmas Inn had been open for more than two months, but the Kennedy Suite was now finished and decorated, and the results had exceeded Carol's expectations. Her natural urge to show it off coincided nicely with her growing realization that a little promotion would be good for business, which had been spotty so far. Although Fayette hadn't exactly shown itself to be rich in well-wishers, Carol was banking on the fact that whatever the populace lacked in cordiality, it made up in simple curiosity. She expected a large crowd. She made another whirlwind check of the bedrooms.

"Now?" Sammy asked again pointedly.

"No, not now. Plug in the Christmas tree."

Dropping the scroll on the floor, Sammy trotted into the foyer and did as he was instructed. The colored lights were reflected deep in the floor, which Walker had coaxed to a high gloss the day before. A fresh wreath with a white satin bow hung on the front door, and sprays of Christmas greens erupted happily on every mantelpiece and windowsill. It was all so festive that, if the temperature weren't already in the high seventies and climbing, one could easily forget there were still 141 shopping days until Christmas and panic about the gifts that remained to be bought.

At 12:45, Walker and Joey Burns drove into the yard. Carol figured that since they had done most of the work, they deserved to share whatever praise might escape from her tight-lipped neighbors. Walker, who had traded in his T-shirt for a white shirt and striped tie, had slipped a few business cards in his pocket, just in case.

He whistled admiringly as Carol hurried down the stairs. "Amazing what a little paint remover and steel wool can do."

"Don't give away all my beauty secrets, Walker," she retorted, secretly pleased with the compliment. "You don't scrub up so badly yourself."

Sammy was at her heels. "Now, Ma? Please?"

"Okay, Sammy, now."

Whooping with delight, the boy retrieved the scroll from beside the living room chair where he had left it and slid open a panel in the front of the large, boxy object that intrigued him so. Carefully, he guided each end of the scroll into a slot, threaded the paper over a flat bar that resembled a large harmonica, and attached the end of the paper to another scroll, already in place. Then, he moved back and threw the switch on the side of the box.

With a protracted wheeze, the player piano slowly shook itself to life, and a rowdy version of "Happy Days Are Here Again" flooded the living room. Sammy squealed and lifted up the lid of the keyboard. The keys were dancing up and down all by themselves in rippling arpeggios and flashy chords. It was as if the instrument were being played by some invisible honky-tonk musician, long dead, who had come back to the mansion for one last triumphant encore.

Carol had stumbled upon the player piano on one of her regular sweeps through the antiques shops in the area. She was scouting for brass doorknobs and fixtures at the time, but the piano had caught her eye, or her ear to be exact. It had been reconditioned and electrified, so that you didn't have to pump away tirelessly at the pedals, but otherwise it was the real thing.

It was huffing out "You Are My Sunshine" when she entered the shop, and she stood, transfixed, amid the bric-a-brac until the merry song was over.

"She's a humdinger, all right. An Aeolian, 1924," commented the antiques dealer, who had noted Carol's interest and sensed a sale. "Mint condition. You don't come across all that many of them in such good shape these days."

Carol knew that she would purchase it. She couldn't say why, but it seemed the perfect addition to the mansion, obligatory somehow, although what could possibly be obligatory about a player piano? The pounding, blustery sound had something of the one-ring circus about it, something of the backroom bar. Listening to it just seemed to take her out of herself to another time. She tried not to appear too eager.

"Tell you what," suggested the dealer. "I'll knock ten percent off the price and throw in the piano rolls for free."

In a wicker basker by the pedals of the mechanical piano, there were about twenty long boxes, ornately decorated, with the song titles in flowing script. Carol pored over them—"Down by the Old Mill Stream," "Harvest Moon," "Katie"—oldies-but-goodies she recalled her grandmother humming. It would be fun to introduce them to Sammy.

"You'll find a little of everything in there," the dealer said. "Stephen Foster, some Rudolf Friml, I believe. Last I looked, there were even some Christmas songs."

Sure enough, Carol discovered "Hark the Herald Angels Sing," "Jingle Bells," and "God Rest Ye Merry, Gentlemen." That clinched it. She scribbled a check on the spot. Two days later, a pair of deliverymen, alternately grunting and cursing, succeeded in maneuvering the instrument up the porch stairs and into the living room.

1 RAGGED RIDGE ROAD

"Happy Days Are Here Again" built to a flamboyant climax and abruptly stopped, as the final bit of paper scrolled through the piano. The keys became inanimate pieces of ivory; the magic spell was broken. Carol congratulated herself on the acquisition all over again. To her, it already seemed as much a part of the mansion as the wraparound veranda or the chestnut staircase.

Her wristwatch showed five minutes past one when the first car pulled into the driveway. Two men got out. The one with shorts and sandals and oversize sunglasses, fire-engine red, looked vaguely familiar to Carol, but she couldn't place him. She had never seen the other one. No sooner had they reached the front steps than two more cars turned off Ragged Ridge Road.

"People!" said Carol, surprised. She threw Walker a nervous smile and headed to the door to welcome her guests.

The man with the red sunglasses spoke first. "Hi, how's your mother doing?"

"I beg your pardon," she replied, mildly puzzled by the question.

"Your mother, who was dropping things. I guess you don't recognize me out of my professional duds. Well, this is the real me." He took off his sunglasses and did a little spin. His Hawaiian shirt ballooned out. "Remember? From the Council on Aging. *A Chorus Line?*"

"Of course, how are you, uh . . ."

"Harry. Harry Watkins. I'd like you to meet my friend, Mark Ridley. Mark runs the White Barn Playhouse, which you may have heard of."

Carol had. The White Barn Playhouse was just what the name suggested—an old clapboard barn on the road to Gettysburg that had been converted twenty years ago to a summer theater. For some residents, summer officially began with the opening of the White Barn's first production and ended, five productions later, when the scenery was packed away and the staff returned to the city. The plays were usually breezy and inconsequential, but they were expertly enough acted so that the playhouse was considered one of the community's cultural resources.

"I've been meaning to get over there. I've just been so busy with this house," Carol said, extending a hand.

Mark Ridley took it willingly. He was a tall, debonair man in his late forties, definitely matinee-idol material. Carol noticed that he wasn't wearing a wedding ring and surmised that all the actresses at his theater must be mad for him.

"Give me a call anytime and I'd be happy to arrange tickets," he said. "You'll be our guest. That way you can personally recommend our plays to your customers. If you've got some brochures, I'll put them out at the playhouse. We've got to stick together, right?"

"We certainly do," she replied, not certain that she had grasped his meaning.

"This place is just *fabulous,*" gushed Harry, spinning around the foyer, agog. "I'd heard you had done great things. My dear, have you ever! Mark needs lodgings for one of the actors who's coming to town next week. Actually, a very big star, thank you very much. So I made him get dressed and come check this place out before the crowds arrived. You know theater people!"

With scarely a pause, he burst into song, "When a Broadway baby says good-night, it's early in the morning . . ."

"Down, Harry," Mark ordered with a straight face. "I can't take him anywhere they don't appreciate show tunes." Carol laughed and immediately revised her earlier opinion. Mark seemed to be one-half of a couple, the other half being a human top in the loudest sports shirt she had ever seen. All those poor actresses were barking up the wrong tree.

"I think we should let the woman greet her guests, Harry," Mark said. Then, training his blue eyes on Carol, he winked. "We'll chat more later."

A small queue had already formed on the veranda—a dozen or so people waiting politely as if they were in the receiving line at the wedding of a distant relative they'd never met before. "Welcome to the Christmas Inn," Carol said, stepping aside and noting their reactions as they entered. Some made a direct line for the bar, but others hung back, vaguely intimidated by the elegance of the mansion and the unmistakable social status it once represented. She spotted several of her neighbors walking across the lawn and wondered whether this meant the barriers were coming down at last.

By two o'clock, at least fifty people were eating her hors d'oeuvres and peeking into her closets. There was quite a party atmosphere. Carol moved through the crowd, thinking that if this kept up, the Christmas Inn was on the map. Walker and an elderly man were having a serious discussion of banister railings. She couldn't see Joey anywhere.

In the dining room, she bumped into Harry and Mark again, who were conversing with a smartly dressed couple.

"This is Carol Roblins, the lovely lady who owns the Christmas Inn," announced Harry.

"Ned Foster," said the man, who gestured to the pleasant woman beside him. "And my wife, June."

"I should have known. You look just like I imagined you would," Carol said, pumping his hand enthusiastically. "I mean, just like your photograph . . . I saw it in the *Weekly Register* . . . a few months ago."

"Right!" Harry jumped in. "Ned is going to be the next mayor of Fayette, if we have anything to do with it. We're throwing a fund-raiser for him at the theater. Ned and June are on our board. You'll have to come, Carol."

"Hold on, Harry," Ned interrupted. "Maybe Mrs. Roblins hasn't decided who she's voting for." He wasn't shy, but he wasn't the usual slick politician, either, pandering for votes. Carol liked that. There seemed to be a gentle soul inside Ned Foster.

"I'm new here. I don't really know anybody," she said.

"Well, now you know us," declared Harry, "and we're the most fascinating people in town. And I'm telling you, Quinn has to go." If Ned Foster wasn't going to climb up on a soapbox, Harry Watkins was. "The mayor's been on this crusade against the theater ever since his fifteen-year-old daughter came to see *Brighton Beach Memoirs* and went home and told Daddy it had the word *fuck* in it. So now the man, who used to attend every opening night—for free, I might add—has decided that we are a corrupting moral influence. Neil Simon? A corrupting influence? Pul-eeze!

This man needs to get a life. If he really wants to clean up this town, he should start with his daughter. Whose back-seat is she occupying this week?"

Mark cut him off with a reproving look. "Harry gets a little carried away with local politics."

"All I'm saying is the mayor could afford to be a helluva lot more tolerant. He's supposed to set the example for this town, and he's our A-number one bigot. Did you know that Pennsylvania has the second-highest rate of hate crimes in the country? Well, it does. We've just got to make things better. And I believe Ned is the man who can do it in Fayette."

"Well, thank you, Harry," Ned said soberly. "Now all I need is a few thousand more voters just like you and I'll have no problems. But I didn't come here to campaign. I came to look at Mrs. Roblins's beautiful house."

"Please do, Mr. Foster. I'm especially proud of the Kennedy Suite." Carol pointed them in the direction of the staircase and turned back to the crowd. There were a lot of new faces. She took it as a good omen that the woman from the Chamber of Commerce had dropped by and waved hello at her across the room. From all appearances, people were impressed.

She caught bits and pieces of conversation.

"Kennedy was big in banking—or was it railroads? No, it was banking. Whichever. He must have had a pretty penny . . ."

"Well, this renovation wasn't exactly done for nothing. A lot of money has gone into it . . . the woodwork alone . . . Did you see the bedrooms upstairs?"

"The place used to be haunted. That's what they say. Of course, I've never believed in ghosts myself, but personally I'd think twice about living here."

Then someone in the crowd, a man, said, "What do you think she's trying to do?"

It took a moment for the words to register on Carol's consciousness. When they did, she stopped short. The voice on the telephone had asked her the same question. Could it be the same person? Was it possible the caller was actually standing in her house, mixing with her guests, observing her?

She looked around and tried to figure out whom she might have overheard. The balding man in the plaid slacks? Or the portly gentleman with the double chin by the bay window? A cluster of people hovered at the bar, although none of them seemed to be paying her much mind. She told herself she was just experiencing an understandable case of the jitters—the renovation was coming under public scrutiny for the first time. As a precaution, however, she studied the faces of the men in the room. She wanted to be able to remember them, if she ever had to.

In the foyer, Walker handed his card to a young couple and told them he'd be more than happy to give them an estimate. Carol saw the exchange and felt a wave of wistfulness wash over her. It was hard to imagine not having Walker around. His arrival in the kitchen every morning had come to mark the beginning of the day, and just the sound of him working in some part of the house picked up her spirits when they were sagging. The mansion was now alive with guests, sipping their sodas and chattering happily, but at times, when she was alone at night with only a twelve-year-old child, it seemed all too big and empty.

"I hope I'm not losing you yet," Carol said, sidling up to Walker after the couple had departed.

"You don't ever have to lose me, if you don't want to."

"You know what I mean. There's still work to do around here."

"Not for much longer. And you know what *I* mean."

Walker reached over and stroked her hair. He had never done that before, and the gesture made Carol slightly uneasy. Everybody could see them. "I'd be lying," he continued, "if I didn't admit that I had once hoped we could have more than a professional relationship. I think about us a lot, Carol."

"Oh, Walker." She backed up a step, patting him on the shoulder as she did, so it wouldn't look too obvious that she was pulling away. "Maybe if things had been different."

"Different how?"

"I'm married. I know it doesn't seem so to you, because you've never met Blake. We're going through a difficult time now, but we're still married. An army wife gets used to her husband being away for long periods. I guess a lot of people don't understand that. This just happens to be a longer period than usual. Anyway, you know how much I care for you. I wish I had the money to keep on paying you indefinitely. In my mind, this inn will always be part yours."

"Well, if I don't start lining up some clients fast, in another couple of weeks I'm gonna be out on the street."

"I doubt that. Now that everybody can see how talented you are and how you've transformed this place. There wouldn't be a Christmas Inn without you. I say it all the time. Word gets around."

"Do you really think things would have been different if you were free? You know, if you and Blake weren't still together?"

He didn't want to let the subject go. Oblivious to the noise and chatter about them, he searched her face for a sign that his hopes were not unfounded and that he had not simply dreamed up a relationship where there was none. It wasn't desperation Carol saw in his eyes, but something sadder—neediness. She'd never seen it in him before.

"How can I answer that honestly, Walker? What if we'd never come to Fayette? What if Sammy were just an ordinary kid? Who's to know about any of it? I'm not free and that's the way it is."

Walker pulled himself together. "Well, I accept that. And I admire it—that you are sticking by Blake, even though times are rough. Not many women I know would do that, believe me." He seemed to be making a veiled reference to his own marriage and divorce, but Carol preferred not to go into it. She shifted uneasily as "Blue Moon" welled up out of the player piano. (Sammy was attending to his duties.) The burst of song gave her an excuse to bring the conversation to a halt.

"I better circulate among my guests and see if I can drum up some business myself. We'll have a chance to talk later. I told the Fosters I'd show them the Kennedy Suite." She gave Walker a quick hug that he tried to prolong.

Going up the back stairway, she took a moment to organize her thoughts. Had she relied on Walker too much? Led him on? If so, that had never been her intention. Walker was the one at fault for misinterpreting the familiarity that had developed between them. Why couldn't men just accept friendship as an end in itself? Unless they were both partially to blame, which was the compromise she had struck with herself as she reached the top of the stairs.

She nodded to several people who were inspecting the Rose Room and hurried down the corridor to the Kennedy Suite. As she was about to enter, a thin, wiry woman came careening out. She was highly agitated and her breathing was heavy. They nearly collided.

"Are you okay?" Carol asked, putting out a hand to steady the woman, who appeared to have had a terrible fright. "Wait a minute, don't I know you?" It was the historical-society lady.

Esther McPherson stole a quick glance at Carol, then with bony fingers plucked a scented handkerchief out of her purse and brought it to her nose. Her face was flushed and splotchy, and her hat was askew.

"I'm Carol Roblins. Remember? We met at the library."

"Oh, yes, nice to see you again," mumbled the woman through the handkerchief. She was eager to get on her way, and social pleasantries were not about to detain her.

"I hope you got a chance to look around."

"Yes, I did. Thank you," she answered crisply.

"Are you all right, Mrs. McPherson? You look awful."

"I'm fine. If you'll excuse me, please." With a surprising burst of strength for one so fragile, she pushed by Carol and scurried down the hall.

Carol joined the Fosters in the suite. "What was that all about? Esther McPherson damn near ran me down."

Harry pulled himself away from the four-poster bed, of which he had just given his rapturous, if vaguely indecent, opinion. "Not particularly friendly, is she!" he huffed. "She was already here when we came in. Going over everything with a fine-tooth comb, the old biddy. I tried to speak to her, but she could barely manage a peep in return."

Mark judged it best to take over the story. "When she saw that picture on the wall, she gasped and kind of went into shock. I asked her if anything was wrong, but she wouldn't answer. Then she dashed out of the room. Beats me." He edged up to the picture for a closer look. It was the photograph of the Kennedys cavorting at the beach. "Who are they?"

"The original owners of the house, Charles and Veronica Kennedy," Carol said. "This was their bedroom."

"She's very pretty. They look like they had a happy life," commented Ned.

"Well, actually, they didn't," admitted Carol. Normally, she was reluctant to tell people about the murder, even though it had occurred long ago. A house with a rich history was appreciated, unless the history was a lurid one. Then, the house just became a magnet for gawkers, a Halloween attraction, and she didn't want that happening to the Kennedy mansion. The purpose of the restoration was to bring life, not death, back into its rooms. But if these people were going to be her friends, she'd have to divulge the past sooner or later.

"Mrs. Kennedy was killed in this very room," she began. Unconsciously, June clutched Ned's arm. "Beaten to death on Christmas Eve. Her husband was so distraught afterwards that he committed suicide. They never found the murderer. It was believed to be"—she hesitated—"a robbery. The Kennedys are both buried in Woodbridge Cemetery. I've been meaning to take flowers out there sometime."

"What do you know!" marveled Harry. "Murder and suicide, huh? A double whammy! No wonder the old lady reeled out of here a minute ago. The picture must have brought it all back."

"That's certainly not why I put it up. It's such a romantic photograph I figured it deserved a place of prominence. The Kennedys were obviously deeply in love. You can see that just from looking at them."

She recalled the care with which she had selected the gold-embossed frame and the number of times she had shifted the photograph from one wall to another, until she had found the perfect spot for it over the cedar chest between the two west windows. Was she being blindly sentimental? It hadn't occurred to her that people would be troubled by the image. Unless they were told, how many would even know it was a portrait of the Kennedys?

"I don't want any more problems. I've got enough as it is," she said, examining the photograph in a new, clinical light. "Do you think I should take it down?"

"No, just keep Mrs. McPherson off the second floor in the future," answered Mark. "And if anyone asks, say it's a picture of your dear, departed grandparents."

Harry's appreciation of the bedroom had taken on a whole new dimension. "You said you wanted to find the perfect place for your star," he interjected. "Guess what, Mark! I think we just may have found it."

Mark went on to explain that the star in question was Will Williams, the television actor. Will had started his career at the White Barn Playhouse ten years ago, and he'd always thought fondly of the theater, apparently, because he had agreed to come back to Fayette and appear in the last show of the season, *Dial M for Murder*. It was quite a coup for the playhouse, and the entire three-week run was already sold out at considerably higher prices than usual. Will Williams, in fact, was practically subsidizing the rest of the season. Carol was not a big television fan, but even she had heard of him and watched an episode of *The Handyman* with Sammy once.

"I can't put him up with the rest of the company," Mark continued. "Well, I could. Will's a great guy. But he's doing me a favor, so I'd like to roll out the red carpet for him."

"I'm sure he'd get a big kick out of staying here," trilled Harry. "Can't you see the headlines? 'Star of *Dial M for Murder* Confronts Ghosts of Christmas Past.' It's like . . . like *Hamlet*."

"Sounds more like Dickens to me," quipped Ned.

"I'm sure we could work something out," said Carol,

getting a little carried away herself. Talk about publicity! Will Williams at the Christmas Inn. Even the Philadelphia papers would take note.

"That's settled, then," proclaimed Harry. "I don't know about anybody else, but I could use a beer." Carol said she thought there were a couple in the refrigerator, and they all traipsed out into the hall.

The crowd downstairs hadn't thinned out. More people than ever were milling about and snatching at the hors d'oeuvres to the emphatic strains of "You Are My Sunshine." With Carol's permission, Harry rustled up two beers from the refrigerator—one for himself, one for Mark. Ned and his wife fell into conversation with friends. By now, the open house seemed to have taken on a life of its own.

Carol went back to her post by the front door and noted with satisfaction that there wasn't a parking space to be had on the property. Cars were lined up on both sides of Ragged Ridge Road. She recognized the battered pickup truck first, even though it was several hundred feet away. Then, the figure in overalls. Leaning up against the hood and smoking a cigarette was Clem. He was back again. She couldn't see the expression on his face, but his casual stance implied he wasn't leaving soon. And up to then, everything had been going so well. It would be just like him to crash the open house and make a terrible scene. Well, she wasn't going to put up with it. Walker would have to tell him to move on.

As Carol turned to reenter the house and find him, a booming voice stopped her.

"Quite a turnout you've got!"

A burly, silver-haired man was climbing up the steps, nodding affably to people on the veranda. He was carrying the jacket of his pale blue seersucker suit over his shoulder, and perspiration had turned his pale pink shirt a raspberry color under the arms.

"Oh, Mayor Quinn, how are you this afternoon?" Carol inquired politely.

"Hot and thirsty. I had to park halfway down the road. You know that's against the rules, but I guess we can make an exception today." He cracked his broad politician's smile, the one-size-fits-all smile that she remembered unpleasantly from his last visit.

"Please come in and cool off."

"Don't mind if I do. Hi there, Karen. Nice to see you, Jim." Barely in the door, Mayor Quinn was already working the crowd, his eyes steely bright with ambition. "Looks like all of Fayette has shown up for your little affair, Mrs. Roblins. I should hold my rally here. You know about my rally on Saturday, don't you? Hope to see you there."

He surveyed the rooms, efficiently sizing up the guests and deciding who, among them, were worthy of more than his polite attention. Then, the smile dried up as his eyes locked on Ned Foster.

"Someone else seems to have had that idea before me," he said. He pushed through the crowd that had gathered around his opponent.

"Well, look who's here. What bad things is this guy saying about me today?"

His voice had an edge, so it was difficult to tell whether the question was meant as a pleasantry or as a rebuke. It was the same with the expression on his face, which was neither genuinely amicable nor overtly hostile, but fell ambiguously in between. Sensing a confrontation, people backed away, letting their sentences die, unfinished, so that the two men stood opposite one another in the center of a widening circle. A smile was back on the mayor's face, but it was taut and forced.

"I've been saying nothing bad at all, I can assure you, Bill."

"Except that I shouldn't be mayor. How does it go? 'One more term and it'll take a crowbar to get him out of office.'" If that was a joke, nobody laughed.

"I merely said that maybe it's time for a change. That's all."

Everybody in the room was focused on the mayor, waiting expectantly for what he would say next. The Quinn temper was well known and justly feared for both its unpredictability and its rashness. But he said nothing. Instead, he rocked on his heels and slowly looked around, taking in one face after another, scouring each one with his eyes, as he might have scrutinized the sorry suspects in a police lineup.

Then he shot his hand toward Ned Foster and said jovially, "What can I say, but 'Good luck, son.'" As they shook hands, the mayor automatically turned outward and smiled, as if he half-expected flashbulbs to record the historic moment for posterity. "You see," he proclaimed in a tone of unassailable authority, "this is what makes America the best country in the world. Anyone can run for mayor. A whippersnapper like Ned Foster here. Even an old fogy like me. All right, all right! I may no longer run, but I do walk pretty briskly these days."

That brought a hearty laugh and a palpable sense of relief from the guests.

"I must say you've got a lovely establishment here, Mrs. Roblins, and I wish you great success." Then, taking a glass of lemonade that had been offered him by the bartender, he raised it above his head in a toast. "Welcome to Fayette."

There was a smattering of applause. The mayor had seized control of an awkward situation and turned it to his advantage. Carol realized that Ned Foster had an uphill battle ahead of him.

Several minutes later, the mayor waved broadly to the guests, who had resumed their conversations, and prepared to leave. Carol caught up with him at the door. "I appreciate your dropping by, Mayor Quinn. I hope the Christmas Inn will become part of Fayette."

"So do I." Then, pulling her aside, he asked, "Do you have a liquor license, Mrs. Roblins?"

"Excuse me?"

"A liquor license. Do you have one?"

"No, not yet." It seemed such an odd question to ask at a time like this! Then, Carol realized what must have prompted it—the two beers that Mark and Harry were holding. "Oh, I'm not selling anything," she stammered. "They're just friends."

"Friends?" The mayor chuckled. "This is a place of business, is it not?"

"Yes, but—"

"We'll let it go this time, Mrs. Roblins, but I suggest in the future you make sure that everything is in order. I don't allow people to break the law in my town. Maybe Mr. Foster will. Maybe that's the kind of change he wants to implement. But there's a little matter of an election first. Good day, Mrs. Roblins."

Perplexed, she stood on the porch watching as the mayor lumbered down the driveway at an impressive clip. His seersucker coat, slung over his right shoulder, flapped behind him.

Harry came out to join her. "So what was that all about?"

"I wish I knew."

"Don't we all," he sighed. "Welcome to Fayette, indeed!"

Twenty-Three

When Carol added it all up, the open house had been a considerable success, despite the unexpected appearance of Mayor Quinn. Or, just as likely, because of it. Several hundred people had streamed through the Christmas Inn and gone away talking, if only to tell a neighbor about the encounter between the mayor and Ned Foster.

She had made some new friends in a town where friendships didn't come all that easily. And now a big television star was going to be staying in her inn. Blake would get a charge out of that. All the time they had lived in southern California, they never saw one famous person, if you didn't count the time Carol sighted John Travolta in a gas station, and Blake, who maintained that it was just a college kid with uncombed hair, didn't. But now that Carol was living in the sticks, a celebrity was actually going to be sleeping under her roof.

She briefly contemplated letting Will Williams have the Kennedy Suite for free, as her contribution to the arts, but a glance at the balance in her checkbook was enough to curb any generous impulses. The arrangement she made with Mark Ridley satisfied them both: the suite would go for $350 a week, a bargain rate, really, and she'd host the opening-night party for *Dial M for Murder,* which meant plenty of free publicity for the inn.

The only downside to the open house was that she had somehow ended up on the wrong side of Mayor Quinn, who obviously divided the world into two categories—those who were for him and those who were not. Ned Foster and the team who ran the White Barn Playhouse belonged to the latter group, and the mayor seemed to find Carol guilty by association. She hoped his animosity didn't run any deeper than that. The permit to open the Christmas Inn had involved a lot of petty wrangling, and her application for a liquor license was still mired in some bureaucratic bog. The mayor could make her life difficult, although she couldn't conceive why he would want to. He had applauded the restoration, so it was probably just certain of her guests that he didn't approve of.

She and Sammy watched *The Handyman* that week, and much as she hated to admit it, she found the show slightly moronic. Will Williams was personable enough, a lanky, loose-limbed guy who at the end of each episode cocked his head, smiled a lopsided grin, and brayed, "Well, what do you think of that!" The signature phrase had entered the popular vocabulary, just as "Sock it to me" and "Mahhh-velous" had in prior years. To Carol's dismay, Sammy had picked up on it right away.

His high-pitched voice sang out at all hours of the day. "Well, Charlie, what do you think of that!" "Walker, what do you think of that!" "Mama, Mama, listen. What do you think of that!" Then he would giggle and try to smile with just one side of his face, and the resulting grimace usually made Carol laugh in spite of herself.

That Saturday, she was nursing her second cup of coffee and Sammy was playing listlessly with his oatmeal when Blake's weekly telephone call came through.

"You have reached the Christmas Inn," she answered in her most efficient manner. "How may I help you?"

"Er . . . is that you, Carol?"

"Hello, Blake. I figured it was you. Just trying out the official greeting. Were you impressed?"

"You're in a good mood. Things must be going pretty well over there."

"They are."

She filled him in on the open house and was pleased that he registered a certain amount of surprise when she told him how many people had attended. His astonishment was even greater when she let it drop that Will Williams would be her first guest in the Kennedy Suite. Even Blake knew who he was.

"Sounds like you're having all the fun. All I do is work."

"That's all I do, too, Blake. A bed-and-breakfast isn't a hobby you can give up when you get tired of it. Didn't you tell me that once? You were right by the way. Not that I'm complaining."

Sammy had lost what little interest he had in his oatmeal and was tugging excitedly at his mother's belt. "Me, me. Please. Let me talk."

"Okay, Sammy. Calm down," she said, angling the receiver away from her mouth.

"Now, please. My turn."

"Blake, we'll have to continue this in a second. Your son is standing here, dying to talk to you."

"Daddy?"

Sammy grabbed the receiver; the listlessness he had displayed minutes earlier had been replaced by a hyperanimation that bordered on breathlessness. Carol wondered what had got into him all at once and hoped it wasn't going to be a day of mood swings. As she retrieved her coffee cup, she let herself gloat over Blake's surprise. There was nothing like a celebrity to lend validity to her little enterprise. If that's what it took to convince Blake she was accomplishing miracles, she would definitely have to find a way to get Kevin Costner to spend a couple of nights.

Amused by the thought, she didn't notice right off that Sammy had slunk into a corner with the phone. An anxious expression had crept over his face, and he had lowered his voice to a whisper. She strained to hear what he was saying, but all she could make out was "soon—tiny soon."

What was that about? She redoubled her concentration. "Shiny spoon" was what her son was saying, over and over, and getting visibly more upset with each repetition. Suddenly, Sammy dropped the phone on the floor, dashed into the living room, and threw himself into the chair by the bay window.

Carol picked up the receiver. "What is going on, Blake?"

"You're asking me? How the hell should I know? He kept whispering, 'Shiny spoon, shiny spoon.' What's that supposed to mean? Is he all right?"

"He was, before you telephoned. Just a minute." She called into the living room. "Sammy, come here." The boy didn't budge from the armchair. "Please, Sammy. As a special favor to me?" Slowly, the child shuffled to the kitchen door, his head hung low to prevent her from seeing he had been crying.

"What's wrong, honey?" She could sense that he was about to retreat into one of his uncommunicative states. "Why were you saying 'shiny spoon' to Daddy?" she asked softly. "Can you tell me?"

Sammy lifted his head and stared at her with injured eyes.

"Can't," he finally responded. "Secret. Our secret."

"Oh, shit," Blake's voice erupted out of the phone.

"What is it?"

"It's a secret code he made up. I forgot all about it."

"Blake!"

"Well, it was six months ago, for chrissakes. Put him back on the line, will you? . . . Hey, Sammy? I'm sorry, old buddy. I got so busy over here our code slipped right out of my mind. Are you mad at me?"

"Nope."

"Are you sure?"

"Yup."

"We can make up another one, if you want."

"Nope."

"Because we can. We can make it up right now."

"Nope." Sammy handed the phone back to his mother. Disappointment had tugged the corners of his mouth downward. Otherwise, his features were devoid of expression.

"I'm afraid we've got a problem on this end," Carol said. She wound up the conversation with Blake, put the receiver back on its cradle, and tried to think what to do next. She was going to have to work hard to get Sammy out of this one.

Then, she remembered that this was the day the mayor was holding his rally. Ned Foster had her vote, but she figured she owed the mayor the courtesy of showing up and listening, and maybe the festivities would distract Sammy. They could get an ice cream cone at Linehan's Candy Kitchen afterward.

"What about it?" she asked Sammy.

"Okay," he replied dully, but she could tell his curiosity was piqued.

The mayor's rally was scheduled for noon in Memorial Park, the site of one of Fayette's chief landmarks, a multi-tiered Victorian fountain guarded by the bronze statue of a Civil War soldier. The graceful monument commemorated the four hundred residents of the county who had fought in the Civil War, and the water that spilled from one tier to the next was supposed to be a symbol of purification and healing. But corrosion had eaten away at the central support, and the municipal authorities had found it advisable to turn off the water to prevent further deterioration. An emergency fund drive, launched by a group of concerned citizens calling themselves the Friends of the Fountain, had so far raised only negligible contributions.

From the unusually heavy traffic on the road to town, Carol concluded that there would be a big turnout. The Quinn name counted for a lot in Fayette, and the weather was flawless, which counted even more. She parked the Toyota in front of the Meadowbrook Market, two blocks away. As she and Sammy got out, they heard the squawk of a microphone and someone introducing "a man who needs no introduction," followed by boisterous cheering.

In the middle of Memorial Park, a large crowd had already amassed before a wooden platform, which had been erected for the occasion and was draped with flags and bunting. The Fayette High School Band in full uniform, sunflower yellow and navy blue, sat to one side, ready to burst into a Sousa march at the first sign of a downward swoop from the drum major's silver baton. Some people were spread out on the grass; some stood in groups, trading gossip and opinions. Were it not for the campaign posters that had been tacked up on every available tree, the gathering could have been mistaken for a church picnic. Indeed, the white spire of the First Presbyterian Church, which overlooked the park, had recently received a fresh coat of paint and reflected the sunlight like a mirror.

Carol grasped Sammy's hand tightly and they hastened to the edge of the crowd, arriving just in time to catch Bill Quinn's speech. It wasn't the same Bill Quinn who had been to her house on Sunday. This one had the confidence of a heavyweight champion entering the boxing ring for a fight that he knows he's going to win. Carol didn't like him any better.

"I can't tell you how good it makes my heart feel to see you all here today, to know you're behind me and my struggle to keep Fayette the town we know and love," he was saying. A warm round of applause proved that his sentiments were widely shared. Carol looked around and thought she recognized several people who had been at her open house on Sunday. A gentleman in lime green Bermuda shorts nodded at her affably, and she returned the greeting. Most eyes were bracketed on Bill Quinn.

"Hey, Tom," the mayor said, pointing to someone in the front row. "I've known you since Miss Marshall's second-grade class."

"Sure have!" the man with the short-sleeved polyester shirt and a John Deere hat shot back.

"And you, Ed and Marion, we've been neighbors for longer than any of us would probably care to remember." Ed and Marion laughed appreciatively and waved to the figure on the platform.

"And what can I say about you, Esther?" the mayor continued, this time singling out a starchy-looking matron who seemed to have overestimated the social significance of the rally and was dressed in a style more befitting Easter Sunday. Carol craned her neck and was surprised to see that it was Esther McPherson, the historical-society lady, he was talking to.

"Why, I went to my junior prom with Esther," the mayor told the crowd. "But she was smart enough to marry Joe

McPherson instead, so she could have a doctor in the family. To me, though, she'll always be Esther O'Hare with the light brown hair." He sang the last few words, and the woman blushed scarlet at the unexpected tribute. Carol judged the girlish reaction a bit excessive for someone who had reached the age and exalted position of the historical-society lady. Youthful amours died slowly in Fayette, apparently.

"Heck, I think I know everyone in this park today. We've been to one another's weddings. We've seen the birth of one another's children. And we've watched them grow up and start families of their own. Through the joys and the tragedies, we have stuck together. That's what a community is. And Fayette is precisely the kind of community that this great land of America is built upon."

A few yelps of appreciation came from the sidelines, where some men were drinking beer out of cans concealed in paper bags. They were unshaven, and one of them carried his cigarettes in the rolled-up sleeve of his white T-shirt. Elsewhere the rally had the homely flavor of a family reunion or a backyard cookout. There were, in fact, hot dogs sizzling on a grill, and bowls of coleslaw and potato salad and coolers of soft drinks had been set out on two tables covered with red-and-white-checkered tablecloths. A group of teenagers were playing with Frisbees that had the mayor's picture on them and the slogan "Keep Fayette Flying with Quinn."

It made for the sort of idyllic scene that used to adorn the covers of the *Saturday Evening Post.* Carol took it all in and wondered how real it was, this image of down-home America, populated by plain and decent citizens who minded their own business, kept their front lawns tidy, and turned up at church without fail every Sunday. Her instinct was not to trust it. There was no such thing as just plain folks in her estimation. Whatever their station in life, people were complicated, their emotions were unruly by nature, and their personal affairs usually tended to the messy. Small towns had no greater claim on virtue than big cities did. And vice knew no boundaries.

Perspiration had begun to glisten on the mayor's forehead, and he was puffed up, like a bullfrog. "You know, I said to my wife, Ruthie, the other day, maybe it's a good thing I have to campaign a little harder this year. I should have to prove myself to the citizens like any other civil servant. It also affords me the opportunity to reexamine my own values and remind myself once again why I do what I do.

"Well, my friends, I believe that the streets of our town should be safe for our children, free of crime and drugs. I believe our schools should perpetuate the beliefs in God and country that have always guided us and not tear them down willy-nilly. But do you know what I believe in most? The family. The traditional family. Why, if we wanted to live in New York or Philadelphia or Baltimore, we would. We'd move there tomorrow. But we want to live *here.*"

That brought a particularly loud round of cheers and even a few whistles. "You tell 'em, Bill!" cried out a man standing behind Carol and Sammy. The mayor was gaining momentum and she was beginning to feel uncomfortable about the course of his speech.

"Now we have these people, people like my opponent, who move here from the big city because they didn't like the smog or the high taxes or something, and they want to change our town. Tell me, why change what isn't broken? Frankly, I would not like to see Fayette become another cesspool of liberalism, one of those cities—and you know the ones I mean—where anything goes and usually does."

Sammy's attention had begun to droop. He tugged at his mother's sleeve. "Can I have a Coke, Ma, please?"

"In just a second, honey. As soon as the mayor has finished talking."

The mayor had hit his stride now—the folksy neighbor having given way to the skilled orator and practiced politician. The transition had been seamless. "Look at this park," his voice rang out. "Look at our monuments. Look at that beautiful white church over there. Every day, I take such pride in Fayette. My family laid the cornerstones of this community. By that, I don't just mean they named the streets and built the buildings. They laid the cornerstones of friendship, fellowship, and family. And, my friends, I do not want to see those cornerstones destroyed."

The drum major's baton came down, and the band lurched into "The Stars and Stripes Forever," drowning out the clapping and the cheering. Volunteers with baskets of campaign buttons waded into the crowd.

"Race you," said Sammy, and almost before Carol realized what he meant, he had scampered off in the direction of the refreshment stand.

"Be careful," she shouted after him, just as a young woman with a baby stroller passed in front of her, blocking the path and giving Sammy an even greater head start.

After listening to the long, boring speech, he was happy to break free. He pretended he was a racing car, threading his way around the other automobiles on the speedway. "Zoom, zoom, zoom," he hummed to himself. The finish line (the refreshment stand) loomed ahead. The fans were screaming. He was shifting the vehicle into high gear, anticipating the last-minute surge of power that would propel him to victory, when he heard the familiar voice.

"Well, if it isn't the eejit! Where you off to in such a hurry?"

Instantly, the boy pulled to a stop and looked around. The band and John Philip Sousa were engaged in a mighty struggle, from the sound of which Sousa was definitely getting the worst of it. With all the noise, it was hard to tell where the voice had come from. To the right, the Frisbee players were bantering raucously. Behind him, a baby was wailing.

"No, over here, eejit."

Then Sammy saw him—seated on the back of a park bench, his feet resting on the lateral slats. The man smiled broadly, exposing his tobacco-stained teeth.

"Ain't you gonna say hello?" He made a movement to get off the bench.

Sammy pulled back. His breath was short from running, and when he tried to respond, nothing came out at first. "Mom, come here," he was able to cry at last. "Come fast."

Carol forged her way through the throng. "What is it? What's the matter, Sammy?"

"Clem," the boy panted. "I just saw Clem."

"Where?"

"By the bench."

Carol spotted the bench immediately and scanned all the faces in the area. An overweight woman had just sat down and was fanning herself with a newspaper. A campaign worker was pinning buttons on people's lapels. There were several young couples, strolling hand in hand, kids milling about, and a man with a dog, but no trace of Clem.

"Are you sure you saw him, Sammy?"

"Yes, he was there, there, right there. Honest," he insisted, jabbing his finger frenetically in the air. Tears had started to trickle down his cheeks.

"*Shhhhh.* It's all right. I believe you, honey."

But "there," where Sammy kept pointing, all Carol could see were women in white straw hats and red aprons, passing out free hot dogs and soft drinks to happy customers.

Two days later, a brown business-size envelope intended for the "Occupant" of 1 Ragged Ridge Road was delivered to the mansion. Carol assumed it was another piece of the junk mail that had reached epidemic proportions and sorted through the bills first. Regrettably, they were reaching epidemic proportions, too. She was pleased to note, however, that Blake had sent a postcard of the Black Forest to Sammy, who would no doubt tuck it away under the eaves, along with his stones and artifacts.

She was on the verge of tossing the brown envelope in the trash when she realized that it had been addressed by hand. Junk mail was usually addressed by machine. Curious, she moistened her index finger and ran it over the *O* of *Occupant*. The ink smeared. With some misgivings, she opened the flap.

Inside was a single piece of yellow, lined paper. It bore no date, no salutation, no signature, only a blunt warning:

This is not a town that needs another whore. How would your husband like to know what your doing? I wont let you destroy the kornerstones of this community. You do not belong here. If your wise, you will go back where you came from.

The writing was so laborious that it could have been a child's scrawl, assuming, of course, that someone hadn't tried hard to make it look that way. Carol remembered reading somewhere that when people wanted to disguise their writing, they used the wrong hand, which is what the author of the letter could have done. The strokes wavered, the *o*'s were lopsided, and the *t*'s were erratically crossed. It occurred to her that the splotches of ink and the spelling mistakes were probably intentional, too.

"The kornerstones of this community!" Those were the mayor's words, despite the ridiculous misspelling. The letter must have come from somebody who had attended the rally on Saturday. That narrowed it down to about four hundred people! Unless . . . it was the mayor himself. Carol entertained that possibility briefly, then dismissed it. The idea of Bill Quinn sending her a poison pen letter was entirely too preposterous.

It didn't take her long to come up with the culprit. Sammy had seen Clem at the rally, even if she hadn't. The letter was just the sort of mean and underhanded thing he would do. Well, matters were getting entirely too personal. She was going to have to put a stop to the harassment once and for all. She promptly picked up the telephone, dialed the Fayette Police Department, and asked the woman who came on the line if she could send an officer to 1 Ragged Ridge Road.

"I think I'm being stalked," she said when the woman asked her what the problem was.

Forty minutes later, Sergeants Johnson and Burke knocked at the front door, none too thrilled with what they regarded as a low-priority assignment. Carol showed them the letter, which Johnson, the burlier of the two, read with mild interest. He jotted a few notations in a notebook when Carol told him about the threats that Clem had hurled at her the night of his eviction. Then there was the incident with Charlie.

"Was the dog in the road, ma'am?"

"Well, the side of the road."

"He didn't actually hit him then. That correct?"

"No, but I know he wanted to."

"I see."

"No, I'm afraid you don't see. What if it had been my son? This man is dangerous."

Johnson didn't seem to take any of it too seriously, and Burke poked around the living room all the while, fingering the Christmas decorations and not even listening from what Carol could tell.

"Mr. Clemson spray-painted some terrible things on the bedroom walls," she said, hoping that might convince them of his long-standing maliciousness.

"Can we take a look?" asked Johnson.

"That was months ago. The whole apartment has been renovated since then."

"Oh," replied Johnson, tucking his ballpoint pen into his shirt pocket.

"Look, Officer, I'm certain it's Paul Clemson who is responsible for this letter. Every so often, he parks his truck on Ragged Ridge Road and just stares at the mansion for minutes on end. My son saw him at the mayor's rally. I don't know what would have happened if there hadn't been a lot of people around. I've received strange phone calls, too."

"Strange?"

"Yes, someone hanging up on me."

From the way Burke and Johnson traded glances, Carol could tell what they were thinking. She suddenly felt exposed and vulnerable—not because they didn't believe her, but worse, because they were humoring her, as they would some hysterical spinster who was forever imagining that a robber lurked under her bed. She wasn't being hysterical, though. She needed protection and she'd called the police. What else did they expect her to do?

The frustration, added to her fears, had her on the edge of tears. She willed herself not to cry. That's all they needed to see. Tears! So like a woman!

"Do you have any enemies that you know of, Mrs.

Roblins? Besides this Mr. Clemson, I mean," Burke asked her.

Carol shook her head.

"And your husband is abroad, right?"

"Yes, he is."

"But you get along? He's never threatened you, has he?"

How could they think Blake was involved? The police were supposed to help in a situation like this, she thought, and instead they were asking her irrelevant questions with a nonchalance that approached indifference. Someone had sent her a vile note, violated her property. Someone was after her. Wasn't that obvious? It was to her. So why was she being made to feel guilty? Things were backward here.

"Officer," she said, struggling to remain calm, "Captain Roblins has been in Germany since February. This letter was mailed last week in Fayette. How can he have anything to do with it?"

"Cool down, lady," said Johnson, patting the air in front of him with his palms. "We're trying to get to the bottom of this." But they weren't trying. They were merely putting in their time, checking out the mansion, before they returned to the police station, where they would fill out a report saying that a female resident of Ragged Ridge Road, aged thirty-five or thereabouts, had received a crank letter in the mail and overreacted.

"Say, isn't this the place that had the big open house, beginning of the month?" asked Burke. "How many people do you guess passed through here?"

"Two or three hundred," said Carol. "Why?"

"That letter could have come from any one of them," Burke answered. "Somebody envious of a big mansion like this. A jealous type. You got a pretty nice place here. I dunno. I wouldn't take that letter too seriously, if I were you."

"But if you receive anything else, be sure and let us know," said Johnson as the two policemen sauntered to the front door. Burke hitched up his pants and took one last look around. Then, they left. They hadn't even bothered to take the letter with them as evidence.

Carol walked back into the living room, picked up the

sheet of yellow paper, and read the message again. "This is not a town that needs another whore." Whatever the police believed, it wasn't the work of a prankster. Clem was trying to scare her. The words were meant to wound.

She sank despondently into a chair and massaged her temples, asking herself if she should show the letter to Walker. He would probably downplay it, too, and all she needed at this point was one more person telling her not to worry. Facile reassurances, like those the police had just given her, only served to lull people into a false sense of comfort, and she knew it was vital to keep her wits about her from now on.

She heard Sammy tripping down the stairs from the attic, reached for the letter, and hid it away in her pocket.

Stopping in the doorway, her son cocked his head jauntily and chirped, "So, Mama, what do you think of that?"

Twenty-Four

She held the note tightly in her hand and paced about the bedroom. The envelope lay on the floor at the foot of the bed, where she had dropped it earlier. Her initial response had been to disregard it as a prank, the act of a puerile imagination, but the more she paced, the more troubled she became.

The maid rapped lightly at the door to tell her that tea was ready in the parlor, but Veronica was in no state to face anyone, not even servants. "I'm not feeling well," she said. "I think I'll lie down for a while. Make sure no one disturbs me, Megan."

Megan O'Hare withdrew down the hallway, wondering if Mrs. Kennedy's indisposition didn't have to do with her being, as they put it, in the family way. Her mistress had been acting more capriciously than usual; she kept to her bed until late in the morning and barely picked at her meals. That had to be the sign of something. A child, if that was it (and Megan had all but concluded it was by the time she reached the kitchen), would enliven the mansion. And there was no lack of bedrooms to fill.

Veronica didn't lie down. She continued to pace, her mind turning over the various possibilities. The letter had

202

arrived in the afternoon mail that Jimmy, the butler, had brought to her, as was his custom, on a silver tray. It was addressed to Mrs. Charles Kennedy, Esq., at 1 Ragged Ridge Road. The "Esq." was curious, but other than that, the envelope was like dozens of others, eggshell white and unremarkable in appearance. There was no return address, naturally, although the envelope carried a Fayette postmark and the day's date. So someone in Fayette had sent it to her this very morning.

But even that wasn't evident. Someone had posted it in Fayette this morning, that was all, someone who could be living in Brickton or Gettysburg or Harrisburg and was passing through town. Or maybe someone from out of state, who had arranged for the letter to be deposited in a Fayette mailbox, for all she knew, which was nothing.

She read the note again, even though there was precious little to read, just three brief sentences, and they were already stamped into her memory:

I wish you were dead. I do. I really do.

She stared at the writing. If she stared hard enough, perhaps she would recognize the hand. But the penmanship could have been anybody's—her husband's, Megan's. The anonymity of the letter was what made it so effective and let her think that anyone and everybody could be guilty. If only she could attach a face to it.

She was tempted to march right down to the bank and show the letter to Charles. She looked at herself in the mirror and immediately turned away from the reflection. Her face was pallid and drawn, and her eyes were puffy from crying. She couldn't go out in public looking like this. She would wait until Charles got home from work and show it to him then.

Clutching the paper in her hand, she sat in a chair by the window and stared out at the leaves that remained on the trees. They were brown and brittle, bled of all their fall colors and just waiting for a gust of wind to blow them to the ground. The sun slowly sank behind Ragged Ridge and darkness settled over the room, but the questions wouldn't go away, the same two questions—Who? Why? Who? Why?—echoing in her head like the mockery of nasty schoolchildren.

She must have drifted off to sleep, because when she opened her eyes, the bedroom lights were blazing and Charles was standing over her.

"Are you all right? Megan said you've been under the weather."

She shielded her face from the light, disoriented, the afternoon a blur in her mind. The letter had slipped out of her hand and was resting in her lap.

"Oh, it's you, Charles."

"Who did you think it was?" The voice echoed strangely in her ears. It took only a few seconds before the anxiety returned, sharp and tingly.

There was a long silence before she dared to look up at him, fearful of what she would see. But his eyes, clear and guileless, told her she had nothing to fear. The concern that furrowed his brow was concern for her. He would protect her, as he always had, because he loved and needed her so much. She was safe. Safe with Charles. A wave of relief came over her.

"I only mean I'm glad you're home, darling."

She reached up, put one hand around his neck, and gently guided his lips to hers. As she did, the other hand found the note in her lap and slowly crumpled it into a tiny little ball.

Twenty-Five

Carol looked across the kitchen table at Will Williams as he nursed his second cup of coffee and studied his script, and it dawned on her how normal the routine had become after only a week. Even Sammy, who had worked himself up to a fever pitch by the time the television star arrived, was beginning to take him in stride.

The Handyman, life-size and in living color! Frankly, Carol hadn't known what to expect. Would he come with an entourage? A manager? A bimbo? No, there turned out to be just Will, and he looked pretty much as he did on television. Taller, though. About six feet one inch, with a lean, muscular body. His hair was blonder than Carol remembered it, or maybe that was because her television set was old and the color constantly needed adjusting. And his eyes verged on gray, which gave him an introspective air when he wasn't conversing.

Mark Ridley brought him by, and the introductions couldn't have been more informal. Will had a couple of bags, that was all, and he insisted on carrying them up to the Kennedy Suite himself. He said he was looking forward to getting away from the West Coast madness for a while and hoped it could be a low-key time for him. Except for the daily phone calls from his agent, there was no knowing that he had the third most popular TV series in the country. When he let it drop that a few reporters from the tabloids and a television crew or two might come poking around, once they learned of his whereabouts, Carol, unbidden, appointed herself as his chief protector. The first week, however, that entailed little more than screening him from the stares of an inquisitive neighbor, who claimed she wanted to borrow a stick of butter, but would have been happier if she had gone away with an autograph.

Blake telephoned from Germany that week, too, saying they were after him to extend his tour of duty another year. Carol hadn't expected that piece of news and, even less, his evasive answer when she asked him what he was going to do about it:

"I haven't made my mind up yet. As you can imagine, there are pros and cons. I've got to give it some serious thought."

Pros and cons? Her patience was fraying. He'd been overseas six months now, and all he could tell her was that his mind wasn't made up. What had been going through his head all this time?

"It's not like you're going to wake up some morning and, bingo, the answers will be there, bright and shining," she said, making an effort to keep anger out of her voice. "Marriages take work, Blake. If you don't want to work at ours, fine. But eventually the only way we'll know what is going on between us is for us to be together. In the same room. Hey, I'd even settle for the same country right now."

"I get two weeks' leave at Christmas. I thought I'd come back to the States and we could talk about it then."

"Christmas is four months away, Blake."

"The tree is still up in the foyer, isn't it?"

"Yes."

"And the wreaths."

"Yes, the wreaths are still up, too. What's your point?"

"Nothing. Just making sure you haven't changed everything while I've been away. I mean, sometimes you sound like a different person to me."

"I am, Blake," she said firmly.

He'd always wanted her to get real. Well, she had made progress on that front. There was nothing like a burst water pipe or a rotting T-beam to hone your coping skills. But lately her self-esteem had risen in other ways, as well. She'd been a wife and mother for so long, she had forgotten that men could be drawn to her simply because she was a desirable woman. Although she had discouraged Walker's recent advances, she knew she would be lying not to admit that some small, still reckless part of herself had found them flattering, just as the prospect of getting to know Will Williams, a rich, successful actor, excited her.

What about Blake? she wondered. Had he changed? Loosened up? She wasn't altogether convinced that Germany was where a person went to learn to let down his hair. (It was just possible you couldn't let down a crew cut!) Too bad he hadn't been assigned to southern Italy or a sunny Greek isle.

"So how about you?" she asked. "Are you getting out of the rut?"

"Was I in one?"

"What do you think?"

"I think . . . we can talk about it at Christmas."

So there they were, right back in limbo again. For every step forward, a step backward. In the days that followed, she was grateful to have Will Williams around as a distraction.

Serving him dinner hadn't been part of their original agreement, but after watching him slap together a ham sandwich late one night—and mostly make a botch of it—she invited him to eat with her and Sammy whenever he wanted. Soon, that became a habit, too. Carol began planning meals, the way she had with Blake, and automatically set three places at the table—for her, Sammy, and Will.

The first time she did, Walker assumed the third place was for him. He was wrapping up work on the last of the suites—the two bedrooms along the front of the house that opened onto a common sitting room—and he'd stayed later than expected. He and Carol had eaten dinner together often enough in the past, so he wasn't presuming all that much when he saw her bustling about the kitchen. Just as he was on the point of telling her that he would need a few more minutes to wash up, Will came through the front door and kiddingly shouted out, "Honey, I'm home."

Walker was peeved and made no effort to hide it. Carol told him to stop being foolish, that he was always welcome, and started to put out another place setting. "No, I wouldn't want to interrupt anything," he replied, a smirk on his face, and he went outside and climbed into his truck without even saying good-bye to Sammy.

Carol dismissed his precipitous departure as a silly, adolescent reaction. Will was a paying guest, and perhaps she did treat him specially. But he was also a famous person, for heaven's sake, and he would spread the word about the Christmas Inn if his stay was pleasant. Surely, Walker's jealous streak didn't blind him to the fact that good business was good business. And Will was nothing if not good for her business.

She paused for a moment. Was she being naive by oversimplifying the workman's emotions? Her own? If so, that was the old Carol back on the job, the one who preferred to sidestep unpleasantness and avoid confrontations. Surprise! Just when she thought the anxious peacemaker in her had gone into remission, who popped up, all fretful and concerned?

Looking back, she realized how much Walker had enjoyed being man of the house, if only by proxy, and how he'd relished the showdowns with Clem, which had allowed him to play defender of the hearth. Sammy's neediness had plenty to do with Walker's becoming the boy's surrogate father, granted, but Walker liked that role, too, especially now that Sammy's adulation was directed elsewhere.

Unquestionably, Will Williams had changed the emotional climate in the mansion. The coolness between the two men, she suspected, was an early manifestation of territorial warfare, a skirmish that she hoped Walker wouldn't escalate into a battle.

It didn't help that there wasn't a whole lot for him to do on the Blue Room and the Cumberland Suite, as she dubbed them, before the second floor would be completely renovated. Her and Sammy's quarters on the first floor were going to have to wait, but otherwise, the Christmas Inn was very nearly a fait accompli with accommodations for five sets of customers. As far as Carol knew, no big new jobs had come through for Walker. He was building a shelving unit for a woman over in Hagerstown, but that was the extent of it, and the reality of running his own business was starting to sink in. He couldn't string out the few remaining chores in the mansion that much longer.

The night he had gone off in a jealous pique, Carol had made a special effort and prepared her chicken cordon bleu. Sammy wolfed down the meal, as usual, and then asked to be excused so he could watch television. Carol and Will lingered at the table, getting mildly, but agreeably intoxicated on a bottle of white wine, an extradry Sancerre. The apprentice from the theater who was supposed to drop by to help Will with his lines canceled out—there was a last-minute rehearsal for the children's show—so Carol wound up with the script for *Dial M for Murder*, cuing the television star.

He was playing the part of Tony Wendice—Ray Milland in the movie version—a former tennis champion and bounder who arranges to have his wealthy wife killed. It was a complete about-face for him, and he expected his fans to be surprised.

" 'I always intended to marry for money,' " he proclaimed over the dinner dishes. " 'I had to. Whilst I was in tennis, I met wealthy—' "

" 'Whilst I was in *first-class* tennis,' " Carol corrected him.

"Right. 'Whilst I was in *first-class* tennis, I met wealthy people all over the world—I was somebody—while my wind lasted! I decided to snap up the first chance I got. I nearly married a . . .' " He went blank. "Shit, what did I nearly marry?"

" 'I nearly married a tubby Boston deb with five million dollars.' "

"Got it," said Will, and repeated the line. For half an hour, it was stop and go. Carol wondered how actors managed to remember so many words, but Will assured her that was the easy part.

" '. . . I dropped into a pub and had a few drinks. As I sat

in the corner, I thought all sorts of things. I thought of three
different ways of killing him. I even thought of killing her.
That seemed a far more sensible idea—and just as I was
working out how I could do it, I . . . I . . .' *did something or
other. Damn! What?*"

"'I suddenly saw something which completely changed
my mind,'" chimed in Carol, who was beginning to get into
the scene.

A yell from the parlor interrupted them. Sammy rushed
into the dining room, panting with excitement. "You're on
TV. You're on TV."

Will shrugged philosophically. "Can't get away from it,
can I?"

Sammy couldn't figure out why his observation hadn't
precipitated a dash for the parlor. He tried saying it louder.
"You're on TV!"

The three of them ended up side by side on the couch,
watching *The Handyman.* Will actually laughed at his own
show. Not at himself, but at the other actors, when they did
something subtle or inventive that wasn't immediately
apparent to Carol. She had to admit that she found the
series a great deal funnier now that she knew Will, and his
passing comments made her feel like an insider.

"Oh, God, she couldn't remember a single line. It was a
nightmare," he moaned, referring to Mildred Nash, who
was making a guest appearance as his feisty grandmother
from Cleveland.

"You've got to be joking. She's a legend," said Carol.

"Yeah, well, she's also seventy-nine years old. But you
gotta give her this: she's a trouper. Off camera, she looks
half-dead. But once she got in front of a studio audience,
boy, did she come alive. She was funny and real. She had
them in the palm of her hand. You can only learn timing like
that on the stage. Doing it eight times a week. When Mark
called me and asked me if I'd like to come back here for a
play, it was just after I'd taped a couple of episodes with
Mildred. I think that's why I said yes. I realized how far I'd
strayed from the live theater."

"Surely, you could do a play anytime you wanted?"

"I guess I do get a lot of offers, but it's hard to go back

after you've been away from it for a while. You get rusty. I haven't been on a stage in eight years. A studio audience isn't the same thing. Hey, I'm not knocking my show. I'm grateful for the success. Whoever thought I'd earn this kind of money? And I know I'm never gonna play Hamlet, although some fool Shakespeare festival somewhere would probably let me make an ass of myself by trying.

"Last year, I was offered a really good play in New York. A bright young director, a much-sought-after role. I turned it down because I was scared. I didn't want to face the critics. As an artist, you're supposed to take risks and I was frightened. So here I am, getting my feet wet again. Reconnecting."

The jaunty *Handyman* theme song started to play and there was a close-up of Will, uttering his trademark sign-off: "Well, what do you think of that?" A protracted burst of canned laughter followed. Sammy looked intently at the set, then at the man on the couch, still not entirely certain how he could be in two places at once.

"Off to bed, Sammy," Carol prodded gently.

She and Will polished off the last of the Sancerre. They were both feeling mellow. A light breeze had picked up, breaking the heat left over from the afternoon and stirring the wind chimes on the veranda.

"But enough about me. What do you think about my career?" He flashed the sideways grin and they both laughed. "Seriously, you've been real good to me. You cook dinner. You help me with my lines. We talk about my TV show, my play, my hang-ups. What about you?"

"Believe me, there's nothing very interesting to talk about. I run the Christmas Inn. I have a twelve-year-old son. It's just what you see."

"Nothing is ever just what you see."

He obviously wanted more from her than that, but Carol didn't know where to begin. They sat there for a moment in silence. She glanced down nervously at her wineglass. She could sense his probing gaze. She looked up. America's favorite comedian had retired for the night, leaving behind a handsome, introverted, mildly insecure actor. His eyes had turned a velvety gray.

"I'm sorry," he apologized. "I've had too much wine. It's none of my business."

"Well, I do have a husband, in case you were wondering. He's not here right now. He's in Germany." She related the events of the past year, how she and Blake had stumbled on the mansion, how she had dealt with some of the renovation problems, and how uncooperative the historical society had been. She even divulged the murder, which intrigued him.

"That doesn't bother you, does it, sleeping in the room where someone was killed?" she asked.

"Why should it? Everybody's gotta die somewhere. Some actors even die on the stage. I'm speaking figuratively, of course."

"Will, you're going to be great in the play," she said reassuringly.

"Let's hope." For luck, he rapped his knuckles on the end table by the sofa. "So you did this restoration all yourself, then?"

"Well, there's Walker and Joey. And a platoon of electricians and plumbers."

"I don't think you're giving yourself enough credit. I don't know what this place looked like before, but it's beautiful now. Your husband must be proud of you."

"Who can say? I don't know what's going on between us. Things weren't exactly great when he left and . . ." She felt uncomfortable continuing. Her feelings about Blake were in such flux. To talk about them to a third party was to give them a definition, a finality, they hadn't yet acquired. Better to let them float for a while longer. "He called yesterday and said they want him to sign up for another year. He hasn't decided. Who knows what any of this means?"

"Do you miss him?"

"Do I miss him? Good question." She ran her index finger around the rim of her wineglass. "I miss having a companion. I miss having someone working alongside me. Yes, I miss the Blake I married. Not the Blake who left. I miss loving someone, I guess." The emotion was welling up inside. If she wasn't careful, she would be spilling her guts to a man she barely knew. Fame was deceptive that way—it pulled you in, disarmed you by suggesting an intimacy that wasn't necessarily there. She had a sudden need to turn the conversation away from herself. "And you?"

"Me? Me. Me," Will sighed. "I messed up pretty bad. I let *me* become more important than *us,* and she filed for divorce. It's very seductive out there. Everyone tells you you're the most important person alive. After a while, you start to believe it."

A quiet descended over the parlor. Will reached for Carol's hand and held it for a second. "You're a very nice woman. You deserve to be in love."

"We all do."

He leaned over and gave her a kiss on the cheek, lingering just long enough so that they were both aware of the warmth of his lips on her skin. Then, he mumbled something about seeing her tomorrow morning, smiled shyly, and went upstairs.

Carol couldn't keep her thoughts off him while she waited to fall asleep. She heard him get up, go into the bathroom, and come back out again. She tried to picture him and what he was wearing, if anything. He had an unassuming sensuality that made him far more attractive in person than on TV. On TV, he was the guy next door, Mr. Average, everybody's pal. But there was more sensitivity to him than that. More depth. She had read in some magazine that he was equally popular with male and female viewers. Men found him unthreatening and related to him. Women found him cute and sexy.

And right now, on a warm August night, he was probably lying naked on a bed, ten feet over her head.

Sammy squinted in the blinding circle of light. It was brighter than the headlights on his mother's Toyota, brighter than a flashbulb going off in his face when she took his photograph.

"Can't see," he said, shading his eyes with his hands. "Where are you?"

"Out here," said the voice in the darkness. "In the audience. You're a star now, Sammy. How do you like it?"

"Can't see."

"Sure you can. Just don't look into the beam. You'll get used to it. Now walk around a little."

Sammy took several steps to the left, and the white light moved along with him. Then he reversed direction. So did the light. He giggled.

"It's chasing me."

"Know what we call that light, Sammy? A follow spot. Because it follows you when you move around."

"Like Charlie?"

"Well, yeah. A little like Charlie, I suppose," chuckled Will.

The actor had no rehearsal that morning, only a costume fitting at ten-thirty, so during breakfast he'd offered to take Sammy to the White Barn Playhouse and show him around, if the boy was interested. Not only was Sammy interested, he was beside himself.

Magically, the white beam turned pink, pale blue, sea green, then back to pink again.

"Rainbow," the boy chortled, enchanted by the colors that made his clothes and his skin pink and blue and green, too. He hugged himself and spun in circles. It was as if no one could see him. He was hiding. Hiding in the bright light. Different from the attic at home, but just as warm and safe.

After the houselights came back on, Will climbed up on the stage and they explored the set together. It was like a big dollhouse, only the front wall had been removed so that everybody could look in. The other walls were panels of cloth, painted to resemble wood. Will said they were called "flats." A pair of French doors opened onto a garden, where Sammy was fascinated to discover that the shrubbery was made of plastic. The rosebush, when he sniffed its blossoms, smelled a lot like new sneakers.

"Fooled you!" the actor said with a laugh.

The costume shop was cluttered with racks of clothes, but the costumer had laid out several suits, shirts, and ties on a couch for the actor's approval.

"Bernice, this is my pal Sammy Roblins," Will said to the middle-aged woman, who had dark hair pulled back into a bun and cat glasses hanging on a chain around her neck.

Two yellow pencils were stuck in the bun, like chopsticks. "He's my personal consultant. Whatever he says, goes."

Bernice opined that two heads were always better than one, especially when one of them was as cute as Sammy's, and pinched his cheek. Sammy squirmed uncomfortably. She handed Will a gray fedora, which he slipped on for size.

"Like it?" Will asked, pulling the brim down over his right eye.

"Yup," the boy answered.

"Sammy says it's all right by him, so it's all right by me."

After the pin-striped suit got a "yup," Bernice made some chalk marks on the sleeve and pinned up one of the pants cuffs. The houndstooth sports jacket and the London Fog raincoat also passed muster. But when Bernice held up the yellow tie, patterned with tiny horses, Sammy frowned and shook his head vigorously.

"Nope."

"Nope?" responded the costumer. "Don't you like horses? What's wrong with you? Every kid likes horses."

"It's silly," Sammy stated firmly.

"But it's British."

"New tie, Bernice," Will ordered.

"Well, there's this one," she said, displaying a silver tie with red triangles. "I think it accentuates the gray in your eyes nicely."

"Nope."

The woman inhaled deeply. "This one, then?"

"Nope."

"Well, just which one meets with your approval, young man?" she asked, her exasperation growing. Will had to turn away to keep from breaking up.

Sammy hesitated for a long time before selecting a blue silk tie with thin burgundy stripes. "This one."

Bernice was about to voice her objection when Will proclaimed, "Perfect choice. I tell you, Sammy, I don't know what I'd do without you. I've never been very good at picking out ties for myself."

The boy swelled with pride. This was the most important thing he had ever done.

"The blue one, it is," replied Bernice flatly.

As he and Sammy left the costume shop, Will heard the woman grumbling to herself, "I suppose the little squirt will demand a program credit now."

They walked down a narrow corridor, turned right, and entered the prop room. Sammy couldn't believe his eyes. Furniture of all sorts was stacked in piles, and chairs hung from the ceiling. Everywhere he looked there was something strange and wonderful—from a stuffed moose's head to a suit of armor. Will showed him a trick knife, a bottle made out of spun sugar that shattered just like glass, and a plastic container of fake blood.

"Someone gets stabbed in my play, but not really," the actor explained. "From the audience, it looks real. But now you'll know better."

"You don't get hurt?"

"Not at all. Watch." He pushed the tip of the knife against his palm, and the blade retracted into the handle.

"It's just pretend?"

"You got it, Sammy. Theater is just pretend."

"I like to pretend."

"That makes two of us."

Twenty-Six

A key rattled in the hall door. The elegantly gowned woman and the sporty young man stopped conversing, put down their drinks, and turned to see who it was. The door slowly swung open, but for a second no one was visible in the vestibule beyond.

Then Will Williams made his entrance.

He was instantly identifiable, even in a Savile Row suit and London Fog overcoat with an umbrella hooked over his arm. The audience experienced a collective shiver of satisfaction, gratified to see that someone they watched fondly every week in their homes didn't have a hunched back or a hook nose or some other flaw that had been concealed from them all this time by makeup or artful lighting. In fact, Will Williams didn't look all that different in person than he did on their TV sets, which was just as they wanted it. The applause that erupted in the White Barn Playhouse was loud and sustained and supportive.

The theater was packed for the opening night of *Dial M for Murder,* and a dozen customers, lined up behind the last row, were more than willing to stand during the performance, which almost never happened at the White Barn. Only the week before, in fact, theatergoers by the droves had stayed away from *Come Back, Little Sheba,* a sterling production, Mark Ridley thought, but one that "had entirely too much drinking in it," according to a disgruntled subscriber. What would they say when they discovered Will Williams was the culprit?

Without question, he was big news. A crew from *The Biz,* the half-hour television show that boasted every morning that it was "keeping an eye on the nation's entertainment," was on hand to film the opening. While Carol and Sammy were waiting to go inside and take their seats, she had spotted several reporters, scribbling in their notepads.

"How about giving me a quote, Mrs. Roblins?" Tony, the young go-getter from the *Fayette Weekly Register,* had picked her out of the crowd.

"It's an exciting evening, isn't it?"

"Yeah, this is bigger than the Ned Foster story."

It was exciting—the bustle and the chatter, the sense of expectation that brought everyone together as the houselights dimmed, then the split second of pitch darkness before the curtains parted and another world, bright and stylish, suddenly materialized on the stage. When Will came on, Carol's heart began to pound furiously. She had cued him so many times that she knew much of the play by heart, and it startled her to hear the leading lady paraphrase her lines. Will had his down perfectly, but beyond that, Carol couldn't tell if the performance was good or not.

He seemed at ease on the stage, he moved naturally, and at times she totally forgot who it was up there. Then, she would recognize the expression on his face as one she'd seen at breakfast, or hear him use a familiar intonation and she was instantly reminded that the actor plotting murder on the stage of the White Barn Playhouse was the very same man with whom she sipped white wine late at night. How could you separate the person from the performance, spontaneous everyday behavior from carefully rehearsed behavior that just looked spontaneous? The two were mingled, interdependent somehow, so that reality became some kind of illusion in her mind, while illusion took on the weight and solidity of reality.

At first, she noticed that the audience members wanted to

laugh at everything Will said. By the third act, though, they really believed he was this smooth, manipulative bastard and took perverse delight in the audacity of his scheming. "It doesn't matter who you really are," Will had explained to her. "The actor is a lot like the hypnotist. You put people in a trance and plant suggestions in their heads. You don't have to be handsome to make an audience think you're good-looking. I've known brutes who are the soul of sensitivity onstage. And take my word on it, some of the most intelligent performances I've ever seen were given by some of the dumbest actors in the profession."

So where was the real Will in all this? Carol wondered fleetingly. She was definitely drawn to him, the supple grace of his body and the promise of tenderness she read in those melting gray eyes. His antic wit delighted her and his concern flattered her. Was all that just illusion, too, more of the hypnotist at work? Had he charmed her as effortlessly as he was now charming a rapt audience in the White Barn Playhouse? An outburst of applause interrupted her musings and she realized the play was over. People around her were clapping enthusiastically. When Will strode through the upstage door for his curtain call, the applause rose several notches and a number of spectators jumped to their feet.

He stepped forward and bowed, scanning the auditorium. On his second bow, he located Carol and Sammy and winked at them. Sammy waved back, which brought a broad smile to Will's face. The audience, happy to catch a glimpse of the Handyman at last, cheered. That smile has made him millions, Carol thought, but part of her still wanted to believe it had been meant for her and Sammy alone. Actors! What an oddly seductive, thoroughly untrustworthy breed!

She grabbed her son by the arm, slipped out the side door of the theater, and ran for the car. She'd left the preparations for the opening-night party in the capable hands of two caterers, but it wouldn't do to have the guests arriving before the hostess. The cast and crew would be coming, naturally, along with the board of directors and "friends" of the theater, as Mark liked to call the more generous supporters. Carol had taken it upon herself to invite Mayor

Quinn out of courtesy, suspecting that he would decline, as indeed he did, through his secretary, who noted tartly that the Quinns would be vacationing that week.

Carol barely had time to check out the buffet table and light the Christmas candles in the living room before the doorbell rang and people started streaming in. If seeing Will Williams onstage had left them giddy, the prospect of actually mingling with him had them positively euphoric. Everyone seemed to be congratulating everyone else on a great show, although most of the guests, to be honest, had done little more than watch it.

The reporter and the cameraman from *The Biz* pushed through the front door.

"So where do you want me to set up?" grumbled the cameraman, who was loaded down with several bags of equipment, which he dumped unceremoniously in the middle of the foyer.

The reporter, a lacquered blonde in a tight dress, took a quick look around. "In front of the Christmas tree should be good."

Carol went over to them. "Can I help you?"

"You must be Carol. Will said he wanted to have the interview here. Is it all right if we do the setup by the tree?" The reporter flashed a perfunctory smile, revealing a row of teeth so blindingly white that Carol asked herself if they weren't painted. Nature didn't make teeth like that; dentists did.

"Whatever 'Will' said is fine by me," she replied, suppressing her instant distaste for the woman, who ignored the sarcastic inflection, if she even heard it.

"This is your place, huh? Cute idea—the Christmas Inn. Hey, I'm even wearing the perfect color. Red! How do you like that!" The cameraman busied himself angling lights, while the reporter fished around in her shoulder bag for a brush and some hair spray. Carol had ceased to exist for both of them.

As if obeying some primal law of the theater, the members of the company arrived in the reverse order of their billing, which meant that the crew showed up first, then the actors playing the various police officers, then the leading lady, and finally, Will Williams himself. He was more dressed up than Carol had ever seen him—beige slacks, collarless white shirt, Italian loafers, and a black silk jacket so thin it caught the breeze.

The guests broke into applause when he entered, bathed in a celestial white glow. The cameraman had turned on the floodlights and was recording the actor's arrival for the millions who would see it on *The Biz* the following morning. The reporter, freshly painted, chirped, "Whenever you're ready, Will."

"In a minute." He waved her off and made his way through the room with the unassailable confidence of one who knows that everyone wants to talk to him. He was used to the attention of others, and his manner, a perfectly calibrated blend of the accessible and the superior, kept people at just the right distance.

"Is this the most *fabulous* actor on the planet or what!" Harry Watkins's voice rose over the noise of the crowd like an air raid siren. Mark Ridley called for quiet and embarked on a series of heartfelt thank-yous that began with Carol, "the White Barn's newest friend," moved on to "the terrific company and crew," and culminated with Will, "our most famous alumnus, whom we welcome back with more gratitude and love than we can ever show." There were toasts and cheers, then Sammy threw the switch on the player piano and a cascading version of "Someone to Watch over Me" filled the living room.

Will took Carol's hand and pulled her into the foyer. "I thought if I did the interview here, instead of at the theater, I could plug the Christmas Inn," he whispered in her ear. His eyes had a devilish sparkle. "Tammy," he said to the reporter, "have you met Carol?"

Tammy remembered vaguely that she had.

"Let's do it, then." Will buttoned his jacket, and the reporter gave a final, needless pat to her hairdo, which would have held up under a hailstorm. "Rolling," barked the cameraman.

"This is Tammy Tulane in Fayette, Pennsylvania, where television star Will Williams made a long-awaited return to the stage tonight in *Dial M for Murder*. The curtain came down only minutes ago, and *The Biz* has the inside story. Congratulations, Will. This must be a big change for you." She thrust the microphone at the star.

"Well, it is, Tammy. No more overalls for the next few weeks. I finally get to wear a suit and tie. Seriously, there's nothing like the excitement of doing live theater."

"All your fans who know you as Sam Love, the Handyman, will be surprised to learn that you're playing a different kind of role, right?"

"I guess you could say that. Sam Love likes everybody, and Tony Wendice, well, he's out to plot the murder of his wife."

"That's certainly a side of you we've never seen before. Tell me, how did you prepare for the part?"

"I think everybody has wanted to kill someone at some time or other in their lives. Haven't you ever had the urge to murder somebody, Tammy?"

"I'm not telling." Tammy laughed, showing off her teeth for the camera.

"I'll bet you have," continued Will. "That doesn't necessarily mean you'd follow through. Sometimes, the urge gives birth to the deed, sometimes not. Why, did you know that someone was killed in this very house?"

Tammy Tulane's face went blank.

"In fact, I'm staying in the actual room where the woman was murdered. So I've been absorbing all the vibes here the past few weeks, trying to figure out what turns an ordinary person into a cold-blooded killer. It happens every day. All you have to do is watch the news."

"So you believe it's something in all of us, then?"

"Sure, don't you?"

Tammy paused, not sure what she thought. Profiting from the break, Will pulled Carol into camera range. "Tammy, this is Carol Roblins, who runs the Christmas Inn. That's why there's a Christmas tree behind me. If you're ever in this area, folks, this is the place to stay." He stepped forward, peered into the camera lens and winked, then stepped back. Carol didn't know where she was supposed to look, so she fixed on Sammy, who was standing next to the cameraman.

"Yes, there was a murder here seventy years ago. It was never solved. But not to worry, Tammy. Carol and I think we have finally figured it out, haven't we, Carol? It's quite a story. Why, I may do a movie-of-the-week about it." He was getting carried away. "We're even going to shoot it on location here at the Christmas Inn. Carol will have a small part in it."

"Will you play the killer?" Tammy asked.

"Aha," said Will, twirling an imaginary mustache. "That's something you never give away until the final reel."

Tammy generously exposed her teeth again. "Well, we'll certainly all be looking forward to that, I'm sure, and to another season of *The Handyman*. Thank you, Will Williams. This is Tammy Tulane reporting from Fayette, Pennsylvania, for *The Biz*."

The cameraman doused the lights and lifted the camera off his shoulder. Will leaned over to the reporter and said, "Be sure and use the stuff about the inn, will you?" Then, he gave her a pat on the fanny and rejoined the party, which was in full swing.

"Movie-of-the-week!" Carol shook her head. Where had Will picked up that idea? Letting your imagination run wild seemed to be an integral part of being an actor. The plug was nice, though. It would be interesting to see how many people commented on it tomorrow.

"What a fabulous dip!" Harry Watkins sashayed up behind her. "I've got to have the recipe."

The cast was the last to leave, and only then when the stage manager announced, "Don't forget, everybody. Matinee tomorrow. The call is for one-thirty." They straggled out onto the veranda, prolonging the good-byes, although they would be seeing one another in twelve hours. The moon had disappeared, and the sky had turned a grayish phosphorescent color that carried the threat of copious rain. Cars were parked at odd angles on the lawn and by the kitchen door, but after a little jockeying and a few blasts on the horn, they fell into a line and proceeded toward town in orderly fashion. Carol looked in on Sammy, who had long since conked out, then went around the house turning out lights and verifying that windows were closed tight. The

Rose Room and the Hunter's Retreat were empty, but they had been booked for the weekend.

She flicked off the lights in the upstairs hall.

Will stood in the door to the Kennedy Suite, a silhouette framed by gold. "Great party," he said.

"It was," she agreed, half-expecting to see him there.

He beckoned with his hand. As soon as he did, she knew she would go to him. No words were necessary. She knew that he would put his arms around her and breathe warmly in the hollows of her neck. And she knew they would kiss, softly at first, savoring the delicate sensation of their lips touching. Then he would lead her into the bedroom, turn out the lights, and undress her slowly in the darkness.

That night, Carol dreamed of Veronica Kennedy in a wheat field, drenched in sunlight and rippled by a restless wind that blew down from the boulders of Ragged Ridge. She had on a simple white muslin dress. "Be careful," she repeated, over and over again.

Twenty-Seven

———

When Carol opened her eyes the next morning, she was disoriented by the milky gray light that filtered through the window. The surroundings were a blur. Maybe she wasn't awake yet or maybe it wasn't morning.

She rolled over on her side and felt a body next to her. As she lifted her head, the Kennedy Suite slowly came into focus, and she remembered the events of the preceding evening. Will's face was buried in the pillow and he had thrown off the covers, exposing his bare back. She reached over and tucked the sheet around him. He had been so gentle with her, so attentive. She looked around for her clothes and saw them on the armchair, neatly folded in a pile. A smile came to her lips.

The clock radio on the bedside table read 7:15. Sammy would be padding into the kitchen shortly, expecting his bowl of cereal. Part of her wanted to remain in bed, cuddle up to the body beside her, and postpone as long as possible the moment when she would have to start her day. She found herself stirring anyway. The night had been a tender, romantic interlude, and now, just beyond the door, reality summoned. She didn't feel guilty about what had happened. She had walked into the Kennedy Suite with her eyes wide open, and that's how she would leave it. No foolish sentimentality. No awkward grasping and clutching. No "What do we do now?" and "Will you always love me?" She knew precisely what she had to do: prepare breakfast for a hungry twelve-year-old son and clean up after an opening-night party.

When she saw the living room, she was sorry she had sent the caterers home early the night before. It was not a pretty sight, and the dingy light of the stormy August morning didn't make it any prettier. Dirty glasses and plates with dried food on them were everywhere. But by ten o'clock, Sammy was up, fed, and absorbed in a comic book, and she had gotten a healthy start on her chores.

She was washing the glasses by hand when Walker trudged up the back stairs into the kitchen, dripping water from the rain that had started to come down in thick, gray waves.

"That looked like some party you had here," he said, taking off his slicker and giving it a shake.

Carol rinsed a wineglass in hot water and placed it upside down on a kitchen towel to dry, alongside all the others. "Yes, it was a big success, I guess. Want some coffee?"

"Must have been, because I saw you on *The Biz* this morning. You're a star now. Sure caused a lot of talk in town, Will boasting how you two solved the murder."

Carol had to think a moment. She had totally forgotten about the television interview. "Oh, he was just kidding. I don't know what made him say that. So, how did it look?"

Walker poured himself a cup of coffee. "Well, he shouldn't go mouthing off about a murder if he doesn't want to upset people. What's all this crap about him making a movie-of-the-week and you having a part in it! All I can say is, it's caused a helluva lot of talk."

"Good! Let them talk," Carol snapped. Walker was starting entirely too early with his jealous act. "Half the people in this damn town don't speak to me as it is."

The workman sipped his coffee. "Why give them another reason?" he muttered sourly.

She turned away from the sink to face him. "I didn't know you were coming in today, Walker."

"I'm just going to finish up the wallpapering in the bathroom. Then I've got an appointment this afternoon in Hagerstown."

"Fine."

The rain lashed up against the kitchen windows. Carol peered outside. The sky was getting gloomier. The summer had been a dry one, and the farmers desperately needed the water, but it was coming down so heavily that she feared it would mostly run off into ditches and gullies, before soaking into the ground. The roads would be slick. She went back to the dishes.

It was well past noon when she realized that Will still hadn't shown up for breakfast and the cast had a one-thirty call at the theater. She knocked lightly at his door and got a groggy "Yes" in exchange.

"You know there's a matinee today." She poked her head inside the bedroom. "It's almost twelve-thirty. I thought you'd like to know."

Will was seated upright in the bed, blinking. His hair was tousled, and he had a crease mark on his cheek from the sheet. He looked about fifteen. "Come here," he said, throwing out his arms.

"I can't."

"Yes, you can."

"You know that three-hundred middle-aged fans are gathering right now at the White Barn Playhouse, worried sick that the play is going to start without them. And the star they're all dying to see doesn't have a stitch of clothing on and is still half-asleep."

"They can wait. Come here."

He caught her by the wrist, pulled her onto the bed, and nuzzled her neck.

"Mmmmm. You smell good enough to eat."

She pretended to fight him off, laughing as she beat on his chest with her fists. He let out a series of yelps, then fell back on the pillow in mock exhaustion.

"Truce. You're taking unfair advantage of a semiconscious man."

She looked down at him and smiled.

"You know, I never realized how blue your eyes are," he said.

"Oh, so you just now noticed the color of my eyes?"

"Of course not," he protested vehemently. "I'm an actor. I notice everything." He pulled the sheet over his head. "You have lovely blond hair. You have unbelievable cheek-bones. You have perfect teeth, except for one on the bottom that is slightly out of line and makes you look like a little girl when you laugh. You have long, delicate fingers. Your lips are unbelievably soft. Your legs are world-class. Your knees don't knock. And you have a tiny, little mole, located in the most amazing place."

His head popped out from under the sheet. "Do you want me to tell the world where the tiny, little mole is?"

"Cad. You wouldn't."

"Only if you kiss me, then."

He wrapped his arms around her, found her lips with his, and lowered her onto the sheets. For a moment, they rediscovered the intimacy of the previous night.

Will whispered in her ear, "Call up the theater. Tell them the matinee is canceled. The star has been suddenly immobilized. Bedridden due to mysterious causes. They'll believe it, if it comes from you."

"You're incorrigible," she said, struggling to her feet. She tucked her white blouse into her slacks, readjusted her belt, and raked her fingers through her hair several times by way of combing it. "I'll fix you some breakfast."

Quietly, she pulled the door to Will's bedroom closed and started down the hall. Walker was standing in the entrance to the Cumberland Suite, watching her.

"So that's how you get parts in TV movies."

Carol jumped. "Oh, it's you. I was just waking Will for the matinee."

"Late sleeper, isn't he! Must have been up until all hours last night, huh? I guess it really was some party, after all."

There was no confusing his snorting with laughter.

"Walker, don't you have work to do?" It came out more curtly than Carol intended.

"Ah, to be rich and famous!" He pivoted abruptly and

stalked into the Cumberland Suite. Soon, a loud pounding echoed down the hall. It didn't sound as if Walker were wallpapering to Carol. It sounded, frankly, as if he were taking his frustrations out on the woodwork.

She debated whether she should follow after him and smooth things over, then decided against it. She didn't want to promote any disagreements, but lately she was having to placate Walker all too often. This was the second time today. He was acting like a spoiled schoolboy. She owed him no explanations for her behavior.

The pounding continued while she hastened down the back stairs to the kitchen. She could see that she was going to have to make an effort to keep Will and Walker apart from now on.

His hair still damp from the shower, Will bounded into the kitchen ten minutes later and polished off the toast and coffee Carol had ready for him. He plucked an apple from the fruit bowl and pocketed it for later. She asked him if he would be joining her and Sammy for dinner, and he struck a snooty pose and replied in an English accent that nothing appealed to him more. Certainly not performing this afternoon for three-hundred damp matinee ladies, who would probably munch chocolates and chat all through the show.

A gust of wind flung a sheet of rain up against the window.

"Wow, when did this start?"

He snatched his raincoat off the hook, hesitated in the entryway, then made a dash for the station wagon that Mark Ridley had put at his disposal. The motor turned over several times, emitting a shrill grinding noise, before it finally caught. The actor depressed the accelerator several times in quick succession and shifted into reverse. The motor sputtered and died.

He came running back into the kitchen, water streaming off the raincoat. "I'm such a jerk. There's no gas in the car. I noticed it yesterday, but with opening night and everything, I completely forgot to do anything about it. You wouldn't mind driving me over to the theater, would you?"

"Just take the Toyota. I'm not going anywhere in this

weather." Carol rummaged around in her purse for the keys and handed them to the flustered actor. "Maybe you should wait a few minutes, until this rain lets up."

Will checked the clock on the kitchen range. "I can't. It's one-fifteen already. The show must go on." He looked back at her and grinned. "And on and on!" Holding the raincoat over his head like an awning, he darted back out into the yard. The Toyota started right up and he was gone.

That afternoon, Carol thought a lot about the preceding twenty-four hours.

For the first time in months, she felt desirable and knew that the feeling was Will Williams's gift to her. Of course, there was no future in their relationship nor did she expect it. They inhabited two different worlds that, against all odds, happened to overlap. If it hadn't been for the inn, she would never have met him. And if Blake hadn't left her to march off to Germany, perhaps there would never have been an inn. Who could figure any of it out? Will would return to Hollywood in three weeks and resume his hectic TV career. On Monday, Sammy would enter a new class at school and she would have to explain why he couldn't take Charlie with him. Life would go on. That much was certain. Not too much else.

Until then, Carol resolved to enjoy the actor's company and keep their relationship as uncomplicated and guilt-free as possible. She couldn't even say if they would sleep together again. For now, she could live, content, with the memory of a special night.

She was unloading the dishwasher, her back to the stairs, so she didn't notice that Walker had come into the kitchen. He tossed his tool belt on the kitchen table. The thud made her jump.

"You startled me. Have you finished up?"

"Yeah," he said, going for his slicker, which hung from a hook by the door. He buttoned up the slicker in silence, then grabbed the tool belt and prepared to leave. The rain stopped him at the doorstep. He watched it for a while. Something was bothering him.

"So I guess things are 'different' now," he finally said.

"What are you talking about?"

"At the open house. Remember? You said if things had been different, if you weren't married, maybe we could have, you know, gotten together. Well, you're still married, aren't you? So I guess you've changed the rules. Women like that—changing the rules."

"Walker, let's not get into this all over again. Whatever you're thinking—"

"Don't make it worse by lying, Carol. I'm not stupid. I've got eyes. I can see. The funny thing is, I didn't think you were like the rest of them. I thought you were different. But I was wrong. I'm always wrong. You're all the same. Determined to make fools of us. Well, I'm no fool, Carol, and don't you forget it."

Without waiting for a response, he gave the door a shove and strode out into the rain. It was just as well, Carol thought. She had nothing to say to him anyway. Maybe the rules had changed. In just a few weeks, she and Will had forged an intimacy that all the months with Walker had failed to create. And just a few minutes ago, she had been telling herself that she was going to have to keep things simple and uncomplicated. Nothing was ever simple, she thought.

She made a quick inspection of the Cumberland Suite. The striped wallpaper was up and looked handsome. She had chosen the colors—ivory and a brownish gray— because they reminded her of birch trees in winter. Walker had left his toolbox in a corner.

Sammy heard the doorbell first.

"Guests," he cried, sending out a high-pitched, all-points alert.

Two policemen, soaking wet, were waiting on the veranda. Through the glass, Carol recognized one of them as Sergeant Johnson, but he had a different partner this time. She figured their visit had something to do with Clem. Maybe they'd finally come around to her way of thinking and had interrogated him about the threatening letter. She opened the door.

Sergeant Johnson spoke. "Mrs. Roblins?"

"Yes."

"Do you own a 1991 blue Toyota?"

"I do, but it's not here right now. I loaned it to a friend for the afternoon." The second policeman shifted uneasily on his feet. "Why? Is everything all right, Officer?"

"Well, no, Mrs. Roblins, I'm afraid it isn't." Sergeant Johnson looked at her apologetically. "There's been an accident."

The pause seemed endless.

"Oh my God," Carol blurted out. "Has Will been hurt?"

Sergeant Johnson took a deep breath. It was at moments like these that he hated his job. "He was turning off the highway onto the road that goes to the playhouse. He seems to have been speeding. The car skidded off the pavement and slammed into a tree."

He stole a glance at his partner, who had his head down and was staring at his feet.

"I'm sorry to have to tell you this, Mrs. Roblins, but Mr. Williams is dead."

Twenty-Eight

—m—

Charles Kennedy was in such a state of shock as he stumbled out of the mansion into the storm that he did not feel the cold or the wind or the ice-crusted snowflakes that pelted his face. He hadn't bothered to put on an overcoat, and his fedora still hung on a hook in the hallway. The rosy warmth with its glowing Christmas lights and the ghostly chill of the woods were the same to him. The sight of his wife's mangled body in a pool of blood at the foot of their bed had so profoundly jolted him that all his other senses seemed to have shut down. A terrified child again, propelled by instinct alone, he ran in search of the man who had always been his closest friend.

He heard voices on the veranda, calling after him.

"Where are you going, Mr. Kennedy?"

"Somebody stop him. He'll do himself some terrible harm."

"Come back, Mr. Kennedy. Please, come back."

But the voices were soon lost in the howling wind. And the rectangle of golden yellow, which was the front door that he had just flung open, quickly faded and then disappeared altogether behind a curtain of snow.

The two houses were less than a mile apart, connected

by a meandering path that followed the stream in back of the mansion, threaded through several apple orchards, and then gave onto a meadow that in the summer months was sweet with the smell of grasses and bluebells. Kennedy had walked it often, but the going was arduous in the snow and he frequently lost his balance and fell. For twenty minutes, he plowed ahead. Tree branches caught his clothes and lashed his body. Finally, he spotted the lights of the Quinn household at the far edge of the meadow, which was nothing but wintry desolation now.

He was numb, his mind near the snapping point. Only a dull gnawing at his inner being let him know he was alive. His goal was to reach the Quinn house. After that, he didn't know what he would do. The future had become a meaningless concept to him.

A large oak at the side of the house creaked in the wind, and its twisted boughs clawed at the slate gray sky. Huddled underneath, visible only to someone who looked closely, and perhaps not even then, was a person in a knit cap, a checkered scarf, splattered with blood, and a navy blue topcoat. As the banker summoned the last of his strength to pound on the Quinns' door, the figure retreated behind the thick trunk of the tree. The topcoat was nearly indistinguishable from the knobby black bark.

Phillip Quinn cracked open the door cautiously, then recoiled at the sight of Charles Kennedy, haggard and half-frozen. Something close to delirium shone in his eyes. Quinn grabbed him under the arms and pulled him into the house, almost as if he were rescuing a drowning man from frigid waters. The wind slammed the door shut.

Cautiously, the figure in the checkered scarf moved out from behind the tree, edged up to a window, and watched.

The two men had withdrawn into the living room. Charles Kennedy, seated with his back to the window, was blurting out the calamitous news to his partner, who appeared devastated by what he was hearing. Veronica Kennedy bludgeoned to death? It was inconceivable. Surely, Charles had gone stark raving mad and was making it up. Incredulity pulled Phillip's features downward, and his mouth hung open stupidly, like the Greek mask of tragedy, only badly drawn. If Charles had expected the solace of comforting phrases or placating gestures, his friend was incapable of delivering them.

Phillip Quinn retreated into a stupor of disbelief. How could their lives, lives full of such promise and joy, have come unraveled in a single night? Things like that just didn't happen of their own accord. There had to be a seed from which the chaos had sprung, a moment when happiness began its irreversible mutation into unhappiness, a turning point. Try as he might, he couldn't identify it. Only minutes before, everything had been calm and ordered and reasonable. And now it wasn't. But there were no transitions, no warnings that he could look back to, no yellow flags, indicating that a violent change in the weather was imminent. The suddenness of it all rooted him, speechless, to the center of the living room floor.

The warmth of the house revived Charles Kennedy. His face lost the cardboard pallor that it had had when he first lurched over the doorstep, and the beads of ice in his hair melted, making it look as if he were drenched in perspiration. Soon, he was back on his feet again, pacing and gesticulating so wildly that he seemed less a man in torment than a flailing drunk. He desperately wanted an explanation for what had transpired, but Phillip had none to offer.

The two men faced each other across a yawning void—each inconsolable and alone.

The figure outside in the snow inched closer to the window, trying to make out what was being said. All that could be heard over the rising and falling of the storm, however, were the sharpest of Charles Kennedy's cries. The banker was taking God to account for allowing murder in His universe and cursing men for their godlessness. No one escaped his anger, not even himself. His breath grew shorter and he clutched at his collar, gasping for air.

Then, as abruptly as he had arrived, he hurtled down the hallway, threw open the Quinns' front door, and *plunged back into the night. A gust of wind swept into the living room, whipped the curtains to a spirited dance, and rattled the picture frames on the wall.*

The figure in the knit cap and the blue topcoat ducked behind the oak tree and pressed up against the bark, so as not to be noticed. Phillip Quinn hovered helplessly on the doorstep, while Charles Kennedy, without realizing it, ran straight toward the killer.

Twenty-Nine

—✦—

The days following Will's death were a blur in Carol's head, and her emotions, seesawing violently between anxiety and remorse, heightened her muddled impression of events. The Fayette police had concluded that in his rush to get to the theater, Will had been driving entirely too fast. The rain had made the roads slick as glass, and the brakes on the Toyota were wet. When it came time for Will to take the turnoff to the theater, the obvious had occurred. He lost control of the vehicle, which spun off the road and slammed into a large maple tree. The tree didn't give. The Toyota did. It folded up like an accordion. Will hadn't been wearing a seat belt, and the consequences were predictable there, too. The force of the crash had propelled him through the windshield.

Everyone in Fayette knew that stretch of the highway was notoriously dangerous. The turnoff to the theater was poorly marked, and the foliage made it even trickier to spot. There were half a dozen accidents every summer—tourists, usually, who were trying to keep an eye on the road, a map, and the scenery all at once. Will was the first fatality in a long time, though.

The county coroner kept the body long enough to determine that the actor had neither been drinking nor ingesting drugs. Then, it was shipped back to California, where a private funeral, along with several ceremonies of public grieving, were scheduled. The media, meanwhile, were having a field day. The network news shows reported Will's death that very night and showed clips from *The Handyman.* Then, the tabloid press and television programs took over, and they were milking the accident for all its morbid drama. "Ghost Calls Williams to His Grave," proclaimed the headline in one supermarket rag, while another ran a fuzzy photograph of a starlet, wearing dark glasses and a kerchief and holding her hand up to block the camera. She was, for those who chose to believe it, anyway, the "Secret Woman in Will Williams's Tormented Life."

The Biz, of course, held the trump card, the interview Will had given to Tammy Tulane at the opening-night party of *Dial M for Murder.* ("Will Williams's last words to his fans," promised the promo. "Tonight exclusively on Channel Six.") Although the interview had run once, *The Biz* aired it in its entirety a second time as part of a half-hour special devoted to "one of America's best-loved stars." Someone at the theater had thought to tape the program for Carol, but she hadn't been able to bring herself to watch it yet.

She felt responsible for Will's death. If only she had driven him to the theater that day, if she hadn't waited until past noon to wake him, and of course, the biggest if of all, if she hadn't slept with him the night before, maybe the scenario would have turned out differently. Religion had never been a strong factor in her life, but in her darker moments, she saw Will's death as an act of retribution, engineered by some glum Old Testament God with blazing eyes and streaming hair.

"Nonsense," she scolded herself. "The brakes failed, the road was slippery, and Will was speeding. That's all." But she couldn't put the guilt out of her mind.

Only a month before, an inner voice reminded her, she had taken the Toyota to the garage for an oil change and a tune-up. Hadn't the brakes been gone over then? And why did the Fayette authorities persist in doing nothing about that impossible turnoff? There were so many questions without answers! She tormented herself with all of them.

She was not alone. Events had devastated Mark Ridley, who was equally convinced that his had been the key role in Will's death. Hadn't he played shamelessly on the actor's loyalties to the White Barn Playhouse to lure him back to the stage? Then, when Will had expressed reservations, Mark had trotted out the old saw that the only real acting is done live, before paying spectators. Now Mark wished he could retract the words.

Will's understudy had taken over the role in *Dial M for Murder* that very evening, but nobody wanted to see him and audiences were dwindling away. The production that was intended to end the season on a triumphantly star-studded note was proving a fiasco. Death was entertaining only as long as it stayed behind the footlights and the corpse got up off the floor and took a curtain call. When real life was mixed into it, most customers, it seemed, preferred refunds.

Sammy did not go unmarked by events, either. He withdrew deep into himself and spent more time than usual in his hiding place in the attic. Repeatedly, Carol would tell him to go outdoors and play, only to realize, an hour later, that he hadn't budged. Next week he'd be returning to school, and she hoped that would draw him out of himself. But whenever she mentioned going to town and buying a new lunch box and a pencil case, he showed no interest. All he wanted to do was huddle under the eaves with his curious treasure trove of odds and ends. This morning, she had issued an ultimatum—fresh air or else—and had stayed at the foot of the stairs until he had actually come down from the third floor and gone outside.

From the kitchen window, she could see him by the stream, which was swollen from the recent rainstorm. Even at a distance, his sadness was apparent. Head hung low, he poked along, aimlessly kicking at sticks and barely paying any heed to Charlie.

The animal was rapidly outgrowing puppyhood, his days as a lapdog now severely numbered. The rain had released a whole range of fresh scents, to which he responded with comical enthusiasm—leaping ahead of his master, falling behind, then scampering ahead, his pincushion nose aquiver. If Charlie couldn't raise Sammy's spirits, Carol found herself thinking, nothing could.

She took one last look out the window just as her son came to a halt. Something had attracted his attention. He stooped down, scooped up an object from the edge of the stream, and put it in his pants pocket. Another stone, no doubt! Carol sighed. Sammy was collecting things again, and unfortunately, she knew what that meant.

Despondent, Carol turned away from the kitchen window. She had promised Mark that she would pack up Will's effects and drop them off at the theater, but so far, she had been unable to make it over the threshold of the Kennedy Suite. Her car was beyond repair, a mass of twisted metal, apparently. While the insurance company had supplied her with a temporary rental, it came with a sheaf of forms that still had to be filled out. There was so much unfinished business to attend to, and Carol had the energy for none of it.

As she started to climb the stairs to the Kennedy Suite, she had a sinking feeling. She stopped and went into the parlor instead, sat down in front of the television, and stared at the blank screen. The tape of *The Biz* lay on the table. She took a deep breath and inserted it in the video cassette player. And there was Will, youthful and loose-limbed, smiling his defiantly carefree grin, as if there were no such things as slippery roads and defective brakes in the world.

An urge to flee the parlor seized her, but she forced herself to stay and watch—the home movies of his childhood, the testimony of his peers, the clips from *The Handyman,* and then ("Will Williams's last words to his fans . . . after this message") the interview at the Christmas Inn. At the sight of Will standing in front of the Christmas tree in the foyer, only ten feet away from where she was sitting, her tears began to flow, blurring the image on the screen. Will's voice faded in and out, as if she were listening to it over a shortwave set.

". . . Sam Love likes everybody, and Tony Wendice, well, he's out to plot the murder of his wife . . . everybody has wanted to kill someone at some time or other in their lives. . . . Why, did you know someone was killed in this very house? . . ."

She tried to control herself.

Will was reaching over now and pulling her playfully into the picture. "There was a murder here seventy years ago," she heard him saying once again. "It was never solved. But not to worry, Tammy. Carol and I think we have finally figured it out, haven't we, Carol? It's quite a story. Why, I may do a movie-of-the-week about it."

She experienced a sudden twinge in her chest that made her sit upright. A terrible thought had just occurred to her, come and gone in a flash, leaving her short of breath and hot all over. She clicked off the television and leaned her head on the back of the couch, waiting for the uncomfortable sensation to recede. What she had thought was crazy, irrational, not worth consideration. It was only an opening-night interview, a spur-of-the-moment remark. Anybody who knew Will knew that.

Then, an image of Walker sprang into her mind. He was standing in the kitchen, saying . . . what? "Sure caused a lot of talk in town." Almost snarling it. The interview had disturbed people. Who, she wondered, was doing all this talking in town? And did they limit their unhappiness to talking?

No, the idea was mad. There was no point pursuing it to its conclusion—a not very logical conclusion at that.

Still, she couldn't shake the suspicion. What if someone had taken Will seriously? Had really believed him when he said they'd solved the murder and were going to make a movie-of-the-week about it? Would they go so far as to kill him? Ridiculous! The murder was ancient history by now.

Carol stood up, swallowed a deep breath of air, and tried to clear her head. It was time to stop all this macabre fantasizing and get some work done. She would pack up Will's clothes and personal effects and call Mark Ridley to come get them. That's what she would do. But like a dark tide, the troubling thoughts returned almost immediately.

It was possible, after all, that the brakes on the Toyota had been tampered with. The police said they had checked out the car, or what was left of it, and concluded it was mechanical failure. But wasn't that the hitch? The Toyota had crumpled like aluminum foil. It was going to cost more to repair than it was worth. Before towing the vehicle away, the police had informed her that she was better off selling it for junk. If they were right about the extent of the damage, how could they tell for sure about the brakes? Carol had the impression that they simply wanted the matter over and done with.

Unlike the relentless detectives on television and in the movies who never gave up, the Fayette police seemed content to put in their forty hours a week with a minimum of fuss and paperwork. Unless someone pushed them to search harder, the simple explanation sufficed. The simpler, the better. And no one was pushing them. Mayor Quinn's antipathy for anyone connected with the theater was no secret. He probably considered Will's death just deserts for going over to the side of the enemy.

Carol had certainly never had any trouble with her brakes in the rain. All at once, she felt the sharp twinge in her chest again. *Her* brakes! Of course. They were her brakes! No one could have known that Will was going to use the Toyota that afternoon. It was her they were after, not Will. Someone wanted her to drive off the road. But why?

In the bottom drawer of the bureau in her bedroom, from underneath the linens where she had tucked it away, she retrieved the anonymous letter that had arrived in the mail. She unfolded it and scanned it quickly: "This is not a town that needs another whore . . . You do not belong here . . . Go back where you came from." Sergeant Burke had advised her to pay it no attention. It was the work of a crank, he'd said. Obviously, he had drastically underestimated the situation. The letter had been written in earnest. And it was because she hadn't taken it seriously that her Toyota was in a junkyard somewhere and Will was in a coffin.

Picking up the phone, she punched the buttons, aware of the discordant tune her dialing produced. It took forever for someone to answer. Finally, a crisp voice said, "White Barn Playhouse, Pennsylvania's professional summer theater. How may I help you?"

"Mark Ridley, please."

"I'm afraid Mr. Ridley is not in his office at the moment. Would you like to leave a message?"

It was some fool apprentice, overarticulating and trying to sound grown-up.

"This is Carol Roblins calling. I have an emergency. Do you know where I can locate him?"

"An emergency? Gosh! Hold on, ma'am. Lemme see if he's in the theater."

Carol tapped her foot nervously. A few minutes later, Mark's voice came on the line.

"Oh, thank God, you're there. It's Carol. Can you and Harry come over here quickly? I'm scared, Mark. I think Will was murdered."

"Murder," shrieked Harry Watkins. "You've got to be kidding."

"I'm serious," Carol insisted.

Mark sat quietly on the arm of the wingback chair, confused and depressed. Seeing Will's clothes in the closet and his toiletries in the bathroom was more of a shock than he had anticipated. It was as if Will had stepped out of the Kennedy Suite briefly and was going to return at any moment. There was even a dog-eared copy of *Dial M for Murder* lying open on the bedside table. Had the actor been brushing up on his lines just before he left for the theater that afternoon? He had always been so fearful of going up in the middle of a scene.

Will's belongings, undisturbed since the day of his death, unleashed such a flood of memories in Mark's head that he was finding it difficult to concentrate on what Carol was saying. She had calmed down considerably since their arrival. The color had come back to her face and her initial panic had passed, leaving in its place a vaguer, although no less real, apprehension.

"If you really think Will was murdered," Harry said, "why don't you just go to the police?"

"I don't want to do that until I've figured out who the killer is."

"Come on, Carol. Isn't that their job?" Harry took several of Will's shirts out of the closet and folded them up. An empty suitcase sat on the luggage rack at the end of the bed. "If there's been a crime, you go to the police. That's generally the way it works."

"It's more complicated than that. Besides, I'm not sure they'd believe me." Mark and Harry waited for her to continue. "Can you promise me that whatever we say will be in complete confidence?"

"Promise," replied Mark.

"I really do think Will was murdered. But it was by mistake. You see, I'm the one the killer is really after."

Harry let a shirt drop on the floor. "Look, Carol. All of us are upset. Everybody feels terrible about what happened. I mean, Mark is absolutely convinced he's the cause of Will's death. And now you're horning in on the act. Aren't we losing sight of the fact that Will is dead? Gone. Probably lying right now in a mortuary somewhere in L.A. until they deposit him in the cold, cold ground, as it is commonly referred to . . . Jeez, let's all try to be a little less self-centered." He retrieved the shirt and tossed it into the suitcase with a huff of indignation.

"Your turn to calm down, Harry," Mark said, outwardly ignoring the outburst, but privately granting Harry his point. He turned to Carol. "Go on."

"I know it sounds crazy, but I'm not just being dramatic." She reached into her pocket and handed Mark the anonymous letter she had been keeping in her bottom bureau drawer. "Read this."

Mark looked it over and let out a low whistle.

"Did you show this to the police?"

"Yes. They weren't interested. They told me to get back in touch if I ever received another one." She took the note and passed it to Harry.

"It's written with pen and ink, you know," he observed. "Well, it could be a fountain pen. What I'm saying is, it's not your usual Bic."

"We could always go on a house-to-house search for

inkwells," Mark commented, not without a trace of sarcasm.

"I'm just trying to help here," Harry said, bristling. He shifted his attention to Carol. "Who do you think sent it?"

She gave him a blank stare. "I don't know for sure. I've got a strong suspicion that it was Paul Clemson. He was a boarder for years in this very suite, before it was renovated. After Blake and I bought the mansion, we let him know he was going to have to move out eventually, but when the time came, he reacted pretty badly. He scrawled threats all over the walls. He shouted at me. Every now and then, I see him parked by the edge of the road, just staring angrily at the mansion."

Harry piped up, "A real gent, in short."

"The thing is, he's an auto mechanic. He works at Broadbent's Automotive Center. So he would know all about car brakes and how to tamper with them."

"Tamper?" said Mark, arching his eyebrows skeptically. "I thought the police already checked out the car and found nothing wrong."

"As much as they check out anything around here," Carol said. "They had no reason to believe the brakes had been fooled with. The car was totaled. Do you think they went over the wreckage with a magnifying glass?"

"Probably not," agreed Mark. "So you think this Clemson guy wanted to kill you just because you evicted him from the mansion?" He threw Harry a dubious look. "Isn't that stretching things a little?"

"I suppose. But there's something else. You saw the interview on *The Biz,* didn't you?"

"With the ever-fabulous Tammy Tulane?" Harry tucked another load of Will's shirts into the suitcase. "Puleeze! I'd rather not think how that woman got her job!"

"Will shouldn't have said what he did," Carol explained. "Tammy asked him how he prepared for the part in the play, and he started rambling on about the murder that happened here in the Kennedy suite and how, after all these years, he and I had finally solved it."

"Well, have you?" Mark asked.

"Of course not. But someone could have believed him.

Someone who really does know what happened back then and wants it kept a secret."

"Like this Paul Clemson, for example." Harry's features lit up briefly, then dimmed. "Wait a minute. I'm not sure I'm following you. You evict this auto mechanic, who turns around and messes with your car, because he believes you know something about a murder that took place decades ago in the rooms he used to rent. Have I got it straight?"

"If you put it that way, I guess it does sound pretty far-fetched, doesn't it?" she said.

Reluctantly, Mark sided with Harry. "Yeah, it does, Carol. We're all overwrought. Nobody's thinking clearly. It's very hard to accept that Will's death was senseless. We all want reasons for why it happened. Let's face it, there were none. Or if there were, they were stupid reasons. A car had mechanical failure. Or the driver wasn't paying attention, which Will probably wasn't. You know what a dreamer he could be. So what we do is make up explanations, invent some dark plot, some conspiracy, because that is somehow preferable to the senselessness.

"This way, somebody is to blame, even if we don't know who that somebody is. And life isn't just this absurd mess. There's a pattern to it, assuming we're smart enough to figure it out. We desperately want Will to be a victim by design, not by sheer happenstance. It serves our sense of justice if some kind of skulduggery is involved. Well, much as I'd like to think you're on to something, Carol, this is life, not theater. The sloppiness doesn't get tidied up in the end. It stays sloppy. Sometimes there is no culprit, just rotten luck."

Mark's voice cracked. "Okay. End of lecture. Class dismissed," he tried to joke. "What can I say? We deal with grief differently. Carol invents plots. I pontificate."

Carol was unconsciously cradling one of Will's cashmere sweaters that she had taken out of a drawer during Mark's tirade. With a sense of resignation, she laid the garment in the suitcase on top of the shirts. Perhaps it was time to call an end to this whole sorry saga of the Christmas Inn. Mark had put his finger on the truth. She had lost her head for a handsome television actor from Hollywood, just as she had allowed herself to get swept away with romantic notions of the mansion. Now, she was concocting an extravagant tale about Clem and the Toyota, to make herself feel better. It was nothing she hadn't done already with the Kennedys themselves.

Who were they, after all? Nothing but a provincial banker with too much money and his self-centered wife, who probably devoted most of her days to her clothes and her jewels.

Harry broke the heavy silence that had descended over the room like a shroud. "Shall we finish up the packing and put all this behind us?"

Carol didn't answer right off. She had left one significant detail out of her account. She wanted to share it with Mark and Harry, but she also needed to believe that they would keep it to themselves. When you were young, Sammy's age, it was so much easier. You made your best friends cross their hearts and hope to die if ever they revealed your secret. What did adults say to one another? "I'd appreciate it if this remained between us." "I'm sure I don't have to explain the necessity for confidentiality here."

"Cross your heart" was better.

Every friendship, new or old, hinged on trust. There came a moment when you had to risk it. Either you ended up with a truer friend as a result, or else your secret got out and all you had for your pains was another passing acquaintance. Carol weighed the alternatives.

Then she said, "Can I show you guys one other thing before we finish up here?" She disappeared down the stairs. When she returned several minutes later, she held an object in the cup of her hand. With care, she placed it in the middle of the quilted bedspread and then stepped back. The diamonds and sapphires caught the light.

"This belonged to Veronica Kennedy," she announced. "It's her necklace. The one she was murdered for. The one the robber took on Christmas Eve. Except that it never left the mansion."

Harry exhaled loudly. "My dear! Perhaps you had better begin at the beginning."

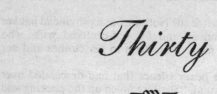

Thirty

So what do we really know?" Harry asked as they regrouped around the kitchen table. "Charles and Veronica Kennedy were married for a year and a half. He was loaded. She was what? Social. Flirtatious. Sexy. They were gloriously happy together."

"Where do you get all that?" Mark questioned.

"From the photograph in the Kennedy Suite. The one that put old Mrs. McPherson in such a swivet. They look sexy to me. Carrying on at the beach like a pair of kids."

"Oh, I think they were a happy couple," agreed Carol. "He built this place for her. The architect's plans are almost like a love letter. He wanted their initials everywhere. Most of those details were destroyed over the years."

"It's all so transitory," Mark observed gloomily. "I swear we're on this earth for ten seconds. Eleven, if we're lucky. Then, it's over."

"And for eight of those seconds," Harry added, "most of us are pissed off or depressed. Puleeze, Mark. Spare us the philosophy." He raised a bottle of beer to his lips and loudly gulped down half its contents. "Sorry, but you know how talk of murder always dries me out."

Irreverence was Harry's coping mechanism. It wasn't that

he cared less deeply about Will's death than the others, but he couldn't see that a sad face and dour platitudes helped in the long run. And it struck him that Carol's suspicions, while intriguing, weren't buttressed by too many hard facts. Harry's levity was not meant to be disrespectful of the dead, but merely of the living, who, as a rule, took themselves too seriously for his taste.

He put the bottle down. "Veronica Kennedy was murdered on Christmas Eve, right?"

Carol recapped the familiar story. "The Kennedys weren't ones to hide their wealth. It must have been widely known in Fayette that she would be wearing her finest jewelry that night. Anyway, the necklace vanished. So did the robber. And Charles Kennedy went berserk when he discovered his wife's body. I never would have questioned any of it if I hadn't found the necklace in a heating duct."

"How the hell did it end up in a duct?" Harry asked, taking a closer look at the jewelry, which Carol had laid out before her on the kitchen table.

"Good question," said Carol. "Someone must have put it there. Don't ask me why. But it does suggest that the robbery wasn't a robbery at all."

"And that Veronica Kennedy was killed for a different reason altogether," Mark concluded.

Carol noted with satisfaction that their skepticism was rapidly diminishing.

"Well, that tells me who the killer is, right there," announced Harry. "Charles Kennedy. Nine times out of ten, it's the husband. Rather than give himself up, he committed suicide. Motive? The green-eyed monster. Jealousy."

"It seems unlikely," Carol said. "The maid was with him when he discovered the body. She told people he was beside himself, sobbing with grief."

"Crocodile tears. He could have been acting." Harry pushed his point. "Look how the husband in *Dial M for Murder* behaves." As soon as the words left his mouth, he regretted them. The three friends had temporarily succeeded in putting Will out of their minds, and mention of the mystery play brought him roaring right back, an invisible fourth party to their deliberations. Carol gazed distractedly out the screen door at where the Toyota had been parked.

"He was an awfully good actor, then," she mumbled. For an instant, Mark wondered if she wasn't referring to Will.

Harry took another slug of beer and proposed a different scenario. "Well, how about this? The maid was having a secret love affair with Veronica Kennedy."

Mark rolled his eyes. "Be serious."

"It's conceivable. You never know. Look at Eleanor Roosevelt and that newspaper woman, for example. What was her name? . . . Hicks. Leanore Hicks . . . Leona . . . Or was it Lila? . . . Okay, forget it."

"I learned something else about that night, after I took out an ad in the *Register*," Carol said, coming back to the discussion. "Before Charles Kennedy committed suicide, he went to the house of his best friend. In his crazed state, he didn't know where else to turn for help. Sue Whiley told me. At any rate, that's what everyone believed at the time. It could just be a story that was circulated after the fact. Everyone pays such lip service to friendship around here."

She paused. "The best friend was Mayor Quinn's grandfather. He and Kennedy were banking partners. Between them, they controlled most of the town."

Mark's jaw dropped.

Harry squealed with surprise. "Is my hearing failing? Testing, one, two, three. Testing, one, two, three. Do you mean to tell us that the Mayor for Life is involved in this sordid affair?"

"No, not Mayor Quinn. His grandfather Phillip Quinn. And I hate to disappoint you, Harry. He's been dead for years."

"Well, I wouldn't put anything past a member of the Quinn family, dead or alive." Harry shuddered. "The hypocrites. Look how the mayor acted at your open house—wishing you luck in front of everybody, then practically threatening to shut you down when he got you alone. What was that about, I ask you."

"Politics, no doubt," speculated Mark. "He was upset. I don't think he expected to run into Ned Foster."

"Politics or old ghosts," quipped Harry. The remark hung tantalizingly in the air. Unlike most of Harry's quips, it seemed to demand a response.

"Funny you should mention that," Carol said. "The mayor visited me several months ago. He claimed it was a courtesy call. He was just passing by and said he liked meeting his constituents in their homes. I assumed he was interested in how the renovation was shaping up—"

"Wait." Mark's mind had begun to click away. He held up his hand. "What if Phillip Quinn and Charles Kennedy were not the best of friends? Wouldn't that put a whole different slant on things? The Quinns are a big deal in Fayette, but you never hear anything about the Kennedys. Until Carol decided to restore this place, the name never came up. Everyone's forgotten them."

"Or maybe everyone just agreed to forget them," Carol added. "Collective amnesia. It comes in handy."

"Well, let's say that Quinn and Kennedy did have a severe falling-out for some reason or other," Mark continued, jiggling the loose change in his pocket, as he did when rehearsals were going well. "That's the sort of thing that splits small towns down the middle. Word starts to get around. People have to choose sides, declare their loyalties. No one can be neutral. Then, Veronica Kennedy is killed and her husband dies soon after. Everybody's shocked. But in some perverse way, they're grateful, too. They don't have to take sides, after all. There's only one side left to take. The Quinns'."

"The police make their routine inquiries, just as they did about the Toyota. But the trail of the robber leads nowhere because there is no robber. Furthermore, no one's clamoring for justice. The official explanation is satisfactory enough. Life goes on and the whole ugly story fades away, a distant memory that grows more distant every year."

"Which would explain why the mansion is allowed to fall into disrepair," Carol said. "Pieces are sold off. The rooms are switched all around. The historical society never makes the slightest attempt to save it. Blake and I pick it up for a song."

"And believe you're doing the town a huge favor by

restoring it," Mark said. "Wrong! All you're doing is calling attention to the past. You actually name one wing the Kennedy Suite and boast that it looks just as it did in 1927. Then, you invite the community to come and see. Will's interview with Tammy Tulane would be the final straw, in that respect. The mansion actually winds up on TV."

Mark considered the implications. "In Fayette, I think you're supposed to let sleeping dogs lie. You seem to have awakened one, Carol."

Harry rattled his beer bottle impatiently on the counter. "Well, I'm glad you two know what you're talking about. Will someone kindly let me in on the big secret. Who did it?"

Carol and Mark looked at one another and shrugged.

"Carol's intuition might be right, though," Mark said. "There could be a connection between Will's death and this old house."

What he didn't add was that he feared Carol and Sammy were in danger. He didn't have to. The faint wrinkling of Carol's forehead told him that she feared it, too.

"I know one thing I'd do in your place," Harry said. "I'd put that necklace in a safety-deposit box tomorrow morning. You don't leave jewels like that lying around the house, unless you live in Versailles. And even there, they had to watch out for the servants." He picked up the necklace and draped it casually around his neck. "Or I could keep an eye on it for you. What do you think? Is it too much for the Council on Aging? Maybe with some tasteful earrings?"

He sucked in his cheeks, lowered his eyelids, and began to sing, "A kiss on the cheek may be quite continental, but diamonds are a girl's best friend . . ."

Mark snatched the necklace back and put it in Carol's hand. "Harry's right. If word ever got out . . ."

"How could it?" Carol asked. "You guys are the only ones I've told about the necklace. Anyway, it belongs here in the mansion."

"The way Harry shoots off his mouth," Mark said, "the safety-deposit box isn't a half-bad idea, Carol."

Harry protested, "I am the soul of discretion." A look of

disbelief from Mark prompted him to amend the statement. "When I have to be."

The sharp rapping noise startled them all. Walker stood on the other side of the screen door, waiting for an invitation to enter. Carol slipped the necklace into her pocket.

"I heard voices," he said, clearing his throat. "I didn't want to burst in."

Carol got up from the table. "You're not interrupting anything. You've met Mark Ridley and Harry Watkins." They all exchanged nods. Walker seemed nervous in their company.

"I just dropped by for my toolbox. It's upstairs. I'll run up and get it." He turned to go.

"Could I ask you something first, Walker?"

"Sure."

"We were just discussing Will and the TV show. The other morning, when you came in, you said the program caused a lot of talk in town. I didn't think anything of it at the time. After what's happened, though, the accident and all, I was curious. What did you mean by that?"

"Is that what I said?" Walker arched his eyebrows.

"Yes. You said a lot of people were upset."

Mark observed the workman closely, trying to decide whether the boyish ingenuousness was real or a mask.

"I feel like I'm on the witness stand here," Walker joked lamely.

No one rushed to fill in the uncomfortable silence that followed. Finally, Walker volunteered, "I, um, guess Joey said something like, 'Did you see Carol on TV with that famous actor?' He was pretty surprised. Well, hell, so was I. There you were on the television screen, and this big-shot Hollywood guy is yapping on and on about a murder that nobody's thought about in years. Why wouldn't people be talking afterwards? I know Joey was, that's all. That's what I meant. Any more questions?"

Carol shook her head.

"I'll get my tools, then."

Mark remained silent until the workman was out of hearing, then he whispered, "I don't believe him. He knows more than he's telling."

"What makes you say that?" said Harry, who had been thinking, much to the contrary, that Walker was a fairly hunky-looking guy and certainly entitled to the benefit of any doubt.

"Gut instinct. A long familiarity with bad acting. A feeling I get every once in a while."

Carol had to admit that her brain was as muddled as Mark's.

"What about the you-know-what?" Harry put a hand up to his throat to indicate he meant the necklace. "Does he have any idea that . . ."

They heard workboots on the stairs. Carol shook her head and silenced him with a quick "No."

"I'll be on my way, then," Walker said to no one specific as he crossed the kitchen. At the door, he stopped and shifted his toolbox from one hand to the other. "Where's Sammy?"

"In the woods."

He smiled. "Tell my old pal that I said hello."

Carol tried to return the smile, but managed only a slight upturning of her mouth—more an involuntary twitch than a smile. She was suddenly very tired. The afternoon had exhausted her. It occurred to her that the Kennedy mansion was booby-trapped from the outset. Stupidly, she had marched right in with her paintbrushes flying, and her swatches of fabric and her Christmas decorations, thinking she was going to transform it into the pride of Fayette. In the end, it was still a booby trap.

She watched Walker's truck grow smaller, then leaned back against the doorframe. "So where do we go from here?" she asked in a toneless voice.

At a loss for ideas, Harry chipped away at the label on the beer bottle with his fingernail.

"How about Broadbent's Automotive Center, for starters," suggested Mark.

"Let me put the necklace away first." Carol was gone for fifteen minutes.

He found it by a bend in the stream, where the rushing water had caused a portion of the embankment to cave in.

Usually, by midsummer, the stream had dried up to little more than a lazy trickle. But the recent rainfall had swollen the waters, which cascaded over the rocks, throwing up spray and turning quiet pools into eddies. Sammy knew that big storms often yielded surprising treasures, so he kept his eyes riveted on the ground, seeing what he could see.

A hooklike shape, protruding from the glistening stones and tangled roots, was all that was visible. When he bent over to pick it up, he realized it was part of a larger object, buried in the ground. He pulled at the hook. There was no give. So he worked the hook back and forth with both hands, trying to free the strange object from the grip of the earth.

Slowly, it came loose.

He giggled with pleasure at the thought of all he could do with it. He could use it as a cane, for instance. Maybe catch fish with it. Now when his wooden glider snagged in the branches of a tree, he could reach up with the hook and gently pull the model airplane down. Not have to throw stones or climb the tree.

It was definitely an important addition to his collection. He dipped it in the water and swirled it around to wash off the dirt. Then, he swung it over his head several times, so it would dry.

Charlie emerged from a thicket, panting excitedly, and rubbed up against the leg of his master. Sammy showed him the object and the dog sniffed it. "So what do you think of that, Charlie?" the boy said, remembering someone he used to know.

Over the babble of the stream, he heard a familiar voice calling. His mother's.

"Saaammmmy! I've got to go out. Come on back to the house. Sammy, do you hear me?"

He yelled back that he did.

"I won't be gone long," the voice echoed off the rocks. "There's a snack on the table. Are you coming?"

"In a minute."

"No. Now, Sammy."

"Okay." He patted his dog on the head. "Come on, Charlie. Going home."

Trudging back through the woods, he thought about how his mother would scold him and tell him that he couldn't bring any more stuff inside. He decided he wouldn't show her his latest discovery. Wasn't hers, anyway. Was his. He would store it away, out of sight, where it would be safe. Unseen.

The house was empty. He scrambled up the stairs to the third floor, dragging the object behind him. It made a clanking sound on the steps. He pushed open the door to his hideaway and crawled under the eaves, relieved that no one had disturbed his collection. For a moment, he just sat and stared at the various pieces—the license plate, the giraffe stick, the smooth gray stones flecked with gold and lined up neatly in a row.

They were nice, but the new object with the hook on the end was nicer. Already, it was his favorite. It deserved a special spot, apart from all the other things. Sammy crawled to the north end of the attic where a fieldstone chimney pushed up through the gabled roof. He liked that corner. Yes, that's where it belonged.

Up against the rough, gray stones, he carefully leaned the poker that had killed Veronica Kennedy.

Thirty-One

~~~

If they had been asked why they looked forward to the annual Christmas party, most of the employees of the Fayette Guaranty and Trust would probably have cited the excellence of the homemade eggnog as their reason. But such an answer would have been less than candid. Everyone knew that the year-end bonuses were the lure.

Charles Kennedy made a point of distributing them personally, while doing everything possible to disguise the nature of the gesture. For one who dealt in movements of currency every day of his working life, he showed a curious delicacy, when it came to handling the actual bills themselves. During the festivities, he'd take each employee aside, solicit advice on how the bank could improve its operations, and extend his congratulations on the progress that had already been achieved. Small talk about the weather or the deplorable condition of the back roads invariably came next, so that business would not seem to be his unique preoccupation. Only then did he reach into his inside jacket pocket for the brown envelope, stuffed with crisp banknotes, which he passed to the grateful employee with a firm handshake and sincere wishes for a happy New Year.

257

He liked to think of the ritual as a conversation between friends and was uncomfortable with the thank-yous that his generosity provoked. "Yes, yes. Think nothing of it," he'd say, cutting them short. "Now, have you sampled the eggnog yet?" In the spirit of egalitarianism that marked the event, Phillip Quinn manned the punch bowl. So Charles would call out jocularly, "How are we holding up, Phillip? Here's another customer for you. We don't want anybody to go thirsty tonight."

Now that Veronica Kennedy presided over the affair, it had acquired a certain social cachet, as well. Not quite on a par with the elegant Christmas Eve dinner that the Kennedys threw for their intimate friends. Employees were employees. Still, the Fayette Weekly Register would make sure to take note of her attire, while the conviviality of the event, compared to that of past years, would be read as an unofficial gauge of the town's prosperity. Since 1928 had been particularly profitable for the bank, rumors had it that "the eggnog" would be better than ever this year.

The party was traditionally held on the Friday before Christmas. The bank closed promptly at three, and clerks and tellers hastened home to change. The women brought out their fanciest outfits. The men put on their Sunday suits and the bright ties that were considered inappropriate during the workweek. Children were scrubbed and polished until they shone like Christmas ornaments. When they all arrived back at the bank at six, it was to discover that the punch bowl and a buffet had been set up by the massive vault, and a three-piece orchestra, consisting of an upright piano, a bass, and a clarinet, was playing popular tunes under one of the brass chandeliers that hung from intricate medallions in the richly patterned ceiling.

Outside, Polly Quinn maneuvered the Packard into a tight parking space, and her two children, eager to get to the party, tumbled out of the car in a jostle of elbows and knees. Main Street had a celebratory air. Small fir trees had been attached to every street lamp, and strands of colored lights crisscrossed the thoroughfare at regular intervals. Polly came around to the sidewalk and gave her *offspring a last-minute inspection. The bow in her daughter's hair, coffee-colored like her mother's, required straightening, and the collar button on her son's shirt had popped open. As she refastened it, she noted that he was developing a prominent Adam's apple and the down on his upper lip had darkened considerably, announcing the onslaught of puberty.*

Reassured that they both looked presentable, she let them race ahead to the bank. Her own step was less enthusiastic. Not yet ready to join the merriment, she hung back, trying to fashion a less than somber demeanor. A crowd of passersby was watching the party through the tall windows on either side of the double door. It wasn't every day they saw people dancing in a bank, which, given the transactions that usually transpired there, was held in the same grave esteem as the Congregational Church next door.

Yet, there were Veronica Kennedy and her husband, waltzing around the marble floor, spinning past the tellers' cages, weaving spiritedly in and around other couples less daring than they. When Charles lowered his wife into a dip, the woman's silvery laughter rose over the music. Several employees broke into applause, and Veronica playfully acknowledged their tribute with a mock curtsy and kissed Charles on the cheek.

Polly pulled back, inadvertently bumping up against a workman standing behind her.

"Hey, lady, careful."

She mumbled an apology and thrust her hands into the pockets of her woolen coat. It was growing chilly, but she was loath to join the party. She could see her children at the buffet table and Phillip coming over to them, a quizzical expression on his face. Her son gestured toward the entrance, and she assumed, from the way Phillip looked up, that he expected to see her walking through the door any minute. She couldn't postpone her arrival much longer without causing comment. Perhaps she could plead a sudden illness and return home. Or claim that she had twisted her ankle on the sidewalk. It seemed preferable to subjecting herself to the gaiety inside the bank.

"Polly? What's wrong? Aren't you coming in?" Phillip stood at the door, beckoning to her. "Everybody's expecting you."

Reluctantly, she detached herself from the crowd of onlookers.

"Just getting a little fresh air," she murmured by way of an excuse as she went to him.

In the entrance area, marked off from the main floor by a low railing, a youthful clerk took her coat and checkered scarf and politely inquired how she was. "Well enough, thank you," she answered distractedly. Her attention was fixed on Charles and Veronica Kennedy, who had seen her coming in and were headed over to greet her.

"Merry Christmas, Polly," said Charles, catching her up in a warm hug.

"Merry Christmas, Charlie," she replied flatly.

The first thought that occurred to Veronica was that Polly was ill. Her coloring was ashen and her eyes lacked animation.

"Are you feeling all right?" she questioned solicitously.

"Of course I am. Why shouldn't I?" There was the slightest edge to Polly's voice, but with the chatter all around them, Veronica failed to detect it.

"Well, you don't look yourself, that's all. I know the grippe has been going all over town. Mrs. Knight was just saying so a minute ago. As long as you're well, that's the main thing." Veronica leaned forward and gave her a gentle peck on the cheek. "Merry Christmas, dear."

"Hypocrite!" Polly hissed in her ear.

Veronica drew back in surprise, wondering if she hadn't misunderstood. A closer inspection of Polly's face assured her that she hadn't. The slight had been intentional. Polly's features were hard and fixed, except for a nervous twitching of the mouth and a faint flaring of the nostrils. Veronica glanced quickly at Charles and Phillip and realized that they had heard nothing.

Barely hesitating, she let out a ripple of laughter, clasped Polly's hands warmly in hers, and exclaimed, "You are such a dear, Polly. What a lovely thing to say. But you really must stop flattering me or I'll get a swelled head. Won't I, Charles? Now come join the fun with the rest of us." Then with perfect aplomb, she bent forward and kissed the woman on the cheek a second time.

Unnerved, Polly fumbled for a response. She should have waited for some other occasion to speak her feelings, but the insult had just slipped out. She was angry with herself for letting it happen. Her instinct to return home had been the right one; there was nothing to be gained tonight. Now for the rest of the evening she would have to endure the humiliation of watching Veronica revel in her role as gracious hostess.

The orchestra struck up "Has Anybody Seen My Gal?" and Veronica squealed delightedly. "Oh, my favorite song. You don't mind lending me your husband, do you, Polly? Phillip promised me a dance." With a triumphant smile, she pulled him out into the center of the floor.

Anyone witnessing the brief encounter between the two women would assume it was a routine exchange of compliments and would pay it no mind. It was only natural for people to curry Veronica Kennedy's favor. She was the banker's wife and certain hierarchies had to be respected, after all. She was also a splendid-looking woman, quite worthy of flattery in her own right. Mrs. Quinn had always appeared older and dowdier in her company. Tonight, more than ever. Her face was drawn and her conversation lackluster. The whispers soon started up that the poor thing was under the weather, while elderly Mrs. Knight couldn't help commenting loudly that a most becoming flush colored the cheeks of Veronica Kennedy.

In reality, much of Veronica's fascination lay in the way she countered other people's moods, used them for contrast. If they were reverent, she was apt to be impudent. Their giddiness tended to bring out her pensiveness. Something was always slightly different about her. Her few detractors said that it was all a calculated bid for attention. Kinder souls maintained that it was simply the actress in her, instinctively setting herself apart, as she had done ever since childhood. Whatever the explanation, the phenomenon manifested itself once again. The more withdrawn Polly appeared, the more expansive Veronica became, almost as if the younger woman were sapping the older woman's vitality.

An oblivious Charles Kennedy clasped his hands behind his back and surveyed the goings-on with satisfaction. The year had been embarrassingly prosperous, and this, he felt, was the celebratory conclusion it merited.

"Are you keeping an eye on that punch bowl?" he asked his partner, who assured him that he was.

"Because we don't want to run out of eggnog before the night is over."

Phillip Quinn agreed that, no, they certainly didn't. That would be a tragedy to reckon with! Out of the corner of his eye, he searched the bank for his wife.

Thirty-Two

—m—

Mark Ridley guided the Buick Regal through the center of Fayette, then headed it south on the old Emmitsburg road, where Broadbent's Automotive Center was located. Although he hadn't yet decided how he was going to approach Paul Clemson, he prided himself on his ability to read most people. As a director, he knew they expressed themselves in a variety of ways, words being only the most obvious and not always the most revelatory.

A psychiatrist once told him that you can learn everything you need to know about a person in the first three hours, if you're observant enough. Temperament, personality, neuroses—it's all there to see. The trouble is, the psychiatrist added, we don't just observe. After a few minutes, we start talking instead of listening, inject ourselves into the relationship, and end up projecting all our own wants and fears onto the person. Mark had always made a special effort to listen.

"So what are you going to say to him?" Harry piped up from the backseat. " 'I hear you're quite the mechanic. Fix any brakes lately?' "

"That ought to get a conversation going," cracked Carol, who was feeling safer now that she had a couple of allies.

263

"I think we should come right out and tell him we're good friends of Carol's," Mark said. "We've heard that he's been pretty unpleasant with her lately, and what does he have to say for himself."

"Pretty unpleasant?" Harry howled.

"Yes. If he's the underhanded bully we think he is, he'll probably yelp like a dog and claim he doesn't have the slightest idea of what we're talking about."

"The 'lady doth protest too much' theory, eh?" noted Harry.

"We may learn something, we may not. Either way, he's been put on notice that we're wise to him and he'd do well to leave Carol alone in the future."

"I hope you're right," she said. "Walker tried talking tough and a lot of good it did."

"Oh, I don't intend to talk tough. I'll be civil about it," Mark said. "Firm, but civil."

From the backseat echoed a fluttery voice, "My hero!"

Broadbent's Automotive Center was Fayette's greatest eyesore. The garage itself, a run-down hangar with corrugated-tin siding, was bad enough, but it was surrounded by several acres of cars in various states of dilapidation. Someone had made an effort to enliven the front of the building by covering it with used license plates, but the effort—or the license plates—had given out after several rows. From a distance, the incongruous effect was similar to that of a brightly colored ribbon on a banged-up cardboard package. The town council had pressured the owner, Jake Broadbent, into erecting a ten-foot fence along the road, which masked some, although hardly all, of the ugliness from view. Everybody knew what environmental horrors lurked behind the fence, nonetheless, and motorists usually trained their eyes straight ahead when they drove by.

Mark gave a sharp spin to the wheel and turned into a dirt parking lot, rippled like a washboard. The yard was bleak and so still it almost seemed abandoned. Most of the cars had been stripped of their chrome and cannibalized for any serviceable parts and were corroding in a sea of goldenrod and milkweed. The Texaco gas pump by the garage door hadn't been functional for years, the numbers in its window serving only as a quaint reminder that gas had once sold for $.52 a gallon and that someone had bought a tank's worth for $6.24. As a cloud passed before the sun, a shadowy veil swept across the parking lot.

"Okay, guys," Mark said, jumping out of the car, "onward!"

Harry looked around at the desolation and burst out singing. "As you walk through a storm, keep your head up high . . ."

"What are you doing?" Mark asked him curtly.

"The big number from the last act of *Carousel.* Remember? Billy Bigelow has died and the townspeople—"

"I know what it's from!" Mark cut him off.

"Well, *excusez-moi.*"

The three of them pushed through a creaky door with flaking decals on the window and entered a small office that smelled of stale cigarette smoke. Behind a chest-high, vinyl-topped counter, two metal desks were littered with manuals and papers. A row of clipboards hung from the wall next to a time clock, and a coffeemaker sat on the far end of the counter. The red light was on, indicating that someone was around, although judging from the black, viscous sludge in the pot, the coffee had been brewing for hours.

"Hellooo," Mark sang out.

Nobody answered. He tried again. "Anybody here?" This time, the sharp whine of a pneumatic wrench came back. Taking the door on the other side of the counter, they found themselves in the garage itself, a large, high room divided into six stalls. Puddles of oil spotted the floor. A wobbly tower of tires, patched and balding, rose nearly to the ceiling. Carol immediately understood why Clem dressed the way he did. You could get filthy just looking at the place. It took a moment for their eyes to adjust to the gloom.

In the first stall, a short, stocky man had his head under the hood of a beat-up Chevy. At the sound of their footsteps, he stood up and wiped his brow with the back of his hand, leaving a smudge. He had a grape-colored birthmark on his cheek and a burned-out cigarette butt clung to the corner of his mouth. Mark started to say something to him, but the man turned away, indifferent, and went back to his work.

"That's not Clem," Carol whispered. Two stalls away, there was another piercing whine from the pneumatic wrench. "That must be him over there."

At first, they could only see him from the waist down. His upper torso was hidden by the body of a Ford Mustang, perched precariously on a hydraulic lift, but Carol knew the workboots. How many times had they tramped across her kitchen, up and down the back stairs, tracking grime into the mansion. She edged closer to Mark and grabbed his arm. From the tension in it, she could sense that he was steeling himself for a confrontation.

Clem came out from behind the car. Only it wasn't Clem. It was someone taller and wirier, who wore his hair pulled back in a ponytail. Carol recognized him as one of the rabble-rousers who had hovered on the sidelines at the mayor's rally, guzzling beer and making wisecracks. It was difficult to tell if he saw them. His face was dull and expressionless. He grabbed an oil can off a shelf and disappeared behind the car again. The series of earsplitting, mechanical whines that followed seemed calculated to drive unwanted visitors off.

Carol's instinct was to get out of the garage right then. She sensed something hostile about the two mechanics. Their sullenness served as a warning to stay away, as plain to her as any No Trespassing sign. She didn't care to know what the penalty was for not heeding it.

"I've seen enough. Let's go back to the car," she said, tugging at Mark's sleeve.

"Wait a minute. What's over there?" Harry had noticed a small room, off the rear of the garage, a lunchroom, maybe, or a locker room for the employees. "Clemson could be on his break."

It was a lunchroom, sort of, with a rickety table and a couple of folding chairs. A rusted soft-drink cooler was leaking water on the floor. They ventured inside. An obese man in a food-stained T-shirt that stopped several inches short of his trousers was eating a pastrami sandwich and drinking a Dr Pepper. "Yeah? What do you want?" he growled.

"Pardon me," Mark said. "We're looking for a Paul Clemson."

"Paul Clemson, huh?"

"Yes, do you know where he is?"

The obese man swigged his Dr Pepper. "Don't work here no more."

"Really?" The three friends exchanged quick glances.

"You wouldn't happen to know where he works now, would you?" Carol inquired timidly.

"Moved to North Carolina. Or is it South Carolina? One of 'em, anyway. Said he had a sister down there." The man spit little pieces of his sandwich in the air as he talked.

"When was that?"

"About three weeks ago. Maybe a month. Why? Did he owe you money, too?"

Carol was too flabbergasted to reply, but it didn't matter. The man wasn't particularly interested in a response.

"Two people already come by, asking after him. Guess he left a few unpaid bills in town. Wouldn't put it past him. Sonavabitch hit me up for fifty bucks day before he left. I can kiss them fifty bucks good-bye forever." He took a gigantic chomp out of the pastrami sandwich by way of signaling that he had nothing further to say on the subject.

"I suppose you have no forwarding address for him," Mark said.

"I told you," the man shot back. "North Carolina. Or South Carolina."

The Buick Regal had baked under the sun, and a blast of hot air hit Carol when she opened the door on the passenger side. She slid onto the front seat feeling discouraged and foolish. So much for her suspicions! All this time she was convinced that Clem was plotting behind her back, and he wasn't even in Fayette! He was somewhere four hundred or five hundred miles away. The investigation had only just begun and it had come to a screeching halt.

It wasn't as easy as they made it out to be in the movies. Movies, indeed! Ever since Will had set foot in the Christmas Inn, she'd been playing make-believe. She preferred not to know what was running through Mark's and Harry's heads right now. At least they had the decency to keep it to themselves. To think she had actually gotten them all fired up for . . . this! She cursed her stupidity.

Mark swung the Buick around and she had a view of the rusting cars in the meadow, skeletons for the most part, their windows gone or smashed, their doors dented, some hanging at an angle from sprung hinges. "Oh, no!" she cried. Mark applied the brakes and the Buick skidded on the dirt.

"What's the matter?"

Carol pointed to a mass of twisted steel by the side of the garage that had yet to be stripped down and put out to pasture with the other wrecks. The hood folded in on itself, like a toothless mouth, and the broken headlights resembled gouged-out eye sockets. Although the windshield had been shattered beyond repair, in front of the steering wheel a few remaining pieces of jagged glass formed a strange, starlike pattern. It was the blue Toyota.

They drove back to town in silence.

The familiar landmarks passed before Carol—Memorial Park, where the mayor had played on the hometown sympathies of the crowd at his rally; the office of the *Fayette Weekly Register*, where she had first learned about the deaths of Charles and Veronica Kennedy; the Fayette Guaranty and Trust, once the keystone of the Kennedy fortune. All the places that were new and exciting to her not so long ago seemed cold and unwelcoming now.

They stopped at a red light in front of the public library. Through the glass door, Carol thought she spotted Esther McPherson, the historical-society lady. She recalled how the birdlike woman, flossily dressed and red-faced, had stumbled out of the Kennedy Suite on the day of the open house. Mark and Harry had witnessed her reaction to the Kennedys' photograph. What had that been all about? Carol was on the verge of bringing it up when the light switched to green and the Buick pulled away.

Fayette sometimes seemed like a cliquish little club, jealously guarding its memberships, she reflected. Would she always be the outsider? Or was she imagining things again, turning every passing gesture and offhand comment into a threatening act, aimed directly at her. Isn't that what paranoid people did?

"Don't worry. Everything will be okay, Carol," Mark reassured her when they reached the Christmas Inn. "You can call us anytime just to talk. We've all been through a bad patch. The thing to do now is let life get back to normal. It will, you know, return to normal. Maybe next weekend we could all go over to Gingerton State Forest. Take Sammy and Charlie. Go boating."

"He'd like that." She leaned through the window and gave Mark a hug. "Thank you both for listening. I'm sorry I led you on such a wild-goose chase. No more conspiracy theories. I promise."

"Hey, better to know that he didn't do it, right?" said Harry. "At least we checked it out."

"Right." She returned his smile.

She went into the kitchen. Sammy had left a glass of milk, half-drunk, on the table. It was still cold, which meant he was probably upstairs, hiding. As she climbed the three flights to his attic sanctuary, she thought sheepishly about the outlandish fantasies she had managed to concoct. Clem, it turned out, had nothing to do with Will's death, just as she was forced to admit that Will's death had nothing to do with Veronica Kennedy's unsolved murder. The one was what the police said it was—an accident. The other? Who knew or even cared at this late date!

She opened the door to the crawl space without bothering to knock or call Sammy's name. He wasn't there. She was distressed to note how much his collection had grown since she had last seen it. There were the usual stones and strangely shaped sticks that so appealed to him. Only there were dozens and dozens of them now. She recognized the license plate and the shiny antique spoon, but where had he come upon the milk bottle with the head of a cow embedded in the glass? People hadn't used glass milk bottles for years. And the dead bird with the molting feathers! She turned up her nose. She was going to have to talk to him about that.

Then her eyes fell upon what appeared to be a piece of fireplace equipment, standing up against the fieldstone chimney. Sammy had polished half of it, starting at the bottom and working up. The top half was still black with corrosion and rust, but the point and the hook glinted even in the fading light. Carol took it by the handle, a knob the size of a golf ball, and the pocked metal prickled her palm. She was surprised by its weight.

Old metal objects—door knockers, andirons, copper kettles—were always so much heavier than she expected when she picked them up in antiques stores. She wondered if metals were processed differently today. Was it the addition of alloys that made them lighter, cheaper, so much less substantial? This object was the real thing—pure and solid and dangerous. Sammy could hurt himself with it.

She contemplated removing it from the attic, but stopped herself. Too many books on child rearing had drilled it into her head that children's privacy was sacred and that it was vital not to invade their space. She would talk to him about it, though. Along with the decaying bird. She put the fireplace tool back where she had found it and noticed that a rusty residue from the handle had come off on her palm.

She brushed her hands together briskly, attempting to clean them, on her way back down the stairs. As she crossed the second-floor landing, the sounds of high-pitched laughter and sharp barking outside attracted her attention.

"You're it," squealed Sammy, racing from one tree to another, while Charlie, in close pursuit, snapped playfully at his heels. Boy and dog were playing a game of tag. Sammy had the advantage when it came to circling the tree trunks, but on the open stretches, Charlie made up for his clumsiness. Carol decided to let them have their fun. Dinnertime would be soon enough to lecture her son about the inappropriateness of some of the objects in his collection. First, she wanted to put the afternoon to rest.

She sank into a leather armchair in the living room and thought how simple it had been to let her imagination run wild. Christopher Ruffo, the architect of the mansion, would have to take the blame for that. Even now, she could hardly look at the grand staircase without seeing Veronica posed coquettishly on the landing, and Charles, dashing up the steps, spinning her around, kissing her.

Their wedding reception had been held in this very room. The guests had been so numerous they had spilled out onto the porch, and the children had frolicked on the lawn. Charles's gift to his young bride that day had been the necklace! Carol remembered the spell the jewels had cast, even caked with dirt, after she had fished them out of the heating duct. How brightly they must have sparkled when they were new and Charles Kennedy had fastened them round his wife's slender neck. The townsfolk must have been filled with awe and envy.

The devil's envy!

That's what Sue Whiley had said. No, it was Sue Whiley's father. He'd said something odd back then about how the devil's envy brings death into this world, and Sue Whiley had never forgot it.

Carol felt herself drawn to the telephone. She had long since thrown away the woman's phone number, but information had a listing for a Mrs. John Whiley on Hancock Street. Carol dialed it and waited while the phone rang. She was prepared to hang up when she remembered that Sue Whiley had bad legs, so she gave it a few more rings. At last, someone picked up and uttered a brusque "Hello."

"Mrs. Whiley?"

There was a pause. "Who's calling, please?"

"This is Carol Roblins . . . from the Christmas Inn . . . the Kennedy mansion."

The voice warmed up instantaneously. "Oh, yes. How are you, dear? How's the house coming? I'm told it looks just like it did in the old days. It's so nice that some of you young people want to preserve the past. Not everything we did was bad, you know. It seems that nowadays everyone wants to blame their parents for all their problems. That's all those talk shows are filled with now—children blaming their parents. I ask you! Why those people would go on TV to blab about matters that should never leave the privacy of their own homes is beyond me. Hold on a second, honey."

It didn't take much for Sue Whiley to get off and running.

"I was just having my afternoon sherry. Helps ease the digestion, you know. Also helps ease you through the afternoon, if you get my meaning." She cackled delightedly.

Carol could hear her taking a gulp. "Are you pulling in any customers over there?"

"Yes, I'm starting to . . ."

"That was so sad about that actor that was staying with you. Do you think it was drugs? They're all on drugs, you know. They have everything in the world, success, all the money they could want, and they throw it away on drugs."

"I don't think it was drugs, Mrs. Whiley. It was just an accident."

"Oh . . . my . . . It's so sad when young people die."

That was certainly true, Carol thought. Will wasn't even forty. Neither was Charles Kennedy. Veronica was in her midtwenties.

Mrs. Whiley gave herself a moment to savor her melancholy, along with the sherry. "I'm sorry I couldn't make it to the open house, honey."

"I'm sorry, too."

"Was it a success?"

"Yes, I think so. I mean, a lot of people came by, which was rewarding. I'm not sure how it will translate into business—"

"Well, from what I hear, you've done a lovely job."

"Thank you. That's good to hear. I finally located the blueprints of the house, so I was able to put the rooms back as they were. When it came to decorating, I had to guess. I'd love to know how close I came."

"And I'd just love to see what you've done! But my legs, you know. And, as I told you, honey, I never was inside that house much, so I wouldn't be a big help there. As long as you captured the feeling, that would be the important thing."

"I did get one odd reaction that day."

"Oh? What was that?"

Go slowly, Carol cautioned herself. She had already made up enough cockamamy plots for one day. There was no reason to fabricate yet another. She was telephoning Sue Whiley on a hunch. Not even a hunch, really. Out of a vague sense of unfinished business. If nothing came of the call— and nothing probably would—she was determined to lay the Kennedy affair to rest once and for all.

She kept her tone casual. "It seems that Mrs. McPherson from the historical society got very upset when she saw a picture of Charles and Veronica Kennedy on a bedroom wall. I did my best to re-create the Kennedys' bedroom suite. It's quite magnificent now. And I thought their picture deserved to hang in a place of honor. Mrs. McPherson couldn't get out of there fast enough. She practically knocked me over."

Carol held her breath. She had thrown out the bait. Would Mrs. Whiley bite? There was a heavy silence on the other end of the line, then a long sigh.

"Poor Esther!" Carol heard Mrs. Whiley swallow another mouthful of sherry. "Esther has spent most of her life trying to forget that her parents were servants in that house. And here you are, bringing it all back!"

So that was the connection! Before she got married, Esther McPherson was Esther O'Hare. That's what the mayor had called her at the rally. And O'Hare was the name of the maid mentioned in the newspaper account of Veronica's death. Carol knew she had seen it somewhere.

She flashed back to the day at the library when she'd made her first innocent queries about the Kennedy mansion and recalled the pained look on the face of Esther McPherson as she snapped, "There is no beauty worth preserving on Ragged Ridge Road."

Little did Carol realize at the time how personal that statement was. Nor could she have possibly known that the desk behind which Esther McPherson sat, haughty and uncooperative, was the perfect place to begin an inquest into murder.

Thirty-Three

———

Esther McPherson knew that someone was standing before her desk, but on principle she liked to make people wait. People were always in such a hurry, jostling and pushing one another, demanding service. As the president of the Fayette Historical Society, she expected and enforced a different code of behavior. Pretending to be deeply absorbed in the volume on her desk, *Betsy Ross: Seamstress and Patriot,* she read to the end of the paragraph, carefully placed a bookmark in the crack between the pages, closed the book, slid it to the upper right-hand corner of the desk, and then, and only then, looked up.

When she saw it was Carol, she had a visible start that momentarily wiped away her habitual expression of glacial superiority.

"Oh, it's you," she said unpleasantly.

"Your mother worked in the house."

"I beg your pardon?"

"Your mother worked in the Kennedy mansion, didn't she? She was present when Charles Kennedy found his wife's body."

Esther McPherson took a deep breath and exhaled it audibly. "May I ask what your business is, Mrs. Roblins?

And allow me to remind you that this is a historical society, not, as you seem to think, a police station."

"Could you please answer one question, Mrs. McPherson? Why did you hide it from me that your mother was Veronica Kennedy's maid?"

"Hide it? Whatever do you mean?"

"When I came here looking for documents relating to the house, you told me not to bother. You claimed there was nothing worth knowing. The historical society had no information about the Kennedys, you said."

"That is quite true."

"Well, maybe the historical society knows nothing, but I think you do."

"Really?" Mrs. McPherson gave Carol one of the scolding looks she usually reserved for noisy children. "And what, pray tell, makes you think you're entitled to such information? Just because you buy a house, Mrs. Roblins, it does not mean that you buy the history of the people who passed through it. Yes, my mother worked for the Kennedys. So did my father. I fail to understand, however, why I should be expected to share that knowledge with a perfect stranger, such as yourself."

Mrs. McPherson waited long enough for the remark to sink in, then added crisply, "Good day, Mrs. Roblins."

Carol ignored the slight. "Something terrible happened that night, and it wasn't the result of a robbery. Did your mother know who the murderer was?"

"I think that's quite enough."

"Why? Did she have something to do with it?"

Esther McPherson sprang to her feet. "I'm afraid I am going to have to ask you to leave immediately." Indignation burned through her chalky powder, coloring her cheeks baby pink.

"Not until you answer my question."

"I will answer nothing. Leave now." The words echoed in the stillness of the library. An elderly man in the reading area lowered his newspaper to see what the fuss was all about, while a librarian, loading up returned books on a cart, stopped what she was doing and called over, "Anything wrong, Esther?"

With an impatient gesture, Esther McPherson waved off the librarian and sat back down. She disliked being the center of attention, much less the cause of a row. She opened a desk drawer where she kept her purse, removed a lace handkerchief from it, patted her brow, then tucked the handkerchief neatly in the cuff of her left-hand sleeve. The methodical actions were her way of reimposing order on a situation that had temporarily slipped out of her control.

When she finally spoke, her papery whisper indicated she was herself again. "You seem to know so much already. Perhaps I should be asking you the questions. It was a tragic night, needless to say. My mother was very devoted to the Kennedys. She said that Charles Kennedy treated her like a member of the family. Naturally, the deaths devastated her."

"Did she have any idea who was responsible?"

"If she did, she never said so. And they never found him."

"Him?"

"Oh, please, Mrs. Roblins. If you think you're going to catch me in some silly slip of the tongue ... I know no more than you do, or anyone else, for that matter. What happened then is of no concern to us today. All this foolishness of yours—taking out ads, playing detective, going on TV—haven't you done enough? Why don't you put this ridiculous obsession to rest and concentrate on running your little inn."

"Why were you so upset on the day of my open house?"

"I wasn't upset at all." She fumbled for the handkerchief tucked up her sleeve.

"You didn't like seeing the photograph of Charles and Veronica up on the wall, did you?"

Esther McPherson exploded, "Charles and Veronica! Veronica and Charles. You're like a broken record. That's all you can think about, Mrs. Roblins. My mother may have been a maid, but she taught me never to speak ill of the dead, and I shall not begin now. If there are any secrets about the Kennedys, they are buried with them in Woodbridge Cemetery. As far as this town is concerned, their lives ended a long time ago. Let me give you a piece of advice. Go home. Mind your own business. Leave the past alone. You'll be better off that way."

Carol thought of Will and the remains of the Toyota. "But an innocent person died, Mrs. McPherson."

A flicker of distaste registered on the old woman's face. "Innocent? What makes you think she was so innocent?"

"She? I wasn't referring to Veronica."

"Then I have no idea what you are talking about."

The anger drained out of the woman. Her powder had crusted in the little lines around her mouth and eyes, and she looked frail and spent. Carol realized she was probably a lot older than she let on.

With as much dignity as she could summon, Esther McPherson stood up, brushed the wrinkles from her skirt, and took her purse out of the desk drawer. "I am sorry to have spoken so sharply. I am also sorry you're so consumed by such a sad and violent episode in our local history. You will kindly excuse me now."

Nodding curtly, she tottered to the far side of the library and disappeared behind a door marked Private.

Carol didn't go home, as the historical-society lady had counseled. She went to Woodbridge Cemetery, instead.

According to the Fayette Chamber of Commerce, the wooded cemetery, which spread over ten acres of rolling land, was one of "the ten most beautiful in America," although who had officially designated it as such, and when, nobody could say any longer. People simply accepted it as fact, the way they believed with no particular evidence that Fayette was "a good town" or that the air in the county was fresher than it was twenty miles away in Brickton.

The entrance was marked by two massive fieldstone pillars and an elaborate ornamental iron gate that was opened every morning at eight and was closed every evening at six, except for weekends and holidays, when visitors were allowed another hour and a half. The wrought-iron arch that bridged the pillars took a longer view of time, advising fortitude and patience "Until the Day Breaks and the Shadows Flee Away."

Just inside the gate, a stone cottage served as the office and home of the groundskeeper, who was watering a bed of orange and yellow lilies as Carol drove in.

She rolled down the car window. "Good morning."

"Mornin' to you." He was short and plump, with a double chin and a tonsure. Only the olive green jumpsuit prevented him from passing as a medieval monk. His name, Jay Stubbs, was stitched into the pocket on his chest. "What can I do for you?"

"Can you direct me to the Kennedy grave? Charles and Veronica Kennedy."

"Kennedys, eh? They're in the old part of the cemetery. One of the mausoleums. You aren't family by any chance, are you?"

"Oh, no. A friend."

"I don't mean to pry. It's just that we don't get a whole lot of people asking for them, that's all. Heck, we don't get any. I can't remember the last time somebody put flowers by their graves. It makes no nevermind, I guess. That's what I'm paid for. To keep the place looking nice and pretty for all our residents."

He retreated into the office and came out a minute later with a small map. "Lemme, see. The Kennedy mausoleum is set into the hillside . . . here . . . and you're at the entrance . . . here." He traced the route between the two points with a pencil. "Keep a lookout for a big oak tree with a metal bench around its base. You can park there and walk the rest of the distance. The mausoleum with the spires is theirs. If you have any trouble, give a honk of the horn."

"Thanks for your help."

As Jay Stubbs had directed, Carol followed Horizon Drive around the edge of the cemetery until she came to a fork in the road. To the right lay the newer section of Woodbridge, where row upon row of marble slabs stood guard, like expressionless sentries, over the deceased. Clumps of hydrangeas and stands of pine trees relieved some of the monotony, but the section had obviously been designed for easy maintenance. Maybe in another ten years, Carol thought, it would look less austere.

The older part of the cemetery, to the left, was another

world entirely. The terrain rose and fell in hills and gullies, and the road was content to follow the natural contours of the landscape. Stately trees formed a canopy of green that filtered the early-September sunshine, and the air smelled moist and earthy, as in a fruit cellar. Everywhere, the vegetation was full and luxuriant. Ivy crawled up the tree trunks, and patches of jack-in-the-pulpit flourished in the damp shade. But the biggest difference was in the grandiose monuments themselves, which advertised their grief openly and melodramatically. Great stone angels, gray-green with moss, hovered protectively over opulent tombs. Classical Greek urns, resting on marble drapery, vied for attention with Egyptian obelisks, while massive granite scrolls and tablets, enscribed with weepy verse, reminded the poor passerby how fleeting was man's life, yet how infinite God's mercy.

As the road came out of a dip, she saw the oak tree with the metal bench straight ahead of her. She brought the car to a stop, edging it over to one side, where a widening of the pavement qualified as a parking space. Built into the sloping hillside were the mausoleums Jay Stubbs had pointed out on the map. There were three. The Kennedys' was the middle one, high Gothic in style, with miniature twin spires, a sharply pitched slate roof, and rainspouts in the form of gargoyles.

From the car, it looked to Carol almost like an illustration in an old book of fairy tales, unreal, overdone, a little creepy. So this was the final resting place of Charles and Veronica Kennedy. They seemed so alive to her in the mansion, almost like her contemporaries, but she had no sense of them here. The ostentatious monument was from another time entirely, foreign to her sensibility. People were so much more discreet about death these days. They hid it, tried to pretend it didn't exist, referred to it euphemistically. In this section of Woodbridge Cemetery, it was still the pretext for a big, gaudy breast-beating show.

She got out of the car and walked up a gravel path edged with brick. As she did, the words of Esther McPherson—"this ridiculous obsession"—taunted her. She pressed on anyway. She owed this visit to herself, as well as the

Kennedys. The grounds were well tended: the grass had recently been mowed and the path raked. Here and there a faded American flag attached to a bronze star marked the resting place of a World War I casualty. Nearing the mausoleum, though, Carol perceived definite signs of wear. Some of the roof slates had come loose, and the stones around the base had begun to crack—the work of frost, apparently. She was dismayed to see that the facade was desecrated with graffiti. The letters *V H O B F* had been spray-painted over the top of the door.

What did that signify? Whose initials were they?

Moving closer, she realized that she had misread several of the letters. What someone had actually written on the marble stones was W H O R E. Some schoolboy had probably done it on a dare from his pals. Teenagers, she knew, loved to sneak into cemeteries at night, drink beer, and scare one another. On Halloween, usually. Still, it was an appalling thing to scrawl on someone's grave, and it should have been cleaned off the wall a long time ago. Her shock translated into a puff of indignation. On the way out, she would have to ask Mr. Stubbs who was entrusted with the upkeep of the mausoleum. No one, from appearances. The years and the weather were taking a toll.

By gripping the iron grating and standing on her toes, she could see through a narrow window in the door into the tiny chapel. It was murky inside, like fetid pond water, but gradually her eyes became accustomed to the darkness and she could make out two oblong shapes, side by side. Carol felt her heart thumping. There they were—the coffins of Charles and Veronica Kennedy, covered with a thick, grayish film of dust and cobwebs. Their sad story ended here in a crumbling mausoleum. They really were dead and forgotten, as everyone kept insisting. In the solitude of Woodbridge Cemetery, Carol found the sobering evidence hard to deny.

She stepped away from the door. For a minute, she could no longer remember what Veronica Kennedy looked like. The playful image of a vivacious woman, cavorting at the beach, had been replaced in her mind by that of a dull, wooden box. The box had lost its bright ebony sheen long ago and was slowly disintegrating in a cold cell. After seventy years, how much could be left of the body it contained?

As Carol retraced her steps on the gravel path, she resolved to try to get something done about the mausoleum. It couldn't be allowed to deteriorate any further. The Kennedy descendants, if there were any, obviously couldn't be bothered. She would assume the duty herself. She and Sammy would have to be the Kennedys' family now.

Jay Stubbs was trimming the grass around the fieldstone pillars with a pair of clippers when she pulled up to the gate.

"Did you find it?" he asked.

"Right where you said it was."

"Pretty in that part of the cemetery, isn't it?"

"Very pretty. Tell me something, Mr. Stubbs. Who's in charge of maintaining the Kennedy mausoleum?"

He scratched his head. "I don't know that anyone is. I try to keep an eye on it myself."

"Well, it's none of my business, but it's not in very good condition. Some of the stones are cracking. And don't you think someone would have removed the graffiti by now?"

"Graffiti? What do you mean?"

"The spray paint over the door. The word *Whore*. How long has that been there?"

The groundskeeper looked dumbfounded. "I don't know. It wasn't there when I made my rounds three days ago."

"Are you absolutely sure?"

"Of course I'm sure. That's one of my favorite places. I eat my lunch there sometimes. All I can think is that it must have happened over the weekend. Because Friday afternoon, I pruned some myrtle bushes in that area and everything was normal. I lock the gate every night, you know. What more can I do? If someone wants to climb over the wall, there's no stopping them."

He stood there shaking his head, afraid that Carol might somehow think him derelict in his duties. "*Whore*, you say? Now why would some crazy person go and do a thing like that? People ought to let the dead rest in peace. Well, I'll take care of it first thing tomorrow morning." He went back to his trimming, muttering to himself that kids were no better than hoodlums these days.

As Carol drove through the gates, the thought began to take shape in her mind. She resisted it at first. There was no point embarking down that track one more time. It was her old paranoia at work. Just more mad fantasizing! But the thought stubbornly refused to go away. If it was true that the past was of no concern to most people in Fayette, one person still cared. And cared passionately.

She had remembered a sentence from the anonymous letter that had arrived in the mail: "This is not a town that needs another whore." *Another* whore? Until now, she hadn't known what the writer really meant by that. Now she did. The black paint on the mausoleum wall spelled it out. Another whore *besides* Veronica Kennedy. In someone's sick mind, she and the banker's wife were linked. Both had apparently violated small-town proprieties and both deserved whatever horrible fate befell them. The only difference was that Veronica was dead and moldering in her coffin and Carol wasn't. But that could change at any minute.

Her hands locked on the steering wheel, and beads of perspiration trickled down her back. She saw what she had to do with a terrifying clarity. If she intended to stay alive, she was going to have to solve the murder at 1 Ragged Ridge Road.

Thirty-Four

———

Phillip Quinn hovered in the door, dazed by the news that he had just learned and unable to force himself out into the storm. He hadn't even known what to say to Charles, who had fled from his presence in despair.

He told himself he should go after his partner and bring him back. But the icy wind, whipping his face, could not rouse him out of his paralysis. A picture of Veronica Kennedy at the foot of her bed—her mouth twisted into a leer of pain, blood coagulating in her jet-black hair—swelled to fill his mind, leaving room for nothing else. Not even grief. He looked out at the darkening blizzard, then turned back and closed the door.

Charles had no idea where he was headed. His only purpose was to put more distance between himself and Ragged Ridge Road. When he realized that he was automatically retracing his steps to the mansion, he reversed direction and ran around the side of the Quinn house, where a large oak tree groaned in the high wind. Light spilling from the windows made squares of brightness on the snow, and he tried to avoid them, as if they were patches of quicksand that could swallow him up.

Then, a sight stopped him dead in his tracks.

He felt feverish, hot and cold at the same time, and thought that his vision might be playing tricks on him. A person, wrapped in a dark blue overcoat and a checkered scarf and wearing a knit cap, was crouched at the foot of the tree. The cap was pulled so low that only the eyes showed—frightened eyes, like those of a small animal caught in the beam of a flashlight. The person got up slowly and mumbled, "I'm sorry. I didn't mean to."

A scream of protest escaped from Charles Kennedy's lips. "Nooooooooooooooo!"

He had just seen something else—the brass poker that the figure was holding. Charles had recognized it as one of the fireplace tools from his bedroom. Instantly, all the fragments of the grisly night came together in his head: his wife's battered body, the poker with a lethal hook at the end, the bloodred splotches on the checkered scarf. It was Veronica's murderer who stood trembling before him. He reached out and yanked away the scarf.

"Oh my God! It's you. Why? Why?"

His horror flamed up into rage and he slammed into the figure, who reeled backward and thudded to the ground, pulling the banker over, too. Although Charles Kennedy was the stronger of the two, the icy terrain made them equals and the murderer's thick topcoat absorbed the savage blows. Locked in an inconclusive struggle, the pair rolled back and forth in the snow, like amateur gymnasts performing an ill-conceived and badly rehearsed tumbling routine.

Only because the topcoat tore open was Charles Kennedy finally able to get his fingers around the throat of the murderer. Once he did, the fight shifted to his advantage. The figure weakened, and the eyes, which had been so frightened moments earlier, turned glassy and began to bulge. Sitting astride the murderer's chest, Charles dashed the limp body into the hard ground, over and over, the way a dog shakes a rat to snap its neck. Brute instinct was governing him. Nothing—not a vestige of reason or a final flickering of conscience—could prevent him from avenging his wife's death.

In his delirious state, he did not sense that someone had

come up behind him, attracted by the cries and the tumult. But suddenly he felt a blinding pain in the back of his head and saw the brilliance of heat lightning in his mind's eye. And he knew, in that instant before he crumpled to the earth, that his life, like Veronica's, was over.

Polly Quinn raised the rock over her head again, prepared to strike a second and a third time, if necessary, but Charles Kennedy's body was motionless. She prodded it with her foot, as she might a dead animal, looking for an involuntary spasm of life. There was no reaction. Convinced that he was no longer a threat, she lowered the rock and cast it aside. Then, she helped the frightened figure wriggle from underneath the banker's inert form.

"I'll take care of it now," she said in a voice devoid of emotion.

Something had to be done, and soon. She looked up at the house. Hiding the body was impossible. It had to be disposed of some other way. As long as the bad weather kept people indoors with their curtains drawn, she was safe. The storm was bound to let up up sooner or later, though, and when it did, children would be swarming outside with their sleds, and their parents wouldn't be far behind. She thought of the Packard in the garage and knew it was useless. Although she might make it down the driveway, all the roads were snowed under and the town wouldn't start plowing them until daybreak. What to do? She was determined not to panic, but few options presented themselves to her.

Then she heard the distant whistle and the solution came to her. The train was still running, if nothing else was. She flipped Charles Kennedy on his back, slipped her arms under his armpits, and hoisted him into a sitting position. His head flopped forward on his chest. Laboriously, Polly Quinn began to drag the body toward Chaldrake Tunnel.

Thirty-Five

———— ◆ ————

"Hey, Mrs. Roblins, good to see you."

Tony, the spike-haired office boy at the *Fayette Weekly Register,* bounded up to the counter.

"Nice to see you, too. Tony, isn't it?"

"Yeah. I'm a reporter now, you know. Got a promotion last week. The publisher was real pleased with the stories I did about Will Williams's death. Said I was turning into quite a journalist."

He beamed like a Boy Scout with a merit badge.

"Well, congratulations, Tony. Your boss wouldn't be in today, would he?"

"He's stepped out for a late lunch. I think he's over at the Molly Pitcher Coffee Shop. He ought to be back in a half hour."

Carol checked her watch. "I was wondering if it would be possible to look at the Kennedy file again. The one you keep in the morgue." The word had a particularly sinister ring to her now.

"I don't see why not." With his newly acquired authority, Tony showed her to the back room.

"You knew Mr. Williams pretty well, what with him staying at your place and everything."

"Pretty well."

"It's a shame what happened. Maybe the town will do something about that turnoff now. I doubt it, though. The police didn't seem any too concerned when I interviewed them. They said we've got country roads around here, not freeways, and any fool who can't tell the difference is asking for whatever he gets. Like Mr. Williams was some nut case or something. He was an okay guy, wasn't he, Mrs. Roblins?"

"He was an okay guy, Tony."

"I thought so."

He flicked on a light switch in the morgue and motioned for Carol to take a chair. "Still looking for information about that house of yours?" he asked as he pulled the manila envelope marked "Kennedy, Charles and family" from a filing cabinet drawer. "Here you are. Let me know if you need anything else. I got to keep an eye on things up front."

Carol removed the yellowed clippings from the envelope. She recalled how astonished she had been when she had gone through them in March to learn of the deaths of Charles and Veronica Kennedy. It was conceivable, she told herself now, that her initial surprise had caused her to overlook some significant detail. Conceivable, if not very likely. But frankly, where else was she to turn?

On top of the pile was the front-page article from 1928 announcing "Bloodshed on Ragged Ridge Road." The headline cut closer to home than she liked to admit. She read through the account again. It referred to "the testimony of the Kennedys' servants," and sure enough, Megan O'Hare, Mrs. Kennedy's personal maid, was quoted extensively. In all likelihood, she was the last person to see Veronica Kennedy alive. She obviously knew a lot. How much had she passed on to her daughter, Esther?

Except for the necklace missing from the dressing table, "the bedroom and its contents were undisturbed." Was the necklace already in the heating duct, Carol wondered, hidden there, perhaps, by someone who intended to return later and retrieve it? Megan O'Hare, possibly, or Charles Kennedy himself? The article mentioned Charles "wailing in a frightful manner" as he ran from the house. But that was Megan O'Hare talking again, and how reliable was she?

Reading on, she came to a comment made by the cook, and her heart skipped a beat. The cook had told police that the player piano, pumping out "God Rest Ye Merry, Gentlemen" in the living room, must have drowned out the noise of the murder. Carol had forgotten that detail, but obviously it had lodged in her subconscious. Could that be why she had been drawn to the player piano in the antiques shop and felt so strongly that one belonged in the mansion? There was a spooky thought for you. Even spookier was the fact that "God Rest Ye Merry, Gentlemen" was in the basket of piano rolls that the dealer had thrown in to clinch the sale. She repressed a shiver.

The rest of the article held no surprises. There was no mention of Kennedy's going to the Quinns' house. Apparently, that story began circulating sometime after Charles Kennedy's suicide. Who was to say if it was true or not? The speculation of the police that the murderer was powerfully built wasn't very helpful, either. All they seemed to be going on was the mangled state of Veronica Kennedy's corpse.

She put the article aside and read the one underneath, the follow-up piece filed one week later:

Kennedys Laid to Rest

No Clues after Weeklong Search

It regurgitated the same few facts about the murder and quoted a Sgt. Michael Stevenson, who "reassured the citizens of Fayette that every effort possible was being made to apprehend the perpetrator of this reprehensible act." The account of the funeral service at Woodbridge Cemetery made note of the Kennedy family mausoleum "set high on a hillside away from the rest of the graves, where it can be seen from considerable distances." The writer seemed to be implying that in death, as in life, the Kennedys were fully aware of their social position. Time had taken care of that, Carol thought. Now the mausoleum was smack in the middle of a little stone city. The names of the most prominent mourners were listed. Carol's eye stopped at that of Phillip Quinn, who was described as being "among the more visibly aggrieved" and "reluctant to leave the cemetery" once the service was over.

Another article, written a few weeks later, was virtually summarized by the headline:

Police at Dead End in Kennedy Mystery

There had been no breaks in the case, and the article was little more than a list of official excuses. The storm on the night of the murder had hampered the search. Because it was Christmas Eve, the Fayette police were operating at reduced force. They had no description of the murderer to go on. No fingerprints. No motive, other than the missing jewels. A farmer had come forward to say that he thought he saw two people in the woods near Chaldrake Tunnel the night of the murder, but he wouldn't swear to it. The personal effects found strewn along the railroad tracks had all been identified as belonging to Kennedy.

Rumors that the Fayette Guaranty and Trust was in trouble were soundly denied by Phillip Quinn, in response, apparently, to those who theorized that the murder and suicide were connected to financial wrongdoing at the institution. The whole investigation struck Carol as almost comical in its ineptness.

A lot of the articles, written earlier, had to do with Kennedy's acquisition of the bank. One revealed his intentions to build a mansion on one hundred acres of land off Ragged Ridge Road and, in a typographical mishap, baptized the architect Christopher Tuffo. The various social activities of Mrs. Veronica Kennedy, "the beautiful and accomplished wife of the eminent banker," seemed to have been generously chronicled. The society pages were more respectful of money and privilege back then, Carol reflected, but as she sorted through the last few clippings, she realized there were no clues here, nothing that might inadvertently shed new light on the old affair.

Then, she came upon the marriage announcement—"Veronica Childers to Wed Charles Kennedy." It was illustrated with formal portraits of the fiancée and her husband-to-be. Veronica's almost jumped off the page. She really was a beauty, Carol thought, with one of those magnetic looks that managed to be innocent and worldly at the same time. She had the sort of "Come hither; no, don't" presence that Hollywood prized. Charles's portrait was something else entirely—serious, conscientious, very much the rising young executive whose worst fear is being thought callow.

There was no hint of the abandon he displayed in the photograph taken on the boardwalk in Atlantic City. Of course, that was a vacation shot, not a posed studio portrait like this one, and it showed him in profile, outdoors in the sun, with the wind blowing off the ocean. His hair was all mussed up and he was squinting. The picture in the newspaper had been taken head-on in a studio under artificial lights. All the imperfections had no doubt been touched up by an obliging photographer who knew the surest way to please his clients was to flatter them.

That wasn't all of it, though. Something else was different. Carol stared hard at the newspaper clipping, trying to figure out what. Then it dawned on her: the hair. The man in the Atlantic City photograph had thick, curly hair, and this man's hair was straight, straight and fine, and he wore it plastered to his head. She put all the other articles back in the manila envelope and slipped the wedding announcement into her canvas bag. The publisher wouldn't mind if she borrowed it for twenty-four hours.

"I left the file on the table, Tony," she said to the cub reporter on her way out.

"Get what you needed?" he asked her brightly.

"I think so. Thanks."

On the drive home, she tried to keep from leaping to conclusions on the basis of a single seventy-year-old photograph printed on a piece of decomposing newspaper. People didn't necessarily look the same from one photograph to the next. In fact, the opposite was usually true: people rarely ever photographed the same way twice. She would be able to tell more when she put the two pictures side by side.

Glancing at the dashboard, she noticed to her consternation that the needle had crept up to sixty without her realizing it.

As she pulled the car into her habitual parking space by the kitchen door, she hit the brakes hard and bumped into a garbage can that the sanitation men had left sitting in the driveway. It rolled up against the house with a clank. In a flash, Carol was in the kitchen, up the back stairs, and down the hall to the Kennedy Suite. As soon as she saw the picture on the wall, she knew that it was another man. The hair was the tip-off, as she had suspected. She took the clipping out of her bag and noticed that the shape of the face was different, as well. The man in Atlantic City, gazing up so adoringly at Veronica Kennedy, had a rounder, fleshier face, whereas Charles Kennedy's was definitely sharper, more angular.

She took the picture down off the wall and turned it over to read the faded inscription: "Atlantic City, September 1928." Then, the initials "VCK," surrounded by a heart. Why would Veronica Kennedy have written her and her husband's initials on the back if he wasn't the man with her on the boardwalk? Carol studied the newspaper photograph again, just to make sure her eyes weren't tricking her. They weren't. Without question, these were two different people. "Veronica Childers to Wed Charles Kennedy," the headline said. There was the answer, right there in black and white. After the marriage, her name became Veronica Childers Kennedy. VCK. The initials were hers alone.

That explained Esther McPherson's dither. She knew it wasn't Kennedy on the wall. After all, there had to be pictures of the real Charles Kennedy in the historical society's archives. Esther's lips were sealed, but when Carol had pressed her, she'd snapped, "Innocent? What makes you think she was so innocent?" Esther could withhold the facts, perhaps, but she couldn't suppress her righteousness.

So! Three months before her murder, Veronica Kennedy was in Atlantic City with someone who appeared to be hopelessly smitten with her. The question was, who? Who was this man with the curly hair and the bright shine on his face? Carol perched on the edge of the four-poster bed, sobered by the realization that it could be anyone at all.

Somebody Veronica had met that weekend at the beach. An old beau. Any one of hundreds of men who lived in Fayette back then and eyed her avidly as she paraded up and down Main Street. Veronica Kennedy could have had any man she desired.

As Carol ran through the possibilities, one person slowly separated himself from the others. One person whose fortunes were entwined with the Kennedys' almost from the start, and whose intimacy with them would be viewed as normal, not suspect. The shine! The shine on the face was the giveaway. Unless her memory was fooling her, she'd seen it already.

The telephone rang. "Hold on," she called out. Sprinting down the front stairs, she picked up the receiver on the sixth ring. Sammy's school was calling.

"I'm glad I caught you, Mrs. Roblins. This is Mrs. Ingelbrook, Sammy's teacher. He's a little upset. Nothing to be worried about. There's a crafts class after school, our first one, and Sammy would very much like to attend. But we need a permission sheet from the parents, you see, and Sammy says he left his at home. I thought if you'd give your consent over the phone, we could make an exception in this case. . . . Hold on just a minute. Your son says he has to talk to you."

Carol sensed that Sammy had been crying. "I want to stay, Mama. Can I, please? Crafts. Everybody making things. Please?"

"Of course you can stay, sweetheart. It sounds exciting." Was it too much for her to hope that he would finally find a friend?

Mrs. Ingelbrook came back on the line and explained a few details about the activities. "Well, that's settled then, Mrs. Roblins. It should be over by five-thirty. You can pick up your son then. Or if you'd like, a school bus is taking some of the children home. Sammy could go with them."

The grandfather clock read three-thirty. Carol made a quick mental calculation. Forty-five minutes to drive there, a half hour or so once she was there, and another forty-five minutes to return, providing there was no traffic. It was going to be tight, but with a little luck she could do it all in two hours and still arrive back at the mansion before Sammy.

"The bus will be fine, Mrs. Ingelbrook."

"I'll keep my eye on him. I'm glad this worked out." Carol heard her son cheering in the background.

She hung up the phone, knowing that every minute counted. She went back up to the Kennedy Suite where she'd left the clipping and the Atlantic City photograph, lying on the bed. She stuffed them into her canvas bag, checked to make sure she had her keys, glanced at her image in the mirror, and quickly concluded that this was not the time for vanity. She was going to Oakdale. Her appearance was of no consequence. What mattered were the family pictures she recalled seeing on the rolltop desk in the living room of Lyle Quinn.

Oakdale hadn't changed at all. The immaculate condition of the grounds, free of so much as a fallen leaf or a withered flower, suggested that they were attended to round the clock, not unlike some of Oakdale's more unfortunate residents. The goldfish pond shimmered in the sun. It occurred to Carol that what had probably changed drastically were the tenants. New ones had moved in. Old ones had left, feet first. That was why the management made such a big deal about keeping the facility in pristine shape. In the midst of so much human flux, there was at least one constant.

As she walked up to the entrance, Carol assumed the same purposeful attitude that had worked so well on her first visit. Confidence was the key, striding in as if you knew exactly where you were going, not stopping to answer questions. Lyle Quinn's apartment was on the third floor—number 311. It was six months ago, anyway. It was entirely possible that his health had declined since then and he had been transferred to the nursing wing. She would find out soon enough.

Preparing to fend off the unctuous greeting of the receptionist, Carol was pleasantly surprised to discover that the woman had stepped away from her desk. The path to the elevator was clear. Carol darted across the empty lobby into a waiting elevator and pressed the close button. There was a ten-second delay. As the doors glided shut, she had a glimpse of the receptionist returning to her station and taking up her watch.

The third-floor corridor was deserted, too, the only indication of activity being a maid's cart at the far end, stacked high with sheets and towels and rolls of toilet tissue. Carol headed directly to 311, relieved to see from the card in the metal holder to the right of the door that Lyle Quinn still resided there. She knocked and, while she waited, speculated on what state he would be in today. If he was lucid, she was fairly certain she would be able to wheedle her way into the apartment and stay there long enough to have a good look around. If not, then she was going to have to play it by ear. The family pictures were all she really needed to see. The last time, he'd stormed out of the apartment, leaving her in his wake. She wouldn't chase after him this time.

She knocked harder and pressed her ear up against the door, listening for the sharp, rapping noise Lyle Quinn made with his cane. No one was coming. He was probably out on his afternoon drive. The apartment was empty. If she could only get someone to open the door for her. She looked around for somebody—the maid. Then she spied the pass key, attached to a large silver hoop, dangling from the end of the maid's cart.

From inside 317, the sound of a vacuum cleaner spilled out into the hallway. Momentarily emboldened, Carol snatched the hoop from the cart, unlocked Lyle Quinn's door, then with a sharp flick of the wrist sent the key flying back. The hoop caught the metal post on the corner of the cart and fell into place. She was aware that what she was doing was generally referred to as breaking and entering and tried not to think of the consequences. The last apartment she'd sneaked into was Clem's. Lyle was older, frailer, but he had a formidable temper, too.

Once she was in the living room, her eyes went directly to the rolltop desk and the black-and-white photographs in ornate silver frames. There were more than Carol remembered. Various sizes and shapes. A veritable gallery. She picked out the mayor in a couple of them, although most of the faces said nothing to her. The family portrait sat in the middle—a husband, his wife, and their son and daughter, posing before a trompe l'oeil backdrop of a formal garden. The woman had a pinched and frowning expression, and the children seemed fidgety and uncomfortable, as children usually are when they're instructed to smile for the birdie. But the man, he had a pizzazz about him. The bright eyes in his oval face lit up the old photograph, even after all these years. That shine!

Carol didn't have to compare the portrait with the Atlantic City photograph in her bag to know that Phillip Quinn was the man in both pictures. It was the classic scenario. Shortly before her death, Veronica was having an affair with her husband's partner and the best man at their wedding. Had they managed to keep it secret, she asked herself, or had Charles Kennedy found out about it? In the small, conservative town, it would have been a huge scandal if word had gotten around. To this day, Esther McPherson still had difficulty talking about it.

No other pictures of Phillip Quinn were on display, but the woman and the boy showed up in a photograph that appeared to have been taken five or six years later. The boy had grown into a strapping young man, while the woman had simply become more severe than ever, with sunken cheeks and fierce, staring eyes. She was holding on to the young man's arm possessively, as if she were afraid that he would run away. It didn't take Carol long to realize that it was a youthful Lyle Quinn she was looking at, and the unhappy woman was his mother. The affair must have ruined her marriage. There was such pain in the faded photograph.

A voice in Carol's head advised her to go home. She had learned what she had come for. It was better to leave before Lyle Quinn returned and had another of his irrational outbursts. But she couldn't resist the urge to open a few desk drawers first. Ten more minutes wouldn't hurt. After all, he might have saved some old letters or maybe he kept a diary.

The top right-hand drawer held nothing of interest. In the

drawer beneath it, she discovered a pad of yellow, lined paper and a sheaf of brown business envelopes with a rubber band around them. The significance of them didn't register until she noticed the handsome cut-glass inkwell on the desk. Then it came together. The antique inkwell wasn't just a decorative objet d'art. Someone actually used it. There was ink in it.

Her suspicions snowballing, she yanked open a third drawer and came upon Lyle Quinn's checkbook. He had made out checks recently to the Prudential Insurance Company and to Brown's Fayette Pontiac and dutifully recorded the transactions on the check stubs in his wavering hand. She recognized the writing instantly. It was the same laborious scrawl that had ordered her to get out of town. Lyle Quinn, not Paul Clemson, was responsible for the threatening letter.

Was he still protecting the family honor after all these years? What possible shame could there be in a seventy-year-old affair? It all seemed utterly crazy to her.

Someone inserted a key in the door.

"Damn," Carol muttered. She had stayed too long. Lyle Quinn was back from his ride. She barely had time to close the desk drawers and duck into a closet. The door cracked open slightly and a voice called out, "Are you there? Anybody in here?"

Carol held her breath.

"It's housekeeping, Mr. Quinn, with fresh sheets and towels."

The door yawned open all the way, and a plump Swedish woman with braids on top of her head waddled over the threshold. "Not home, are we? Thank the Lord for small favors." She pushed on into the bedroom. Soon after, Carol could hear her operatic rendition of "You Light Up My Life" over the splash of running water.

She made a dash for the door and nearly collided with the maid's cart in the hallway. Racing down the service stairs, she emerged in the lobby a minute later, flushed and breathing heavily.

"Are you looking for someone?" asked the receptionist,

tucking away a movie magazine and putting on her most efficient airs.

"Yes. Mr. Lyle Quinn." The receptionist didn't remember her.

"He's not here. I believe he went out earlier."

"What time does he usually get back?"

"Is he expecting you?"

"No, I just dropped by."

"Well, he could be back anytime, then. You never know with him these days."

"You mean, they drive him around for as long as he wants?"

"Drive him?" the receptionist replied with a faint snicker. "He drives himself. Mr. Quinn has his own car now."

"His own car?"

The receptionist picked up right away on the surprise in Carol's voice. "Oh, I know. I know. I didn't think it was a very good idea, either. But he made such a stink, the mayor finally gave in and bought him one. Now he takes off at all hours. There's no stopping him. Once he didn't come back all night. After that, I expected the mayor to lay down the law. But no. Well, it's hardly my place to criticize—"

Carol didn't wait for her to finish. "I'll come back another time." She was out the door and into the parking lot, running for her car and fishing for the ignition key in her shoulder bag as she went. Her watch said ten to five. If she didn't hurry, Sammy was going to arrive home before her. And Lyle Quinn was out there somewhere with crazy thoughts rattling around in his head. The car roared to life and careened down the driveway, throwing up gravel and tar.

Thirty-Six

———∾———

The snow came gently—in dry, feathery flakes that slid off the gabled roof, floated down the chimneys, and settled, like gossamer silk, on the slopes surrounding 1 Ragged Ridge Road. The knit cap of the figure standing in the shadows outside the mansion looked as if it had been sprinkled with confectioners' sugar. He'd been standing there since dusk, careful to stay out of the golden light that shone from the windows. Every now and then, a face from inside pressed up against the glass—someone checking on the progress and the intensity of the snowfall—and the figure took a few steps backward. With his navy blue topcoat, he blended into the darkness. It was getting cold. He pulled a checkered scarf up over his nose.

The living room was ablaze with lights, and the large windows afforded him a good view of the servants, coming and going, as they readied the house for the Kennedys' annual Christmas party. Veronica Kennedy was talking to someone just out of his sight, gesturing animatedly, giving orders probably. He didn't know how, but he would teach her a lesson tonight. Scare her. Scare the wits out of her, that's what he would do. Kill her, maybe.

The butler sat down at the player piano and began

298

pumping the pedals. After a few seconds, a lusty version of "Jingle Bells" rose up out of the instrument. There was clapping and laughing, and soon everyone in the living room was singing along. The voices carried outside, rising and falling like waves, bringing merriment to the night: ". . . oh, what fun it is to ride . . . dashing through the snow . . . laughing all the way, ho, ho, ho . . ." The cook came in from the kitchen, her cheeks beet red, and the chauffeur grabbed her apron strings and twirled her around. Before long, all the servants were caught up in an impromptu dance, their arms linked together as the piano huffed and puffed out the jolly notes.

Now was his chance. He quickly went around to the back door. He could see the kitchen was empty, the steaming pots on the stove momentarily unattended. Megan O'Hare had broken out in a jig in the living room. She had one hand planted firmly on her hip. The other, arched over her head, waved a sprig of mistletoe. She was daring the men to kiss her. A whoop of laughter went up when the chauffeur puckered his lips and lunged playfully at her. Veronica was laughing along with everyone else.

Taking advantage of the distraction, the figure in the knit cap slipped through the kitchen door, stole up the back stairs, and made his way down the long hallway to the Kennedys' bedroom.

Carol was barely in the kitchen when she started calling, "Sammy, Sammy." She cast an eye about the room for the telltale signs that her son had returned: his lunch box, a dirty milk glass in the sink, cookie crumbs on the counter. Sure enough, the lunch box was sitting on one of the kitchen chairs.

"Sammy? Where are you?" She tried not to let the apprehension she was feeling creep into her voice.

For a while, with Will around the house, Sammy had really started to come out of his shell. He was laughing more, doing that silly imitation of the Handyman at every opportunity, and Carol had allowed herself to think that her son was finally outgrowing his shy, withdrawn stage. Then, Will's death had driven the child even deeper into himself, and he had gone and found dozens of new places to hide. She realized he could be in any of them right now.

She pushed open the kitchen door, cupped her hands around her mouth, and shouted into the woods behind the mansion, "Time to come in, Sammy! It'll be getting dark soon." There was no answer. She walked around to the front of the house and sat for a while on the veranda steps, scanning the front lawn, hoping he would come sprinting across the grass, Charlie tagging behind him. Neither boy nor dog was anywhere to be seen. Just the lengthening shadows cast by the setting sun.

In the foyer, she noted that the Christmas tree lights were on and concluded that Sammy had plugged them in. He was probably in the attic. She stood in the stairwell, looking up as she yelled, "No more hiding, Sammy. Come on down now. Please, I'm being serious. We're not playing games anymore." The rich chestnut paneling amplified her words.

Usually, he was incapable of remaining silent for long. He eventually called back or made a noise to indicate his general whereabouts—that was part of their ritual. So why wasn't he answering? Carol was beginning to worry. He could have fallen and hurt himself.

She made an effort to keep from panicking and running up the stairs to the third floor. Still, she was breathing heavily when she reached the dormer room with the little door that gave onto the storage space under the eaves. She knocked softly—"Are you in there, Sammy?"—then cracked the door open gently, afraid of what she might discover. The early-evening light from the dormer window washed into the storage space, which Sammy had turned into a virtual museum.

"Sammy?" she whispered urgently into the gloom beyond the pale strip of illumination. Her heart sank. He wasn't there, either. Her eyes raced over the stones and the sticks, the decaying bird and the milk bottle and the license plate. Something was missing. With a shudder, she realized what it was. Sammy's prize item, the brass poker that he kept by the fieldstone chimney, was gone, too.

She wasn't sure where to search next. One of the guest suites was a possibility, although the guest suites had always been strictly off-limits. And what about Charlie? He was generally underfoot at suppertime. As she turned to go back downstairs, she heard it, coming up the stairwell, as if to meet her. "God Rest Ye Merry, Gentleman" was being played on the player piano. The notes, loud and assertive, almost seemed to be saying, "Fooled you! Here I am! Come get me!" Carol scrambled down the stairs, fully expecting to find Sammy at the pedals of the antique instrument. But when she got there, the piano was playing all by itself, filling the whole house with the swelling strains of the stately Christmas carol.

Two small lamps on the dressing table made circular pools of light on the floor of the Kennedys' bedroom. The fire in the fireplace had recently been stoked, and it threw off reddish yellow flickers that danced on the walls and skittered over the ceiling. With a sharp crack that sounded like a rifle shot, a log broke in two and a shower of sparks rained into the grate.

He had been standing outside in the snow for so long, he was immediately drawn to the warmth. He extended his gloved hands in front of him and held them there immobile as the chill slowly lifted from his body. The snow on his knit cap melted, and he felt drops of water trickling down his neck. The checkered scarf still masked the lower half of his face. There was no expression in his eyes beyond a glassy fascination with the fire. Mesmerized, he watched the flames leap and fall.

Then, he slowly stirred to life as if the heat of the burning logs had thawed him and looked around at the bedroom. The velvet curtains had been drawn shut to keep in the warmth, and a fancy evening dress had been laid out on the bed. He guessed it was Mrs. Kennedy's dress for the party. That was her, gazing down from the oil painting over the fireplace. It was a good likeness, but what the artist had captured best, it seemed to him, was her smile, so playful and so superior. He hated that smile.

He looked away. Just to the right of the door by which he had entered, another door, already opened, led to a dressing room. The ghostly forms that hovered in the dark, he realized, were only clothes, hanging from wooden bars, just like in a department store. And the ghostly feet were men's shoes, that's all, polished and lined up in a row. With his knuckles he rubbed his eyes, making them red.

The sound of someone coming down the stairs from the third floor gave him a start, and a surge of adrenaline coursed through his body. He seized the brass poker from the fireplace set to protect himself and ducked into the dressing room. No one would know he was there, concealed behind clothes that smelled vaguely of sweet perfume and tobacco. He had to strain to hear the footsteps. They were growing fainter. Whoever it was had continued on down to the first floor.

He stayed put in the dressing room, gripped the poker tightly, and waited.

Carol stared at the player piano. The ivory keys were moving up and down of their own accord, producing the majestic chords of "God Rest Ye Merry, Gentlemen" that were shaking the living room. She knew that Sammy hadn't done this. Sammy could never tear himself away from the instrument while it was playing. He loved to watch the white paper scrolling from one roll to the other—amazed, every time, that a bunch of punctures in the paper could produce music. But Sammy was nowhere to be found. Somebody was toying with her, somebody who knew the circumstances of Veronica's murder.

The empty mansion simply had far too many nooks and corners for a child to hide in. Or a stranger to lurk in. Fighting to hold the fear at bay, she decided to telephone Mark and Harry. They would come over and help look for Sammy, or at least keep her calm until he showed up. She punched their number on the kitchen phone and put the receiver to her ear. There was no ringing. The call hadn't gone through. She replaced the receiver on its cradle, then picked it up again, listening for a tone first. The telephone was dead.

She checked the cord. It seemed all right. That meant the problem lay with the outside line, unless the phone in her bedroom was still working. Her uneasiness intensified as soon as she reached the bedroom door. Because it opened onto the foyer, she always made a point of keeping it shut. Otherwise, guests just wandered right in, thinking it was part of the inn.

The door was ajar.

"Sammy? What are you doing in there?" she called cautiously, not daring to raise her voice too loud. When no answer came back, she nudged the door with her foot.

The bedroom had been totally ransacked. All the drawers had been pulled from the dresser and emptied on the floor. Clothes were strewn everywhere. The mattress and the box spring were pitched at incongruous angles on the bed frame, and the mattress was disgorging some of its stuffing, where someone had slashed it with a knife. What was going on? She tried not to step on her clothes as she entered. Even the curtains had been yanked from their rods. She couldn't believe the mess.

Then, behind her, she heard humming. A man's voice, humming "God Rest Ye Merry, Gentlemen" along with the music from the player piano. She spun around and found herself facing Walker White. He was leaning up against the wall, a thin smile on his stubbly face.

"Where is it?" he asked softly.

"Where is what?" She backed away.

"The necklace."

"What are you talking about?"

"Quit bluffing, Carol. I know all about it. Where is the necklace?"

"It's in a safety-deposit box," she lied.

"No, it's not."

"I took it to the bank this morning."

"I don't believe you."

"It's true, I swear. Where's Sammy?"

"Why didn't you tell me about it when you found it? I did all the work on this place. And now you've got a big beautiful house and money coming in. You said yourself it should be half mine. But I don't have shit. I want that necklace, Carol. You never would have found it if it hadn't been for me. I was entitled to at least part of it. But no, you had to keep it for yourself. Well, I want the whole thing now. So give it to me."

As he came toward her, he pulled a pair of pliers out of his back pocket and played with them casually. She tried not to look at them. The clinking of the pincers unnerved her.

"I told you. I don't have it here."

Walker laughed. "That's the one thing you've never done very well, Carol—lie! Oh, you pretend to be Miss Goody Two-shoes, but Clem was right. Underneath, you're really just a lying whore who fucks the guests while her husband is out of town. Here I was trying to be such a gentleman, all this time, and protect innocent little Carol. You sure made a fool of me. The minute I turn my back, you shack up with some Hollywood pretty boy. Did you show him the necklace? You showed it to those fairy friends of yours."

He brushed her cheek lightly with the pliers.

"Stop it, Walker." She winced. "Where's Sammy?"

"You should have been more concerned about that when you were gallivanting all over town, leaving him to come home to an empty house," he snapped. "Just give me the goddamn necklace. And don't tell me it's not here, because I know it is." The smile was gone; he was turning brutish.

"It's upstairs in the Kennedy Suite."

"Oh, yeah? Show me then. You first."

He let her pass in front of him, but as she climbed the stairs, he followed close behind, keeping the pliers pressed in her back. Neither spoke until she had opened the door and they were inside the Kennedy bedroom.

"There." She pointed to the brass heating grate, formed by the initials VCK, that they had discovered under the old carpeting.

"You're a lot smarter than I gave you credit for. This is the one place I never would have looked." Now that he sensed that the jewels were within his grasp, Walker seemed to relax. He made Carol sit on the bed and knelt down in front of her. With the screwdriver he carried in his tool belt, he promptly set to work removing the brass screws that anchored the grate to the floor.

"Do you think you can just take the necklace?"

He looked up at her. "Yes, I do. And do you know why? Because you're going to let me."

Carol squirmed uncomfortably.

"Because if you don't, I tell your husband you've been fucking the guests. And if he doesn't give a damn, I can think of someone who just might. Mayor Quinn. Yeah, Mayor Quinn was running a clean, upstanding town, until you came along. I don't think he'd be any too happy to hear what's been going on at the Christmas Inn."

He had already removed three screws. Three more remained. Carol could sense his mounting excitement. "Hell, you're not going to say anything about the necklace because, if you did, an accident could very well happen to that beloved little pooch of Sammy's." He snickered. "Accidents have a way of happening around here."

"You wouldn't do that."

There was hardness in his face. "I don't believe you're curious enough to want to find out."

When he spoke next, his voice was almost playful. "But we're forgetting the biggest reason of all. This necklace doesn't exist, remember? It was stolen a long time ago and never recovered. Disappeared into thin air. Anybody who says otherwise is just making up a crazy story."

He pulled out the last screw, lifted off the grate, and tossed it to one side. "Okay, where is it?"

"Open the louvers. It's down there."

He angled the cast-iron louvers so they were straight up and down. "Oh, baby, it sure is." His hand was too big for the job, but he wedged it between the flaps anyway, forcing his arm down until he could feel the jewels with the tips of his fingers. He was tantalizingly close to his goal. Only a few more inches. Drops of sweat pearled on his forehead. He jammed his arm deeper into the duct, closing his eyes with the effort and rolling on one shoulder. He grimaced. Carol realized from the fleeting expression of pain that he was momentarily caught, like an animal in a sprung trap.

She leaped off the bed and bolted for the hallway.

With a howl, Walker wrenched his arm free of the louvers and started after her. His shirt was torn and his arm was bleeding. Carol reached the top of the stairs first, but he was only a few feet behind and gaining fast. She knew she could never outrun him.

Instead of continuing down the stairs, she dropped into a crouch, reversed direction and braced herself for the collision. Walker hadn't expected that. She clipped him just below the knees. Unable to stop, he plummeted headfirst over her crouched body, then tumbled down the chestnut staircase, until he reached the bottom with a sickening thump.

As Veronica Kennedy climbed the wide staircase to the second floor, she breathed in the pungent scent of the Christmas tree. The spontaneous display of good spirits from the servants had put her in a good mood. She had even detected the outlines of a smile on the face of Jimmy when Megan burst into her jig, and that was certainly a rare sight. Two rare sights, actually, if you counted Megan dancing.

The mansion was beautifully decorated, and the snow that had begun falling a few hours ago provided the perfect, if unexpected, final touch. She would tell her guests that she had ordered it specially for them. Christmas really was her favorite holiday, an opportunity to file away old rancors and renew friendships that had frayed or been neglected during the year.

The butler switched over to "God Rest Ye Merry, Gentlemen" on the player piano, and the notes reminded Veronica of little gusts of wind, flurries of melody swirling up the staircase and nipping at her ankles. She glided down the hallway to her bedroom and shut the heavy door behind her. Megan had already put out her dress, and the necklace was in the velvet-lined box on the dresser. Charles's freshly starched tuxedo shirt hung on the silent butler, waiting for him to put it on and assume the role of magnanimous host. Veronica sat down before the oval mirror and gazed at her image. Her face was still unlined and free of blemish, with only the faintest suggestion of creasing around the eyes. She still had years of youthful beauty ahead of her.

She took the necklace out of its case and held it up to her cheek. The light from the dressing table lamps, catching the platinum chain, was reflected onto the ceiling, where the silvery glints warred with the flickering firelight. Fire and ice, the endless combat. Veronica let her thoughts go to the future and, in no time at all, was lost in dreams of happiness.

Walker's body lay crumpled and still at the foot of the stairs. His left leg was bent underneath him and twisted in such a way that it looked as if it had been whacked off at the knee. The handsome face was a yellowish white, the color of souring cream. A trickle of blood from his ear oozed down his cheek.

Carol realized he was unconscious, maybe dead. Dizzy with emotion, she held on to the banister to steady herself, waiting for her breath to return and the vertigo to pass. She had to phone the police and get an ambulance here fast. The thoughts rushed through her head in a blur. She made herself concentrate. The kitchen phone was out of order, but it was conceivable that the extension in the Kennedy Suite was still working.

She ran down the hall and back into the bedroom, careful to avoid the open grate. The phone was on a table by the four-poster bed. She grabbed the receiver off the cradle and listened for the reassuring tone. The silence seemed to mock her.

"Oh, no, no, no. Please work, please," she pleaded as she jiggled the button up and down with her finger. But wishing couldn't bring the line to life. All the phones in the mansion were dead. She would have to make the call from a neighbor's house.

Turning to leave, she noticed that the bedroom door was shut. For a second, she had a terrible vision of Walker pulling himself to his feet, staggering back up the stairs, and preparing to lunge for the jewels again. She scolded herself for letting her imagination flare up just when she needed all her senses about her. Then, a rustling coming from the dressing room alerted her that someone really was in the suite.

"Who's there?" she cried. "Did you hear me? . . . Who are you?"

The only response was a protracted moan. Almost a growl.

"Sammy, is that you? . . . Are you hurt? Say something . . . Walker?"

On the far side of the bedroom stood a figure in a heavy blue topcoat. All his features, except his eyes, were concealed by the knit cap and the checkered scarf. The eyes were so red and watery that Veronica Kennedy fleetingly wondered if the person hadn't been crying.

The fire brightened, illuminating the flash of yellow at his side. He was holding a long brass object in his hands, the poker from her fireplace set.

"Who are you?" she asked indignantly. "What are you doing here?"

The figure didn't budge.

"Didn't you hear me? Who are you?" The very idea that someone had stolen into her bedroom angered her, and the anger, for the time being, overcame any fear that she might be courting danger. She could have been addressing an errant child. She hadn't even thought to put down the necklace and held it, cupped, in her left hand.

"Get out of here immediately or I will have my husband throw you out." Even as she sputtered out the words, part of her couldn't help thinking what a silly, idle threat that was. Charles hadn't come back from the bank yet, or if he had, she hadn't heard his heavy, galumphing step on the stairs or the exasperatingly hearty "Anybody home?" that he insisted on shouting every time he crossed the front door. Furthermore, the player piano would surely drown out any calls for help. The irony of her situation didn't elude her. Her only trump card, she sensed, was psychological.

"I'm going to ask you one more time to leave," she said firmly.

He lowered his head. Ashamed? Confused? Veronica allowed herself to venture closer. As she did, she thought she perceived a deep sadness in the red, watery eyes. She made herself blot out the knit cap and the scarf and tried to picture the tormented face underneath. All at once, it dawned on her that she knew the person standing before her.

Her whole attitude softened as she reached out a hand to him.

"Sammy? Is that you?"

Carol stood before the darkened dressing room. The rustling noise had ceased, but she knew someone was hiding in there. She could hear heavy breathing. It was more than just breathing. It was a panting sound closer to . . . whimpering. Her son must have had a terrible scare to be cowering like that in the back of the dressing room, too petrified to show himself. What had Walker done to threaten the boy?

"It's safe now. You can come out, Sammy. Mama's here. Walker won't hurt you anymore, I promise."

Slowly, the small figure emerged from the shadows. His hair was snowy white and his face was wizened. It was Old Man Quinn. His eyes were bright with exaltation and he was pointing a gun at her.

"Mr. Quinn," she gasped.

"So, we meet again."

Words stuck in Carol's throat like bits of bone. "What . . . what are you doing here?"

"Is that you? . . . Is that really you, Lyle?" Veronica said. "What's come over you? You look like you're absolutely freezing. Here, let me take your coat and your scarf. You can warm yourself by the fire."

"Stay away from me," the adolescent barked.

"What's wrong?" She took a step toward him.

"I said, stay away."

For emphasis, he swung the poker at her. It cut through the air, perilously close to her face. Instinctively, Veronica threw up her arms for protection, letting go of the necklace, which flew out of her left hand and landed on the heating grate. It hung there for a second before gravity did its work. Like a glittery snake, the precious chain slithered through the brass initials and fell into the sooty blackness below.

Veronica didn't dare look away from the boy. "Lyle, put the poker down," she commanded.

"You are not going to destroy my family!"

"What are you talking about? I'm not trying to destroy your family. Where did you get that idea?"

"Yes, you are. Mama said so. She said you're going to take Daddy away from us and we will never see him again."

"That's not true."

"I wish you were dead," he screamed. "I do. I really do."

"Lyle, calm down. You mustn't believe everything that people tell you. Things are going to be all right. Trust me. Your mother didn't mean what she said."

As she spoke, Veronica inched backward, trying to keep her voice steady and not excite the boy. "Lyle, you know what tomorrow is? Don't you want to go home and get ready for Christmas?"

She reached behind her for the button on the wall by the dressing table that would summon the maid. In an instant, the boy was upon her, the poker raised high over his head like a hatchet.

Lyle Quinn held the gun in front of him with both hands. Carol realized that it wasn't whimpering she had heard in the dressing room. It was the sound the old man made every time he exhaled, an unconscious vocalization, not unlike the creaking of a bellows.

"I told you to get out of Fayette," he said in a raspy voice as he shuffled into the room. "Didn't I tell you? Why didn't you listen to me? Now you'll have to suffer the consequences."

Carol remembered the violence of his mood swings at Oakdale. Anything could set one off. It was vital to talk quietly, behave as normally as possible, if she didn't want to provoke a tantrum. The only difference this time was that he was gripping a gun and it was trained directly on her.

"I didn't know the letter was from you, Mr. Quinn," she murmured apologetically. "I'm sorry."

"You should be. After all you've done to destroy my family. You couldn't leave us alone, could you?"

"But I haven't done anything to destroy your family."

He snorted derisively. "That's what she said, too. I tried to warn her, you know. I sent her a letter, too. She wouldn't listen, either. She did whatever she damn well pleased."

"Mr. Quinn, I'm listening to you. Can't you see?" Her words weren't registering with him.

"My mother told me you were nothing but a whore. A filthy whore who wants to take my father away from us. It was all ruined because of you." A white froth had formed on his lips. Lyle Quinn was raving. "Now you're trying to hurt me and destroy my son." He waved the gun erratically at Carol.

"I never hurt anyone, Mr. Quinn. I never even knew your mother or your father. You're talking about the past. It's over. Gone."

"I had to protect my mother from you once," he shouted, "and now I'm going to have to protect her all over again."

"Oh, my God, please don't—"
The poker came down with a furious thwack, carving a bright red furrow in Veronica Kennedy's forehead. The next blow caught her on the side of the head and sent her sprawling at the foot of the bed. She pulled herself into a sitting position, but the boy couldn't restrain himself now. He was yelling at her, venting all his rage and fear and youthful frustrations on her slender body.

"You've got everything you could ever want. I'm not going to let you take my father on top of it all." As she put up a hand to protect her face, he thrust the poker forward and penetrated her throat.

The words entered her consciousness as broken fragments of sound, shards cutting the inside of her head, shredding her memories and her identity.

"You . . . ver . . . ould . . . not . . . athe . . . ll" was all
that Veronica heard before sensation left her body altogether.

The present had ceased to exist for Lyle Quinn. He stood
there in the Kennedy Suite cursing Carol but seeing someone else. Or maybe, in his disturbed mind, the two had
merged into one. The mansion, after all, hadn't changed.
The bedroom was as he'd remembered it all these years—
brand-new, with the smell of fresh varnish and nice, clean
paint. Even the Christmas decorations were up, as they were
that night. Time hadn't budged.

"I wanted everything to go back the way it was, but it
didn't," he said bitterly. "It changed forever. Why didn't
you leave us alone? My father never looked me in the eye
again, because of you. Why did you do it?"

He cocked the gun.

The saliva in her mouth dried up, and her tongue felt too
thick and heavy to move. She forced herself to speak
anyway. "Wait, Lyle. It wasn't your father's fault. He never
wanted to leave you. He really loved you and your mother
all along. So don't blame him, Lyle. You did what you had
to do. But can't you see I'm not Veronica Kennedy? She's
gone. She's forgotten."

Over his shoulder, Carol saw the door inch open and the
iron hook of a poker appear in the crack.

A look of vindication lit up the old man's face. He had
been perfectly justified in killing Veronica Kennedy, just as
he had every right now to kill . . .

He had no time to finish his twisted thought. The hooked
end of the brass poker bit viciously into the back of his
neck, knocking him off-balance and shooting needles of
pain to his brain. He let out a screech and the gun clattered
to the floor. As he turned to see who had attacked him,
Sammy swung the poker hard into the old man's ribs. It
knocked the wind out of him and he crashed up against the
wall, panting for air. Then his body slid to the floor. From
his open mouth, a trickle of yellowish saliva ran slowly
down his chin. He looked like a corpse fished out of chilly
water.

Sammy's face was puffy and tear-stained, but it was not the usual hysteria that gripped him, splintering his concentration and sending him scurrying for a hiding place. This time he wasn't running away. His frenzy had a purpose, protecting his mother, that pumped strength into his flailing limbs. Carol had never seen such determination in him. Pushed beyond his limits, her son was almost unrecognizable, a child possessed.

As he raised the poker a third time, she grabbed the weapon in midair. She had Lyle Quinn's gun now.

"Stop, Sammy. That's enough."

It took a minute for the words to register on the boy's consciousness.

"It's okay. Everything's okay. Mommy's all right."

Slowly, the softness crept back into Sammy's face. As it did, his eyes darted about the room as if he were seeing it for the first time, and he began to tremble with fright. She pulled him to her and enfolded him in her arms. Only then did she notice that she was trembling, too.

"Why did that man come here?" he stammered.

"Shhhhhh. It doesn't matter now," she whispered in his ear.

"But why?"

"He was lost, honey. Lost and scared."

She stroked his hair gently, each stroke bringing the boy closer to calm. For a while, they sat there and took comfort in one another's closeness.

In the living room, "God Rest Ye Merry, Gentlemen" came to an end.

The only sound in the mansion was the flap-flap-flap of the piano roll turning on itself.

Epilogue

————

Harry Watkins caroled at the top of his voice as Mark steered the car onto Ragged Ridge Road.

"'For we need a little Christmas, right this very minute, candles in the window,' dah, dah, dah, dah, dah . . ." He turned to Mark. "How does it go?"

"How does what go?"

"You know. From *Mame.*" Harry ran through the lyrics. "'Need a little Christmas, right this very minute, candles in the window,' something, something, something. What?"

"You're asking me?"

"Mark, think."

"I don't know. 'Tinsel on the turkey.' 'Glitter on the mantel.' Don't look at me like that. 'Frost on the pumpkin.'"

Harry slumped down in the car seat. "I can't tell you how it drives me nuts to forget the words to a song. And I did that show, too. So it was fifteen years ago in Pittsburgh . . . 'Right this very minute . . .' What rhymes with *minute?*"

"Linnet."

"What the hell is a linnet?"

"A bird."

"They don't sing about birds in *Mame.*"

"Just trying to help, Harry."

Mark squeezed the car between Carol's station wagon and a green Volkswagen Jetta that was unfamiliar to him. He reached in the backseat for a pastry carton, tied with string. He had spent the previous night baking an apple crumb cake and was hoping that the bumps on the drive to Carol's hadn't radically increased the crumb quotient.

Harry pulled on his snowy beard, slipping the elastic band behind his ears, adjusted the red velvet cap, and fluffed up the white fur trimming on the sleeves of his jacket.

"How do I look?" he asked, hoisting a duffel bag packed with Christmas gifts over his shoulder.

"Fraudulent, but jovial."

Usually, they walked right in the kitchen door without knocking, but this was a holiday, and Harry felt a more formal entrance was called for. The front door of the mansion was outlined in white lights, and two holly bushes, pruned into lollipop spheres, stood decoratively on either side, the red ribbons around their trunks reminiscent of the floppy ties on choirboys. Mark pressed the bell.

"Spinet!" Harry exclaimed.

"Spinet?"

"Yes. Rhymes with *minute*. 'Candles in the window, carols on the spinet.' Thank God. I wouldn't have been able to think of anything else all during the meal."

Sammy opened the door and shrieked delightedly at the sight of Harry Watkins in full Santa Claus regalia.

"Ho, ho, ho. Meeeeeery Christmas," Harry chortled. He tossed his head back, clapped his hands on his belly, and tried to make the down pillow under his jacket jiggle convincingly. "Have you been a good boy this year? Tell Santa now. Ho, ho, ho."

Sammy galloped off to get Carol. "Mama, Mama. Come quick. Guess who's here? Harry and Mark."

"I knew this fool pillow wasn't going to work," Harry grumbled. "I should have used the foam-rubber one."

Laughing, Carol came in from the kitchen, just behind her son, who was jumping up and down and spinning in circles. "Are you absolutely sure that's Harry, Sammy? I thought Harry had blond hair."

"Surprise!" Harry pulled down the beard and gave her a kiss. "I tried to get Mark to come as one of my helpers, but he would have none of it. He said green isn't a flattering color for him."

"Dressing up isn't my forte," Mark said.

"Sure, he just makes other people do it. The voyeur! No, a voyeur is . . . what do you call someone who likes to watch people put on strange clothes and parade around in public?"

"A director?" Carol volunteered.

"Touché," Mark said.

"Well, at the risk of repeating myself, you're only on this planet once," Harry philosophized. "At least, that seems to be the operative theory. So what's the point of holding back? Lighten up. Let go. Dress up as Santa Claus. Dress up as Mrs. Claus, if you feel like it. Who cares, right?"

Mark snatched the velvet hat away from Harry and slipped it on his head. "All right, will this do?"

"Superb," said Carol.

Harry rubbed his chin and looked at Mark appraisingly. "You know something, Mark, red isn't your color either."

If there was anything consoling about Will's death, Carol sometimes thought, this was it: Harry and Mark becoming part of her life. They were like family now. The turning point in the friendship had been "that day." That was how they had all come to refer to the day Walker had plummeted down the staircase, breaking his leg in the fall, and a crazed Lyle Quinn had terrorized Carol in the Kennedy Suite. Afterward, she had wanted to flee the mansion and never return, but Mark had convinced her that running away would be conceding defeat after she had fought so hard for the mansion. And won. The house was hers now, the past had been put to rest.

Mark and Harry had stayed that night in the mansion, and in the weeks that followed, one or the other made a point of sleeping over. They had been her support, too, all during the police investigations and court procedures, which dragged on through the fall. Walker had spent almost a month in the hospital, where there was a bedside arraignment. Besides the broken leg, he'd cracked several ribs and suffered from internal bleeding. After entering into a plea agreement with the DA's office, he went before the judge in November. He pleaded guilty to attempted robbery, in exchange for which the charge of assault with a deadly weapon (the pliers) was dropped. Because of Walker's cooperation and his lack of a criminal record, the judge handed him a two-year sentence. He would be eligible for parole in twelve months.

Carol was relieved not to have to testify. Once she calmed down, she even felt a certain sadness for Walker. She knew she hadn't led him on or made any rash promises she hadn't kept. But she had repeatedly minimized his interest in her, reducing it to the status of a friendship, because it was more convenient that way. And she had preferred not to see all the anger bottled up inside him. If he was guilty, then so was she—guilty of misreading him. She wondered if she hadn't committed that crime more than once in Blake's presence, too.

In light of all that had happened, the investigation into Will's death was reopened, and the Toyota, which still sat in a patch of weeds at Broadbent's Automotive Center, was reexamined. Carol regularly called the detective to find out if any new information had surfaced. He informed her that two of the brake-fluid lines had been severed.

"So the car *was* tampered with," Carol said.

"Well, we don't know that. It could have happened in the crash."

"Isn't there some way to tell?"

"Yeah, if they were both sharp, clean cuts—if both were exactly the same—you might be able to conclude it was deliberate. In this case, the cuts are jagged. They could just as easily be the result of the impact."

"Or else someone knew how to cover their tracks."

"Or that."

Old Man Quinn, questioned about the car, confessed that he was "just trying to scare her." But that was also the answer he gave when asked what he was doing with a gun in

the Kennedy Suite. Just whom he meant by "her"—
Veronica Kennedy or Carol—was not clear, either. Frequently, he seemed incapable of making a distinction
between the two, and his ravings, which had always bordered on incoherence, gradually lost all touch with reality.
Authorities ruled him unfit to stand trial, and he was sent
away to Farview State Hospital, an asylum for the crimi-
nally insane in the northeast corner of the state.

An official statement released by Mayor Quinn acknowledged that his father had been ailing for several years and
expressed "complete and total shock over events." The
Quinn family, the statement concluded, "trusts that the
community of Fayette will extend its understanding and
sympathy in this difficult time."

While there was no proving the old man had hired
someone to tamper with the brakes on the Toyota, it seemed
likely to Carol. Unless a guilty conscience prompted the
person to come forward and confess, however, she would
never know for sure. She was free to blame the accident on
mechanical failure or human perversity. On men or the
gods. On foul weather or rotten luck. Not much of a choice
whichever way she looked at it, but hers to make.

There was an initial swarm of reporters and newscasters,
but without a celebrity of Will Williams's magnitude to
drive the coverage, interest in the story waned rapidly.
Carol no longer craved publicity, although she felt it was
important for Fayette to know what had happened. So she
gave her exclusive interview to Tony at the *Fayette Weekly
Register* and told him everything about "that day" and the
events leading up to it. The article ran under the banner
headline "The Story of 1 Ragged Ridge Road" and took up
two full pages. In it, readers learned that Lyle Quinn, then
fourteen, had murdered Veronica Kennedy, whom his father was having an affair with at the time. Whether the boy's
mother had encouraged him, actively or unwittingly, was a
matter for speculation. Most memories people had of Polly
Quinn dated from years later, when she had become a tense,
high-strung woman, little given to socializing.

The article inferred that both Phillip and Polly Quinn
had covered up for their son, but since all the principals

were dead, with the exception of Lyle Quinn, that, too, was speculation. Many readers found it hard enough to imagine that the rheumy old man had ever been a youth.

The Fayette Historical Society, in an unusual act of cooperation, provided a series of pictures to illustrate the article—Charles and Veronica Kennedy on their wedding day, Charles Kennedy and Phillip Quinn in front of the bank, their arms clapped affably over one another's shoulders; Lyle Quinn's high school graduation photo. The newspaper also secured the photo of Polly Quinn gripping her son's arm protectively that Carol had seen on the rolltop desk at Oakdale. As much as anything else, the fading photographs told the story and put it in perspective.

There was even a picture of the Kennedy Suite, just after the mansion had been built, which the paper ran beside a photograph of the restored suite. The furnishings were different, but even Carol had to admit the rooms were eerily similar nonetheless. Sue Whiley had been right: capturing the feeling was the important thing.

The first outbursts of public reaction, shock and indignation, were replaced by the buzz of gossip at the Molly Pitcher Coffee Shop and at the Meadowbrook Market. Carol sometimes heard people whispering her name as she passed by. More often, there was a nod and a knowing hello—an acknowledgment of her newfound fame. But without an infusion of fresh indignities to spur it on, the gossip eventually waned.

And then she sensed it was over. It was nothing specific, just a feeling she had, the way she knew, before the signs were visible, say, that spring had supplanted winter. One day, it just seemed to be over for Veronica and Charles, for Polly and Phillip and Lyle. Most of all, over for her and Sammy. The Kennedy saga had played itself out. What she had to do now, she realized, was to forge her own history in the house, make her life where they had once tried to make theirs.

This Christmas dinner would count for a lot.

There were footsteps on the chestnut staircase. A pleasant-looking man in his early forties, with short, black hair and soft eyes, was coming down from the second floor.

His bearing was a little stiff, and he seemed ill at ease in a sports jacket and tie.

"I'd like you to meet my husband, Blake," Carol said. "This is Mark and Harry."

"Harry's the one dressed up like Santa," Sammy pointed out.

"Just in case you thought it was Santa himself," Harry said. Blake put out his hand. "I sort of feel I know you both already."

Blake had been home for two days, but he was still finding his way about the mansion, which no longer looked remotely as it had the day he left for Germany. He knew his marriage had changed as well, but neither he nor Carol could yet say what it had changed into. The prospect of exploring what was new about each other lent both an excitement and a wariness to the relationship.

Carol had waited for Blake's weekly phone call before telling him about "that day," and then she'd played it down. She didn't want him rushing home—the white knight to the rescue of the bumbling damsel. Mark and Harry were there, helping, and things were slowly coming under control.

"What about Sammy? Where was Sammy in all of this?"

"He saved me from a crazy old man, if you want to know the truth."

"Saved you? Is he all right?"

"More than all right. He was a real hero. You should be proud of your son, Blake."

She assured him that she would keep him posted and that they would see one another at Christmas, as planned.

Now that he was back, the sorting-out would begin, the reaccommodating, the redefining that would give them a future together, or maybe not. She perceived a certain hesitancy in his manner, which had always been so categorical beforehand. His emotions weren't so hard-edged. There was a blurriness to them, a new vulnerability that Carol found touching.

"Well, if Santa has to lug this sack of presents any farther, he'll slip a disc," Harry announced. "What about giving a hand, Sammy? Which tree do I put them under? There are so many."

"Presents!" squealed Sammy. "Over here." He gave a little skip and ran into the living room, where a small mountain of packages already hugged a plump blue spruce in the bay window. As the rest of them followed, the doorbell chimed.

"I'll answer it," said Blake, turning back. Then, he stopped and checked with Carol. "If you want me to . . ."

"Of course. This is your house, too. I'll get the eggnog."

Ned and June Foster had arrived, bearing a large poinsettia and more gifts. Blake introduced himself, and Harry bellowed another "Ho, ho, ho" from the living room. At the sight of the glossy packages, Sammy came running. And soon a merry confusion prevailed as coats and gloves were doffed, kisses exhanged, hands shaken, small talk mumbled. Before long, the group had spilled into the living room.

"Your place is festive, as always," said June as Carol glided out of the kitchen, bearing a tray of crystal cups filled with creamy eggnog. The smell of rum and nutmeg mingled with the scent of pine needles.

"Yeah, and she's finally in season," noted Harry.

"No, Sammy," Carol said. "That one is for Mr. Foster. Yours is the one on the end, without the rum." Sammy took his cup and skipped away, and Carol offered the tray to Ned. "Listen to me! *Mister* Foster," she said apologetically. "Blake, did you know that we are having Christmas dinner with Mayor Foster and his wife?"

"Mark was just telling me."

"Not quite yet," Ned said. "It's still citizen Foster for the time being. I don't get sworn in for another two weeks."

"And are we ever counting the days!" Harry stepped forward. "I would like to propose a toast." He raised his eggnog high in the air. "To the new Fayette."

Everyone followed suit.

"Sammy," said Blake. "Come join us." His chin resting on his hands, Sammy was kneeling on the sofa and staring raptly out the window. A dreamer, as always, Blake thought, then caught himself. Not true. The kid was a hero, too. The doctor's words came back to him. "He can't express all he knows. There's a lot more inside Sammy's head than he is able to share with you."

"What are you looking at, Son?" Blake put his hand on the boy's shoulder.

Sammy didn't answer immediately. Then a little voice piped up in wonderment, "It's snowing."

Everyone moved to the window, and sure enough, it was snowing. The weatherman had been predicting a white Christmas for central Pennsylvania, and the forecast was accurate for once. As they watched, the lawn disappeared under a dusting of pristine flakes.

"Falling. Pretty," said Sammy to no one in particular.

Soon, the bushes were blending in with the lawn, which blended in with the driveway, which blended in with Ragged Ridge Road and the hills and fields and railroad tracks beyond. Everything was connected and still. No animal or person or skidding automobile had yet sullied the expanding whiteness. The noise of the living was absorbed by a soft murmur that seemed to rise off the landscape.

For a while, it was just as Carol had always wanted it.

For a while, it was all perfect.